At the
JOURNEY'S END

At the
JOURNEY'S
END

A novel

Annette Lyon

Covenant Communications, Inc.

Covenant

Cover art: woman portrait © William Whitaker; *St. George Temple* © Al Rounds. For print information go to www.alrounds.com

Cover design copyrighted 2006 by Covenant Communications, Inc.

Published by Covenant Communications, Inc.
American Fork, Utah

Printed in United States of America
First Printing: September 2006

11 10 09 08 07 06   10 9 8 7 6 5 4 3 2 1

ISBN 978-1-59811-176-7

ACKNOWLEDGMENTS

Many people have helped make this book possible, and I must express my gratitude to them. Foremost, my husband Rob and our children, as always, have been a huge support in all aspects of my writing. Thanks for living with a woman who digs up bizarre historical details at all hours and has characters talking in her head!

With research, I had significant help. First, I'm grateful to Norma B. Ricketts for her generous support and guidance. If she hadn't shared with me her book, *Arizona's Honeymoon Trail and Mormon Wagon Roads*—and continued to guide me in my research after that—this book never would have been written. I'm also grateful to historian and writer Linda Shelley Whiting for steering me in Norma's direction.

Steve Whisel at the Arizona Railway Museum was very helpful in answering multiple e-mails from a pesky writer seeking to be accurate. He consulted reference books to answer my questions and helped me get the details straight. I am grateful for his help.

More direction came from David Allen of the Appalachian Blacksmiths Association, who read over the scene in Seth's blacksmith shed—more than once—to ensure its historical and technical accuracy. He jumped on board immediately with his expertise, even sending me photos and diagrams of the type of horseshoes (and the method of punching holes in them) that my characters would have used.

When I asked some medical questions of Beth, my nurse practitioner sister-in-law, she didn't just answer with what she already knew about the history of medicine and surgery. Instead, she discussed my questions with colleagues and did some digging for more information, then pointed me toward some excellent resources. The result is a much better portrayal of 1880s medicine than I would have been able to come up with on my own. A big thanks to Beth.

I was thrilled to discover *History of the St. George Temple,* a thesis written by Kirk M. Curtis, at Brigham Young University. While I consulted other texts about the St. George Temple, I relied heavily on this well-researched volume and am thankful for Kirk's meticulous work.

A small world (and some pretty neat parents) connected me to Judy Caldwell, who directed me toward further literature and resources about Snowflake, Arizona.

One of the highlights of my publishing experience has been working with the best editor in the industry. Angela, if you ever move away, I will be forced to track you down and bribe you with chocolate to make you edit me!

Finally, I can never go without thanking the six writers who take my work, shred it to pieces, and help me put it back together better than it was before. I'm a much better writer due to all of your insights. I treasure your friendship and every red ink mark—plus all those salsa drippings on the pages. Oh, wait—most of those are mine.

DEDICATION

Dedicated to the four little people who have the greatest hold on my heart—Daniel, Samantha, Megan, and Allison. After researching and writing about faithful Saints struggling to receive temple blessings, I am even more grateful to have those same blessings in my life—and because of them, the promise of being your mother for eternity.

PROLOGUE

April 1881: Near Lee's Ferry, Utah—on the bank of the Colorado River

A rifle shot split the air with a crack.

The sound halted Maddie in her step, and she looked around for the source. Maybe Peter or James had bagged some game for dinner—a wild rabbit, perhaps. It would taste good after eating dried fruit and jerky for nearly two weeks. But something told her that wasn't right. *The shot did come from the river where animals would be drinking,* she thought.

Curious, she flung her dark braid over her shoulder and picked up her pace, hurrying to the river with a water pail in each hand. A second blast rang out, this one accompanied by a cry—a man's cry. Her heart speeding up, Maddie dropped the buckets and ran to the river. Just as she rounded the last rise, she saw an Indian walking with his gun leveled at Roland, who gripped his upper arm with one hand. His horse whinnied with fear and pulled at its lead rope tied to a shrub. Feet frozen in place, Maddie took a sharp breath when she realized Roland had been shot. As the Indian drew closer, Roland held his hands up as if in surrender.

"Please . . ."

Before he could say another word, a third shot blasted and sent Roland staggering backward. He collapsed to the ground.

Horror washed over Maddie; she couldn't even scream as she stared at Roland grasping his chest. She couldn't breathe either, only gaze at her beloved fiancé as a dark circle spread across his shirt. The Indian simply stood there, looking as calm as the wisp of smoke curling from the tip of his rifle.

A cry finally ripped from her throat. "Roland!"

The Indian's face snapped to the side, and he stared at her. He wore a torn shirt, buckskin leggings, and moccasins. His brown skin sparkled with sweat in the springtime sun. In one smooth motion, he raised the rifle, leveling it toward Maddie. She sucked in her breath and stared at him, hating the man for shooting Roland. Defiant, she dared him to try the same with her. Her knees threatened to buckle with fear, and for a moment she thought she might faint, but she refused to show it on her face. When she didn't flinch, the Indian lowered the gun and looked at her, clearly surprised she hadn't run.

Even this close, he seemed to have no life in his black eyes—no emotion, no regret, only a fierce glare that seemed to imply that he took what he wanted when he wanted it. A shiver went down Maddie's back, knowing he could do anything. The man grabbed the lead rope on Roland's horse, drawing the animal away from the river. In one swift movement he mounted the horse and rode away, throwing a final, threatening glare over his shoulder.

As he galloped off, Maddie regained the use of her legs. She raced to Roland's side, stumbling over rocks and holding her skirts high. She sank to the ground and leaned over him, caring nothing for staining her dress. She held his head between her hands and tried to make eye contact. "Roland? Roland!" His eyes were half open, but they couldn't focus.

His breathing was labored and frighteningly shallow. Blood soaked his shirt. "Roland, please talk to me."

Hurried footsteps sounded behind her, and she looked back to see James and Peter, running at full tilt from camp. "What happened?" James asked breathlessly as they arrived at the scene.

"Move over," Peter demanded of Maddie. "Let me check him." He edged her aside to examine the wounds.

Maddie pulled back only slightly and watched, praying that Peter could save the man she loved. Her hands clasped together at her chest, and she felt Roland's ring. The reminder made her clutch her fingers so tightly that the band bit into her skin.

How far were they from a doctor? She had no idea but guessed too far. Days and days away from St. George, where she and Roland were to be married in the temple—but her thoughts stopped there. She couldn't let herself think about that now.

Trying to retard the flow of blood, Peter pushed his fist into the worst of the wounds. But the color in Roland's face was draining. A heaviness in her chest told Maddie that it might already be too late. The thought made her cover her mouth as a wail choked her.

Roland managed to look over at her. "Maddie." His voice was breathless, and with it came bubbles of blood from the corners of his mouth.

She pushed Peter to the side and knelt against Roland. "What is it?"

His mouth opened a fraction of an inch, but he didn't say another word. Instead, his body went limp, and his eyes rolled into the back of his head.

"No!" Terror swept through Maddie, and she began patting Roland's face. "Open your eyes, Roland! You can't leave me." Her voice rose as she cried, "You *can't!*" She began pushing against his chest, frantically shaking his body to try to bring him back.

Peter and James tried to pull her away, but she yanked out of their grasp with ferocity. "Don't!" She patted Roland's face again. "You'll be fine. Just look at me. Talk to me. Breathe!" She waited for a response, and when none came, she sat on her heels and looked up into the heavens.

"Father, make him *breathe!* Please!"

Sobs overtook her, and she lowered her head beside Roland's, holding his head in her hands. The reality of his death suffocated her as she wept.

He was gone. And there was nothing she could do about it.

"Maddie, go with Ellen." Peter spoke softly and put a gentle hand on her shoulder. His voice broke through a hazy fog into Maddie's consciousness. She didn't know when her sister had arrived or how much time had passed since the moment her life had changed forever. In a matter of days, they would have been sealed for eternity. She looked up at her older sister, whose tears had washed rivulets into her dusty cheeks.

"Come with me," Ellen said, urging Maddie to her feet. Dazed, Maddie took a few steps toward camp. But the thought of abandoning Roland by the river kept her from moving farther. She couldn't walk away from him, not yet. She tugged her hand from her sister's and stepped backward, shaking her head and wrapping her arms around herself.

"I can't."

She sank to Roland's side, then stroked his face lovingly and closed his eyes. The action made her squeeze her own eyes shut as uncontrollable pain welled up inside her chest. "I love you, Roland, more than life itself! I always will." She pressed his hand to her cheek and kissed the back of it, tears falling onto their hands as she rocked back and forth in despair.

CHAPTER 1

Salt Lake City, Utah—August 25, 1883
Almost two and a half years later

"Lazy good-for-nothing Lamanite. Ruined my plow."

"What did you expect, hiring one of them?"

The voices stopped Abe midstep. The paper in his hand crinkled as his hands fisted. Teeth clenched, he looked to the side of the road where two men stood talking as they leaned against a fence. Did they realize he was there, or was it pure coincidence that he, a so-called Lamanite by birth, happened to be walking by at that moment?

The men caught his eye and stared him down. For one wild moment, Abe wanted to lash out and tell them his mind. But that would only validate their view of Indians. Better to move on, say nothing—especially for his mother's sake. If he made a ruckus, it would impact her as well.

It's not just me anymore, he reminded himself.

Jaw working, he unclenched his hand, nodded in their direction, and forced his mouth to curve into what he hoped looked like an easy smile. "Good day," he said, then kept walking, his cheeks burning with anger.

After rounding a bend in the road, Abe let out a big breath. This was supposed to be his home, and yet, as an adopted Shoshone, he knew he'd always be an outsider. Always had been, always would be. To everyone but his mother.

He shoved his hands into his pockets and continued down the road, trying hard to shake the look of distrust in the men's eyes. His thoughts were so preoccupied that he didn't notice the young woman walking toward him until he bumped into her.

She pulled back in surprise, dropping a package. "Oh, excuse me." She bent down to pick up the parcel, but Abe had already reached for it.

"I wasn't paying attention. I'm sorry," he said, holding the package out to her. His hand paused as he looked at her for the first time, and his heart lurched. She looked so much like Lizzy. The same playful smile, the way she swept her hair off her neck. She even had similar brown eyes. Eyes that held no fear when she looked at him, though they surely saw someone different from herself. It was the same refreshing lack of prejudgment he had found in Lizzy.

"Thank you," she said with a nod, gently tugging the package away from him. She glanced over her shoulder and smiled as she continued down the road. Abe stood there staring at the bumps and divots in the dirt. Would he *ever* get over Lizzy? He hadn't seen her in what, about four years? And every time he thought he had moved on, something happened to remind him that his heart still belonged to a girl in Logan—a girl who was now married to someone else.

With a grunt of frustration, Abe kept walking toward the pharmacy on an errand for his mother. *I've been home a full year now,* he thought. *And I can't take it anymore.* He had thought at first that being in Salt Lake would be easier—at least here he was known as Clara Franklin's son, not just an "outsider" as he had been in Logan. And here there weren't the constant reminders of Lizzy, who would never be his. But there were reminders enough.

And he was still miserable. Maybe it was time again to sit down with his mother and discuss moving to California. He walked on toward the pharmacy, his mind troubled with every step. Just as he rounded the final corner, a voice boomed from the front of the store.

"Drop the rifle!"

Abe came to an abrupt halt, nearly bowled over in shock at the scene before him. Three men stood together, looking into the barrel of a rifle held by a Negro man. Abe recognized the speaker, the man in the center, as Marshal Burt. At his sides were Wilcken, who had been a bodyguard to Brother Brigham, and Brother Elijah, a faithful Negro Saint.

The anger in the gunman's eyes sent a shiver down Abe's back. The man wouldn't think twice about pulling the trigger, Abe was sure of it. A coldness in his eyes told Abe that this wasn't the first time he'd aimed a gun to kill.

"Sam Harvey, there's no reason for this," Marshal Burt said.

"Then why're you trying to cart me off to jail?" Sam sneered, his gun still pointed at the marshal.

"Because you pulled out a pistol, then threatened Grice and his patrons, that's why," Marshal Burt said, his voice surprisingly calm and even. He had his own weapon out, but his face had drained of color. "We're just trying to keep the peace. You've had a bit too much to drink. I suppose you're not thinking as clear as you should. So I'll say it one more time—drop the gun."

As he stepped forward, the gunman took a matching step. A bright flash exploded from the end of his rifle, sending the marshal reeling backward, clutching his chest. Hazy smoke curled from the tip of the gun. The shot missed Wilcken by inches, but he didn't flinch. Before the smoke had cleared, he jumped forward and wrested the weapon away from Sam. He threw it to the side, where Abe kicked it out of reach. Sam took a step back, fear registering in his eyes as he looked around. People were watching him, and Wilcken was coming for him. Sam glanced at his gun, lying on the ground behind Abe, then took another step and had started to turn when Wilcken and Elijah pounced on him, one of them gripping him by the throat.

"You don't think you're gonna get away after shooting the marshal, do ya?" Wilcken said between huffs.

"Let me go!" Sam roared, trying to yank his arms away. The men continued to fight, saying nothing between kicks, punches, and the occasional curse.

Behind the scuffle, Marshal Burt staggered backward into the pharmacy, blood flowing from both sides of his chest. The bullet had gone in one arm, through his torso, and into the other arm, leaving him with several bleeding wounds. Through the pharmacy window, Abe could see the marshal collapse on the floor.

More cries from Wilcken, Elijah, and Sam brought Abe back to the scuffle. He glanced around at the crowd; some had run screaming at the first shot but had since returned. Dozens of people watched tentatively, but seemingly assured that all would turn out right. A few men hesitated on the fringes as if wanting to help but not sure what to do.

A second shot cracked the air, and Wilcken let out a cry. He gripped his left arm and stumbled away. Sam boldly stepped forward, holding a pistol at arm's length and pressing it against Wilcken's body. His finger moved on the trigger, ready to release another round.

With strong hands Elijah grabbed the pistol away just in time. Sam brought his arm back, aiming a punch, but Elijah ducked. Abe rushed forward. If they could only get Sam onto the ground, they could tie him up and wait for the authorities. Abe focused on Sam's arms. Who knew if the man had yet a third weapon to brandish.

Abe held onto Sam's right arm with all his might, trying to pull it behind his back and hold it there. The smell of alcohol and Sam's unwashed body came over Abe like a cloud, making his nostrils burn. He had to stifle a gag and focus on keeping the man under control, but Sam managed to work one arm free, landing a punch square on the right side of Abe's head, making his ear ring and his head pound as he held on.

"No you don't, Harvey." Wilcken had reentered the fray, grabbed the arm, and yanked it behind Sam's back, making their captive wince with pain. Blood poured from Wilcken's arm, but he didn't back down. He pushed Sam's elbow up, twisting it from its natural position and making the man cry out and fall to his knees. Even then he wouldn't be subdued. He lashed out with his legs, making Abe and Elijah dodge kicks until they shoved him face-first into the ground. Wilcken turned his face toward Elijah, looking pale and disoriented—clearly ready to pass out.

"I got him," Elijah said, taking Wilcken's hold on the arm before he fainted. Wilcken stood, staggered to a building, and leaned against it, cradling his arm. Sam writhed on the ground, threatening violence. As Abe helped hold Sam down, he feared that he and Elijah wouldn't be able to subdue him for long; Sam was surprisingly strong. The punch to Abe's head had him seeing stars, and he worried he'd pass out.

"We need more help!" he called. A man hesitated only a moment before adding his strength in holding down Sam Harvey. Several other men rushed forward, allowing Elijah to get off Sam and tie him hog-style. Sam still pulled against the restraints, fighting like a mad dog.

"I'm tellin' ya, Sam Harvey," Elijah called as he pulled the ropes tighter and ducked to avoid a kick. "Stop fightin' and ye won't get hurt." With Sam secured, Elijah stood back, hands on his waist as he puffed with exertion.

Abe stood and let out a shaky breath as he stepped backward, thinking just how much worse the situation could have been if Elijah hadn't taken away the pistol when he did. Abe tried to rub his hands, but they wouldn't stop shaking. He turned away, still trying to catch his breath, when he heard snippets of stunned conversation around him.

"Who got shot?"

"That's Brother Wilcken."

"Who else? I heard another shot."

"I think it was the bishop."

"No! Are you sure?"

"Wasn't it the marshal?"

"The marshal *is* a bishop."

The onlookers continued to gasp and point at Sam Harvey on the ground, Wilcken rocking by the sidewalk, and then inside the pharmacy, where Marshal Burt lay. As Abe looked from the crowd to the spectacle, his throat grew dry.

The officers arrived in two wagons, and the crowd made way. The lawmen hopped off and quickly took control of the situation. They dragged Sam to the first wagon. Two men picked him up and tossed him into it like so much cargo, Sam landing on the wooden planks with a thud and a groan. Another man emptied the ammunition from the offending rifle then threw the gun into the wagon beside the perpetrator, muttering, "Stupid Negro."

A fellow officer nodded. "What did he think he was doing coming to Utah anyway? His kind don't belong here."

The words pierced Abe. *So this isn't just about a murdered bishop.*

Several men jumped on board, but instead of taking seats, they took turns kicking Sam. With each blow, he cried out and curled up in pain, which only spurred the men on more. Nausea bubbled up, and Abe covered his mouth, turning away. He couldn't believe what he was seeing—or hearing. Sam Harvey may have been a cold-blooded killer, but these men were no better. Some in the crowd applauded.

"You show him, brothers!" one called out. "No Negro's gonna kill our bishop and get away with it."

They left the second wagon behind for the injured and moved the first one out. The wheels creaked as Sam Harvey was taken away. A good number from the crowd followed behind the wagon. The shooter was in custody—surely that was the end of the spectacle. Why were they following? The thought made Abe's stomach clench.

A moment later Dr. Benedict raced through the street, carrying his black bag. "Where's Burt?" he demanded. Abe pointed to the pharmacy, and the doctor raced to the door. But he stopped when he saw Wilcken and knelt down to probe the wounds.

"Is it just this arm, or are you hurt elsewhere?"

Blood trickled from Wilcken's upper arm, but he didn't look at it. Pale and visibly shaken, his voice remained clear. "Burt." He nodded into the pharmacy. "Check him first."

The doctor glanced over his shoulder. His brow furrowed as he turned back and hastily tied a handkerchief around Wilcken's arm to staunch the bleeding before entering the pharmacy. Abe stood in the doorway, watching as Dr. Benedict stepped inside and worked over the injured marshal. Even though Abe could only see the marshal's feet, there was a dark red pool around him. Something in the doctor's expression said that Marshal Burt wasn't long for this world.

With solemnity, the doctor reached forward and closed the marshal's eyes. "Bishop Burt is dead," he said in a low voice as he stood. He glanced at the waiting crowd outside and sighed. Abe felt his stomach sink. He stepped closer and lowered his head in respect. The doctor withdrew a handkerchief, opened it, and covered the marshal's face. Then Abe, Dr. Benedict, and several other men helped carry the body to the waiting wagon.

At seeing the body of their beloved marshal and bishop, the crowd began to moan and gasp. A woman covered her face with her hands and burst into sobs.

"I say *hang!*" came a gruff voice from the street. "Who goes with me?"

A chorus of people calling, "I do! I do!" followed.

Hanging? As soon as the marshal's body was safely inside the wagon, Abe stepped back into the shadows, a shudder going through him. The feeling increased as the sentiment gained acceptance. As he stood in the pharmacy doorway, his hand gripped the frame. What were they thinking? Wasn't this a people whose own prophet had been slaughtered by a mob only a few decades earlier? Shouldn't they recognize the need for justice through the courts, even if it was one of their own bishops who had been murdered?

The sheer energy in the air mounted as anger and outrage became almost palpable. Abe glanced around at people eyeing him furtively in a way he recognized all too well. Their eyes narrowed as they stared at his black hair and brown skin. He was an outsider for sure. Fear prickled his scalp, and he eased a few steps backward. He wasn't a Negro, but he *was* different. Plenty of people regarded any of his race with suspicion. Just like they did Sam Harvey.

Only I've done nothing, Abe thought as he pulled the brim of his hat over his eyes and scanned the crowd, wondering how Elijah felt, but the man was nowhere to be seen. *Must have hightailed it out of here,* Abe thought. *Not a bad idea.*

"Let's go tell 'em about the marshal!" The suggestion came anonymously from the crowd, but almost everyone seemed to agree. The throng began moving toward city hall, where Sam would be searched in the marshal's office. Abe thought of Sam Harvey in the wagon, the men who had followed it, and now the people headed that way who wanted Sam hanged.

"Kill him!" This time the call came from a young voice, and Abe looked over in horror to see a boy of no more than ten punching his hand in the air just as his father did beside him. "He killed a bishop!"

"Stop!" a voice called from the middle of the crowd. Only a few people heeded it; most kept walking, but a handful paused and looked back at the man speaking. He was probably in his thirties, with blond hair and a moustache. Abe didn't recognize him, but the man was clearly frustrated. "I said stop! You can't do this. *We* can't do this. Let the law see to the man. Trust that he'll get justice."

"*We'll* see that he gets justice," came a faceless response from somewhere in the crowd. Most of those who had paused continued going toward the city hall.

The blond man jumped on top of a hitching post and tried again, calling at the top of his lungs. "Are you going to let a murderer turn you into the same thing he is? Are you? Is that what we've lived and taught?"

Someone walked by and pushed the man, who fell off the post and onto the wooden sidewalk. He grunted and sat up, the look on his face one of defeat. Abe crossed the road and helped the man up.

"At least you tried," Abe said. "Thank you."

"Didn't do any good," the man said with a shrug. He headed in the opposite direction of the crowd. Abe almost followed, but something kept him connected to the mob going the other way. He had to know what lay in store for the mob and the man they hated. He slipped into the crowd and tried to blend in, but knew he'd stand out no matter what he did. Perhaps it didn't matter—the crowd was so focused on their goal.

"What's a person like him doing here anyway?" a woman beside him asked her friend.

For a moment Abe thought she meant *him,* then realized she referred to Sam.

"He's a vagrant, just come from Ogden or someplace up north," came the response of a man near her. "He was out of work but refused a farm job, they say. Bickered in Grice's restaurant or something."

"No surprise. Don't know what else you can expect from colored folks but laziness."

"Naturally," a friend of hers agreed with a shudder. "They all make me nervous."

The first woman tilted her head. "Except the ones who are Saints, of course." Her tone implied charitable acknowledgment. "*They're* different. Like Sister James."

"Oh, of course," came her friend's reply.

So drawing lines by race and religion makes it all acceptable? Such talk made Abe's heart cold and heavy. As he walked along the street and listened to several such conversations—hat still pulled low—he never once heard anyone refer to Sam by name. He was only *the Negro, the colored man,* or worse.

A year ago Abe's mother had asked him to give the Saints a chance. "We're not all like your father," she had assured him.

Unfortunately, enough *were.*

Heartsick, Abe felt drawn to continue with the crowd, to not leave Sam. Both curiosity and dread drew him along as they walked to the city hall. The crowd grew in number, and by the time they reached First South, Abe could hardly see where it began—there had to be a couple thousand people by now. He snaked his way closer to the front, afraid for Sam. But when Abe arrived at the building, the wagon was nowhere to be seen.

A few moments after the crowd had gathered before the city hall, someone ran inside the building and yelled, "He killed the marshal!" The man turned back to the throng and repeated the words. "The Negro killed our marshal!"

The people were getting antsy—they wanted some action.

"Get a rope!"

"Hang the heathen!"

"I bet they're moving him out the back door to the jailhouse. Let's go get him!"

Another voice was so quiet Abe almost missed it. An elderly woman a few feet to his left was shaking her head and holding a handkerchief to her mouth as tears rolled down her cheeks. "Is it come to this?" she cried, presumably to herself. "Oh, Brother Joseph, at least you aren't here to see this!"

The crowd stampeded down an alley on State Street to the yard between the city hall and the jailhouse. At the door, Officer Salmon met the crowd.

"You are hereby ordered to disband," he yelled at them. "Go home. This is a matter for the law to decide."

As he looked over the yard, his eyes shifted back and forth. The crowd jeered and cried out, mocking him for his weakness, demanding he turn over the murderer. He took a step back, obviously unsure what to do with the number of people screaming at him. Half a dozen men pushed forward, grabbed the officer, and fought briefly before tossing him to the side and rushing into the jailhouse. The mob cheered. Abe looked around, hoping to find another kind face, but the woman had left, and everyone else had wide eyes and faces flushed with rage and energy.

The men raced into the jailhouse and moments later dragged out Sam Harvey. He tried to walk, but his legs kept buckling beneath him, so the men resorted to dragging him. Sam's face was red and swollen, and his lips bled.

The crowd cheered, and the anger in Abe's chest intensified. Someone cut leather straps from a horse's harness and passed them into the crowd. Like a wave on the sea, onlookers raised their arms to keep the straps moving forward, and Sam's captors grabbed them. A man tried to tie them into a noose, but they were too short.

"A whip!" someone called, and the man obliged, using the straps to beat Sam while someone else found a rope. Sam grimaced with each stroke, eyes filled with fear as he strained against his bindings.

This can't be happening, Abe thought. *Surely of all people . . . They won't really . . .*

But his disbelief gave way to horror when his eyes saw the truth. Men from the front of the mob gripped Sam under his arms and dragged him to a stable shed at the end of the yard. Sam fought with all his might, his heels making chaotic tracks in the dirt as he kicked. They opened the stable doors wide so more people could see the spectacle. By the time they had the rope secured on a beam, Sam's body was almost spent from fighting. They tied him, hoisted him up, then stepped back to view their handiwork. The mob roared their approval.

The sudden loss of air sent Sam struggling against the ropes and groping at the restraints. Abe wanted to scream, to run into the stable loft and cut Sam down. But fear kept him from moving; if he were to say or do anything, his fate might be the same. And Sam wouldn't be any better off.

When Sam's body finally went limp, Abe felt bile rise in his throat, and he turned away to retch onto the dirt road. He stayed there, doubled over, his eyes pressed closed as he tried to catch his breath. A moment later, he wiped his mouth with the back of his hand and stumbled away from the crowd, too sick to view the dead man and hear the cheers.

He ran hard all the way home, arms and legs pumping to take him away. Every so often he glanced over his shoulder, afraid someone might be following—someone who might see him as another intruder, another threat. With the farm in sight, he scrambled behind an old oak tree and collapsed against the trunk. Holding his head in his hands, he tried to catch his breath as tears streamed down his face.

I've never felt at home here, he thought. *But now, am I even safe among the Saints?*

He leaned his head back against the tree and closed his eyes. *Saints. Ha.*

What would they do next—to someone like him, another not of their race, not of their religion? Abe glanced over his shoulder, horror still coursing through his veins.

Enough.

With or without his mother, he had to leave. And the sooner, the better.

CHAPTER 2

Snowflake, Arizona

"I understand if you would rather not take the trip with us," Ellen said, fingering the quilt she and her sister were working on. She stood from her chair and rubbed her back to ease the strain her growing belly put on it. "It would certainly be much easier with another set of hands to help with the little ones, but . . ."

Maddie accidentally pricked her finger. Sucking on the tip, she was painfully aware of her older sister waiting for a response. How was she supposed to react? *Surprised* would be a good word to describe her feelings. Maddie hadn't realized Ellen and Peter were planning another trip to St. George so soon.

So soon. Well, not really. Their last attempt to get the family sealed was nearly two and a half years ago. It also would have been Maddie's wedding trip, if Roland hadn't been killed on the way. Even now she struggled to bury the images seared into her mind.

The Indian and his rifle. Roland falling to the ground. Kneeling over him as he took his last breath.

Ellen's suggestion brought the memories back with vicious clarity. After Roland died, the entire party had turned back to Snowflake, shaken and frightened. Peter and his brother James had wrapped Roland's body in a blanket and put it in the wagon to carry it home for a proper burial.

That return trip was ten days of agony. Maddie spent her time cooking and helping to care for her niece and her pregnant sister while trying to keep a brave face and not completely fall to pieces.

Every hour she expected Roland to come up and walk beside her, only to be torn back to the realization that he wouldn't, not ever again. Instead, he lay inside the wagon, wrapped in a blanket. She often walked beside the wagon with her hand on the box as if that would keep her close to him. Sometimes when they stopped at night, she crept to the wagon and stared at his stiff form, yearning to pull back the blanket and have one final look at the man she had loved.

The memories of his face returned with force. This was the first time in over two years that Maddie had allowed herself to think this much about Roland's death. The sudden request to join the party had turned the key and let all the memories out.

Ellen pulled out a chair and sat down beside her sister, speaking softly now. "You hadn't talked about—Roland—in so long, I thought perhaps it would be all right . . . but I understand if it's too hard."

"Thank you," Maddie said, carefully weighing each word and trying not to show emotion. "But it has been a long time. And I wouldn't feel right about sending you and the children on the wagon road without some help."

"We could use it," Ellen said, sounding relieved. "Peter will be good for protection and driving the horses, but a man can't care for children the same way another woman can. And the children are so used to you being here. You're practically a second mother to them."

"But are you sure it's wise to go with a baby on the way?" Maddie asked.

"We'll have plenty of time to go up to the temple and come back before the baby will be here," Ellen assured her sister. "I don't think this one will come before November, and if it follows the pattern of our first two, it'll be closer to the end of the month. That's three months from now. We'll be home at least a month before we see him—or her." She reached onto the quilt and began absently picking at some of the stitches. "The truth is, I desperately want a child born in the covenant. Mary and Lorenzo didn't have that. This child has a chance to be."

"I know," Maddie said with a nod. She put the needle into the fabric and turned to her sister. "I also know that you can't travel with a newborn, so you'd have to wait at least another year if you don't go now."

Ellen nodded and swallowed. "I don't want to wait any longer to be sealed."

Maddie paused for a moment, evening out her breath and managing a more relaxed smile. "I'd be happy to come."

"Are you . . . are you *sure?*"

With the worst of it past, Maddie embraced the decision. The six-week round-trip journey wouldn't be easy, but she couldn't live in a cocoon her entire life, making decisions based solely on the past—on what would or would not cause her pain. Facing the road where she had lost Roland might help her to move past that time and embrace her future with Edward. Besides, how could she send her pregnant sister on an arduous trip alone, when she could go along and ease the burden?

"I'll go," Maddie assured her sister. "For Mary's sake. She can be quite a handful."

Ellen let out a laugh that ended in a snort. She covered her nose in embarrassment. "A *handful* is the least of it. You're the only person who can manage that girl. I don't know what we'd do on the trail without her favorite aunt. And Lorenzo is getting old enough to cause plenty of mischief of his own." Leaning forward with her belly awkwardly between them, Ellen gave her sister a hug. Then she pulled back and looked down, stroking her stomach. "Thank you."

"You're welcome," Maddie said, reaching for her sister's hand. For the first time in months, she drew aside the curtain she had pulled across Roland's memory and allowed her thoughts to linger on him.

The first time he asked to walk her home.

The day he asked for her hand.

The day he died on the bank of the Colorado River.

With a shake of her head to rid her mind of the images, she returned to working on the quilt, determined to be calm—not the least bit ruffled.

And promptly pricked her finger.

* * *

Abe shoved his belongings into a duffle bag as quickly as he could, as if another mob had already assembled outside, ready to lynch him, too. His heart pounded between his ears as he tried not to think of the scene, but trying not to actually made it stand out in his mind in even greater relief. With the last of his things packed, he surveyed the room and began pacing.

Both hands roughly combed through his hair. He needed something to do before tomorrow morning when the railway would take him west. His mother appeared at the door, looking old and fragile. A handkerchief covered her lips and she coughed, eyes closing at the discomfort.

"Mother, are you well?" Abe asked, going to her side.

When the coughing spell was over, she lowered the handkerchief and nodded. She slowly folded the square cloth in her hands and avoided her son's eyes. "I'm fine. Just choked up thinking how much I'll miss you." Her voice wavered.

"And I you," Abe said, reaching for her hands. This was the first time in the last year she hadn't tried to convince him to stay. Not after today's events.

"Not all Saints are like that," she told her son as she embraced him.

"I know." Abe pulled back and lowered his face to look into her eyes better. "I know *you* aren't. And I know dozens more who are good people. But there were plenty of 'Saints' in the mob, acting like sheep."

"All the same, I don't want to say good-bye."

"Neither do I." They gazed into one another's eyes, equally horrified at the day's events, both fearing for his safety.

"Why—why California?" she asked, still looking at her frail, white hands in his strong, brown ones. She attempted a weak smile. "The Gold Rush ended about the time you were born. You don't expect to get rich out there, do you?"

Abe returned the wan smile. They both knew it was never about money, only about starting a new life. "Come with me, Mother. California is warm all year round. You wouldn't have to fight the snow and your rheumatism."

His adopted mother stroked the top of his hand with her fingers. Her thin bones were prominent. Thick, blue veins showed through her transparent skin, spotted with age. "I'm old, Abe. I can't start over now." Her voice was tinged with sadness, and for a moment Abe wished he could stay. "Come. Let's go outside and sit on the swing once more."

In silent agreement, he followed her outside and sat beside her on the old porch swing. After watching the lynching, memories of the past assaulted him as he looked over the farm and the stable and remembered Brother Franklin's whippings when he tried to "civilize" and "save" the Indian boy he had adopted. *Enslaved is more like it,* Abe thought, though the cynicism lacked the bite it once had. His father was dead, and Abe mostly felt regret now—for his own anger, his father's missed opportunity, and his mother's wasted years with such a man.

"You aren't so old, Mother," Abe said quietly.

"Seventy-eight isn't old?" she countered, then chuckled.

"You could start over with me, get away from this place and its memories."

"Hmm." She looked out at the farm and got a faraway look in her eyes. "You know, memories make it hard to think of leaving here." When Abe's eyes flashed, she shook her head. "Oh, I don't mean that they're all good ones, far from it. But this has been my home for over forty years. I built it with my husband. Flawed as he was, I toiled at his side. This place is a part of me."

Abe had never thought of the farm in those terms. It had only been a location to him—one bursting with heartache and resentment.

"This is also where I became a mother," she added, "at the age when my friends were grandmothers." She reached up and put a hand on his cheek. He leaned down so she could kiss his forehead as she did when he was young. When her lips pressed against his skin, he closed his eyes. He was her only child, and he entered her life as an eight-year-old boy, not a baby.

Running a hand along the outer wall of the house, she said, "This place has a spirit about it, Abe. How could I leave it behind? But . . ."

When her voice trailed off, Abe's heart fluttered with hope. "But?" he prompted.

"But I don't want to be away from my son any longer," she said after a few moments. "Truthfully, I'd be willing to leave this home if it didn't mean leaving the Saints behind with it."

Abe sat straighter and looked at her. "Really? You'd be willing to leave the farm?"

She raised a single finger in protest. "I said *if* I didn't have to leave the Church. I've given my life to it."

They settled into the swing, Abe feeling sullen after that brief moment of hope. Gently moving back and forth, neither said a word as the old wood creaked beneath their weight. Abe wished he could enjoy it as he had so many times in his boyhood. The two of them used to sit together on the rickety swing and read aloud from his mother's small collection of books.

"I suppose I may never see you again." Her hands covered her face now, and Abe gently pried them away. Her statement hung in the air, and Abe didn't know how to respond. She was right—it might be years before he ever returned, and only heaven knew how many more years she had left. Her rounded shoulders began shaking, and Abe took her into his arms, unable to bear her sorrow.

Somehow he had to find a way to make things right with her— for them both. "Mother, everything will turn out," he promised as she wept into his chest. He wondered if his words were hollow. Her body was so much thinner than it used to be—she seemed so fragile. "A lot of cities out West were settled by Mormons, weren't they? If I find a group of Saints in California, will you join me?"

The petite gray head rose, and she looked into his eyes hopefully. She nodded and sniffed. "And if you can't find any?"

"Then I'll keep looking. I'll find another place with Saints, and we'll live there. Together."

"Someplace away from here," she said.

"Away from here," Abe agreed. If going west to California didn't work out, they would have to go south. Perhaps to American Fork or Provo. To the north lay Cache Valley—and the girl he could never have. He'd prefer something out of Utah altogether. Abe gazed into his mother's pale blue eyes. "Wherever we go, Mother, you will be with the Saints. I promise."

She wiped at her wrinkled cheeks and gazed over the acres she had helped cultivate most of her life. The farm work was hired out now, and the harvest would be coming in soon. Alfalfa rippled in the evening breeze.

"Perhaps I could trust the farm to Roger Clements," she said. "He's offered to buy the place more than once since your father died."

"He's a good man," Abe said. "He'll take good care of the place, and that will let you join me sooner." He put an arm around her shoulders and held her close, his chest feeling lighter already. Her head leaned against him, and he kissed it. Surely he could find a settlement of Latter-day Saints; California must have plenty of them, especially around the Gold Rush cities where Mormons had been the first to discover gold at Sutter's Mill.

"I love you, Mother," Abe said.

She patted his leg. "Not as much as I love you."

CHAPTER 3

Maddie sat before the fire, her embroidery forgotten in her lap. She stared, unseeing, at the fireplace at its ribbons of red and orange.

"What's wrong?" Ellen asked as she took a seat in the rocking chair.

Her voice broke Maddie's stare. She blinked away the lights dancing in her eyes as she turned from the flames. Ellen spoke again. "What are you thinking of?"

Maddie lowered her head. "Edward."

For a second, Ellen's face registered a smile, until she realized the look on Maddie's wasn't one of happiness.

"What's wrong? Did you two have a row?"

"No," Maddie assured her with a shake of her head. "Nothing like that. Edward is the same as ever." She gave her sister a grim smile and shrugged. "I can't help but compare Edward with Roland. But I suppose that's inevitable . . . isn't it?"

Picking up her knitting, Ellen nodded. "I imagine so. Roland was very different from Edward. It would be hard *not* to compare them. Why do you ask?"

"Because . . . I don't love Edward," Maddie said miserably.

"I know," Ellen said softly. It was no secret that this engagement wasn't the same as Maddie's first. She faced matrimony with someone she respected and liked, but didn't love. That's how life went sometimes. Ellen leaned forward. "Does it bother you more now?"

Maddie raised her head and gazed at the rafters as if they held some answer. "It's silly, I suppose, but it does. Edward is kind and faithful in the gospel. He'll have his own farm soon, so he'll provide

for me and . . . our children. That's all a woman can ask for, isn't it?"
She looked at Ellen, eyes pleading for confirmation.

"A good husband, a home, and sustenance? That's a good life,"
Ellen said. "It's much more than many women ever get."

"I know." Maddie leaned into her chair, feeling ashamed that she
worried about something as flippant as wanting to be "in love," to
feel as she had for Roland. "I keep reminding myself about Brother
and Sister Horace," Maddie said. "And the Fosters, the Cliftons."

All of those couples, and more Maddie could easily name, had
married out of—for lack of a better term—logic or convenience. In
the Horaces' case, both had been widowed. Both had small children.
He needed a housekeeper and a mother for his children. She needed
someone who could provide for her and her little ones. He marched
up to her porch one day, and holding his hat in his hands, he intro-
duced himself and proposed marriage to her on the spot. She
accepted, and they wed a week later. By all accounts it had been a
successful marriage.

Yet Maddie didn't envy them.

The other couples had various reasons for marrying, satisfying
similar needs.

"Sometimes love comes after," Ellen said. "I cared for Peter when
we married, but today I can say I truly love him. It might be the same
with you and Edward."

"Perhaps," Maddie said, trying to smile her gratitude for her
sister's comforting words. "Although Edward says he loves me already.
It feels unfair to him that I can't say the words back and mean them."

She tried to return to her embroidery, but her mind remained elsewhere, and she had to pick out loose stitches made in distraction.
Ellen sat nearby, rocking slowly and knitting a pair of socks for Peter.
As much as she tried to sympathize, Maddie knew that her sister didn't
fully understand. She had never been consumed by love as Maddie
had, only to lose it. And she had never been twenty-four, facing the
prospect of being an old maid and the trials that went with it.

On one hand, Ellen understood the need to marry for security.
She probably knew as well as Maddie did that a woman couldn't
provide for herself for the rest of her life as a schoolteacher. It just
wasn't enough money.

But Ellen knew nothing of two other reasons prodding Maddie to marry Edward. First it was the feeling that she had outworn her welcome in her sister's home. She had stayed there since the death of their parents from cholera almost four years ago. She had slept in her niece and nephew's bedroom. Ellen and Peter had welcomed Maddie, but she knew they needed more space, especially with a third baby on the way. If she didn't leave soon, she would be sleeping on the couch, and if that didn't make her feel like an outsider, nothing would. It was time for her to leave.

More than that was a deep yearning inside her to be a mother—a desire that only increased the longer she stayed with Ellen and Peter and their sweet children.

* * *

"I'll be fine, Mother," Abe said as he stood on the back porch. He was packed and ready to leave for the train station. The sun hadn't yet crested the mountain peak, and the chill of the morning air hung around the two of them. In a matter of hours the day would be sweltering hot, but for the moment they both shivered.

Abe leaned over and took his mother into his arms. "I'll send a telegram as soon as I can," he said. "And then I'll come back for you."

Nodding bravely—and obviously trying to will back tears—she said, "And while you're gone, I'll get the farm sale arranged with Brother Clements. I'll be ready when you come."

A warm smile curled Abe's mouth. "You have that much faith in me?"

"Land sakes, no," she said with a teasing grin. She gave his arm a playful swat. "I have faith that the Lord will bring us together in a place we can both call home."

She turned and craned her neck to see onto the lane, where Brother Huff was supposed to be coming to take Abe to the train station. Abe had assured her he could walk or go by horse—he could surely pay someone to return it—but she insisted. "After all," she had said, "what good is calling each other 'brother' and 'sister' if you can't ask for a spot of help now and then?"

As if on cue, Brother Huff drove up. Abe's mother jumped and clapped her hands as if she had just remembered something. She scurried back into the house and emerged a moment later carrying a cracked, worn volume. "Here," she said, pressing it into Abe's hands. "You'll need something to read on the train."

Abe looked down at the thin collection of poems, and his eyes misted. When his father had thrown him out all those years ago, his mother's books were the one thing he got to take with him—the possessions he valued most. "Thank you," he said, trying to keep the huskiness from his voice.

"Mornin', Clara. Mornin', Abe," Brother Huff said, nodding his head and tilting his hat. The buggy jostled, the wheels crunching over the rocky ground, then came to a stop.

"I'm ready," Abe said, blinking to clear his eyes. He moved toward his bag, which he picked up, and then he slung his bedroll over his shoulder. "I sure appreciate you coming for me."

Brother Huff reached for the bag and lifted it into the buggy as Abe climbed in. "No problem at all," he said. "Happy to help a neighbor."

Sister Franklin went to the edge of the buggy and reached up to her son. Abe leaned down and kissed her on the forehead. She closed her eyes at his touch. "Good-bye, Mother."

"God speed your journey," she said, waving as they moved away. She stayed there until she could no longer see or hear the buggy, and only then did she let out a sigh and walk toward the house.

* * *

"I do love nothing . . ." Eighteen-year-old Paul stood on the platform at the front of the schoolhouse. Most days it held just Maddie's desk and the blackboard, but next week it would act as a stage for the school festival. Paul's face tightened in concentration as he tried to remember his line. "I do love nothing in this world so well as you—is that not strange?"

"As strange as the thing I know not. It were as possible for me to say I lov'd nothing so well as you." Mary Jane, who played opposite Paul, turned around in protest as she went on. "But believe me not; and yet I lie not: I confess nothing, nor I deny nothing."

Maddie sat at one of the desks, presumably following along with the script. But the scene had taken her mind elsewhere.

To Roland. To the two of them saying very similar things to one another. Roland was the first to confess his feelings. Maddie had been hesitant to admit how deep her affection ran. The thought of living without Roland was inconceivable; she wanted nothing more than to be with him for the rest of her life. She imagined sleeping by his side at night, working in the fields together, enjoying food and rest—and children—together.

She shook her head and returned to the present, knowing she had missed several lines but assuming her students had delivered them correctly.

"Why then God forgive me!" Mary Jane went on.

"What offense, sweet Beatrice?" came the reply.

"You have stay'd me in a happy hour, I was about to protest I lov'd you."

Paul stepped closer to Mary Jane, and she gazed into his face as he spoke. "And do it with all thy heart."

The look in Mary Jane's eyes was almost laughable; no one could accuse her of not trying to act struck by Cupid's arrow. But someone who had truly felt deep love for a man could tell that fifteen-year-old Mary Jane had yet to travel the same road.

"I love you with so much of my heart that none is left to protest," Mary Jane said, clasping her hands earnestly.

Despite the over-acted performance, Shakespeare's words made the classroom vanish for Maddie. For the moment, all that existed was Roland's warm hand in hers and his soothing voice, moonlight hitting his dark hair as they walked together and proclaimed their love for each other. At the time, Maddie was overwhelmed with how much she felt for another person. She spent hours thinking of Roland and planning their life together. What would he look like at fifty? Much like his father, perhaps, with gray at his temples and gentle lines around his eyes. She spent months working on her trousseau—quilts, pillowcases, doilies, and many other items for her home. After his death, all of those pieces of needlework were quietly stored away.

Why was it that ever since she agreed to go with Ellen's family, she couldn't stop thinking about Roland?

"Miss Stratton?" Paul called. "Miss Stratton, what's my next line?"

With an unpleasant start, Maddie came back to the moment. Riffling through the pages of Shakespeare, she tried to find where they had left off. She finally set the pages down and smoothed them on the desk.

"Let's stop for today," she said, standing and putting on a smile. "You have both been working so hard every day after school that you deserve a break."

"But do you think we'll be ready in time?" Mary Jane asked. She bit her lip. "The performance is only a week away."

"You've worked so hard, I'm sure you'll be ready," Maddie said with a confident nod. "And your parents will be duly impressed."

Paul and Mary Jane exchanged pleased looks, then scampered off the platform to gather their belongings. Maddie couldn't help but notice how tall Mary Jane had grown in the last year. She stood almost as tall as Maddie.

"Thanks, Miss Stratton," Paul called over his shoulder as he walked out.

Mary Jane hung back, her books close to her chest. "Can I ask you something?"

"Of course," Maddie answered, gathering her papers and tucking a loose bit of hair behind her ear.

When Mary Jane didn't speak right away, Maddie raised her head. The girl shifted from one foot to the other and started chewing her lip. Her eyes were focused on the door.

Maddie looked from her student to the back of the room, realizing what the question would be about. Apparently the expression on Mary Jane's face had meant something—puppy love. The same thing Maddie had felt toward a young man nearly ten years ago in Bountiful before her family came down to settle Arizona. All he had to do was glance her direction, and her insides would flutter uncontrollably. Thank goodness Maddie was beyond such childish nonsense now.

"Do you think . . ." Mary Jane's voice was quiet and tentative. "That Paul likes me?"

With another glance at the door, Maddie wondered what to say. "The two of you are great friends. Of course he likes you."

"No. That's—that's not what I meant," Mary Jane stammered, the toe of her boot digging into a floorboard. "Acting these scenes with him sort of makes me . . . you know, *really* like him. More than other boys."

Maddie sat on the edge of a desk and pressed her lips together. What could she tell the girl? That she might as well save herself the trouble of love, because it hurt so much to lose it? That she should realize she would eventually settle for someone stable, with good morals?

Someone like Edward?

With a sigh, she wondered if perhaps she should warn Mary Jane that her teacher wasn't the best person to seek romantic advice from.

"To be honest, I haven't paid enough attention to make a guess about how Paul might feel. Remember, sometimes boys start eyeing girls years after the girls start eyeing the boys."

"I don't think Paul's like that," Mary Jane said with a shake of her head. "He gave Lillian a flower on her birthday last spring. You should have seen his face—beet red. He liked her, I could tell. But that was way back in April."

Apparently five months was an eternity in the life of an adolescent. Maddie put an arm around the girl's shoulders, and together they headed for the door. "The best thing you can do right now is to push the entire thing out of your mind."

Mary Jane opened her mouth in protest, but Maddie raised a hand. "I know, I know. It's much harder to do than to say. But you're probably a few years away from marrying. There's no reason to worry about Paul or any other boy. Just be yourself."

She closed the schoolhouse door behind them and locked it, realizing that many women she knew were married at Mary Jane's age. Ellen was married only a year older, at sixteen. Maddie and Mary Jane continued walking together.

"Being myself doesn't seem to work," Mary Jane said, staring at the path.

"Why do you say that?"

With a shrug, Mary Jane said, "Because I'm not like Lillian."

Maddie stopped in the road and wagged a finger at her student. "Who says you *should* be like her? You're Mary Jane Allen, the brightest star in my class."

A pleased smile crept onto Mary Jane's face in spite of herself. "Thanks, Miss Stratton." She kicked a twig to the side of the road and began walking again. "But I still wonder if I should act differently so people will like me more. Lillian says boys don't like smart girls—you know, since book learning doesn't help run a household."

"People" meaning "boys," or more specifically, Paul, Maddie thought.

"Whenever it's just us girls," Mary Jane went on, "Lillian behaves differently."

"Oh? In what way?" Maddie had only ever seen the flippant, flirting version of Lillian.

"For one thing, she doesn't bat her eyes all the time or use that high voice. And she's a lot more clever than you might think. You should hear the games and plans she makes up—and the gossip she passes on. Or invents."

Maddie's brow furrowed. "But why would she act such an elaborate part?"

"So boys will like her more than the rest of us girls," Mary Jane said. "And it works."

They walked in silence for several minutes, Maddie feeling somewhat disturbed at the news. Mary Jane was right about how boys responded to Lillian—they practically hovered around her like the proverbial moths to flame. No wonder Mary Jane was considering changing herself and putting on an act in public instead of just on the stage.

"Don't be another Lillian," Maddie said firmly. "The world has enough of them. Every class has one. When I was your age, her name was Sophia," she said, grateful that Mary Jane had no way of knowing or judging Sophia, who had married young and moved away from Bountiful years before Maddie came to Arizona. "My point is this." They had reached the lane to Mary Jane's home, and Maddie turned to face her pupil. "You will want to spend your life with someone who admires *you,* not who you *pretend* to be."

"Thank you, Miss Stratton," Mary Jane said, pausing at the gate by her home. "I'll try to remember that."

As Mary Jane opened the gate and made her way up the walk, Maddie turned, continuing down the lane as she wrapped her arms around herself. Her final words to her pupil repeated themselves in her mind. *You will want to spend your life with someone who admires you.*

Maddie scoffed. Who knew that one day she'd use the word *admire* to refer to a mate? That was the best way to describe her relationship with Edward. They admired each other and were willing to make a life together based on that respect. Such a far cry from the fairy-tale notions of love that she had once entertained. Her life would have turned out very differently had Roland lived. She increased her pace and headed toward home. Blinking, she realized a tear had escaped down her cheek, and she promptly wiped it away with the back of her hand.

One simply didn't find a second Roland in a lifetime.

CHAPTER 4

Another coughing fit gripped Clara Franklin, one so intense she couldn't even reach for her handkerchief on the end table. Her frail body curled up against the pain piercing her chest with each cough. As the spell ended, she found her hands clenching the bedclothes like claws. She had to consciously release each finger and make her breath even out.

She lay on the makeshift bed in the kitchen, the same one Abe had slept in as a boy. She had slept there every night since he left four days ago; it made her feel closer to him.

A glass of day-old water sat beside her handkerchief on the end table, and she longed for it to cool her parched throat. But the effort to push up and reach for the glass was too much—she might as well try climbing Ensign Peak. The water continued calling to her, and after a quarter of an hour just staring at it, Clara could take the yearning no longer. She edged herself up on one elbow and reached her trembling fingers toward the cup. They closed around it and brought the water closer. She lost her grip, and the glass fell to the ground, shattering and creating a pool around the shards. Clara closed her eyes and fell back against the pillow, tears forming in the corners of her eyes. The chills began again, and she shivered in spite of the three quilts piled on top of her.

A knock sounded at the door, and for a moment Clara wondered if she had imagined it. After a second knock, the door opened a crack and a voice called out. "Clara? Are you home?"

A moment later, Joanna Clements peered inside. Her eyes took in the fireplace, with not even glowing embers left, the table and sink littered with dishes. Her nose twitched at the acrid smell of a filled chamber pot, and Clara closed her eyes in shame. Another day or two and she would have been fine, could have made her house in order. If only her dear neighbor hadn't seen her like this.

"Clara!" Short, quick steps brought Joanna to Clara's bedside. In alarm, she sat at the edge of the bed and put a hand to Clara's forehead. "You're burning with fever. And you're trembling. You poor thing!" At the sound of shoes on crunching glass, Joanna noticed the broken cup on the floor and the puddle around it. "I'll go fetch you a drink," she said, hurrying to the empty pail across the room, then disappearing through the back door.

Mind muddled, all Clara knew was that she felt a mixture of embarrassment and relief as Joanna bustled out the door. A minute later, her friend returned with fresh, cold well water. She ladled a cup for Clara, then sat at her bedside. Without another word, she helped Clara to a sitting position and held the cup to her lips.

She wished she could drink long gulps of water but had to content herself with slow sips against her raw throat. In relief, she lay against her pillow and closed her eyes, vaguely aware of Joanna hurrying to the pail. A cold, wet cloth was soon placed on her forehead, and once again Clara sighed. Something so small didn't relieve all her discomfort, but after a day and a half of absolute misery, the cold compress felt like nothing short of a miracle. The illness had been coming on for over a week, she realized. But it didn't hit full force until the day before last.

Joanna bustled about the kitchen, lighting the stove and washing dishes, and within no time, she appeared at Clara's beside with a bowl of broth. Spoonful by spoonful, Clara had her first meal in two days. She felt stronger, although she wasn't sure how much was from the company and how much was from the broth.

"Would you like more?" Joanna asked with the last spoonful. When Clara shook her head, Joanna rose and began tidying the place again.

"I came to deliver a telegram from Abe," she said, sweeping glass fragments from the floor. With a shake of her head, she made tight, quick strokes with the broom. "You're in no position to be on your own, you know."

"My son was with me," Clara said. She swallowed uncomfortably, her throat still feeling sore and tight.

With a sigh, Joanna wet the washcloth again and put it back on Clara's forehead. Her expression was one a mother might give a child. "Abe's not here anymore."

Clara didn't protest; she hadn't the strength. She and Abe would be reunited soon.

Ever since he had left, she had been missing him and praying hard. And she felt the assurance that she would be with him again, which is why her sickness hadn't worried her unduly in spite of her years. "The telegram?" she croaked.

"Oh, of course." Joanna reached into her waistband to remove a folded paper. She opened it. "Do you want me to read it to you?"

Clara gave a weak nod; her eyes were useless without her reading glasses, and she couldn't think where they were right now.

"'Arrived safely. Stop,'" Joanna read. "'Staying in San Bernardino. Stop. Looking for work and Saints. Stop.'"

A smile from Clara was Joanna's thanks. Her neighbor clearly didn't understand the meaning of the final sentence. She refolded the telegram and placed it into Clara's tired, trembling hands. "Do you want me to respond to it?"

"Not yet. When I'm well."

"Of course," Joanna said with understanding. A mother didn't want to worry her child. As Clara rested, Joanna lapsed into silence and worked—cleaning dishes, emptying the chamber pot into the outhouse, opening the windows and curtains to let in sunlight, scrubbing the smell of illness out of the house. And, finally, making a more filling soup for Clara to eat.

She brought a chair to the bed and sat beside it. "It's a vegetable soup, easy on the stomach," Joanna said. "I'll go home soon and bring you some bread and cheese. Tonight I'll stay with you."

"No need."

"Just see if I don't," Joanna said with a curt shake of her head. "I can't leave you alone."

"Thank you," Clara said.

True to her word, Joanna stayed at Clara's bedside. Several hours into the night, when Clara couldn't sleep, Joanna offered to read aloud. She reached for a book of poetry on the end table.

She opened to the bookmark and began reading Lord Byron's "Prometheus." One line into the poem, Clara protested, "I'd rather not hear about someone in pain if you don't mind terribly." She smiled sardonically, her throat feeling much less raw than before.

"Sorry," Joanna said, returning the grin. She flipped through the book. "How about something by Wordsworth?"

Clara gave her approval, and Joanna launched into "The Thorn."

There is a Thorn—it looks so old,
In truth you'd find it hard to say
How it could ever have been young,
It looks so old and grey.

A chuckle began rumbling in Clara's chest, turning into a series of coughs. Joanna brought another glass of water. After Clara drank it down and could speak again, she waved her hand as if chasing the poem away. "I don't think I'm in the mood for that one, either. I don't need a reminder of my age today."

She also didn't need any thoughts of losing her only child, which is what "The Thorn" was really about. Joanna looked wary of trying a third time, so Clara decided for her.

"'The Rime of the Ancient Mariner' is benign enough."

Joanna apologized as she looked for it. "I confess I'm not familiar with much poetry."

But Clara's mind had drifted elsewhere. "How long do you think a trip to St. George would take?" she asked suddenly.

The book closed in Joanna's lap. "I don't know, two or three weeks there and back altogether, I should imagine. Why?"

The old lady took a deep breath before speaking. "The temple was one of Bart's lifelong wishes. I've been praying to live long enough to reach the temple and carry out his wishes."

"What about the Endowment House?" Joanna asked. "It's right here in town."

Clara shook her head adamantly—or as much as she could in her weak condition. "Bart insisted it be in a dedicated temple. You know how stubborn he was."

Clara and Bart had been unable to receive their temple blessings in Nauvoo before the Saints had to leave. For years, Bart was sure the Salt Lake Temple would be completed in his lifetime, and he was willing to wait. When Brother Brigham closed the Endowment House to urge the work forward, Bart felt his position was vindicated.

"See," he had told Clara. "Even President Young thinks the Endowment House isn't good enough. I'm waiting for a temple."

Of course, President Taylor's reopening of the Endowment House after President Young's death didn't change Bart's opinion. And by the time the St. George Temple was dedicated, Bart was too ill to travel, and he died unendowed.

"I'll be leaving Utah to be with Abe soon," Clara said. "So the next few weeks may be my last chance to go to a temple in my lifetime. I want to go."

Joanna spent another hour at Clara's bedside before returning home to take care of her own family matters. It was then that Clara's thoughts returned to her late husband and his temple wishes. And of their son, of how Bart had treated him so cruelly over the years.

"I wonder," she whispered, as if her husband were there in the room with her, "if you're worthy to have temple blessings." She sighed and rearranged her blanket. How soon would Abe come for her? Would she have time to go to the temple first? Perhaps Abe could take her on their way west; it would almost be on the way to California. After Abe's experiences in Logan, she wouldn't have had the heart to ask him to take her up there, even if the temple there was completed.

The embers in the fireplace were orange and slowly fading. Clara closed her eyes and nestled against the pillow as she fell asleep, wondering where her boy was at that moment—and hoping he was well.

* * *

"The name's Ben," the bartender said, reaching a hand across the bar. By the gray streaks in his hair and the lines around his eyes, Abe guessed he was around fifty.

"I'm Abe," he said, shaking hands and then dropping his bag beside a stool.

"Can I get you something?" Ben asked, turning around and grabbing a glass from a shelf behind him.

"Actually, I'm hoping you can help me in another way," Abe said. He figured that while most Mormons didn't frequent bars, someone who owned a tavern would know the community better than almost anyone. "I just arrived and—"

"And let me guess," Ben interjected, folding his arms awkwardly with the glass in one hand. "You're looking for work."

"Eventually, yes. But maybe not here. First I'm looking for a group of Mormons."

Ben cocked his head in surprise and squinted, making the wrinkles by his eyes deeper. "Which group might that be?"

With a shrug, Abe said, "Doesn't matter much, so long as they're practicing Mormons."

"The Mormons are gone." Holding the glass to the sunlight pouring through the window, Ben eyed some smudges and wiped them with a cloth.

Abe leaned toward the man and said, "Gone? What do you mean they're *gone?*"

Ben jabbed a thumb at the window, eastward. "Just that. They're gone. You won't find them at Sutter's Mill or anyplace else. Brigham Young called the lot back at least ten years ago. Most of 'em picked up and left before you could blink."

A sliver of hope crept into Abe's heart. "Most? What about the rest?"

The man's mouth turned down as he wiped the counter. "A good number followed in the next years. A few stayed behind with Sam Brannan. At least, that's what my sister told me."

On his feet now, Abe felt like interrogating Ben. *Just get on with it,* he thought. *Tell me where I can find the rest of the Saints.* But aloud he said, "So where are Brannan and his Saints?"

Ben looked up from the counter, a wet rag still in his hand and his eyebrows raised. "Tell me why it is you want to find them. Are you a Mormon?"

"Oh, no," Abe said with a shake of his head and a nervous laugh. "Not hardly."

Ben took a step back. "Neither am I, but my sister is. I respect them, and I ain't gonna help someone who's planning mischief. They've been through enough, from what I hear."

"I'm not an enemy," Abe said, suddenly raising his hands in protest. "My mother is a Latter-day Saint. I want her to come out west with me, but she won't budge from Salt Lake unless I can find her a solid group of Mormons she can live by."

Ben visibly relaxed, but gauging by the creases in his forehead, he didn't look less troubled. "Glad to hear that at least," he said. "But if you're lookin' for a substitute for Salt Lake City, I don't think Sam Brannan is the answer."

"How do you figure?" Abe asked. The conversation was starting to feel as endless as the rail trip getting to San Bernardino had.

"Remember, this is just what I've heard from my sister and the conversation over drinks here at my bar, mind you. But word has it that your Brigham Young—" He stopped, noticing Abe's reaction to the word *your.*

"Rather," Ben corrected himself, "*their* Brigham Young all but disowned the Mormons who stuck around these parts. Heard it had something to do with Brannan holding back Church money instead of sending it to Utah. Only the obedient returned. Sam Brannan sort of left Brigham Young and his leadership and went on his own merry way."

Once again, Abe sat back on the stool. This time, his face dropped into his hands. "Wonderful. Now what?"

Ben eyed Abe for a moment, then turned around and fixed him a drink. Sliding it across the counter, he said, "Here. Take this. On the house."

The hot summer day made the drink more tempting than usual. "Thanks," Abe said, gulping most of it down in a single swig. Clapping the glass down, he wiped his mouth on his sleeve and began fingering his hat, which lay on the counter beside him.

"So what is it that you really want?" Ben asked. "To be here with your mother?"

With a rueful laugh, Abe shook his head. "No offense against this place, but no. I just wanted to find work away from Utah, but my mother is adamant about living among Saints. I thought coming here would make us both happy."

"Hmm." Ben nodded, deep in thought. He rounded the bar and went out to the floor, starting to clear tables and push chairs back. It looked like the slow time of day, after the midday break but before supper and evening. He and Abe were the only ones in the small tavern.

When he returned to the bar, he eyed Abe again. "Like I said, my sister's one of the Mormons. Two years ago she up and left."

"For Utah," Abe filled in.

"Actually, no. She moved to Arizona. To a town named Snowflake. According to her letters, quite a lot of settlements of Mormons are springing up in that area."

"But are they of the Sam Brannan variety?" Abe asked, his voice lackluster, his hopes the same. He twisted his empty glass back and forth.

"Nope," Ben answered with a hearty shake of his head. "Not if Marie's involved with them. She's got neighbors who are in Snowflake on missions. People are still being called to go down and settle there, last I heard from her. They were mighty tickled to get a second black-smith for the area—her husband Seth. Mighty fine one, too, if I say so myself."

Abe's heart skipped a beat. Snowflake might be exactly what he had been praying—or rather, hoping—for. *Fine.* He might as well admit that he had offered a prayer or two that he could find a place to take his mother where they could both be happy. But that didn't mean he was becoming religious.

CHAPTER 5

"What do you think Mother and Father would say if they were here?" Maddie asked. She hadn't meant to say it aloud, but had. She and Ellen were canning tomatoes, and after nearly a quarter of an hour working in silence, the question made Ellen stop her work and look up.

"I don't know," she said. "I'd hope they'd approve of our lives. Why do you ask?" She continued drying jars.

"No reason," Maddie said. She leaned against the table and twisted a dish rag. Steam from the pots made wisps of hair cling to their heads. Maddie watched Ellen bustle to the other side of the room, where she gathered more jars from the stack waiting to be cleaned. She didn't seem to notice that Maddie had stopped working or that she was concerned about something.

Yet the question wasn't a general query as Ellen assumed; Maddie had been wondering what her parents would think of her and Edward. She already knew what her sister thought of the pending marriage. Another discussion wouldn't help sort through her tangled web of emotions.

If only Mother were here, she could counsel me.

Tomorrow was Sunday, and Edward would walk her to church. Then she would sit beside him in the hard-backed pew during sacrament meeting and count all of the marriages which, as far as she knew, were not based on love. She'd make herself look up at Edward from under her hat, and smile, determined to go through with her engagement—and the rest of her life.

Ellen glanced over and furrowed her brow. She put down a jar, then wiped her hands on her apron and crossed the room. "You seem worried. Is it about your school?" She shook her head as if already knowing what bothered Maddie. "When Peter and I first discussed the possibility of you going with us, he worried that a six-week trip might be too much for the school to do without you—"

"My students will be fine," Maddie interrupted. "Sister Brown agreed to cover my post."

"Oh," Ellen said, taken by surprise. She smiled and turned back to the jars. "What a relief. That's certainly nice of her."

"Yes, it is," Maddie said absently, picking up a bushel of tomatoes. With a large, slotted spoon, she lowered one ripe tomato after another into the steaming pot. When their skins began to come loose, she placed them into a basin of cold water.

Sister Brown had taught school for twenty years in Utah before moving to Snowflake six years ago. She and two other spinsters made the trip with Maddie's family when they were called to settle the area. The three ladies worked hard to support themselves. They got along quite well most of the time, but periodically the Church had to help them out. Within four years of their arrival, the work and upkeep of the schoolhouse became too much for Sister Brown's rheumatism, and that's when she passed the post to Maddie. The former teacher missed it sorely and had jumped at the chance to teach again even for a short time.

As Maddie blanched the bushel of tomatoes, her thoughts strayed, and twice she burned her fingers in the water. She thought about the three spinsters and their difficult time trying to eke out a living—the same challenges she would face if she didn't marry. She thought about Edward—dear, *good* Edward—and about what her parents would tell her to do if they were still here.

The last question, she supposed, should be easy to answer. They would worry about their daughter's future and her physical well-being. They would probably tell her to marry and be grateful for the good man who had promised himself to her.

There was really only one answer: she had to let go of the past. The trip with Ellen's family would be just the thing. She would see the place where Roland was killed. She would face the memories a final time and say good-bye once and for all. Perhaps she would bury her engagement ring at the site of his death. She would leave all her memories behind.

And when she came home, she would belong to Edward completely.

She turned slightly so Ellen couldn't see her face and the tears forming in her eyes. She bowed her head. *Father, take away my love for Roland. Fill my heart with love for Edward.*

* * *

"You're sure about this?" Joanna asked, sitting across the kitchen table.

From her seat on the opposite side, Clara gave a nod and struck the table with her palm. "Absolutely."

Joanna didn't look convinced. She poured a cup of water and slid it across to her friend. "I'm glad you've mostly recovered, but you still don't have your full strength back. It might be better to wait a few more weeks."

"No," she said, reaching for the cup. "It's now or never. I'm feeling quite well, thanks to you, and I don't want to waste another day apart from my son that I don't have to. The Wilsons' leaving for the temple so soon is nothing short of providential. I want to get there before Abe does so I can see him the first possible moment." She patted a piece of paper on the table. "The telegram said he's leaving for Arizona right away. As soon as he finds a place for us in Snowflake, he's coming for me in St. George. So you see, Joanna, I have go there anyway. Might as well leave sooner and go through the temple while I'm at it."

"But surely you could go later, when your strength—"

Clara waved her hand, chasing the words away. "If I wait, who would I hitch a ride with?" She took a drink and wiped her mouth with the side of her hand, then put the cup down. "I may have to wait *weeks* for another travel party."

Joanna had spent the better part of the last week trying to convince Clara that she wasn't well enough to undertake such an arduous journey. And while Clara appreciated the concern, nothing her friend could say would sway her from going—and being that much closer to Abe.

In another three days she would be riding with the Wilson family to St. George. While there, she would stay with her friend Miriam

Willis, who had been called on a mission to the city years before. They had been dear friends in their youth, and Clara couldn't wait to visit—and finally go to the temple while she waited for her son's arrival. When he made it to St. George, the two of them would go to Snowflake and begin a new life together there.

She looked around the small kitchen, at the stove, bed, and china hutch. "You know, it's funny," Clara went on. "I thought leaving this place would be much harder. But looking forward to the temple and being with my son again means so much more. I'm almost giddy to leave."

Joanna reached across the table and put a hand on her friend's. "And if you ever want to return, the farm is yours. Roger and I discussed it, and we both agree."

Pulling back her hand, Clara said, "No, no, no. You and Roger have paid for it and given me a fair price, plenty to get Abe and me settled."

"But if you ever need a place to stay," Joanna said, "please consider this your home."

A smile curled Clara's lips. "That means a lot to me. Thank you." She reached to the side and slid a sheet of paper across to Joanna, her voice and manner becoming more practical. "Now, let's get that telegram sent."

"All right," Joanna said, dipping the nib of the wooden pen into the ink bottle. "What do you want to say?"

"Hmm. I don't know how the 'stop' thing works," Clara said, pursing her lips.

"I think the telegram office will take care of that part," Joanna assured her.

"In that case, let's see . . ." Clara's eyes narrowed in thought. "I suppose it must be short, right? How about this: 'Leaving for St. George Tuesday. Meet me at C. Willis home when you arrive. Love always, Mother.'"

Joanna scribbled the dictation, dipping the metal nib into the ink bottle twice. When she finished, she looked up with approval. "Sounds good," she said, putting the pen down. "How soon do you think he'll come for you?"

"I don't know. A month, perhaps. His letter said that a rail line was completed right through to that part of Arizona not long ago, so he can ride the train most of the way. It'll be finding a house and then traveling up to St. George that'll take him the most time."

Joanna's brow furrowed. "I'm still worried about you. I heard that Arizona's awful hot and dry. Are you sure you're up to it?"

"It's hot in some places, no question," Clara said. "I've even heard the devil himself would feel at home there." She chuckled at the thought. "But word has it that Snowflake isn't like that, which is why Abe picked it. The city's higher in the mountains and has a more temperate climate."

Sighing, Joanna said, "I'm grateful for that, at least." She plugged the ink bottle and wiped the pen's nib on a cloth, then blew on the note to dry the writing. "But I must say I'll miss you something fierce."

"I'll miss you too," Clara said.

Joanna went on as if she hadn't heard. "And I'm still worried about the trip from St. George to Arizona. I've heard frightening stories about it."

"You needn't worry about me. I'll be in the Lord's hands, and He's assured me that Abe I and will be together again." Clara stood as if emphasizing her regained health and took the page from Joanna's hand. She read over it, holding it close to her eyes and squinting to make out each letter. With a nod of satisfaction, she returned it. "Thank you for sending it."

"Of course," Joanna said. Holding the paper in one hand, she put on her shawl with the other and headed for the door. She paused before leaving and turned back. "Clara, if there's anything I can help you with before you leave, will you tell me?"

"Oh, I'm fine," Clara began.

Joanna interrupted, her voice insisting. "I know. But I'd like to help you while I still can."

Their eyes locked for an emotional moment. Although thirty years separated Joanna and Clara, their hearts knew no difference. "Could you help pack my clothing trunk tomorrow?" Clara asked, her voice suddenly husky.

"I'd love to," Joanna said, opening the door. "I'll see you then." She walked out, and the latch clicked shut behind her.

Clara released a deep breath and looked around the room again. "I'll miss these walls, but, Joanna, I have a feeling I'll be missing you even more."

* * *

It was midmorning when Abe came down from his room above the tavern. Ben had generously lent Abe a spare room, where he had stayed until he received his mother's telegram. At that point, he knew it was time to head east toward the next chapter in his life.

The tavern was empty save for Ben sweeping the floor. The owner looked up, stopped his work, and rested his hands on top of the broom handle.

"Mornin'," he said. "Hungry? I've got hash browns in the back that I doubt are cold yet."

"No thanks," Abe said. He was too anxious to get going. He gestured toward his bag and bedroll. "I'm heading out now."

Ben stopped working and looked up. "Oh?" He looked disappointed.

"My mother's on her way to St. George in southern Utah, and I want to meet her there as soon as I can. Didn't want to leave without saying thanks for all your help—for the room and for pointing me toward Arizona. I don't know if I would have known where to go otherwise."

"My pleasure," Ben said, "on both counts. You be sure to find Marie and her husband, now. She'll take care of you until you find your own place." Ben recited the address and how Marie had explained how to get there.

"I'll remember," Abe said, then recited the address back to Ben. "I put the letter and the other envelope with the address in the bottom of my bag for safekeeping." It was a note from Ben to Marie on behalf of Abe, asking her to help Abe out when he reached Snowflake.

Ben leaned the broom against the bar and headed toward the back room, calling over his shoulder. "You wait there a second. I've got one more thing for you to take along." A moment later he reemerged with a book in his hands, which he held up for Abe to see. "Would you have room in that bag of yours to take this back to Marie?"

"Sure." Abe took the pack off his shoulder and untied it. A book would fit perfectly on top. Ben handed it over, and Abe glanced at the title as he put it into his sack, then whipped it out from the burlap and stared at the cover. The Book of Mormon.

"Marie wanted me to read it," Ben explained. "Gave it to me near two years ago, right before she left."

Abe's heart began beating quicker, and his fingers gripped the side of the book. "Did—*did* you read it?" he asked, surprised at his own eagerness to know the answer. Abe hadn't ever cracked the cover of the book, partly because he wanted nothing to do with his "father's" religion and partly because he was afraid of what he might find out if he did. If Brother Franklin's beliefs were right, then what? Abe had never come across a "Gentile" who owned a copy. He wondered what someone like Ben would think of it.

But Ben just shrugged. "Never could get myself to read more than a few pages here and there. Don't think I'll ever get through it all, so I figured it was high time she had it back, and you're the best way to get it to her."

With a nod and feeling a slight wave of disappointment, Abe put the book back into the bag. He wished Ben had read the book and prayed about it. Then he could ask Ben what he thought—a pure, objective opinion from someone nowhere near "Zion."

Abe retied the sack and swung it onto his shoulder. "Thanks again for your help," he said, putting out his hand.

Ben took it, shook hard, then drew Abe close and pounded his back. "You're more than welcome," he said, pulling away. "It was good to find someone else who has a loved one among the Mormons. It made me feel a bit closer to Marie for the time you were here." He put his hands on his hips and stared at the floor for a moment as if warding back emotion. "You'll be sure to give my love to my sister?"

"Of course," Abe said. "Delivering your letter will be my first order of business. Thanks again." He waved, heading toward the door when Ben stopped him.

"Wait. One more thing." He went behind the bar. Abe paused and turned back while Ben pulled out the cash box. He opened it with a key and dug out a fistful of coins.

"Here," he said, "take these for the trip."

"Oh, I couldn't," Abe said, waving a hand. "I mean, I've got enough for my rail fare. You've already done so much."

Ben walked around the counter, grabbed Abe's hand, and soundly planted the coins into his palm. "Take them. They're yours. Maybe you can hitch a ride part way so you don't have to walk the soles off your feet getting to Waterman."

Abe tried to return the money. "I couldn't," he began again, holding his hand out.

"Please. For Marie's sake," Ben said. "Before she left, she was always saying how we get blessings for such things." He glanced around his tavern and shrugged. "This place is a bit run-down. I suppose I could use some blessings, and what better way than helping someone who's out to help another Mormon?"

Abe looked at the coins but didn't answer right away. There had to be nearly two dollars in his hand—more than he earned in a full day at some jobs.

Closing his fingers around the money, he said, "Good-bye, Ben. And thanks."

Abe headed out the doors and up the street. He had over a hundred miles ahead of him before he would reach Waterman, where he'd buy his ticket and ride the train into Arizona. It would make sense to join someone heading that direction on wheels. He hefted the coins, wondering how far they'd take him.

He pocketed Ben's gift, hitched his pack and sleeping roll higher, then headed along the dusty road, eager to find a home in Snowflake for his mother.

CHAPTER 6

Maddie closed the book and pushed it across the table. "I don't think this was such a good idea," she told her sister, massaging her head.

"Why not?" Ellen asked as she wrestled with little Mary, trying to wipe her dirty face. "The teacher always performs at the school festival. You can't break tradition."

Sister Brown had started the tradition when she had the school, and when Maddie inherited the position, she had kept it up.

Lowering her hands, Maddie blew a stray hair from her face and gazed out the window. "It's not performing that's bothering me."

"Well, that's good," Ellen said, returning to the basin and wetting the cloth again to deal with her daughter's sticky fingers. "Goodness, Mary, how *did* you manage to get so covered in strawberry preserves?"

An ache went through Maddie. She knew motherhood wasn't all hugs and smiles, but she couldn't help but think that had Roland lived, they would probably have had a child together by now.

Of course, if she and Edward were to marry in the spring as planned, she might have her own little one the following winter. She wondered what that child might look like. She imagined a boy toddling into the house, face and hands covered with mud—then realized with a jolt that the boy in her mind had Roland's eyes and dark hair. He didn't look anything like Edward.

She coughed deliberately to clear her throat—and her mind. It seemed like Roland had a way of sneaking into her thoughts at the slightest provocation. Which was exactly why she could *not* recite the poem she had promised to.

Ellen's voice broke through, and Maddie realized her sister had been talking. "After all, you're known as the best elocutionist in town. You can't disappoint everyone."

"I suppose not," Maddie said. "But perhaps I could recite something else. Maybe Keats?" She pulled back the book and opened it, deliberately avoiding the poem marked with a piece of pink ribbon, "Valediction: Forbidding Mourning." It had always been a favorite of hers. Considering the theme of the poem—a loved one going away— it had become even more dear to her after Roland's death.

Two months ago, when she agreed to perform it at the festival, she hadn't been faced with the prospect of traveling on the road where Roland was killed. She hadn't been thinking of him by day and waking from her dreams of him by night.

After letting Mary down from the chair and watching her trot off, Ellen finally sat at the table. "So what *is* your concern?" she asked, leaning over to look at the poetry book.

With a flush of color that Maddie hoped her sister didn't notice, she just shrugged and turned the page. Bringing up Roland wasn't something she wanted to do right then. Admitting how hard the last two weeks had been would only make Ellen feel guilty about asking Maddie to come on the trip. "It's nothing," she said with a forced smile.

A knock sounded, the door opened, and Edward peered inside. "Hello?"

Maddie thrust her emotional thoughts into a dark corner of her mind and smiled broadly. "Edward!" she said, rising to meet him. She took his hands, stood on her toes, and kissed his cheek.

He rocked back with a grin. "To what do I owe such a warm welcome?"

For just a moment, Maddie froze. What could she say? That she was forcing herself to feel excited about marrying him? "I was just admiring little Mary," she finally said. "And thinking about having children of our own." That was true, for the most part.

Edward traced her cheek with his finger, a look of tenderness in his eyes. Maddie smiled back. *I will love him,* she thought. *I will. He is a good man and deserves no less.*

"I came by with an idea," Edward said, leading Maddie back to the table, where they sat down. Ellen quietly excused herself, taking Mary with her to leave the two alone.

"What is it?" Maddie asked. She closed the poetry book and slipped the ribbon from its spot, as if marking that poem somehow meant she was being disloyal to Edward.

His eyes lit up, and he leaned in, pale cheeks slightly flushed. "I know we weren't planning on the wedding until spring," he began.

Instantly her middle tightened. "Yes," she said in a timid voice. They were waiting until spring when they would have their own home.

"And of course with my taking over the farm in the spring, it would be another year or more after that until we could get to the temple to be sealed," he went on.

"At least that long," Maddie agreed, her stomach suddenly feeling unsettled. She didn't like the direction this was going.

"What if . . ." Edward said, smiling.

Maddie did her best to smile back, eyebrows arched in curiosity. He took her hands in his. "What if I come along with you—and we make it *our* wedding trip as well?" He squeezed her hands, which had gone numb. "Just imagine. We could be married in a matter of weeks."

"Oh!" Maddie pulled her hand back, and it flew to her mouth. She couldn't prevent a slight cry from escaping her throat.

This won a full-on grin from Edward, who obviously mistook her reaction. "I knew you'd love the idea! Just think—before the first snowfall, we'll be man and wife."

Maddie's hand stayed over her mouth, and tears welled in her eyes. *No.* She couldn't make that trip *to be married.* Not again. And she wasn't ready to be Edward's wife. Not so soon.

She shook her head back and forth, making his brow furrow. He took her shoulders and tilted his chin down to look into her eyes. "What is it, Madeline? What's wrong?"

Still shaking her head, she walked a few paces away. After a sniff, she managed to speak. "When I go to the temple," she said, facing the window, "it will be with my *husband,* not with my fiancé. I can't go through that again."

"I'm—I'm sorry," Edward said, his voice quiet. He stepped behind her and held her arms. Maddie wanted to pull away but didn't. It wasn't Edward's fault that he wasn't Roland.

"I'm sorry. I should have realized," he said. "I hadn't thought of it that way. We'll wait, and when we go, we'll be going to be sealed, not to be married."

She turned around and wiped at her eyes. "Thank you, Edward. You're so good to me."

CHAPTER 7

On his way out of town, Abe fingered Ben's coins in his pocket. He hoped he could find conveyance at least part of the way to Waterman, saving him several days of walking.

Ironic, he thought, that it could take him nearly a week to reach a city relatively close by, yet only fifteen or twenty hours on a train to get all the way to Holbrook. Amazing what machines could do. Although, to be honest, the rail trip from Utah to California had held more smoke, dust, and heat than Abe wanted to experience for the rest of his life. He hoped this next train ride would be his last, even if it could take him as far in one hour as he could walk in a day.

An inn with a stable out back stood near the side of the road. Abe paused. It looked like a stopping point for wagon caravans. He might have a good chance of finding a ride here.

Taking his hat off, Abe entered the building and wiped his sleeve across his brow. He was tired of the heat. First Utah's, now California's. He knew he might as well get used to it, at least until he reached Snowflake.

"Can—can I help you?" A small, balding man sat behind a desk, waiting for a response. He eyed Abe warily, his gaze moving up and down Abe's figure. The man's glance flitted toward the log book on the desk in front of him. Abe followed suit and saw that it was perhaps half full. The man leaned forward and covered the book with his arms. "I'm afraid we don't have any rooms available," he said, although several keys still hung from the peg board behind him.

The reason for the man's sudden suspicion wasn't a mystery. Abe's hand unconsciously reached for the nape of his neck, where his ponytail had been not too long ago. Apparently cutting it off wasn't enough to hide his heritage from people who cared about such things. His hand absently rose to touch the burn scars on his cheek, but he pulled his thumb away before it reached his face. The scars had faded considerably, and he was grateful that they no longer supplied more reason for stares.

"I'm not looking for a room," Abe said, wiping his palms on his pants and flashing a smile to reassure the man. "Mr.—"

"Hill," the man supplied.

"Mr. Hill," Abe repeated. "I hoped you might know of someone going toward Waterman that I might *pay* to join." He made sure to mention payment. Abe knew from experience that sometimes money could make things possible when moments before they hadn't been.

"I'm headed that direction myself right now." The voice came from behind Abe as a young man about his age walked in the front door.

Mr. Hill's eyes narrowed, and he seemed to want to shake his head at the idea, but the young man thrust a hand toward Abe. "The name's Davis. Davis Hill. This here's my father. I'm running up to Victorville on business. It's maybe thirty miles out of Waterman. I'm leaving right now, and I'd be happy for the company if you want to join me."

"That would be great." Abe shook Davis's hand, completely ignoring the father.

Mr. Hill spoke up. "We'll need at least a dollar. It's a two-day drive, you know."

"I'm happy to pay it," Abe said over his shoulder.

Davis turned toward the door and was about to head out with Abe, when he stopped, remembering why he had come inside. "Hey Pa, is there anything else you want me to take care of while I'm gone?"

But Mr. Hill was obviously distracted at the prospect of Abe riding with his son, and merely shook his head. "Just hurry back. Your ma and I need help in the stable."

"I will," he said with a half wave. "Bye, Pa."

With that, Davis and Abe left the inn. For Abe, stepping outside felt like a weight had been taken off his back; the inn—or, rather, Mr. Hill—had been oppressive and stifling. Abe realized how fortunate he had been to find Ben and his tavern. And Davis.

The latter proved to be a quiet man, saying little to nothing as they rode along the road behind a dapple gray horse. Abe didn't ask what business Mr. Hill had to attend to, although he assumed it was something like picking up supplies. Likewise, Davis didn't ask why Abe was headed to Waterman.

While the silence was pleasant, it had one uncomfortable side effect for Abe. He had nothing to distract him from recurring thoughts of the book in his sack. Several times he found himself glancing over his shoulder at his bag, the sharp corners clearly visible through the cloth. He was a little annoyed with his newfound interest.

Well, I can't very well get it out and read it right here on the road, Abe thought, turning forward again, this time with finality. Beside him sat Mr. Hill's son, after all. Davis might not care that Abe was Indian—or, more likely, hadn't realized that's what he was—but he might care if he saw a Mormon Bible.

Abe wouldn't look over his shoulder again. It took serious resolve not to do so for the remainder of the trip—sometimes to the point of Abe digging his fingers into the bench—but he managed to keep it. It didn't do much good; he was still *thinking* about the book most of the way.

Why *now,* was his biggest question. He had been around the Book of Mormon most of his life and never once had any urge to open its cover.

As the sun set, they reached Cosy Dell, where Davis pulled the wagon up to an inn. He secured a room for both of them—refusing Abe's offer to pay half, saying he would have had to pay full price without Abe anyway—then invited his companion to join him at a tavern.

"Are you coming?" Davis grinned, a piece of straw stuck between his teeth. "A lot of pretty girls live here."

"I'll bet," Abe said. "But go along without me. I'm exhausted."

"You sure?" Davis prodded. "Come morning, you'll regret not coming with me."

Abe laughed. "I'll take my chances. Day after tomorrow I'll be walking to Waterman. I'd better rest up."

"Suit yourself," Davis said. "Sweet dreams."

He closed the door and left his roommate alone. Abe shoved his sack under the cot and lay down, saving the straw tick for Davis, which was only fair since he was paying for the room.

The coverlet was thin, but with the warm night, Abe needed nothing more. He pulled the blanket up and stretched, then closed his eyes and tried to sleep, fully expecting to drift into blissful oblivion until morning.

The book is right under me. The thought came to his mind unbidden and unwelcome. He grunted and shifted position, shaking off the idea.

I ought to read it.

He opened his eyes and stared at the wall for a minute, then reached under the cot and felt the hard shape of the book. But just as quickly, he pushed it closer to the wall and readjusted his position. No sooner had his eyes closed than another thought popped into his head: *Just open it and get it over with.*

He rolled onto his back and threw the blanket to the side in disgust. *It's late. If it's so all-fired important I can look at some of it later as I walk. Then again, I'm also alone for the first time all day. This is a good time to look at it. Yes, but it's late and dark. I'd have to read by the light of the moon. On the other hand, it's a full moon, so there's plenty of light.*

With a groan of frustration, Abe sat up, snatched his sack from under the cot and yanked open the strings that tied it shut. He pulled out the book, marched to the window, and opened it randomly in the middle.

He read a single paragraph—something about Lamanites chasing down someone called Teancum. *There. I read some.* He slammed the volume shut and returned it to the bag, then lay on the cot once again. *And all it showed once again was that the Lamanites were bad.*

The nagging urge to read the book had finally left. He loved books in general, but he wanted nothing to do with this particular one. He had spent his life thus far successfully avoiding it.

He had been called a Lamanite more times than he could count. And the first words he ever read in the book, the very first passage, gave him proof that Lamanites were a bad lot. If that's where he came from, maybe there was a reason to be ashamed of his blood. That wasn't a pleasant thought. But it was an idea that would quell any desire to read more for now. It would stop the book from niggling at his brain all night. And if the urge ever returned, he'd be able to fight it now that he knew for sure what it contained—more prejudice.

He flipped the blanket into the air and pulled it back onto his legs. With a deep breath, he closed his eyes. *Good thing I finally gave in and read some,* he thought. *I'll get some peaceful rest tonight.*

* * *

The school morning had gone smoothly. Everyone arrived on time and was well behaved. Most worked quietly at their desks with their various assignments while Maddie worked with the primer class at the front of the room.

Maddie should have known it wouldn't last.

Out of the serene quiet, a shriek erupted from nine-year-old Eva Ellsworth. Maddie's head snapped up, and she jumped to her feet.

The Hancocks. Whatever had happened, the Hancock boys were always responsible for it.

"Boys and girls," Maddie said to her primer class, who sat with wide eyes. She tried to keep her voice calm. "Wait here quietly. Look over your primers until I return."

Eva stood by her desk screaming, hands clasped behind her neck.

"What's the matter?" Maddie asked, striding up the aisle and wondering, *What can the problem be this time?* She thought through the possibilities—maybe Avery Hancock had gone back to sliding snakes down the girls' collars again. Or putting bugs into lunch pails like he had all last week. Or perhaps he had poured cold water down Eva's back.

Annoying and upsetting. But nothing permanent or catastrophic.

"What happened?" Maddie insisted as she reached Eva, who continued her wails. Avery sat behind her with an angelic grin on his face, hands hidden in his lap.

Letting out a cry of absolute sorrow, Eva turned around and removed her hands to reveal stubby, uneven ends of hair where her long, sleek blond braid used to hang. Maddie's eyes flew open, and her hand went to her mouth.

"Avery! What have you done?"

Her reaction set Eva off into howling even louder. Maddie urged the girl toward the coat hooks. "Go fetch your hat. You can wear it for the remainder of the day to cover your head."

Eva nodded and raced to her hook by the back door. Maddie almost went with her, but instead she stopped cold. She couldn't give Avery time to hide the evidence of his actions.

"Hand it over," she demanded.

"Hand over what?" Avery asked, his voice so tickled with his success that he failed in sounding particularly innocent this time.

"The hair and whatever you used to cut it off with." She put her hand out and waited.

Avery merely stared back. "I don't know what you're talking about."

Twitters floated around the room, mostly from Avery's five brothers, who had certainly been in on the prank or at least knew about it beforehand.

"You are lying to your teacher. Stand up."

After a moment of hesitation, Avery stood, a look of triumph in his eyes. A pair of shears clunked to the floor, but there was no sign of Eva's long braid. Maddie turned in a circle, eyeing her students. "Who knows where the hair is?"

Several students flushed pink and clamped their mouths shut, avoiding her eyes. Maddie couldn't blame them; anyone who tattled on the Hancocks was sure to be their next target. "Give me the shears," she commanded Avery. He leaned down, picked them up, and set them in her palm. She pointed to the front of the room. "Now march to the blackboard. I expect you to copy the text from *Pilgrim's Progress* until school is released."

As Avery strutted to the front, Maddie wondered whether she should try using the switch on him again. It hadn't changed his behavior the two times she had used it before, and it probably wouldn't if she tried it a third time. Furthermore, she hated the idea of hitting her students.

Avery selected the book from the shelf beside the blackboard and began copying the words, not looking at all remorseful for his actions. Maddie practically yelled at the other Hancocks. "Jesse, Adam, George, Nathaniel, and Thomas, line up at the back of the room."

"Why?" Adam said, his dark hair sticking up in ten directions.

Maddie often wondered if his mother ever bothered combing his hair or if it simply wouldn't behave. She assumed the former, considering how little Sister Hancock seemed to care about their appearance—they arrived at school with dirty faces and dirty clothes every day.

"You will obey without asking questions," Maddie said, shepherding the children to the back. With the five of them lined up, they looked like a force to be reckoned with, and Maddie had to resist the dread of what her future teaching years might bring.

Sister Hancock called her children "rambunctious," but the town called them "wilder than coyotes." Two Hancock boys had already graduated under Maddie's care and another child would be joining her school next year—the youngest, a girl. Maddie nurtured the hope that perhaps the little one would have a gentler nature. But with eight miniature devils as older brothers, what were the chances of that?

She proceeded to inspect the boys' pockets and desks for Eva's missing braid, not finding it anywhere. Suddenly an acrid odor filled the room. Maddie looked around and realized that Avery had escaped her notice. He had run to the stove, where the awful smell emanated from. With a smirk on his face, he closed the door and rubbed his hands with satisfaction.

Understanding dawned on Maddie. She rushed to the stove, opened the door, and saw, to her dismay, the last of the braid going up in smoke. Every student in the room gasped, and Eva screamed in horror as if her head were on fire. Maddie snatched the poker, pulled the last remaining stump of charred hair out, and dumped it into an empty pail. She used the poker to smother the flames.

As the final wisps of smoke trailed lazily into the air, Maddie blew away a lock of her own hair that had fallen into her face. She put the poker away and walked to Avery's side, her finger wagging at him and her anger boiling.

"You have gone too far today," she said, her voice even and tense. "Just you wait. You will be sorry you did this."

"Yes ma'am," Avery said, turning to the blackboard with a smirk on his face. He consulted the text, then wrote the next few words on the board.

Maddie could do nothing but return to her class, calm them down, and try to get everything back to normal—then come up with a fitting punishment. "Everyone, go to your seats. Yes, you Hancock boys too. Please pull out your arithmetic books and work the sums on your slates. Raise your hand when you're ready for me to check them."

She slumped into her chair in defeat. Soon she'd have six weeks away from the Hancocks. But then images of Sister Brown came to mind. Could she handle such terrors in Maddie's absence? When the elderly spinster gave up the school, Avery—the mastermind behind all the schemes—might have been young enough that his true wild side hadn't shown itself yet.

An hour later, she rang the bell for dinner. Her students raced out the door, food pails in hand. Avery paused at the blackboard, but Maddie shook her head. "You aren't going outside. You will eat at your desk, and then you will return immediately to your lines."

"Yes ma'am," Avery said, the vexing smirk still on his face.

Maddie swept out of the schoolhouse to check on her students while Avery ate his meal. The girls had hurried over to the creek where they had stashed their cold milk bottles, then settled under the shade of trees in groups. The boys virtually inhaled their food, then turned to playing games and climbing trees. She watched them at their activities, having no desire to end the dinner hour or go back into the schoolhouse to be sure Avery would return to his lines.

But she knew that leaving him alone for long periods would be unwise at best, so she went back inside, half expecting to find Avery up to new mischief. Instead, he sat quietly at his seat, chewing a piece of cold chicken. The reprimand she had assumed would need to be given choked off midword. She walked past him and settled at her desk to keep an eye on him as well as to eat her own meal. He still wore that perpetual smug look of his, and Maddie wished madly that she could read his mind and see what devious plan he was concocting.

The few times Maddie had managed to foil the Hancocks' plots were some of her greatest triumphs. If only Avery wouldn't rile his brothers. If only she could find a way to make him behave. If only . . . but she stopped her thoughts there. She wouldn't wish harm on the boy—although last fall she had two blissful, peaceful months when he broke his leg and had to stay home. The worst pranks then consisted of Adam and Nathaniel tying some of the girls' boot laces together. They lacked the imagination and intelligence of their brother. She had almost wished Avery would be homebound again for a few weeks, but that was an uncharitable thought.

If only Avery could take his qualities and direct them into something . . . not destructive.

That would be her ultimate accomplishment.

At the end of the dinner hour, Maddie reluctantly rang the bell to call her students inside. They all filed in and sat at their desks, including Avery.

"Haven't you forgotten something?" Maddie asked him pointedly. "Unless you've managed to copy the entire book already, you are supposed to be at the blackboard."

"Wish I could," Avery said with a shrug.

Frustration mounted, but Maddie held it in. "And pray tell why you can't?"

"No more chalk." He sat back, thumbs behind his suspenders, and grinned smugly.

Confused, Maddie went to the blackboard and looked for the chalk. There had been plenty earlier that day. But now patches of yellow dust littered the floor. He must have crushed every last piece he could find. She searched the room, realizing that even the students' chalk was destroyed.

For a moment she had to turn away to hide a smile; as aggravating as Avery could be, his tactics were brilliant. No wonder he had looked so satisfied with himself when she returned from outside. Rolling her eyes, she turned to her desk for the chalk she kept there.

When she opened the drawer, the box lay on top, not in the back as usual. And her other belongings had obviously been rummaged through. Her stomach tightening at the sight, she opened the box. Not surprisingly, it was empty.

She replaced the lid, looking back at the drawer and her personal items. Avery had rummaged through them. *Her* things. He might even have touched the wooden box at the bottom of the drawer, which she kept locked. The thought evoked a new wave of anger. Her desk was the one place in the world she could call her own. Even her bedroom at home really belonged to Mary and Lorry. Maddie didn't keep her most precious treasure there. Instead, she used her authority as teacher to safeguard her desk.

Until today, it had worked. No student had ever dared to cross the line of her privacy. It would never have occurred to any student to do so—except for Avery Hancock.

"Get out of my school," she ordered, pointing to the back door. "Leave now."

Avery's expression went from triumphant to stunned.

With four quick strides, Maddie walked to Avery's desk. She grabbed his ear and yanked him to a standing position, then marched him to the back door.

"You can't do that, Miss Stratton," Avery protested, wincing with pain as he reluctantly came along, his head tilted in pain. "My mother—"

But Maddie wouldn't hear him. "You will pay for the chalk," she said. "And you will not return until you have done so and can show clear remorse. I do not want to see you darken my door for at least a week."

She shoved him out, closed the door, and bolted it. With a satisfying sense of justice, she wiped her hands and returned to the front of the class, suddenly refreshed. Her students stared at her, eyes as large as saucers.

At least for a little while, she wouldn't have to worry about Avery Hancock.

CHAPTER 8

The Wilson party pulled out of Salt Lake and moved toward St. George. With each step, Clara's heart throbbed in her chest. Her trunks were in one of the two wagons with what few belongings she and Joanna had decided would be best for her to take along. Clara wore a bonnet to keep some of the glaring sun out of her eyes. Since the party headed south, there would be a lot of squinting against the rays, but she wouldn't mind; with every passing moment she drew closer to her son. If anything, her heart might burst with joy before reaching her destination.

Two hours into their journey, Olive Wilson crooked her head around to make sure all the children were close by. Her lips moved as she counted each one. She nodded with satisfaction and turned to her companion.

"You've walked all morning." She put an arm around Clara. "How are you feeling?"

Clara lightly slapped Olive's hand. "I'm perfectly fine. Joanna shouldn't have told you about my sick spell; I knew it would only worry you. Besides, the fresh air and exercise are good for me. But I thank you for your concern."

They walked in silence for a moment, but Clara noticed Olive and her husband, Theodore, exchanging glances. Perhaps they both had worries that an old woman like her wouldn't be able to make the week-long trip and would instead become a burden within a day or two. Not for the world would Clara have admitted that about a quarter of an hour ago her right hip had started the hint of an ache that always forewarned a painful night. Or that one of her boots pinched her toes.

"Please ride for a spell," Theodore said from his perch on a wagon. "I feel just awful having you walk the whole way."

Clara's lower lip jutted under her top one, and she shook her head. "I'm fine, Brother Wilson. I walked to Zion from Winter Quarters. I can manage another few days on my feet."

Theodore took off his hat and wiped his brow with his sleeve, then replaced the hat. "Of course you had to walk the whole way; they didn't have room for everyone to ride." He patted the spot beside him. "But I've got half an empty bench right beside me and no reason why I couldn't enjoy your company on it."

Too stubborn to admit that a ride sounded good, she said, "Then let one of the little ones sit beside their father. I can walk circles around any one of you."

"I don't doubt that," he said with a chuckle. "But surely you wouldn't prevent me from being a gentleman, would you?" He pulled on the reins and stopped the horses, then tipped his hat in his most cultured manner. "Would you do me the honor, Sister Franklin?"

His unexpected change of strategy took her off guard. If it were still pity he offered, she could refuse, but denying a polite request to a lady was another thing altogether. Besides, the other wagon was already ahead of them, and they really should catch up.

And the aching in her hip was growing worse . . .

With a dramatic sigh, she nodded. "Very well." She allowed him to take her hand and help her up. She sat down and arranged her skirts primly. Theodore clucked to the horses, and the wagon jolted forward.

For nearly an hour Clara clung to the sides of the bench in an effort to keep upright. The constant bumping and jarring of the wheels shook every bone from her toes all the way up her back and into her head. Even her teeth felt as if they were about to fall right out.

When they stopped to let the horses have a drink at a river, Clara shakily climbed off the wagon and planted herself on a fallen log. At first no one noticed her, with Theodore and his oldest son concerned with the horses, and Olive taking care of the younger children's needs. But finally Olive discovered her sitting there with a tight look on her face.

"Clara, are you not well?" she asked, rushing over with a metal cup of river water. "Here, drink this."

The water was cool and refreshing, and Clara drank it eagerly. "Thank you," she said, handing the cup back. "I didn't mean to alarm you."

Theodore had heard his wife's exclamation and joined them momentarily. "What's wrong?" he demanded. "Are you ill?"

"No." Clara felt bad for their sudden concern, when the reason for her discomfort was something as silly as bumpy wheels. She held her sides, laughter finally bubbling up. Shaking her head, she tried to control herself enough to speak. Tears coursed down her cheeks, and as she wiped them away, she managed, "Riding that wagon 'bout killed me. I felt ready to fall to pieces after ten minutes on that thing."

The Wilsons looked at each other, not sure whether to be relieved or concerned. With another chuckle, Clara managed to stand up, although her joints creaked and ached as they resettled, and she winced at the increasing pain in her hip.

Olive stepped forward in an effort to steady Clara. "You're in pain," she said. "You can't keep walking. Please ride."

"No, no." Clara took several more steps. "If you let me get my bones moving again, I'll be fine." She pointed a finger at Theodore. "I do appreciate the offer, but I'd much rather walk than have the life shaken out of me. Or, for that matter, my good sense. I'm afraid much longer on that rattletrap and my very brains would be nothing more than scrambled eggs."

Her jovial tone put Olive and Theodore at ease, and they left to finish watering the horses and taking care of the children. Clara walked over to some trees, her back toward the wagon. She folded her arms and furrowed her brow. With the humor of the moment past, the seriousness of what it meant settled in. They weren't a full day on the road yet, and if she were already having such trouble, where would she be by the end of the week?

Help me, Lord. I can't walk the whole way like this.

She rubbed her hands up and down her arms, suddenly feeling a bit cold. At least Brother Wilson could give her a blessing if necessary, she thought. She hated being a burden on the family, but somehow they'd get to St. George, where Abe would care for her.

All would be well. She turned back toward the group, putting a smile on her face in spite of her pain, and began to hum the music that she had sung walking across the plains.

All is well. All is well.

* * *

The second day of riding for Abe, from Cosy Dell to Victorville, proved as uneventful as the first, although Davis grew more talkative as the day went on. It helped keep Abe's mind off Ben's—or, rather, Marie's—book. He couldn't believe he was still thinking about the book, but he felt unable to avoid it.

They arrived in Victorville shortly after dusk and paid for a room at an inn. This time Abe insisted on covering the cost. After getting the horse and their belongings settled, Davis once more invited Abe to go out for some evening fun.

"No thanks," he said, sitting on the cot. "Tomorrow I've got a long walk ahead of me."

Davis folded his arms across his chest. "When I first saw you, I pegged you as a fun-loving, adventurous type."

Abe looked up from his mug of water. "Maybe I've outgrown the wild life."

"Outgrown? That doesn't bode well for my future," Davis said with a roll of his eyes. "I can't be more than a year or two younger than you."

Abe laughed. "Oh, I don't think you're in any danger of the humdrum life."

"Come on," Davis said. "Don't you want to spend the evening with one hand on a beer mug and the other wrapped around a pretty girl?"

For just a moment, Abe reconsidered. He remembered the previous night all too well and had no desire to fight the blasted book in his sack again. But he also knew that going out with Davis for a drink wouldn't be enjoyable. Abe really had outgrown such things; he never had much of a taste for alcohol to begin with, and if he ever spent time with his arm around a girl again, he'd want it to last longer than an evening.

"Go without me," Abe said, lying on his cot and hoping that would finalize his answer.

"Suit yourself," Davis said. "See you in the morning."

No sooner had Davis closed the door than the persistent thoughts of the book began battling in Abe's mind again.

You're alone. Go ahead and read some more.

What for? I know it's a bunch of malarkey.

But Mother believes it. She'd be happy to know you read some.

With a grunt of disgust, Abe sat up. No point in arguing with himself further. Might as well give in early so he could get to sleep quicker.

He pulled out the book and began thumbing through the pages slowly, reading chapter headings as he went. Half an inch or so from the back he noticed the word *Lamanite* in big letters in a heading. He stopped there—and felt surprised at the rest of the heading.

THE PROPHESY OF SAMUEL, THE LAMANITE, TO THE NEPHITES.

Shaking his head, Abe squinted and scanned the words as if he had misread them. Surely there hadn't been a *Lamanite* prophesying to *Nephites*. But there it was. He had heard the term *Nephites* before, and he was certain it referred to a group of people that were supposedly good. *How odd.*

It was the first sentence of the chapter that drew him in.

And now it came to pass in the eighty and sixth year, the Nephites did still remain in wickedness, yea, in great wickedness, while the Lamanites did observe strictly to keep the commandments of God, according to the law of Moses.

Abe leaned against the wall in surprise and stared at the page. He had never heard about this part of the Book of Mormon.

Out of curiosity, he read about how this Samuel person—a Lamanite, no less—climbed onto a wall and told the Nephites that they were wicked. Abe couldn't help but smile at the irony; it felt good in a twisted sort of way to have the Nephites be chastised by someone they considered evil, just as so many people considered Abe evil because of his heritage.

He finished the chapter, then put the book away, a smile still toying at the corners of his mouth. As he drifted off to sleep, he wondered what ever happened to Samuel, as he was never seen again after calling the Nephites to repentance. As Abe lay there trying to fall asleep, he thought again of Samuel's fate and wished he could have seen the faces of the Nephites when the stones and arrows couldn't touch him.

Abe rolled over on the cot and laughed to himself. Who knew the Book of Mormon had humor in it? And such ironic justice.

* * *

The shadows were long, and the evening breeze sent tree limbs waving gently as Maddie trudged along the road toward the home where Sister Brown lived. They had arranged to discuss school matters this evening so Maddie's departure and return wouldn't disrupt the students' studies. The sun shone brightly, and a light breeze made the world look light and happy. But it all conflicted with how Maddie felt inside as she dreaded the task of preparing Sister Brown for Avery.

Only another ten days. In ten days I'll have six full weeks without him. The thought wasn't quite as nice as it should have been, however, with the image of poor, elderly Sister Brown handling the Hancocks.

When she reached the house, Maddie paused and took a deep breath, wondering how she could possibly break the news about the Hancocks to the aging lady. "Here we go," she said to herself and marched up the steps.

She raised her fist and knocked three times, then waited for the door to open. When no one answered, Maddie wondered if the ladies weren't home. She leaned over and peeked into a window, where a shadowy form approached, but Maddie couldn't make out who it was. As the door creaked open on its hinges, she straightened and waited. Before her stood Sister Palmer, her face pink and puffy, and a damp handkerchief clutched in one hand.

"Oh, it's you," Sister Palmer said, her voice catching.

For a moment Maddie wondered why that was a bad thing; perhaps Sister Brown had heard about the terrors at the school.

But Sister Palmer raised the handkerchief to her nose and whimpered, drawing Maddie into the house. "What's wrong?" she asked, putting her arms around the short, stout woman.

The elderly lady melted into Maddie's embrace, tears erupting. "It's Florence," she cried.

"Sister Matthews? Where is she?" Maddie looked around for a sign of the woman.

Sister Palmer went on as if she hadn't heard Maddie. "I thought you were Bishop Hunt."

Maddie pulled back and looked soundly into the lady's face. "Is something the matter with Sister Mathews?"

Nodding miserably, Sister Palmer clenched her handkerchief and turned away. Confused and worried, Maddie saw Sister Brown coming down the stairs and hoped that she'd be able to shed some light on the situation. As Sister Brown approached, Maddie could see she also had eyes bloodshot from crying, and her hair, normally in a smooth and tight bun, hung slightly askew, with wisps framing her wrinkled face. But instead of crumpling into a mass of tears like Sister Palmer had, she took each step stoically and deliberately.

"Is Sister Matthews ill?" Maddie rushed to the stairs. "Shall I fetch the doctor?"

Sister Brown gave no answer until she reached the bottom step and laid a hand on top of Maddie's, which gripped the banister. Her head moved back and forth. "No. But thank you for the concern. Florence passed not twenty minutes ago."

Fingertips flew to Maddie's lips. "I'm so sorry. I didn't know she was sick."

Beside the door, Sister Palmer choked out, "She *wasn't*. That's the hardest part. For nigh unto twenty years she hasn't had a sick day. Not one. Until yesterday morning." Another round of uncontrollable sobs burst out, and in despair, Sister Palmer scurried past them to the kitchen.

Maddie felt frozen to the wood floor, unsure what to do or say. All thoughts of the Hancocks and Avery had vanished. "Can I do anything to help? Anything at all?"

With a dab at her eye, Sister Brown nodded. "Could you stay with Caroline for a spell? I can take care of Florence and—and the matters at hand. We sent the Gardner boy from across the street to fetch Bishop Hunt, so I imagine he'll be here soon."

"I'll stay as long as you like," Maddie said, moving toward the kitchen. She took a few steps, then stopped and turned back. "Have you eaten supper yet? I can make something to help keep up your strength."

"Thank you. We haven't eaten," Sister Brown said with grateful, tired eyes. "A small bite would be wonderful. For Caroline, especially."

As Maddie headed for the kitchen, Sister Brown called to her. "About the school . . ."

"Don't worry about it," Maddie said. "I'll see what I can do about finding someone else to teach while I am away."

"That's not what I meant," Sister Brown said. "I was going to say I still plan on teaching. I'd appreciate you coming by again next week—after the funeral—to discuss the matter."

"Are you sure?" Maddie asked. "I know a girl in Woodruff—"

"Please let me teach," Sister Brown said. "I've missed it. One final chance would be a pleasant way to say good-bye to Snowflake."

Maddie returned and took Sister Brown's aging hand in hers. "You're leaving? Why?"

Sister Brown lowered her head, staring at the grain in the floorboards. "We've been considering such a move for a long time," she said quietly. "We don't *want* to go, I assure you. We came to Snowflake as old ladies, but it still feels like home."

"Then why?" Maddie repeated. Spring evenings wouldn't be the same without the three old ladies sitting on the porch in their rocking chairs, working on needlepoint. The town fair would have a hole in it without the ladies' famous jams and pies. An overwhelming—and surprising—sense of loss swept over Maddie. She couldn't imagine the town with the three spinsters gone. *Two* spinsters, she corrected herself.

"For starters, this house is becoming too much for us to care for." Sister Brown looked up at the walls and ceiling. "It was built for a large family originally, if you recall, the Kelseys. As soon as President Young released them from their mission, they returned to Utah, and we moved in. It's always been a bit much for three old ladies in the final years of their lives."

"Don't say that," Maddie said. "You have plenty of years left."

Sister Brown reached up and cupped Maddie's cheek. "It's hard to imagine the end of life when you're young." She smiled wanly and sighed. "But when most of the people you once knew and loved have passed on, you start to realize that your turn isn't too far in the future."

Maddie walked around the banister and sat on a step, Sister Brown sitting beside her.

"Fact is, Florence was the one supporting us for nearly three years. Caroline and I haven't been able to help much. I'm just too old and rickety to do much anymore." She smiled sadly and smoothed out her skirts before looking out the window next to the front door. "With Florence gone, it makes the most sense to move now. We'll go to Woodruff and join the United Order there. They'll put us to the best use we can be—whatever that is—and take care of us, too."

"But everyone in Snowflake loves you. We'd care for you—"

"And live on charity until we die?" Sister Brown broke in with a shake of her head. "You understand us wanting to contribute, I'm sure. In Woodruff they'll find the best way for us to give to the order. Perhaps I'll teach again."

"But—"

Sister Brown just shook her head and patted Maddie's hand. She grasped it back, and their four hands were held together. With her voice growing tight, Sister Brown said, "This is the best thing for us."

Maddie nodded, understanding the reasoning but hating the facts anyway. "If you must go, wouldn't it be better to leave soon, before it gets cold? Are you sure you want to wait six weeks until I return?"

Sister Brown wet her lips with calm precision. "Perhaps. But we—the money from teaching will help us move," she said, her voice so low that had Maddie not been sitting a foot away she might have not heard. "I'd thank you to not tell anyone."

"Of course not," Maddie said. "I won't breathe a word."

"Thank you."

The two women sat in silence for a moment, Sister Brown's gnarled and spotted hands clasped in Maddie's smooth, fair ones.

A knock sounded on the front door, and Sister Brown pulled her hands away and wiped her eyes. She stood and went to the door, then paused as she reached for the handle. "I think Caroline would appreciate some dumplings."

CHAPTER 9

As dusk turned to twilight, Abe walked into the outskirts of Waterman with a slight sunburn and achy feet. He had just enough of Ben's money left for rail passage. He wanted to save most of his own money for when he arrived in Arizona, so instead of finding an inn for the night, he sought out a cozy spot under some trees. He soon happened upon the perfect location—near the road but secluded. He dropped his sack to the ground beside a tall tree, grunting from sore muscles as he sat and leaned against the trunk. He pulled the brim of his hat down over his eyes as fatigue washed over him, and he fell asleep.

Birds woke him, and Abe had trouble returning to consciousness, his body crying out to rest a little longer. He took in his surroundings, trying to focus his eyes and his mind, when everything returned to him in a rush—he was in Waterman. Soon he'd board a train to Arizona. He wished he had a way to exchange letters with his mother. For now, neither knew exactly where the other was. Had she left for St. George? Was she safe? Had she arrived?

Thoughts of his mother urged him to get moving. He did a quick swipe of his face with his sleeve, adjusted his hat, and got back on the street, the sack once more slung across his shoulder. It didn't take long to find the rail station and buy his ticket. What seemed to take a lifetime was waiting for the train to arrive, and then depart.

It must have been nearly ten o'clock when Abe realized he hadn't had so much as a bite to eat all morning. He had been so tired the night before that he hadn't even found any supper in town. After making sure—for at least the fifth time—that the train wasn't leaving yet, he walked along the streets of Waterman, discovering a small bakery around one corner. There he bought two hot cinnamon buns and wolfed them down as if he hadn't eaten anything in days. He really hadn't eaten much on the journey, and certainly nothing this delicious, Abe realized as he licked the last of the sugar from his fingers.

A loud whistle rang out, sending Abe's heart pounding. He snatched his bag in one fist and raced through the streets to the train station and onto the platform. He jumped onto a car with more energy than he knew he had and walked down the aisle to look for a seat.

Next came waiting as more passengers boarded. Abe's leg kept bouncing with anticipation until at long last the train lurched into motion. It moved so slowly at first that it felt as if the platform were melting away. During his trip to California, a fellow passenger had told him that a train clipped along at about twenty-five miles per hour—a staggering speed to contemplate.

He sat for hours in the half-filled rail car, staring out the window. The pale brown desert landscape of rocks and sand seemed never ending. The vegetation—tumbleweeds and occasional dried grasses— provided little visual interest, and Abe dozed off. When he woke, the sun was still high in the sky, so he guessed it hadn't been more than an hour or so since he'd fallen asleep. He stretched in the hard wooden seat and wished for something to read. A glance at his sack was all it took to remind him about the book again. But this time he didn't have the agonizing internal debate over it—not since he'd read about Samuel the Lamanite.

Reading couldn't hurt, and it might help pass the time. Abe took the Book of Mormon from his bag and rifled through the pages, trying to decide where to begin. Quickly scanning the text here and there, he decided against the first section, where the name Laman cropped up a lot, and nearly always in connection with something bad. The Book of Enos caught his eye. He read part of the first sentence, which talked about the writer's father being a "just man," then kept thumbing the pages. A "just" father wasn't exactly some-thing Abe could relate to or had any desire to read about.

The Book of Mosiah looked more promising. A cursory look at the first few pages revealed only a few Lamanite references, so Abe delved in, ready to skip if needed.

King Benjamin captured his interest. *Serving others is serving God—a far cry from Brother Franklin's "religion." But it makes so much sense, and it's obviously what Mother believes.*

Abe spent much of the trip looking out the window, thinking about his mother and her constant love and service. Periodically he'd open the book and read. It didn't take long for Abinadi to join the ranks with Samuel as one of Abe's favorite characters. He admired Abinadi's tenacity—he didn't take no for an answer and didn't care a thimbleful what anyone else thought.

Abe stopped reading somewhere in the book of Alma where evil Lamanites were, of course, trying to slaughter the good Nephites. That's when he put the book away and retied his sack, then rested his head against the window and closed his eyes to get a little more rest. Until he joined his mother in St. George with the proceeds of selling the farm, Abe wouldn't have a lot of money and might not be able to get another ride. He'd need his strength; he'd have at least one more long day of walking from Holbrook to Snowflake.

As he drifted to sleep, thoughts of his mother filled his mind. Happy times sitting together on the back porch swing as the sun set, a book between them. Joyful moments in the kitchen when she let him lick the bowl after making a cake. And then a different set of thoughts tumbled out. His mother spending all day and all night with him for a week when he had scarlet fever. His mother helping a neighbor woman through labor—and then through the death of the baby. His mother knitting socks and making shirts for the poor, even though her own dresses were in constant need of repair. It seemed like she spent every day blessing another person's life.

Blessing my life as much as anyone's. If there's a person walking this earth like King Benjamin walked it, Abe thought, *it's Mother.*

* * *

We're halfway. The thought didn't bring any comfort to Clara as she hobbled from the wagon to the glowing fire pit. *Only halfway.*

Both hips throbbed, crying out with each step. Blisters on her feet made walking almost unbearable. A cough threatened to erupt from her chest, and Clara paused, hand to her mouth, to stifle it. Olive had become more concerned over her, and the last thing the Wilsons needed was an invalid on their journey. The cough insisted on coming, but Clara kept it quiet. She hoped no one noticed. Then she turned back to camp and put on a happy face, giving all her effort to not limp on both legs.

As she approached the fire, Theodore dragged over an old log for her to sit on. She smiled her thanks and slowly lowered to it. The Wilson children chatted noisily, and Olive kept busy with their demands, dishing food and keeping the baby from touching the fire. Then she hurried to one of the children who had gotten scratched on a tree branch, leaving Clara and Theodore alone. Clara gazed into the fire, trying not to think about the pain. Even her head hurt—from the constant heat, she figured.

"You feeling all right?"

Theodore's voice broke through her thoughts. She straightened her posture and put on a smile. "Fit as a fiddle," she said, but a sudden cough contradicted her words.

He shook his head as he took another spoonful of stew. "What is it about you women, trying to pretend you're made of metal? Put even metal under enough pressure, and it'll break." His face softened, and he let the spoon fall into the bowl, which he set aside. "Listen, Clara. I've been watching you for the past two days, and—"

"And I don't want to be a burden," Clara said, her jaw set.

"Riding in the wagon wouldn't make you a burden!" Theodore looked exasperated. He grunted. *"Women."* He picked up his bowl and began shoveling stew into his mouth.

Clara bit the inside of her lip, hating the fact that Theodore was right. Tonight she could scarcely walk twenty feet; how could she expect to walk miles tomorrow?

"I suppose I forgot that the last time I walked beside a wagon was decades ago. I'm not a spring chicken anymore." She tried to chuckle, but it faded, and she ended up staring at the fire with a furrowed brow. "I—" Words stuck in her throat, but they had to be said. "I'd better ride."

"Good," Theodore said. "Olive and I will make some room in the back of the wagon and arrange a couple of blankets so you can even lie down if you like. That might be less jarring than sitting on the bench by me."

The rest of the family joined them at the fire. After everyone ate, the youngest ones fell asleep—the boys under the wagon and the baby snuggled in Olive's arms. A peaceful quiet set in. Stars glittered above them, and bright orange flames crackled in the center of the circle. Everyone seemed lost in the magic of the evening.

"Sister Franklin," ten-year-old Elsa said suddenly, the glow of the embers lighting her face. "Is it true you walked across the plains?"

Clara looked up and smiled. "Yes, it is."

The young girl moved around the circle and settled beside Clara on the log, her eyes sparkling. "Did you ever meet the Prophet Joseph?"

Once more Clara had to smile. Elsa couldn't have gazed up with more admiration if Clara had been Joseph himself. "I did, several times," she said. "He even shook my hand."

Elsa's mouth opened into an *O*. She stroked Clara's hand with a finger. "This one?"

"Yes. He shook this hand," Clara said, offering it to Elsa, who took it in both of hers and stared at it as if trying to see some remnant of the Prophet's touch.

"What was he like?"

The memories were decades old, but Clara had no trouble bringing the image of Brother Joseph to mind. "Very tall," she began. "With startlingly blue eyes and light auburn hair. And he walked with the slightest limp. Most people don't talk about that. I liked watching him walk down the street. You had to look closely to notice it. But I liked it. Made him different, you know? Word had it that the limp was from surgery on his leg when he was a child—surgery he endured without any restraints, and no medicine to dull the pain."

At this, Elsa's face scrunched up in concern, and she stroked her own leg. "Ouch."

"If anyone assumed that limp meant Joseph wasn't strong," Clara said, "they learned that lesson soon enough." A chuckle escaped as she recalled the perfect example. "I remember one summer day, when a stranger came to town. He had the idea of lowering the Prophet a few notches. I saw the man strutting along the street toward him. Then the stranger approached Brother Joseph and challenged him to a stick-pulling contest."

"And the Prophet just sent him away, didn't he?" Elsa said. "He probably wouldn't bother with something like that."

"On the contrary," Clara answered, another laugh shaking her body. "Joseph never could resist a good stick-pull. And he never lost one that I heard of. They had barely got in position when the man was thrown head over heels. Joseph stood up, wiped his hands on his trousers, and offered to help up his opponent. The man just scowled and headed the other direction."

The memories made Clara feel younger. When Joseph was alive, she had been close to his age. He could have been her brother, and his death had crushed her deeply.

"Tell me more," Elsa said, her voice full of awe. She leaned into Clara, who put her arm around the girl and began stroking her hair. "More things I don't know about him."

"Let's see," Clara said, wondering what the younger generation might be ignorant of. They had surely heard about his many revelations and miracles, of all the significant events of the Church. To Clara, it was the smaller details she liked to remember.

"He had a chipped tooth. Made him speak with a bit of a whistle. Emma said it was from some evil men trying to get him to drink poison while they tarred and feathered him." Clara shuddered at the thought, then returned to stroking Elsa. "You know, it was those little things—his limp, his whistle—that some people might have assumed were signs of weakness."

"But they weren't," Elsa said indignantly, sitting up.

"Exactly," Clara said with a nod. "Both of those things were almost like medals he would wear the rest of his life, showing his true bravery."

Elsa relaxed into Clara's arms again. She seemed to be pondering the woman's words. "Your limp shows your bravery too, doesn't it?"

Taken aback, Clara wasn't sure what to say. She hadn't realized the children were watching her hobbling attempt at walking. It was Theodore who answered.

"That's exactly what it means, Elsa. Sister Franklin is a very brave woman."

She and Theodore exchanged warm looks, and the family lapsed into silence again. She continued stroking the girl's hair as Elsa fell asleep. Clara thought on old times . . . the early, grand days of Nauvoo. Building the temple. Learning the horrific truth of the Prophet's murder. Being one of the many who were turned away from the temple doors because there was no time left before the Saints had to escape. Walking the endless miles to Zion, facing harsh cold, inadequate food, and unspeakable losses along the way.

After several minutes, a song seemed to come from Clara of its own bidding. In the stillness of the desert night, without any trace of a cough, her voice rang clear.

"Come, come, ye Saints, no toil nor labor fear."

She went on singing, her voice swelling on the chorus of, "All is well! All is well!"

When she reached the final verse, the very air around them seemed to grow more reverent. Clara's voice lowered and she sang in hushed tones, "And should we die before our journey's through, Happy day! All is well!"

CHAPTER 10

The morning of Florence Matthews's funeral arrived without a cloud in the sky. The sun shone brightly, and it seemed to Maddie as she sat with Ellen's family in the chapel during the service that birds chirped in nearly every tree. The sound of buzzing bees came through a window, and Maddie couldn't help but think that the cheery day must mock the two old maids Florence left behind.

"We have lost a fine lady," Bishop Hunt said from the pulpit. Several heads in the congregation nodded in agreement, and a loud sniff came from the front pew, where Sisters Palmer and Brown sat together with an arm around each other's shoulders.

"Surely now that she is on the other side of the veil," Bishop Hunt continued, "she has taken up the mantle of teacher she wore so well here. She will have new students to teach, but instead of the three *R*s, she will instruct spirits on the lessons of eternity."

No one in the congregation gave the slightest hint that the bishop had the three spinsters confused with each other. Pearl Brown had been the teacher, not Florence Matthews. Maddie hoped others noticed the error as she did. A feeling of deep sadness settled over her. Poor Florence. In death she wasn't even remembered for her own life. Granted, being a laundress and seamstress wasn't nearly as honorable sounding as "teacher," but all people deserved to be honored for what their lives consisted of. Sister Matthews had filled hers with hard work and devotion to God. She was an adoptive mother to many children. She made clothing for missionaries and others who had little, even though she was often in need herself.

Didn't any of that bear mentioning?

A simple look around the room sent another wave of sadness over Maddie—Florence had no family to mourn her. At her age, living parents would have been unlikely for anyone, but as the youngest in her family, she had no living siblings, either. And no husband. No children.

No one but this room of fellow citizens and Saints. People who would go on with their lives and within a year no longer think of Florence Matthews with more than a passing memory.

There but for the grace of God go I, Maddie thought.

She placed her right hand over her left, cradling the small diamond in its gold band, the object that would assure her a future along a very different path.

Bishop Hunt concluded his remarks and announced, "The closing song will be 'How Great Thou Art,' sung by Sister Stratton's pupils."

As Maddie rose to shepherd them to the front and lead the song, the bishop added, "A fitting tribute from another fine teacher."

She cringed, not realizing until that moment why her students had been asked to sing. Tears of both anger and sorrow sprang to her eyes, clouding her vision. As the children took their places and Maddie raised her hands, she couldn't tell through her blurry eyes if the boys and girls looked nervous. She worried that Avery would try something truly dreadful during such a solemn occasion. He hadn't yet returned to school, but to appease Mrs. Hancock, Maddie had allowed him to sing at the funeral. She desperately hoped his punishment would keep him from acting out.

The song went well, and Avery didn't do anything besides pull a face at the beginning, although later Maddie couldn't remember much about the performance. It felt like someone else stood there, moving her arms and prompting the younger children. When the final note cut off, she guided the students back to their seats.

As she found her own seat, her thoughts returned to poor Florence. *I will be known for my actions when I die,* Maddie vowed. *And I will have a full life when I lay it down.*

Caroline Palmer offered the closing prayer. The poor old lady managed nothing more than, "Our Father who art in heaven," before her voice broke and she was overcome by sobs. The congregation had to wait as her weeping escalated for several moments, eventually quieting to a high-pitched whimper. Maddie cracked open an eye to see Caroline's shoulders shaking, one hand covering her face, the other still in position as if folding her arms.

"We—we are so grateful for the life of Florence Matthews," she managed, then covered her mouth again and sniffed horribly.

Her emotions went on in the same way for several minutes, and when she finally closed, Maddie sighed with relief. It had surely been one of the most painful moments for Caroline. The congregation stood, heads bowed, as the pallbearers carried the pinewood coffin, lid piled with flowers, including a wreath of pink azaleas Caroline had made. Down the aisle they went and out the back doors of the chapel, with the people slowly filing behind it.

Maddie and Ellen had stepped into the bright sunshine for only a moment when Caroline approached them. She wiped her eyes with a handkerchief so wet it surely couldn't absorb any more moisture, and said, "I understand you're leaving soon."

Her voice wavered, and her bloodshot eyes made Maddie's heart ache, although she wondered why Caroline insisted on talking to them at that moment. People slowly walked to the cemetery only a few blocks away. It seemed odd that Caroline wasn't concerned with being one of the first to see her dear friend laid to rest. Ellen's children pulled at her skirts, energetic after being cooped up for the entire service. Peter led them to the procession, Ellen waving them on.

"I'll catch up," she called, then turned to Caroline to answer her question. "We'll still be around for about a week before we leave, so please, let us know of any way we can help you and Sister Brown in this difficult time."

Caroline's face broke into a strained smile with eyes puffy from crying. "I was hoping you would say that," she said, clasping her hands together.

"Oh?" Maddie and Ellen said in unison.

"There *is* something you can do." Color rushed into Caroline's cheeks. "Something very specific. And it cannot wait." For the first time since she walked into the chapel, Caroline had the slightest hint of something in her eyes besides absolute despair—hope and expectation.

"What—what is it?" Ellen asked.

Caroline took a deep breath as if steadying herself. Then she plunged into an explanation. "The hour Florence took her last breaths, she had one thing on her mind—one horrible, horrible regret." She held up a single finger to punctuate her statement.

Maddie and Ellen exchanged concerned glances. What could Florence have possibly regretted so intensely on her deathbed?

With fingers interlocked, Caroline gazed at the sky as if in prayer. "I promised to fulfill her wish. Moments before she died, I said, 'Florence, I know it's important to you. Before you're laid to rest, I'll do all I can to start fixin' it.' So I had to talk to you about it before that, right now."

She clasped her hands and again looked up at the sky. "I also made myself a promise that day. I said to myself, said I, 'When I meet my Maker, I will not have the same regret as Florence did when she met hers.'" She looked at the two sisters, eyebrows arched with intensity, and she wagged her finger at them. "And as you both well know, I'm no yearling. I'm strong as a bear, but so was Florence. My time could come faster than one of the trains I hear can crisscross the country. 'Course, I have no intention of going into the next life belching black smoke."

Maddie wasn't used to Caroline's way of meandering thoughts and odd comparisons. "I'm sorry," she finally said, interrupting and placing a hand on Caroline's arm. "I don't quite follow."

"What exactly did Florence regret?" Ellen added. "And what can we do to right it?"

Caroline looked from one sister to the other, her wide eyes as innocent as a doe's. "The temple, of course. Florence never received her blessings, and neither have I."

Understanding dawned on them, and they reeled back as Caroline rushed on.

"Bishop Hunt says to find a party to travel with. He doesn't like the idea of me going with the newly married couples heading up next month. Said it would be better to go with another group. I think he really meant they're too young to handle an old coot like me." She added under her breath, "It's not like I haven't walked every day of my life. I wouldn't be no trouble."

Images of traveling the rough road with this elderly—and eccentric—woman jumped to Maddie's mind. The trip would be hard enough. Ellen's children—and her pregnancy—posed increased challenges already.

Taking a step forward, Ellen asked, "Did the bishop suggest coming with us, then?"

"No." Caroline patted her chest. "It was my idea. Florence would be so pleased to know I'm already taking care of it so quickly." Her eyes grew weepy as she stood between Maddie and Ellen. Without another word, she hooked one arm in each of theirs and trudged down the road toward the cemetery, trailing the end of the procession.

"The way I figure," she said, striding along, "I'll get *my* blessings, then I'll get them for Florence."

Over Caroline's head, the two sisters looked at each other, wondering what to say or do. Both shrugged and kept walking. Maddie figured they'd talk it out with Peter and the bishop and have one of them tell Caroline that it wouldn't be the best idea for her to come with them.

But as they walked to the cemetery, Caroline continued to chat in eager anticipation of the day she could receive her own endowment and serve as proxy for Florence. Maddie listened, her heart dropping. How could they tell her no, when all she wanted was heavenly blessings? Who were they to deny the poor old woman her one hope and dream, even if it meant a dangerous and difficult trip? If she were willing to risk it, why shouldn't they allow her to come with them?

Caroline suddenly stopped walking and stared into the sky. "I can't wait for the moment when I catch my first glimpse of the temple. I hear it's white. So heavenly." Eyes closed, she breathed in deeply as if imagining the moment in all its splendor.

Maddie noticed Ellen's eyes—they were teary. The sight made Maddie's throat tighten, and she tried to ward off tears of her own.

"Won't it be wonderful?" Caroline said in a whisper.

"Yes," Maddie said, putting an arm around her. "It certainly will be."

* * *

At the side of the road, Abe emptied his sack to locate the folded letters at the bottom. He took them out, brushed off some dirt, and carefully put them in his shirt pocket. He stuffed the rest of his belongings into the sack and tied it, then looked at the two envelopes Ben had given to him. One was sealed and was addressed to his sister, Marie Ellsworth, with a letter of introduction for Abe.

The other held a folded piece of paper with Marie's address and instructions on how to reach her house. While Ben had never visited his sister, he still had the instructions she had sent him when she first arrived in Snowflake. Abe hoped the instructions were easy to follow. He pulled them out and read through them.

"Simple enough," he said, folding it and continuing down the road. Since Mormons laid out their cities in blocks, finding a location was relatively simple. He cleared his throat, feeling as if his lungs were full of dust from the rail trip. He must have swallowed a bucketful along the way. About an hour ago he had stopped at a creek to wash his face and hands, but without a mirror, he didn't know if it had helped. The train smoke smeared on his hands wouldn't come off completely without soap, and he figured it was still on his face as well. He didn't want to imagine what a sight his hair must be—not to mention that he hadn't shaved in a week. His hand rubbed the stubble. He was glad he had never grown much of a beard.

Even with dusk falling, Abe found the Ellsworth cabin without any trouble. He paused before it and chewed the inside of his cheek as he looked at the yellow glow of the windows and heard the quiet sound of people talking. His heart suddenly began pounding as he realized that this place—this town—was now his home. For better or worse. He hoped it was for the better, that nothing the likes of the Sam Harvey situation would ever happen here. That he and his mother would both feel welcome.

He glanced around the street at homes in different sizes and shapes, in various stages of construction or improvement. Where would he find one for his mother? It didn't need to be big or fancy, but it must be secure from the elements, something cozy his mother could feel at home in. He could picture them rocking on a porch swing, reading until sunset. The sooner he could find a home here and meet his mother in St. George, the better. Abe trudged up the walk bordered by flowers that looked like small, gray mounds in the twilight.

He rapped at the door and waited, holding Ben's letter of introduction in his hands. The letter was damp with nervous perspiration. He wiped his hands on his pant legs, feeling anxious and unsure of himself and once more wishing desperately that he had gotten a bath and a shave before coming. A woman probably in her early forties appeared. She had light brown hair smoothed off her forehead and pulled back in a loose bun. Her dark blue eyes had fine lines around them.

"Hello," she said, eyebrows raised. "May I . . ." She cut off midsentence and took in his appearance. Dirty clothes, his shirt missing a button that had fallen off somewhere between here and Victorville. A rip in his pants knee. Threadbare sack. Stubble. He probably looked like a transient at best.

"You are Marie, I presume?" Abe tried to break the awkward moment and sound somewhat cultured.

Her brow furrowed. "How do you know my name?"

Abe thought he detected the slightest spark of fear as she glanced toward the fire where her husband sat in a chair. He had turned around in his seat, arm resting on the back, and made a move to stand as he kept his eye on their visitor, who rushed to reassure them by holding out Ben's letter.

"This is from your brother in California."

"Ben?" Her eyes widened, and she snatched the letter as her husband walked to her side and peered over her shoulder. A quick inspection of the front of the envelope and Ben's scrawling script, reading, "For Marie," convinced her. "How—how did you get this?" She tore the envelope open and pulled out the two pages inside.

"I stayed at Ben's place a few nights. He gave this to me when I left to come here. Told me to find you and deliver this."

She nodded, reading the letter with her husband. They both looked up at Abe at one point, surely where Ben explained Abe's situation and asked Marie to give him a hand. Feeling awkward, Abe shifted side to side, when he remembered her Book of Mormon. He should get it out and give it back to her. He let his bag flop to the ground, then untied it and fished around for the book. He stood up and brushed the dust from the cover. Abe suddenly felt reluctant to hand it over. He wished he had finished it; yesterday he read about Christ's visit to the Nephites—and surprised himself by getting a bit choked up. Not that he would admit it to anyone—except perhaps his mother. But on second thought, not even to her; it would only raise her hopes of seeing her son enter baptismal waters, something that would never happen.

"Sounds here like you're planning on staying in Snowflake?" the man asked.

"That's the plan," Abe said. "My mother wants to settle someplace with the Saints, but nothing with a harsh climate like some other places in Arizona. Snowflake made the most sense."

Marie folded the letter and replaced it in the envelope. "Ben says you'll need a place to stay. Would you like to spend the night here?"

Abe gripped the Book of Mormon in his hands tighter as he smiled broadly. "Yes, thank you. I would like that very much, if it isn't too much trouble."

"Not at all," she said, stepping back to let him in. "A friend of Ben's is a friend of ours."

Before going in, Abe offered the book to Marie.

"What's this?"

"It's yours," Abe said with a smile of anticipation. He hoped to see her eyes spark with joy from the surprise. "Ben asked me to return it to you."

"It's *mine?*" Marie said with a touch of awe in her voice. She reached for the book, and Abe forced his fingers to release it.

"Seth, look," she said to her husband, fingering the cover gingerly. Her finger went up and traced the lettering where she had inscribed her name. Her hand went to her mouth, eyes filling with tears. "It was the newest edition, the first with numbers for the paragraphs like this." Her fingers flipped the book open and scanned the pages, stopping on the numbers. "Our old copy doesn't look like this." She tilted her head, as if her mind turned back the years. "Remember when Charlotte first gave this to me? It brings back so many memories."

"And all that has happened since then," Seth said quietly.

The reverence in their voices said volumes, and Abe could only imagine what they were thinking and feeling. Ben said his sister was baptized right after reading the book. The course of their entire lives had clearly changed drastically after that, down to where, how, and with whom they lived.

Did they ever miss their old life in California? Did they ever regret the decision to join the Church and uproot their lives by going to Arizona? The thoughts flitted into Abe's mind, and although he wished he could ask, they weren't questions you could pose to someone you had just met, so he tucked them away.

The man extended his hand. "Seth Ellsworth. Thank you so much for bringing this. And you are Abe . . ." He searched his memory and looked back at the letter in his wife's hand as if he could see through the envelope to remind himself of Abe's last name.

"Franklin. Pleased to meet you both." Abe gave Seth's hand a strong shake and inclined his head toward each of them. "I know I must look a sight. I've been traveling for several days." He gestured toward his shirt and tried smoothing his hair. "I'm afraid even my own mother wouldn't recognize me."

Marie smiled as she wiped the back of her hand against her eye. "It's perfectly understandable," she said and stepped back, opening the door fully and gesturing him inside. "Please come in, Mr. Franklin."

"Thank you very much." He stepped inside and took off his hat. "And please, call me Abe."

Seth led the way to the fireplace and motioned for Abe to take a seat on a wooden chair with a pretty embroidered cushion on it. Seth settled in as well, and Marie soon joined them, carrying a glass of water for Abe.

He thanked her as he took the glass. He was sorely tempted to gulp the whole thing down, but tried to show manners by drinking it slowly in spite of his parched throat.

"Tell us," Marie said, sitting in the rocking chair. She leaned forward and clasped the Book of Mormon between her hands. Her cheeks flushed as she looked down and thumbed some of the yellowing pages. "What did Ben think of it?"

A frog formed in Abe's throat, and he had to cough to clear it. What could he say? He didn't want to disappoint Marie, but he couldn't very well say anything but the truth, either. "I'm afraid he never read more than a few pages." At the look of disappointment on her face, he added, "I'm sorry. I'm sure you hoped he'd be baptized."

Marie's lips pressed together, and she shrugged. "Yes, well, I also knew the chances were slim. But of course, one has to have hope in these matters. I'm sure you understand."

Tilting his head backwards, Abe emptied the last of the glass while trying to figure out how to respond. Marie and Seth must assume he was a Mormon. The moment he admitted he wasn't, they would see him as an outsider. He had enjoyed a few minutes of conversation with friendly people who had welcomed him into their home. Too bad it had to end.

"I do understand. In a way." Abe cleared his throat. "My mother is a Mormon. I'm not."

"Yes, we know," Marie said, her hand resting on her precious scriptures. "Ben explained about you and your mother."

Abe didn't know how to respond. They had treated him well— *knowing* he wasn't a Mormon? If everyone in Snowflake were like this, perhaps this town would work out better than he hoped.

A young, fair face appeared around the corner. "Ma? Who's here?"

Marie turned and held out a hand. Her daughter scampered across the floor in her white nightdress and a ruffled nightcap. She clambered into her mother's lap and barely fit there at probably nine years of age. The sight warmed Abe's heart. As her mother held her close, Abe hoped that someday he'd have a similar picture in his own home.

"Eva, this is Mr. Franklin," Marie told her daughter. "He'll be staying with us for a little while until he finds his own place."

She shyly peered at Abe from under her cap, face half turned toward her mother and her eyes barely making contact with his. She bit her lip and asked, "What about your wife and children?" The question was so quiet that Abe almost missed it.

"I'm not married," Abe said.

An embarrassed smile broke across Eva's face, and as she flushed, she buried her head in her mother's arms. A hand went to the nape of her neck, as if she were trying to hide it.

"My mother will be living with me." Abe leaned forward, hoping to make her feel more comfortable. "She makes the best pie you'll ever have. Do you want to taste some?"

Eva nodded eagerly but didn't show her face. Marie translated. "I think Eva would love some of your mother's pie."

CHAPTER 11

Each bump of the road lurched the wagon and sent shocks of pain through Clara's body. She lay hunched inside with two blankets for cushioning and another on top for the chills that came in spite of the heat beating down on the wagon cover. Over the last week, the lingering cough that had never quite left from her previous illness had taken hold once more. The fever had returned with it, and Clara could hardly stand the shaking and pain the second time around.

With her last bout of illness, she was at home, surrounded by familiar things—her own walls, furniture, and dishes. The only face was Joanna's, one of the few people in the world with whom Clara could lay aside any pretense and silly courtesies.

But here, in the middle of the wilderness, she had nothing from home—the familiar needlework hanging on the wall, the blanket with the scent of home on it, and a blissfully stationary bed. Instead, the landscape changed every minute yet cruelly remained the same. The blankets were of rough wool, scratchy on her sensitive, feverish skin.

And the jolting of the wagon. Oh, if she had thought her bones had been jostled to death that first time riding in it, she had been sadly mistaken. At this rate, Clara was sure her insides would be nothing but tapioca by the time they reached St. George—*if* she reached St. George.

Hours must have passed since their last rest stop, and Clara felt like crying out in misery for another one. But once more she reminded herself of her situation as the Wilsons' guest. These people, as nice as they were, didn't have familial bonds with her, or even deep, friendly ones like Joanna had. Clara refused to be a source of frustration. So even in her misery, she wouldn't voice her greatest desire—for the wagon to stop and for someone to fetch her a drink of water.

"Almost there, Sister Franklin," Theodore called to her. He glanced over his shoulder and did a double take. Then his eyes searched the landscape. "Olive! Sister Franklin needs you."

Moments later, Theodore halted the team, and his wife climbed onto the wagon with a canteen. Clara sighed in relief at the stillness, but the wagon moved again. Olive braced herself against the box to avoid falling onto Clara, who couldn't stifle a moan at the pain shooting through her every muscle and bone. A coughing fit erupted, making her chest feel as if a dozen knives slashed at her insides. Olive patted her back, then gently rubbed it when the fit subsided.

Clara rolled over and stared out the back of the wagon at the dry, faded landscape. As Olive opened the canteen, Clara managed to speak in a quiet voice. "Why—didn't we stop earlier?" She wouldn't have dared asked it of Theodore, who apparently was bent on reaching St. George. But he must have heard the question, because he and Olive exchanged worried glances.

"It's to make up for lost time, isn't it? I've held you up." Her voice croaked, and she tried to clear it without triggering another coughing attack. Neither of the Wilsons answered at first; Olive lowered her head, and Clara assumed that was confirmation enough.

"I know I'm a burden. I'm sorry." Clara wanted to say more, to explain her pain and infirmities, perhaps to offer them payment for their trouble, but she lacked the strength.

"You haven't been a burden," Olive insisted. She wore a smile and held the canteen ready. "Having you along has been a blessing. Thanks to you, Elsa finally understands why it's so important for us to obey the call to settle in the south."

A long pause followed. Clara hadn't the strength to say more, although Olive's reassurances had helped. But she knew they would have reached St. George earlier if it hadn't been for her slowing them down, first with her walking pace hampered by her hips and back, and then from lying in agony inside the wagon.

"We want a doctor for you," Olive said suddenly, then rushed on. "That's why we haven't stopped. It's not because we're in an all-fired hurry to reach the city. It's for you."

"I'd prefer a rest," Clara managed, then closed her eyes; talking through the jarring bumps took too much effort.

"I—I know," Olive said. "But Theodore feels you need a doctor without delay, or—" Her voice cut off sharply, making Clara open her eyes again.

A doctor? She had never been seen by a doctor in her life. One had come right before Bart's death, but . . .

At the thought, she gasped. "You think I'm dying."

An agony of a different type went through her. She clutched the blanket to her chest. "I cannot die," she moaned. "No!" Her head rocked back and forth, fearing she might lapse into delirium.

The thoughts kept swirling in her mind. *My temple blessings. Abe.*

As she slowly slipped into unconsciousness, the thought kept repeating itself in her mind.

I cannot die. I will not die.

* * *

As Ellen sat at the kitchen table, she grunted. Her growing belly protruded more these days, even though she still had over two months before the baby would come.

"It's harder for me this time," she told Maddie as she pulled a piece of paper and a pencil closer to her. "My back, my feet, my knees—they all hurt so much more than with my other babies. I hope I don't have to walk much."

The unspoken concern wasn't lost on Maddie; with Caroline Palmer coming along, any extra space in the wagon might end up belonging to the elderly woman.

"It'll work out," Maddie assured her sister. "If need be, Peter will make two trips every mile if he must to bring both you and Sister Palmer along."

"If I thought it would come to that, we wouldn't be making the trip right now," Ellen said. "The baby is still over two months away, you know." She wrote *food and supplies* across the top of the page and said, "Now, let's make that list."

She made a line under the heading and looked up. "How much flour do you think we'll need?" Ellen began counting on her fingers.

"The two children are small enough they count as no more than one adult. So they are one, plus me and Peter, you, and Caroline. The equivalent of five adults." She leaned forward and began figuring how much flour they'd need for everyone. "We've been saving for months. We should have enough even though we hadn't taken another person into account."

Her pencil flew on the page, and Maddie watched, suddenly realizing that Peter was the only man going on the trip. She hadn't really thought about it before, but the idea made her stomach clench; the three women and two children would be safer if they had at least one more man along. Not that even a dozen men could necessarily prevent catastrophe. Last time they had three—Peter, his brother James, and Roland.

Maddie took a deep breath and chased the thoughts from her mind, focusing again on Ellen's list. "And of course we'll need plenty of feed for the horses, since there's so little for them to eat on the trail this time of year," Ellen was saying.

"Of course," Maddie said.

"That will take a lot of room. I hope we have enough space. We really can't take a second wagon, can we?"

"No, but wouldn't that be nice?" Maddie said absently. A second wagon and team of horses was one more reason they could use another man on the trip; neither of the women knew enough about driving horses.

A knock sounded on the door, and Maddie rose to answer it. Waiting for them stood Caroline Palmer with a small wooden cart behind her. It was loaded high with all kinds of things—a quilt, cooking pots, what looked like three bags of beans, and who knew what else.

Caroline stood there, grinning ear to ear, her teeth showing. "I've brought provisions," she announced. "Florence would have insisted on my contributing. Naturally." She stepped aside and waved her arm to reveal her offering. Maddie tried to hide a smile at the elaborate gesture.

"Sister Palmer, thank you so much," Maddie said. "We certainly didn't expect anything like this, but we are truly grateful for your generosity."

"Yes," Ellen said, joining Maddie at the door and looking over the pile. "Thank you."

"Poppycock," Caroline said, and for a moment Maddie thought their thanks offended her. But that wasn't it. "Of course I have to provide something for the trip. I couldn't ask you to take me along *and* feed me on top of everything else, could I? I won't stand for it, and Florence wouldn't have, either. This trip is for her as well, remember. And call me Caroline."

She turned around, wrapped her arms around a big quilt, hoisted it out of the cart, and marched into the house. Maddie stepped aside to let her pass, and Ellen showed her a corner where she could deposit the load.

"That's just the beginning," Caroline said, wiping her hands together in satisfaction as if she had just brought in a pile of gold.

Maddie and Ellen helped Caroline bring in the rest of her supplies—a bag each of flour and brown sugar, a frying pan, a large pot, a small sack of salt, a tub of lard, a box of dried onions, and a few odd items, like a spare sock—which Caroline insisted might be needed on the journey. "You never know," she said, tossing it onto the pile.

The final item, a lumpy burlap sack, lay in a corner of the wagon. Caroline presented it to the sisters with a flourish. "And this," she said, waving it in their faces, "has almost any remedy we might need on the trail. Including," she added significantly to Ellen, "dried raspberry leaves. They're good to help prepare your body those last couple of weeks before your baby comes."

She shuffled once more into the house and gently placed the last item on the top of the pile as if it were nothing less precious than diamonds. "Take care of that one, now," she said to the sisters, wagging her finger. "We'll need it. Don't let the little ones, sweet as they are, get their hands on it, or everything in there will be ruined."

"We'll take care of it," Ellen promised. "In fact, I'll put that bag on a high shelf right away just to be sure Mary can't reach it."

Caroline stared the two of them down for a moment as if determining whether she could trust them, and finally nodded. "Very well." She moved to the door, then stopped abruptly and turned around. "You," she said, pointing at Ellen, "might want to use those raspberry leaves soon. It don't take much to make a difference with labor pains and pushing and bleeding and such. I used to work as a midwife, you know."

"Yes, we know," Maddie said, stunned that even with that background someone would refer to such private birthing details in the open. Ellen and Maddie exchanged glances revealing that neither of them knew exactly how to respond to this unpredictable lady. What manners and customs did one hold onto when one's guest seemed to flout all such conventions?

But Caroline saved them any need to answer. She didn't seem to notice their discomfort as she headed for the door again. "I'll bring by my clothes and underthings the night before we leave," she said. "Of course, I won't bring them earlier. I'll need them until then." She laughed at her own joke, wiped a tear from her eye, and picked up the cart handle from the ground.

Maddie tried hard not to look shocked at Caroline's reference to underclothing.

Caroline did a little hop and clapped her hands. "I won't be able to sleep until we leave. Don't tell Pearl, but I've made a paper chain to help count down the days." She giggled, then breathed out in satisfaction. "I'll see you girls soon. Stay close to the Lord."

She marched down the path, pulling the cart behind her. Maddie and Ellen stood at the front door and watched her leave. The sight reminded them of a little girl pulling her toys behind her. Caroline Palmer was such an enigma, Maddie thought. The lady turned and waved at them, giving one of her big grins. The sisters waved back, and Maddie leaned against the door frame.

"She's certainly excited about coming with us."

"A paper chain is more than excited," Ellen said with a laugh. "*Ecstatic* would be more apt. She'll make the trip interesting, that's for sure."

CHAPTER 12

Leaning down, Abe tugged at the ties on Eva's bonnet. "So why do I never see you without something on your head? I'm sure you've got pretty hair tucked up inside."

Eva lowered her head and shook it back and forth. "My hair's too ugly."

"One of the students at school pulled a prank," Marie explained, coming up behind them. She rubbed the back of her daughter's head wistfully. "She had the longest, prettiest hair in school, didn't you?"

The girl nodded miserably. "Until Avery cut my braid and burned it in the school stove. He's no better than the devil."

"Eva!" Marie's voice went up an octave in surprise. "We don't say such things."

"Even if they're somewhat true?" Abe couldn't help but smile wryly. "Sounds to me like an apt description."

With a quick turn away from her daughter, Marie covered her mouth to hide the beginning of a laugh. She closed her eyes, breathed in and out a couple of times, then changed the subject. But as she spoke, her eyes still danced with merriment. "Please come to the school festival tonight," she said to Abe. "It's the biggest event around here each September. And the children would love to have you there."

Samuel looked up from a book on the sofa and nodded. "Oh, do come with us! You could write Uncle Ben and tell him about how well we performed."

Even Eva managed to not look quite so forlorn at the loss of her precious braid when her mother mentioned the festival. "Oh, *do* come," she said, pulling at Abe's arm.

"I'm singing two songs with my grade," Samuel piped up, leaving the sofa and crossing the room. Abe was no good at judging ages, but the boy barely came above his waist, so he couldn't be more than or six or seven.

"And I'm reciting a whole poem," Eva interjected. "It's a sonnet— and I'm doing it all by myself." She folded her arms with satisfaction and gave her brother a "so there" look. The shyness she had shown on his first night at their home had gradually left, and she was eager to get his attention any time she could.

Samuel took Abe's other arm, and together they begged, "Please?"

Abe eyed their pleading faces, their hands tugging at his, and shrugged. "How can I say no? I'll come, and I promise to write your Uncle Ben all about it."

The children cheered and clapped, then scurried out of the room to finish getting ready. "I'm sure you'll enjoy it," Marie told Abe as she wiped down the kitchen table. "And you'll get acquainted with lots of people, which is good, since you're planning on staying here."

Not half an hour later, Abe walked behind the family to the schoolhouse. Seth and Marie were in front, baby in her arms, and the four little ones trailed behind. Dusk had already fallen, making faces shadowy and vague. More and more people joined them on the road. Marie hadn't been exaggerating. This was *the* event of the season.

When they entered the schoolhouse, it was already near stifling; people were packed inside like pickles in a barrel. Abe decided to stand in the back so Marie's family could fit on a bench. Samuel scurried onto the platform stage and behind a curtain hung on a rope. Eva came close behind, her bonnet strings flying over her shoulders. The drape moved and swayed as students behind it prepared for their parts, sometimes shoving one another, at other times yelping out in frustration things like, "Teacher, he pulled my hair!" and "Miss Stratton, I can't find my hat!"

Finally a pretty young woman appeared from behind the drape. She smoothed her dark brown hair and her skirt, then turned to face the audience, cheeks flushed probably from both the heat and the effort of controlling her rambunctious class. The crowd gradually quieted, and she spoke.

"Thank you for coming," she said. "Your students have worked especially hard for this year's program, and I am proud of every boy and girl. Let's show them our appreciation." She began clapping, and the room joined in. Abe clapped hard, somehow feeling from her words that the teacher's pride was well deserved and that the children had earned the ovation. As the noise died down, the sound of tittering behind the curtain could be heard. He laughed to himself, realizing that it had been some time since he had been around so many children.

"As usual," the woman, who had to be Miss Stratton, went on, "we will begin with the younger grades and end with the more advanced students."

"What about you?" came a loud voice next to Abe. It belonged to a tall, blond man leaning against the back wall. He smiled broadly at the teacher as if they were friends.

She flushed, then nodded at the crowd. "I promised to recite a particular poem, and I will do so near the end. But now, without further ado, I present to you the primer class singing, 'Don't Kill the Birds.'"

As she backed to the side of the makeshift stage, she clapped, and the audience followed suit. Everyone waited for several seconds. When the little ones didn't appear, Miss Stratton went behind the curtain to arrange them in their proper line and lead them out front. Three of the four youngest students stood there with round eyes, just staring at the audience in pure terror while the remaining student sang at the top of his lungs. After the song, the would-be quartet went down into the audience and sat with their parents, mostly on the floor, as that was the only space left.

The evening went on, the performances gradually improving as the age of the students increased. The windows and back door were opened, letting in the evening breeze, which helped ease the heat to some extent.

As students joined their families following their performances, the curtain no longer swayed with jittery youngsters. The teacher appeared from behind it, her demeanor solemn. As she took her place at the front of the stage, the look on her face dissipated any urge the audience had to clap. Instead they quieted and waited, her pensive eyes sending a hush across the room.

"'As virtuous men pass mildly away,'" she began, her voice soft and rich. "And whisper with their souls to go . . . '"

From her first word, it was as if she were telling her own story. Abe couldn't help but wonder who the man was that she spoke of. Every word, every tone of her voice, every movement of her face, showed how she faced her beloved's absence with the quietness and dignity of royalty because, "'Twere profanation of our joys To tell the laity our love."

For a moment, nothing existed in the world besides Abe and the teacher. He stood in the shadows, transfixed with the passion and clarity of her voice, emotion in every word as she declared that their love was as refined as gold, that though they were apart they were yet one. Abe's throat constricted as he thought back to losing Lizzy. This woman knew what that felt like.

She *knew.*

At the end, she bowed her head, and the room erupted in a standing ovation. For just a moment, she kept her head down, pausing before lifting her face and smiling softly to the crowd. Abe thought her eyes looked glassy, as if she were actually feeling the loss in the poem. She gave a curtsy and bobbed her head in recognition of their favor, then raised her hands to quiet them.

"Thank you," she said. "Thank you so much. We have one final performance tonight. My two senior students have worked tirelessly on it, and I think you will find it especially well done. For our final scene of the night, here are Paul and Mary Jane performing a scene from William Shakespeare's *Much Ado About Nothing.*"

She went behind the curtain, and two students emerged. They began a scene where the characters Benedick and Beatrice profess their love for one another. It was well done, for the most part, but Abe thought it was somewhat anticlimactic after Miss Stratton's spell-binding performance. Abe glanced at the blond gentleman who had called out before who seemed to know Miss Stratton.

"She would have been a more suitable finale," Abe said quietly.

At first the blond man at his side didn't respond but continued to stare at the stage. Curious, Abe looked to see what he had missed, when the man finally registered that he had been spoken to.

He spoke absently. "Suitable finale? Yes, it certainly is." He turned his gaze to the actors, apparently mesmerized by the young woman's Shakespearean performance. "She's quite talented."

* * *

The Wilson party rolled into St. George with the moon rising gold in the east, and Clara nearly incoherent in the back of the wagon. Every so often, the mental darkness would fade, and she would come into semiconsciousness. It was enough to recognize some things around her—the moon hanging above them like a polished brass doorknob, the sound of other horses and wagons, and the glimpses of buildings with the subtle glow of candlelight burning behind their windows.

The horrid jolting had stopped. Somewhere in the fog of her mind, Clara thought that perhaps they really were in a city with streets instead of the uneven, rutted path of the wilderness. The thoughts came one after the other like a row of cows walking along, with no emotion connected to them. It felt almost as if she were watching the situation from some other place, detached.

Too weak to cling to the coverlet through the chills, she blinked wearily as Olive dabbed a washcloth to her brow. The last coughing attack had left her so spent that she couldn't manage a thank you to Olive for her attentions. The wagon stopped at a two-story building. Without any talk, Theodore jumped off the wagon, bracing himself with one hand and landing on both feet. He took only the slightest moment to tie the team to the hitching post before racing inside.

Clara stared out at the night, curious about where Theodore had gone but not really caring. For the first time in hours, her eyes fixed on an object—the tip of a white tower peeking above some buildings along the road. A sensation of warmth entered Clara's heart, and she smiled, something she hadn't managed since the fever came on. The warmth counteracted the chills, at least temporarily. She was near the temple. For the moment, nothing else mattered.

This was St. George. Here she could receive all the heavenly blessings waiting for her. And Abe. He'd meet her here. Her heart leapt at the thought.

"Clara? Clara!" Olive's voice broke through the haze of her mind, and she managed to move her eyes and focus on Olive.

"Mmm," Clara said, the closest she could get to an actual word.

"You frightened me," Olive said, putting a hand to her own chest. "You looked like Mother before—" She cut off, then paused and repeated, "You frightened me."

A moment later Clara heard the sound of feet thundering down stairs. The door of the building opened with a violent shove, and two men emerged, Theodore and an older gentleman. The two climbed onto the wagon, while Olive retreated, giving them room. The second man took in Clara's appearance. He touched her forehead, felt her pulse, and looked into her eyes.

"Let's get her upstairs," he said briskly to Theodore.

Together the men hoisted Clara's fragile body off the wagon. Theodore took her and cradled her in his arms as if she were a sick child. Supporting her head on his shoulder, he followed the man into the house and up the stairs, where she was deposited onto a davenport.

Once they got her indoors, with a pillow under her head and an afghan over her body, the older gentleman examined her more thoroughly. Clara concluded that the older man was a doctor, from the orders he barked at people in the room. "Get some water." "How long has she been like this?" "When was the last time she ate?" He put a contraption on her chest with a metal circle on the end—so cold it made Clara's entire body curl up. Then he eased a glass stick into her mouth.

At that point he stood and tucked the afghan around her. Clara lay still, eyes closed, mouth clamped shut over the thermometer. She still felt so weak she couldn't talk or move, but the wracking pain from before had subsided somewhat.

I wonder if that means this is the end. She felt oddly surprised that the thought didn't hold any fear for her, just an aching sadness that she wouldn't partake of the temple first or see her son again in this life.

"It doesn't look good," the doctor whispered in a low voice. He stood a few feet off, talking to Theodore and Olive.

He must think I can't hear him. Curious about why she could think more clearly than before, Clara figured being practically in the shadow of the temple had strengthened her mind.

"A few days at most," he went on, replying to something Olive had said.

Clara opened one eye a crack and saw him shaking his head. An older woman stood beside him, a handkerchief to her nose as she cried. The woman looked familiar. Clara forced the other eye open and took in the woman. She had wrinkles, and the gray hair didn't fit any memory she could summon, yet . . .

With sudden clarity, Clara recognized her dear friend Miriam. Of course—her husband Charles had studied medicine, one of the reasons they were called to St. George.

Miriam, Clara thought. *Miriam Willis!* But she couldn't get the words out. What should have been a happy reunion between old friends turned instead into a time of anxiety. The group of four muttered in concerned tones, throwing foreboding glances in Clara's direction.

Just tell me. Talk to me. Where is Abe? Please say that's what you meant. That he'll be here in a few days.

The effort of those thoughts made her tired, and she decided to rest, pictures of her son playing in her mind. She let her eyes close and began breathing deeper as she imagined seeing him again. He had grown into such a remarkable young man, one she could be proud of. Oh, how she missed him. After getting her own temple blessings, nothing could increase her joy more than being sealed to her son. Perhaps it would happen, someday.

A few minutes later, the circle broke apart, and both Charles and Theodore came to her. Charles took the thermometer from her mouth. He held it up to a candle and examined the results, then shook the mercury down to the end. After laying it on the side table, Charles retrieved a tiny bottle with a cork in it and bent low as he spoke, showing her the bottle. "Would you like us to administer to you?"

"Mmm," Clara said, attempting a nod but unsure if her effort was visible.

Theodore proceeded to anoint her with a drop of oil, and Charles sealed the anointing. Clara held her breath, clinging to every word and shred of feeling that came with the blessing so she could remember both later. In the middle, Charles stumbled.

"You will—" His voice cut off suddenly. "You will—" Again Charles paused. This time the silence dragged out. In her younger days, Clara might have opened her eyes and asked what was wrong, but she knew better now. Charles was listening to the Spirit, and she was content to wait until he was ready to speak inspired words. His voice lowered, and in a reverent tone he said, "You will live to receive your endowment. And you will be with your son again."

The warmth that had pricked her heart at first seeing the temple spire now flooded throughout her body. She had felt the same assurance before, back in Salt Lake, but here, as she hovered between two lives, she questioned if it were still true. But it was. The Lord wouldn't take her quite yet. She smiled inside and closed her eyes, aware of a pen scratching on paper somewhere across the room. The sound lulled her to the first restful sleep she had found in days.

* * *

The school festival ended, and the crowd applauded as the final two actors bowed. Miss Stratton appeared again, her eyes looking red and tired, perhaps as if she had been crying. But she smiled broadly and clapped along with the audience. As the noise died down, she thanked everyone for coming and dismissed the crowd.

Abe had an urge to stay and meet the teacher, to ask about her poetry recitation. He wanted to know how she had come to choose that particular poem, and to perform it with such power. But Marie and Seth had already gathered their children together like chicks and were ushering them toward the back door and the fresh night air.

Eva nudged her way to Abe's side and slipped her arm in his. He looked down at the girl, whose eyes were bright. She smiled. "Did you like my sonnet?"

"I did. Very much," Abe said.

"Really?" She held onto his arm with both of her hands, her cheeks glowing with pleasure. Abe had to bite his lips together to avoid laughing at what seemed to be a crush Eva had on him.

"Do you really think I was good?"

"Absolutely," Abe said with a firm nod as they passed through the schoolhouse door. He looked over his shoulder toward the teacher and saw her talking to parents and students, yet looking around as if searching for someone. The throng urged Abe forward, so he couldn't stop to watch any longer, but as he stepped outside, he leaned over to Eva.

"Go along with your parents," he said, extricating himself from her young grip. Something drew him to the teacher, and he wasn't yet ready to leave without getting a better look at her. "I'll follow presently."

"Then I'll wait for you," Eva said, standing her ground.

To Abe's relief, Marie came to his rescue. "Come along, Eva," she called to her eldest daughter. "I need your help getting the little ones to bed."

"Coming, Mother." The girl reluctantly turned around and walked away, the gravelly road crunching under her shoes as she went.

Abe stepped to a window in the schoolhouse and peeked inside. Parents were still talking with the teacher, and she continued to look for someone. Suddenly her eyes brightened, as if she had found the object of her search, then clouded almost as quickly. Curious, Abe traced her gaze to the blond gentleman he had spoken to earlier, who was now deep in conversation with the young actress from the finale. The man nodded, then touched her arm.

Abe suddenly felt guilty and pushed away from the window sill. He had intended to simply see the teacher once more, but had stumbled upon something he had no right to know. It looked like Miss Stratton had feelings for the blond man—who in turn found the young actress appealing. Sighing, he headed back for Marie's home.

The corner of his mouth curled when he thought of Eva waiting for him. If she were ten years older, perhaps he would be flattered. He chuckled to himself. In a sense, he and Eva were part of another triangle; she admired him, and he now admired Miss Stratton. He'd have to be careful not to bruise the young girl's tender ego.

CHAPTER 13

The schoolroom was finally emptying, but the heat hadn't abated much. Sweat trickled down Maddie's back as she talked with parents and students, wishing she could discretely wipe the moisture from her face. It wasn't the heat, however, that kept Maddie glancing at the clock on the wall. Ever since her poetry recitation, she had felt as if her heart were ready to burst.

She needed a moment alone—more than the few minutes that Mary Jane and Peter had taken with their scene, during which Maddie had sat behind the draped sheet, tears streaming down her face. The poem brought up unexpected emotions, completely overwhelming her. Another set of parents expressed their pleasure at the evening. Maddie shook their hands and smiled her thanks. Edward came up beside her. Before she could say anything, he leaned in.

"Mary Jane's parents had to leave early," he said quietly. "Their youngest broke out in a fever halfway through the evening."

Concern over one of the many families she cared about went through Maddie, and she searched the room for the Parkers, wondering why she hadn't noticed them leaving earlier. Then again, she had been so preoccupied with the program that lightning could have struck the building and she might not have noticed. "Is the baby going to be all right?"

"That's all I was told," Edward said. "But with her family gone, Mary Jane said she is planning on walking home alone."

"Oh, she can't do that," Maddie said, her voice taking on her schoolmarm tone.

As she gathered her skirts with the intention of catching Mary Jane, Edward touched her arm. "I thought I could walk her home."

For a moment, Maddie's heart dropped just a little. Had she imagined the look in Edward's eyes when he had gazed at Mary Jane a few minutes ago? Was she jealous? On the other hand, if she were feeling envy, that was a good sign—it meant she cared for Edward. Her heart picked up its rhythm again, and she nodded. "I'm glad you thought of it."

"I shouldn't be long."

"No need to hurry," Maddie assured him. "I have to tidy the place and lock up. This way you won't have to wait."

"I'll go right away." His hand lingered just a moment on her arm, quelling the fears that had bubbled in her middle a moment ago. Silly to think that Edward had eyes for someone else. Hadn't he spent the last two years seeking her hand? That should be proof enough of his love.

As he turned away, he joined Mary Jane, who stood expectantly at the door with her wraps. Edward put out his arm, and Mary Jane put her hand through it. As the two walked out, the moon caught Mary Jane's hair, which had been pinned up for the evening. Her neck looked tall and stately, and for a moment Maddie saw in Mary Jane more than a schoolgirl—at fifteen, she wasn't all that far from womanhood.

"Miss Stratton," a voice said, bringing Maddie back to the present.

"Yes?" Stifling an internal groan, Maddie forced herself to smile as she turned, knowing who the voice belonged to—Sister Hancock. Avery hadn't returned to class yet. While Maddie had enjoyed every minute of his absence, she knew that his mother was angry, even though he was allowed to sing at the funeral.

"Wonderful evening," she said, swooping toward Maddie, her broad hips nudging chairs out of her way. The buttons on the front of her dress pulled so tight they threatened to pop off.

"Thank you," Maddie said, bracing herself for the onslaught.

"But my Avery belonged in the festival, don't you think?"

Maddie was unsure how to answer the pointed question without being rude. "I'm sure his absence was noticed," was all she said. That was an understatement, in addition to being the absolute truth. "Let's discuss Avery another time, shall we?"

Alone. She wanted to be alone.

The Hancock children jumped on and off desks, then raced through the aisles as Sister Hancock launched into a litany of reasons why her son should be back at school. At the top, of course, was the "fact" that he was innocent of any wrongdoing, at least of anything serious.

"Of course boys will be boys," she said. "You can't think they'll act like miniature adults. They're children, for heaven's sake. What do you expect?"

To be able to teach without fearing for my life. Although tempted to say as much, Maddie merely nodded. "I understand what you're saying, but really, Sister Hancock, sometimes Avery goes beyond typical boyish behavior." She knew this discussion was about as productive as planting baked beans and hoping for a harvest, but what else could she do? At least a dozen times she had gone to Sister Hancock with the details of her sons' antics. Not once did she believe the story or take any action toward her children. Maddie had since given up trying.

"And aside from Avery not being part of the festival," she went on, "I couldn't help but think that all of my boys could have had larger parts, been given more attention."

More attention was the absolute *last* thing the Hancocks needed. Maddie could picture next year's festival with the boys at the center—the audience pummeled with overripe fruit, children shrieking as they ran from the stage with toads down their shirts, and for the finale, the schoolhouse itself burning to the ground.

"My Avery would be able to do Shakespeare every bit as well as that Peter boy did tonight," Sister Hancock was saying.

"Really?" Maddie's mind raced to find a way to get the Hancocks and their mother out of her school. She began walking toward the door, trying to lead Sister Hancock in that direction, just as Jesse and George performed flying leaps from behind the drape—surely they had been standing on Maddie's desk—and landing with a sickening thud on the floor. They jumped up with a yell of glee and raced around the drape to repeat the stunt.

With a shudder, she hoped they wouldn't hurt themselves, the desk, or anything else. She wondered again if Sister Brown were up to the task of taking over the school for over a month. Before leaving for

St. George, she needed to warn Sister Brown about the scissors. And the grasshoppers. And she'd leave a new box of chalk or two just to be on the safe side. To Maddie's dismay, Sabra, the Hancock's youngest, began climbing the desk and throwing herself off it too.

"Joseph, for example," Sister Hancock droned on, following Maddie across the room. "He has such a beautiful voice. Next year you should give him a solo."

This time Maddie had to force back a chortle. Her experience with Joseph's voice had been more of the high-pitched screaming variety. "We'll see," she said noncommittally, then waved at the door. "I'm so sorry, but I must ask you to leave." Maddie felt a twinge of guilt, but didn't feel too sorry. "My fiancé will be back soon, and I must get the room ready for school tomorrow before he returns." Not the full truth. But she *really* needed a moment to herself.

"Oh," Sister Hancock said, somewhat taken aback.

"Thank you so much for your comments," Maddie said in a rush. "If only all parents were so involved and supportive, the festival would be as good as anything in Salt Lake City."

At the compliment, a smile slowly crept along the corners of Sister Hancock's mouth. "You're so welcome," she said. "I have many more ideas."

"And you'll have to share them with me sometime," Maddie said, holding the door open. The two women watched the children, typhoons of energy. Maddie hoped their mother would say something, but knew that even if she did, the children were unlikely to mind her.

With a glance at the clock to see the time ticking away, a flutter of panic swept through Maddie. No longer caring for manners and formality, she marched down the aisle with determination. She pulled the drape aside and stood in front of her desk. "Stop!" she called. The suddenness of her arrival and her loud voice stunned them into momentary quiet. "It's time for me to lock up," she said firmly. When no one moved, she pointed to the door, no longer caring how rude she sounded. "It's time for you all to go. *Now.*"

Shocked into compliance, they meekly filed toward the door. Maddie wished them a good night and closed the door behind them, making sure to bolt it. With a sigh, she collapsed into the nearest desk, grateful she was finally, blissfully, alone. After a moment, she stood and walked around the room, blowing out the lamps along the walls until she stood in darkness, the only light being a sliver of moon peeking through the southern windows.

She paused for a moment, taking in the serenity, the night, the silence—save for the crickets singing outside. After another deep breath, Maddie went to her desk. She sat and straightened the mess the Hancocks had made, then pulled out a candle, candlestick, and matches from a drawer. She lit the candle, its warm glow creating a small circle of golden light.

Maddie sat back, gazing at the flickering flame, and let herself think of the performance—and of all the emotion it had evoked in her.

Love. Sorrow. Grief. Love again. And surprisingly, peace.

For the first time since Roland's death—and, more importantly, for the first time since her engagement to Edward—Maddie felt a quiet inner peace. She wasn't sure what that meant, but something in her heart said there was a message in the evening, a message from Roland, waiting to be discovered.

For a moment, this moment, *her* moment, Maddie didn't want to think about Edward. She would allow herself the luxury of pondering about Roland. After tonight, she would put him away and keep him in a corner of her heart until she could give him a final farewell at the riverbank where he died.

Earlier that evening as she had stood on the platform and spoken, she had felt so close to Roland, as if he were watching from the window. It felt almost as if—had she been able to look quickly enough—she could have spied him. But of course when her eyes strayed that direction, she saw nothing but curtains billowing with the wind and a branch of a nearby tree swaying, almost like an arm waving hello.

Maddie pulled open the bottom drawer of her desk. She rummaged through extra slates, textbooks, and reading primers. At the very back of the drawer, under everything else, lay the locked wooden box. Her hands gripped it tightly as she withdrew it and lay it on the desktop. With trembling fingers, she removed the chain that hung around her neck, where she kept the key. It made a click as she turned it in the lock. She opened the lid and peered inside, heart pounding at what she knew lay there.

The light of the candle glittered off a ring sitting on top. Maddie slowly removed the one she wore, setting it carefully to the side of the box, and slipped on Roland's. It was only glass and tin—Roland had promised to replace it with better as soon as he could—but to Maddie it felt far more precious than the real diamond Edward had given her. She extended her fingers and put her hand out, palm down, to look at the ring. She tilted her hand so the glass could catch the moonlight. Then she turned back to the box and pulled out a thin stack of letters tied with a pink ribbon. A pull of the ribbon untied the bow, and she lifted the first letter and unfolded it. A smile broke across her face as she read Roland's awkward attempts at poetry.

The second held similar effusions, nothing close to Shakespeare's sonnets, but heartfelt and genuine nonetheless. Maddie lifted a finger to her lashes, and it came back wet. Sweet, dear Roland. Farm boy through and through, with a heart of gold.

Some letters had brief sentences with additional rhymed lines, others longer as Roland expressed the deepest desires of his heart.

She took her time reading the final letter.

Maddie,

My greatest wish is for you to be happy. For so long I feared that your happiness would not coincide with my own, that you would find it with another man. But if another would make you happy—if you loved him—then I would rather you be with him than with me. I would rather be miserable without you, knowing you are happy.

But miracles happen—you do *love me! When you first spoke those words, they were nothing short of music and angelic choirs. I could have danced in the clouds for joy and not come down 'til morning.*

I cannot see how it is possible that anyone could love me as much as I love you, and yet when I look into your eyes, I see you do. I promise to do everything in my power until my dying breath to make you happy.

Maddie cringed at the final line, the image of his dying breath all too vivid in her mind. She had knelt beside Roland's body as his life bled away, as he fought for each gulp of air and finally gasped his last breath. And there was nothing at all that Maddie could do but let her tears fall onto his still body and plead with him not to leave her. The earlier lines begged to be read again, so she might erase this picture from her thoughts, to hear Roland's voice in her mind once more as he declared his deep love for her. As she looked over the words, she paused and read them a third time.

It wasn't as if she hadn't read the letter dozens—if not hundreds—of times before. But somehow she felt that this was the message she was to get from the evening. Roland was releasing her to be married. Above all else, her happiness was his greatest concern.

The words became blurry as tears formed in her eyes, and one hand covered her face. She would let herself grieve Roland tonight. For this moment, she belonged to him. She put the letter down and gazed at the ring, wishing with everything in her that she could have worn it for the rest of her life—without any replacement. Glass and tin would have been good enough if it meant she could have had Roland.

She glanced at the clock and realized with a start that Edward would be returning shortly. The room was still a cluttered mess, but she didn't mind; she could come early before school tomorrow to clean up. Slowly, reluctantly, she refolded the letters, retied the pink ribbon around them into a perfect bow, then placed the stack gently in the box. Outside, footsteps sounded, followed by a knock on the door.

"Maddie?"

Edward. She looked at the door with a sudden intake of breath.

"Madeline, are you in there?"

"I'm coming!"

In a burst of panic, she scrambled into action, pulling off the ring and shoving it into the box. Her hands shook so much she had trouble with the lock, but finally managed to return her treasure to its place in her desk and cover it.

"Is everything all right?" Edward called through the door, jiggling the handle.

"Fine. Everything is fine," Maddie called, smoothing her dress and adjusting her hair as she stood. As she leaned down to blow out the candle, she noticed her engagement ring sitting beside it. With a puff of air, the flame went out, and she put her ring back on.

"Maddie, let me in! It's dark in there. What's going on?"

She flew across the room, heart pounding wildly as she opened it and put on her broadest smile. "How is the Parker baby?" she asked, trying hard to keep her voice light. She slipped outside and closed the door behind her so Edward couldn't see the mess inside. Then he wouldn't ask what she had been doing—and she would avoid either having to tell him the truth or lie, neither of which she wanted to do.

Her hands fumbled with the key. Knowing her face had flushed warm, she was grateful for the protective darkness. Edward put his hand on hers, causing her to pause in her haste, and she looked up. A crease had formed between his brows, and his eyes had worry written in them.

"Maddie, what's wrong?"

A quick assurance caught in her throat. "I . . . I . . ." She lowered her head and fiddled with the key. "I'm tired," she finally said. "It's been an exhausting evening—and an exhausting several weeks preparing for it."

Edward was not so easily assuaged. For a moment Maddie feared that if he kept gazing at her, he'd read her very soul. "Is that all?" He leaned closer.

Maddie kept her eyes on her hands as she measured her words. Nothing could be gained by telling Edward about her vigil with Roland's memory; it would only cause him pain. Roland had already given permission for her to seek happiness with another man. The thought brought a smile to her lips. She looked at Edward, once more feeling the peace that had come over her earlier. Her pounding heart quieted, and the anxiety left like a tide receding.

"Thank you for worrying," she said, putting her left hand to his cheek. Her diamond sparkled in the moonlight. For once, the sight didn't feel like a burden. "I'll be just fine. It's nothing a little rest can't take care of."

Edward hesitated just a moment before reaching for her hand. "If you say so." He put her arm through his and led her down the path, his hand covering hers protectively. His was warm and secure over hers. He would try to make her happy. She knew that. Dear, sweet Edward.

And in return, she would do all she could to make him happy, too.

CHAPTER 14

Saturday morning, Abe rose with the rooster and helped Seth and Marie with their chores, the least he could do in exchange for room and board. He spent most of the morning with Seth, in the shed out back.

"I don't know the first thing about blacksmithing," Abe warned him as they went inside. "You don't need to," Seth said, hefting a hammer. "The horseshoes are already made, but I can't make the holes without another set of hands. I've been planning on hiring the help, but since you're here, I won't have to." He looked Abe over. "You look like you've got a strong arm on you. We can take turns holding and swinging and finish up the shoes before noon."

"Show me what to do, and I'll do it."

First Abe held the shoes in place on the anvil while Seth used a punch and hammer to make the holes—usually eight in each shoe, sometimes more or less, depending on the size and purpose of the shoe.

"Do you make the nails?" Abe asked between hammer strikes.

"Oh no," Seth said with a shake of his head. He paused, his breathing heavy. "I've tried that a few times, but it takes so much work, it's not worth it. With the railway complete, we can ship them in from factories that can make more nails in a few minutes than I can in a day." He returned to his work, adding, "It's thanks to the nail factories that we've got so many nice houses getting built instead of just cabins." They worked in silence for several more minutes, when Seth asked if Abe wanted to try punching the holes.

"I'll give it a try," Abe said, taking the tools from Seth.

"You fixin' on buying a place or building one?" Seth asked, taking Abe's place. He reached for the next shoe and held it firmly.

"I was hoping to buy," Abe said. He raised the hammer and let it fall—precisely on the punch, making a clean hole.

"Not too shabby for your first try," Seth said.

"Thanks." Abe raised the hammer again, thinking how similar this task was to his work in the quarry all those years ago. Back then the hammer was heavier and the work harder—he was drilling into rock, not punching holes into metal, after all—but the basic action was the same.

"Not too keen on building?" Seth asked between strikes. "There's plenty of land."

Abe shook his head. "That's not it. My mother isn't as spry as she once was. I don't exactly relish the idea of living in a wagon box all winter like I've heard some folks did when they first got here. She needs someplace warm and tight right away."

"I understand that, all right." Seth counted the finished shoes, which were stacked and sorted into three sizes, before saying, "I'm sure I can speak for Marie when I say that you and your mother are welcome to stay with us until you find something else."

"Thank you so much," Abe said, pleasantly surprised. "I don't know what to say." He turned to the stack of unfinished shoes, which had quickly diminished—only half a dozen remained. It felt good to see the result of his work; it was the one thing he could do to show his gratitude.

"Don't know that you'll need to stay with us long." Seth gripped the shoe Abe held out. "Word has it that a house down the street and around the corner is for sale."

Abe paused, hammer in the air. "Really? Do you know how much?"

"No," Seth said, nodding toward the shoe. Abe punched out three more holes, and Seth went on. "But I doubt the old ladies who live there would need much; they're moving over to Woodruff to join the United Order. They inherited the house from a family who left Arizona when their mission was up. It's probably bigger than you'd need, but it's a nice place."

As Abe worked, he thought about Seth's words. He hadn't even seen this house yet—unless he had passed it on the way to the Ellsworths' home. Even then he might not have noticed it in the fading light. Yet the more he thought about it, the more he felt the house had been dropped in his lap like a gift from above.

Careful, he told himself. *That almost sounds like religious talk.* In spite of the warning to himself, he had to smile. His mother would be pleased that the idea of a gift from God even presented itself to her son.

He and Seth finished up the shoes—several dozen in all—mostly working in silence. When Seth stacked the last shoe, he stretched his back and said, "Thanks, Abe. The helper I usually use couldn't come 'til next week, so you saved me time and money today."

"You're welcome." Abe put the hammer down and rubbed his hand.

Seth nodded toward the door and said, "Let's see if Marie's got something for us to eat. I don't know about you, but I'm famished."

"Sounds great," Abe said, following Seth outside.

The afternoon meal of stew and bread was hearty and filling. Abe enjoyed every bite, especially after eating so scantily for several weeks in a row. It made him miss his mother's cooking all the more. Afterward, Seth offered to take Abe up to visit the ladies selling the house.

"After all," Seth had said during dinner, "I've gotten a lot more done so far today than I would have by myself. We can spare an hour to find you a home."

The walk to the house was brief, and as they approached it, Abe pictured himself walking along the road with his mother's arm in his. He could see them sitting on the porch. The house faced due west, perfect for enjoying sunsets. It seemed welcoming, and as they knocked on the front door, Abe half expected to see his mother appear. It felt right. Like home.

The door opened to reveal a white-haired woman with a jovial smile. "Why, hello, Brother Ellsworth," she said. Then she looked at Abe and exclaimed, "And who the dickens are you, looking like Geronimo himself?" Her hand clenched the brooch at her neck.

Seth smiled with sparkling eyes, obviously trying very hard not to laugh. "Hello, Sister Palmer. This is Abe Franklin. He's interested in purchasing your home for his mother."

The lady squinted both eyes and stared at Abe. Normally such a reaction would have bothered him, but this old lady seemed innocent.

Abe too found himself trying to hold back a chuckle. He held out a hand just to see if she'd take it.

"Nice to meet you, ma'am," he said with a nod and the most charming smile he could muster. To aid his cause, he added, "You're mighty pretty today in that dress."

Sister Palmer looked at his hand, then his smile, and back again. Almost imperceptibly, her lips rounded upward. The hand on her brooch relaxed, and she patted it. "This old thing?" She blushed and looked at her dress. "You think so?" She patted her hair.

"Is Sister Brown at home?" Seth asked.

"Pearl's in the kitchen," she said, her eyes fixed on Abe, who was doing his best to maintain the charming smile tacked to his face. "I'll—I'll go fetch her." She stepped backward, keeping her gaze on Abe until the last moment, until she had to turn around. Then she scurried into the kitchen with small, quick steps, throwing glances his way as she went.

"My, Abe, I believe you're a beau," Seth said. The laughter he had been holding back came out, and he had to wipe tears from his eyes. A full-on laugh erupted from Abe too, and by the time Pearl Brown appeared, they had to quickly gather their wits. Abe cleared his throat, wiped his eyes, and shoved his hands into his pockets.

"Good afternoon, gentlemen," she said, eyeing them with curiosity, most of which was surely because of their merry behavior. "Can I help you? Caroline was a bit flustered when she came in the back, so I'm not exactly sure what it is you're here for."

Both Seth and Abe bit their lips together and somehow managed to maintain some semblance of decorum. Abe wondered why exactly he found it so amusing to have an elderly lady suddenly smitten by him. Perhaps because he had found precious little in recent times to laugh about, a pressure valve had suddenly released.

Seth made the introductions, and Abe shook her hand. "You have a beautiful home."

"Yes, I do," she said, looking around at the furnishings. Most of them were obviously handmade, and Abe admired the craftsmanship. Between two windows sat a Swedish-style sofa with wooden spindles on the back and arms. To the untrained eye, the table looked like mahogany, but Abe knew the grain was painted, probably on top of pine or oak. Still, the grain looked better than most attempts he had seen. Floor-length curtains flanked each window, and a braided rug adorned the floor. It was likely made of old rags, although the colors were so beautifully blended that Abe wouldn't have guessed it had his mother not created equally pretty rugs for her own house.

"We'll be leaving it soon," Pearl said. "I don't know if you've heard."

"Yes, we have," Seth said. "That's actually why we're here."

"Oh?" She looked from one man to the other. "How so?"

Abe no longer waited for Seth to take the initiative. The elderly woman reminded him so much of his own mother. He ached to see her again. "You see, my mother is coming to Snowflake as soon as I can purchase a home for her. Yours is perfect, and I'd like to buy it from you." He paused, waiting for her reaction, then rushed on. "My mother has the money with her from the sale of the farm, so we couldn't actually pay you until we return from St. George, but—"

She raised a hand to stop his words and nodded slowly, her eyes closed and her lips pressed together. For a moment, Abe feared that she was about to reject his offer. Her chin began trembling, and she sniffed. "You are an answer to prayer." She opened her eyes and raised her head to look at Abe. She placed a hand over his cheek—a hand that felt just like his mother's. "You'll take good care of my home, won't you?"

Abe nodded, but before he could speak, she went on. "Yes, of course you will. I can tell. Otherwise, the Lord wouldn't have sent you. He knew we needed this. The house is yours."

"Thank you," Abe said, feeling surprisingly emotional as she pulled her hand back. A pang of homesickness washed over him.

"Please, sit down." Pearl gestured toward the Swedish-style sofa, and they sat on it. "To be honest, Caroline and I don't need much for the house. We didn't pay for it in the first place, just got to use it when the Kensleys left. And we'll be entering the United Order when we reach Woodruff, so everything will be given to the Church, of course. What we really need is travel expenses and such. That's all."

The final payment arrangements took only minutes to make. Abe could hardly believe his good fortune in finding such a perfect home so easily. Some might call it a miracle, but he couldn't quite come to that conclusion.

Pearl served them cake, and as they ate, Caroline kept peeking around the kitchen door but didn't venture into the room. All too soon, they had to leave. As they walked back to Seth's home, Abe thought back to the exchange with Sister Brown. It made him more eager than ever to get on the road to St. George. He hated that he would have to wait at least two or three weeks to see his mother—and that counted just the time it would take to get to St. George from Snowflake, a trip he might not begin for a while. He had heard nothing from his mother since their brief communications about the plan for Abe fetching her. If only he had some idea of how the trip from Salt Lake City had been, how she had fared, and what she was doing now. The itch to get moving north bit him hard.

"Next order of business—finding a party to travel with to St. George," Abe said suddenly, turning to his companion. "The other night Marie mentioned folks going to the temple. How often does that happen?"

"Pretty often," Seth said as they headed along the road. "A few groups go each fall and spring. Often it's couples going up to be married. Sometimes they marry first at Bishop Hunt's home, then, if they have the money, they head on up right after that to the temple to be sealed. And of course some folks who've never managed to get sealed want to go up and get it done."

Abe squinted at the sun and adjusted his hat to block the light. "Know of any fixing to head that way anytime soon?" He tried to keep the eagerness out of his voice.

"I've heard of two," he said. "One's a group of three couples, all going to get married. They'll be leaving at the end of the month, I think. The Hampton family, though, is going sooner than that." Seth stopped suddenly and snapped his fingers. "Just remembered. I saw Peter Hampton at the store the other day. Said he was the only man in the party and was wishing for a second to come along. This might be exactly what they—and you—need."

Providential. The word leapt into Abe's mind. *First I found Ben. Then Davis. Then came the Ellsworths, the house, now this. I suppose I* might *have to start saying a few "thank you's" of my own, 'cause this can't be all coincidence.*

As they turned the corner, a brunette woman rounded it, coming toward them. She smiled and nodded when she saw Seth, but when her gaze landed on Abe, her eyes went wide, and she picked up her pace, passing them quickly. The men turned to watch her hurry around the corner.

She's the schoolteacher, Abe suddenly realized. *Miss Stratton.*

He had an urge to reverse his direction and catch up to her, to introduce himself and explain what her poetry recitation had meant to him.

"She's going with the Hampton family to help out with the children," Seth said, gesturing toward her as she bustled around the corner.

"Really?" Abe said.

"Yep. That's Ellen Hampton's sister."

Abe's thoughts turned back to the night of the festival—her even voice and the intensity of her words as she recited the poem, how he felt in his core that she knew exactly what he had felt.

She's traveling in the same group? Thank You, Lord.

CHAPTER 15

As if the usual Sabbath preparations weren't enough, Maddie and Ellen spent hours on Saturday packing and cleaning and otherwise getting ready for their departure on Monday. They counted bags of wheat flour and beans, boxes of hard biscuits and dry fruit, tins of molasses. For the horses, both grain and hay, since the road had a sad amount of grasses. As they piled up quilts and cooking supplies they made sure to include Caroline's odds and ends.

Walking back and forth from the house to the wagon, they both eyed Peter's gunpowder and bullet sack. More than once they gave one another the same look. Maddie knew what it meant. Neither of them would forget to remind Peter to bring his rifle. It was the one thing they could use as self-defense if the need arose. By the time the sun's rays slanted from the western horizon and the shadows around them had lengthened, both women were so tired they would have been tempted to call off the trip if it hadn't been such an important one.

After hefting a load of cast-iron pots and sliding them into a corner, Ellen sat on the back of the wagon to rest. Little Mary and Lorenzo played inside, having gotten tired of the heat and loose dirt hours earlier.

"We still have to fill the water barrels," Ellen said wearily.

Maddie joined her sister at the back of the wagon and sat on the edge, which folded out. The empty barrels were attached to the sides, and filling them would take more energy than either of them had. "Let's let Peter do that Monday morning so the water's fresh."

Ellen made a face. "As fresh as it's going to be. I've washed and rinsed those things a hundred times if I have once, and they still make the water taste like whiskey."

"Let's just hope there's more water on the road than we've heard," Maddie said.

"I can't believe how much my feet hurt," Ellen said, rotating her ankles. "Doesn't bode well for walking as far as I'll have to for the next few weeks. If they swell much more, my poor feet will look like misshapen squash."

Maddie laughed. "I'm sorry. But just think about what's on the other side of the journey—an eternal family."

Ellen nodded emphatically. "If it weren't for that, no one would be able to get me on the trail, even if they drove me with a pitch-fork." Her face grew more somber, and her hand went to her belly. "To be honest, getting sealed has been on my mind for some time, nagging at me. I wanted to go last spring, but with the high waters, Peter didn't dare."

"It makes more sense to make the trip in the fall," Maddie agreed.

Shrugging, Ellen sighed. "That's what I keep telling myself. I've heard some of the neighbors saying we're foolish to be leaving when I'm so close to having the baby, but it's still plenty far away, and besides . . ." Her voice trailed off and she gazed at the setting sun, her eyes threatening tears.

"You want this one to be born in the covenant," Maddie finished for her.

"Yes," Ellen said quietly. "It's a gift within my power to give this time. I didn't have the chance with Mary. I tried my best to get to the temple before Lorenzo was born. This child deserves no less." Maddie nodded, remembering their previous conversation about the matter, and Ellen's deep feelings regarding it.

They saw two figures walking toward them down the road a stretch. One appeared to be Peter; with sun shining off his blond hair and his unusual height, he was easy to spot. The man beside him didn't seem familiar, but with the light behind them, Maddie couldn't make out any features.

"Ho there!" Peter called, raising a hand.

"Hello," Ellen called with a wave. She edged off the wagon to await his arrival, too tired to run to meet him this time. Maddie joined her and waited for the men to arrive.

Peter jogged forward, his companion following suit, and soon they were within speaking distance. "Good news!" Peter said, a grin on his face. "I found someone to travel with us."

The men stopped in front of Maddie and Ellen, and Peter gestured toward his new friend, who pushed the brim of his hat up. As she caught her first glimpse of him, her stomach immediately knotted up. It was the man she had seen walking on the street with Seth Ellsworth that afternoon.

His cheekbones, nose, eyes, hair, coloring—it all reminded her so much of the man who killed Roland. Everything but his attire and his smile. And his eyes, which stared at her. Her heart thumped hard, and she drew in a quick breath.

"Abe here is heading north to bring his mother back from St. George," Peter said with satisfaction. "Terrific, isn't it? I know we were all hoping for another man on the trip—especially with Caroline Palmer coming—and here he is. This is Abe Franklin."

Ellen nodded. "Pleased to meet you, Mr. Franklin."

A similar greeting caught in Maddie's throat, and all she managed was a nod as she stared at the Indian dressed as a white man. "Likewise," she said, but her voice sounded weak.

The Indian smiled broadly and tipped his hat in her direction. "Pleased to meet you." He sounded like any other person in Snowflake. If her eyes had been closed, she'd have assumed he was like any one of the hundreds of men in the town. But he didn't *look* like any of them. And it was his appearance that made her stomach roil and sweat break out across her forehead.

I have to get away, she thought. *Now.*

As if hearing her inner plea, Mary came to the door of the house. She flung a braid over her shoulder and pouted in her best tattling voice, "Lorenzo's playing in the cinders."

Maddie flew into action. "I'll take care of it," she said, swooping past Peter—and the Indian. The walk to the door felt twice as long as usual, as if she were moving through sand. Once inside, she slammed the door, bolted it, and leaned against its hard planks. It took a moment to catch her breath, which was oddly shallow and rapid.

"Aunt Maddie, look at Lorenzo," Mary demanded, pointing at her brother. "He's a mess."

But Maddie's thoughts were elsewhere. Why had she reacted so strongly to this man? He had done nothing even remotely suspicious or dangerous. For all she knew, he might not really be Indian—although with that nose and cheekbones, she would be surprised if he wasn't.

But even if he *was* Indian, so what?

"They're not all savage warriors," Maddie reminded herself in a whisper. "They're *not*." She closed her eyes and breathed deeply. *It's a good thing we'll have another man on the road. He's just another man. He's more protection. He's going to fetch his mother, so he's a good son. Good sons are kind and caring and . . .*

"Aunt Maddie?" Mary's voice had risen a notch. She looked scared. "What's wrong?"

Mary's voice forced Maddie to leave the moment behind and address the situation. She took a cleansing breath and wiped her forehead with the back of her hand, then bent down to her niece's level. "I'm sorry. I got a little distracted. How about we make sure Lorenzo doesn't coat himself completely with soot?"

Mary rolled her eyes. "That's what I've been trying to *tell* you."

"Yes, of course," Maddie said. She stepped away from the door but paused, realizing she should unbolt it. Her hand trembled as she reached out and turned the lock. She stared at it for a moment, wanting to secure the house again but knew her reaction was silly at best.

"Aunt Maddie," Mary said, her voice sounding impatient as she pulled on Maddie's skirt.

With a shake of her head, Maddie smoothed her bodice with both hands, smoothed her hair back and turned away from the door. "Lorry," she said, approaching Lorenzo, who stood by the fireplace—which, fortunately, hadn't born a fire in hours. "You look like a little black bear cub. Let's clean you up before your mother thinks you're here to eat up her honey."

She picked up the squirming toddler, doing her best to avoid getting smeared with soot and cinders herself. Cold water in the metal tub out back would have to do, and the lye soap should be strong enough to do the trick. As she stepped out the back door, she heard voices from the front. Peter, Ellen, and that Abe Indian person. Her foot paused midstep, as if she shouldn't give away her location by walking on the rock-strewn ground.

Ridiculous, she thought. She grunted to herself in disapproval and marched to the tub, where she plopped down little Lorenzo, whose eyes looked shockingly white against the soot covering his face. In spite of her raw nerves, Maddie laughed. She wondered if there was still any warm water left that she could use to fill the tub, or if she'd have to scrub him clean with cold water. As she looked around, her attention was drawn to the path that led to the front as if an Indian would come screaming around it with war paint and a tomahawk at any moment.

I didn't realize the old wound was still so raw, she thought.

With Lorenzo safely away from the fireplace—and contained in the empty tub—Maddie couldn't help but edge closer to the front of the house to listen. What would Peter and Ellen say about her sudden escape? What did *he* think? She leaned close to the tall shrubs and listened.

* * *

Abe had watched Maddie hurry into the house, long strands of dark hair trailing down her back. He had flinched when the door slammed shut.

Maddie. So that was her first name, the woman he had seen perform that poem. The one who knew exactly what he felt when he lost Lizzy. She looked so different from Lizzy—much darker, with amber-brown eyes and hair the color of molasses. Taller, too. Somehow, he found her strikingly beautiful.

"You all right?" Ellen asked, jarring him back to the moment. "You look a bit peaked."

After clearing his throat, Abe said, "I'm fine. I just—" He pointed at the house. "Is *she* all right? She seemed to be in quite a hurry to get inside."

Ellen's hand flew to her lips. "Oh my. I didn't realize—of course she'd—" But her words cut off, hanging in the air.

Abe looked from Ellen to Peter and back again. Peter shook his head miserably, then looked away, wiping his face with his hand. The two of them seemed to know what the problem was, and Abe wished they'd let him in on the secret.

"Is it something I said?" It couldn't be; he hadn't said more than half a dozen words. He thought through the brief exchange, trying to figure out when her eyes got that look in them. A look of *fear*, he realized.

"No, no, you didn't *do* anything," Ellen said hurriedly. "It's just that Maddie . . ." Once again she paused, this time looking to her husband for help.

Abe searched his memory. He had seen that fear before, in the eyes of the people lining the street after the Sam Harvey lynching. Some people's eyes had held hatred or anger. But others showed fear, like Maddie's had moments ago and on the street earlier that day.

Today he had *done* nothing, but apparently he had *been* something. "It's because I'm . . . the way I am . . . isn't it?" he said, saving either of them from having to explain. Countless times in his life he had faced his heritage as a brick wall. He felt no pride at being Indian; he remembered nothing about the tribe or mother who had given him away as a toddler. But he also refused to feel shame over it, no matter how many people disdained him for his blood. He couldn't change what he was, and people simply had to accept who he was—or not.

Ellen merely nodded, but Peter said, "Afraid so. You see, two years ago—"

"What happened doesn't matter," Abe said, waving him quiet. The details were irrelevant, but he could wager a guess that Maddie had experienced something shocking and difficult at the hand of an Indian. Whatever it was, it had probably been as disturbing as Lizzy's mother's encounter with Indians more than two decades ago. Such stories were so plentiful that a person could trip over them if he wasn't looking. "It was painful and frightening, I'm sure."

"Yes, it was," Ellen said quietly. She pulled out a handkerchief and dabbed at her eyes.

"Maybe it would be best if I find another party to travel with," Abe said with reluctance. "My mother's taken care of. She's staying with good friends. We're both anxious to see one another again, but waiting another few weeks won't hurt anything."

An awkward pause followed where no one tried to change his mind, but Peter spoke up. "I'm sorry. I hadn't anticipated this. But we shook on the arrangement, and I won't back out. We still need another man to come, and if you like, you can be him."

"But—" Abe began, noting Ellen's concerned expression.

"It was just the sudden shock," Peter said. "I'm sure once Maddie gets to know you—"

"I'd hate to be a burden on her," Abe said. It was sad to picture the trip to St. George without her. He had imagined her there ever since Seth mentioned that she was coming—and he had rather enjoyed the image. But to travel in the same party while knowing she felt afraid and disturbed by him the entire time? That would be even worse.

"Abe!" The voice came quite suddenly, and all three turned to see to whom it belonged. Marie Ellsworth raced toward them, running along the road and waving an envelope.

"Abe!" she called again as she drew nearer. She stopped running and walked the remaining twenty feet, her breathing labored. Several inches of her hem were covered in dust.

"What is it?" Abe asked, alarmed at the wild look in her eyes.

"This just arrived for you," she said, then stopped to catch her breath. "It's from a Dr. Charles Willis in St. George, and it has *Urgent* written across it in big letters. I figured if it's from a doctor, it must be serious."

Abe took the letter and ripped it open, having no idea who this Dr. Willis was, but figuring it must concern his mother. How else would the man track Abe to Snowflake? Then the connection dawned on Abe—this was Charles Willis. Abe was to meet his mother at the Charles Willis home in St. George. His mother's friend Miriam must be the doctor's wife.

Dear Abe,

Your mother is gravely ill. When she arrived at our home last night, I didn't expect her to live 'til morning. While I am giving her the best care I know—including a priesthood blessing—I fear for her life.

She doesn't know I am writing to you; she insists that she will soon be well and will have a long and happy life with you in

Snowflake. I hope she's right. But for both her sake and yours, please hurry as fast as you are able to join her at our home in St. George.

Respectfully yours,
Dr. Charles Willis

Abe's stomach dropped. His eyes flitted back to the date the letter was written—over a week previous—and he felt them burn as he folded the letter.

"Well?" Marie said, waiting anxiously to hear the contents of the missive.

He smoothed the crease in the paper several times, put the letter back into the envelope, and turned it over, eyeing the word *Urgent* on the front. The trip between Snowflake and St. George took wagons up to three weeks. Someone must have ridden hard to get it here so fast.

"My mother is very ill. I must leave for St. George immediately in case she—" He stopped, not trusting his voice. He pressed his lips together until he managed to ward off the emotion grasping at his throat. "I'll go alone so I won't disturb your family."

From the side of the house, they heard Maddie step forward. "Come with us."

Abe looked up to see Maddie standing on the path between a dogwood and a large bush that had already lost some of its leaves for the fall. Soot covered her hands, and her bodice and skirt had more smudges, as did her face. She pushed a lock of hair out of her eyes, where Abe could still see some measure of fear.

"You can't go alone." She straightened. "And your mother needs you."

He hardly dared speak, afraid of terrifying her. But he managed to ask, "Are you sure?"

The slightest hint of hesitation crossed her face before she nodded. "Yes. Please come. For your mother . . . Abe."

Hearing her say his name melted any final reservations. He couldn't help but smile—and hope that perhaps the journey might be an enjoyable one after all. Relief flowed through him at the thought of reaching his mother. "Thank you," he said, tipping his hat in her direction. "I'm mighty obliged."

Her lips parted ever so slightly in what might have been the beginning of a smile. She gave a slight curtsy, turned on her heels, and hurried behind the house. As he watched her leave, he imagined the two of them talking as they went to St. George. In his mind, Maddie wore a smile—and soot—on her face.

CHAPTER 16

"When I wrote asking to intrude on your hospitality, this wasn't exactly what I had in mind," Clara said with a wry smile.

She sat propped on the bed in the spare room, pillows stacked behind her. A quilt and an afghan both lay across her lap. She sipped a cup of steaming hot water with lemon and honey, which Miriam made to help clear Clara's chest and soothe her throat.

"I'm afraid I have been a burden from the moment I arrived," Clara said sadly.

Miriam wagged a finger at her. "What nonsense, calling yourself a burden. It's been nothing short of a treat to see my dearest friend again. And I'm so grateful that Charles could help with your illness."

"And administer to me," Clara said. She coughed gently to clear her throat, a far cry from the violent, hacking coughs of just two days before.

"Yes, of course," Miriam agreed quietly. "I'm so pleased that . . ." She opened her mouth to say more, then paused, catching herself before saying, "That you've improved so quickly."

Clara had a sneaking suspicion Miriam had been about to say something else—that not only was it a miracle that Clara felt worlds better, but that she was alive at all. After another sip of hot lemon water, Clara asked, "Did you find my temple recommend, then?"

"It's safe and sound in my jewelry box," Miriam said. "Found it just where you said it was, tucked between the Old and New Testaments."

"Wonderful," Clara said. She took another sip and closed her eyes as the drink eased its way down her throat. She noticed Miriam's hands twisting at a handkerchief.

"Clara," she said suddenly. "I know you had hoped to go to the temple this week."

"Monday morning, with the first sign of the sun." Clara took another sip of hot lemon water.

"But you can't go on Monday," Miriam began.

"Just watch me," Clara said, jutting her chin into the air defiantly.

Miriam laughed. "Really, Clara, you can't. They don't do endowments on Mondays."

"Oh." Clara sat back against her pillow meekly. "Then when *do* they?"

"Thursdays and Fridays."

She folded her arms and declared, "Then I'm going Thursday morning, with the first sign of the sun."

Miriam bent her head and sighed. "Charles fears even that's too soon. Going through the ceremonies takes most of the day. It's taxing even for the young and—"

"And the young at heart?" Clara asked with a mischievous look in her eye. The two laughed, but then Clara shook her head. "You disappoint me."

Miriam looked defensive. "How do you figure that?"

"I'm only doing what you taught me on the trail to Zion," Clara said, her voice soft. She put her cup on the side table, then reached over and took her friend's hand in both of hers. "Don't you remember what happened at Chimney Rock?"

Lowering her head, Miriam nodded. "Haven't thought of it in years, but a body can't forget that kind of thing." She looked up, eyes sparkling with tears at the memory.

"The blessing promised you'd get to Zion, just as mine promised I'd get to the temple. I saw you walk into Salt Lake Valley. Now I'm holding onto the same faith you showed when no one believed you would live to see another day."

With a hard swallow, Miriam nodded again. She wiped at an eye with the back of her hand. "I just knew."

"Yes," Clara said. "But on the trail, I had my doubts. Looking at you—no color in your face, lying still as a stone, bleeding. Everyone hoped, but not many of us believed."

A sad smile curved one side of Miriam's mouth. "Not even Charles, at first, remember? Although he's the one who said the words in the blessing."

They once more lapsed into the silence of the past, memories rushing back. For a moment Clara felt as if they were the young women they had been, vibrant, full of life, with their futures in Zion ahead of them. She could still see their faces free of wrinkles, their brown hair unstreaked by gray, their backs straight. As Clara looked at Miriam, the image dissolved into reality. They were old. Wiser, more experienced. Sadder, in some ways.

Miriam sniffed and tried again. "I believe in the blessing Charles gave you. I do. But surely it couldn't hurt to wait a bit. I know you're gaining strength every day—"

"Every hour," Clara interrupted.

"Even so. Charles thinks another few days would be wisest to ensure—"

Clara mustered a laugh. "Charles, Charles. One would think that after witnessing your full recovery—how long was it again, two days?—you'd think that even a man of medicine would believe in miracles, especially when he's the one they both came through." She slapped her hands on her lap and declared, "Thursday morning as the sun comes up, I will be going up to the temple. And that is that."

"But—"

"I'm more stubborn than you are, Miriam Willis," Clara said, giving a mock angry glare. "And nothing you say is going to stop me."

Miriam broke out in laughter. "I know. Who am I to protest a miracle *and* the illustriously stubborn Clara Franklin? You know my only concern is your well-being." When Clara nodded, Miriam finally agreed. "Thursday it is, then. I'll inform Charles that we're paying him no mind."

"Thank you," Clara said. "Tell him we've decided to mind the *Master* Physician."

Miriam stood, her handkerchief no longer twisted beyond recognition. "I will, Clara. Thanks for reminding me."

* * *

Monday morning dawned bright and clear in Snowflake as the Hampton party gathered minutes before their departure.

Maddie stood inside the doorway, watching the preparations with a queer feeling of familiarity in the scene: Peter making a final check of the horses' gear, Ellen chasing Lorenzo around the side of the house the same way she had scurried after Mary two years ago. Her belly bulged, this time with a third child instead of little Lorenzo.

Maddie sighed and stepped outside to bring out the last of the cooking tools, freshly washed. She hoped that Ellen's desire to give birth to a child in the covenant would come to fruition this time. In a strange way, Maddie felt guilty that Lorenzo hadn't been born in the covenant. As she placed the frying pan and wooden spoons in place, she adjusted them to be sure they wouldn't rattle around the wagon, and the guilty thought still bothered her.

For two years Maddie had silently felt that she was, in part, to blame for Ellen and Peter never making it to the temple. Had Maddie not insisted that she and Roland had to be married *in* the temple that summer instead of sealed the following spring when it was more convenient, he wouldn't have died. And the company wouldn't have been forced to turn back.

She tried to chase away the thoughts; after all, she reasoned, such an argument really made no sense. If Roland and Maddie hadn't been on the trip, Ellen and Peter still would have been. The same Indian would have probably attacked. And instead of Roland, it might have been Peter's body—or James's—in the cemetery.

Maddie eyed the sun, which had broken over the horizon not half an hour ago. They needed to get going soon if they were to make the forty miles to Joseph City before dark.

She turned around and headed back to the house to check for any final items they might have forgotten. Most of the packing had been completed on Saturday, leaving little to worry about over the Sabbath or this morning. Their clothing was all packed. Peter had loaded all the food and oats for the horses. Cooking supplies, blankets, rifle, ammunition. She mentally checked off each item as she stared at the ground and strode toward the house.

"Morning."

The voice made her stop, and she looked up suddenly. Not five feet away stood the Indian man, Abe. In the morning light, he somehow looked different than he had on Saturday. She noticed a lighter patch of skin on one cheek, almost silvery with the early, slanted morning rays hitting it, as if it were scarred. At first she wondered why she hadn't noticed it before, then realized that she had taken only a quick look at him before her heart began racing with fear.

"Good morning," she replied when her voice returned. She wondered what the scarring was from, unable to stop an image from popping into her mind—Abe involved with some savage Indian attack. Ridiculous as it was, she couldn't help it.

Abe touched the brim of his hat, nodded, and smiled, then walked to Peter's side, where he began helping with the horses by untangling a set of reins Mary had just twisted into a knot.

Maddie watched him, thinking that the image of savage didn't fit him. Nor did it fit the man she had seen and heard Saturday, the one whose voice had a desperate edge to it when he learned his mother was ill. He was willing to brave the wilderness by himself if it meant reaching her sooner. Someday, perhaps, she would ask him about the scarring. The thought came quickly, surprising her with the fact that it wasn't unpleasant to contemplate knowing this man beyond the trip.

"Is that everything, then?" Ellen called, holding Lorenzo squarely on one hip.

"I was just about to do a final check," Maddie said. She hurried to the house and scanned the rooms, confirming that everything was in order. By the time she came back out, Ellen had Lorenzo confined rather reluctantly in the wagon on top of a bunch of blankets. He sat there with his lower lip pushed out and his pudgy arms folded, displeased with not being able to run free.

Caroline walked up the lane and greeted them. "I'm not late, am I?" she asked, clutching her shawl around her shoulders.

"You're right on time," Peter said. "Why don't you sit on the bench with me? I'll be driving the wagon for the first spell, and I'd like the company."

Getting Caroline to agree required no coaxing. She took Peter's offered hand and climbed, a little unsteadily, onto the wagon, where she deposited herself on the bench and waited primly. Her eyes widened suddenly when her gaze landed on Abe, and Maddie stepped forward, curious. "Are *you* coming with us too?" Caroline asked Abe. The balls of her cheeks were suddenly rosy.

"Yes, I am," Abe said. "In fact, I'll be spelling Peter at the reins."

"How nice," Caroline said. She clasped her hands tightly and pressed her lips together, trying to hide a smile and avoid his eyes. "So I'll get to sit beside you."

Maddie couldn't help but smile to herself. Poor Abe; what was he to do with an admirer of three or four times his age?

"Gather around, everyone," Peter called, stepping down from the wagon. Maddie and Ellen stood on Caroline's side of the wagon. Peter and Abe stood at the head of the team. "Let's have a prayer before we depart." Peter removed his hat, and Abe did the same. "Considering the paths that have brought us together and how long this journey has been in the making, I think every one of us could use the blessings of the Lord on our trip."

Everyone bowed their heads, but Maddie cracked open an eye and peered at Abe to see what he would do. No one had said as much, but something in his manner suggested that he wasn't Mormon. But, like everyone else, he folded his arms and bowed his head. Maddie quickly closed her eyes, feeling a bit guilty. After all, if anyone needed a blessing to make it through the next several weeks without falling apart, it was her, so she should be taking this prayer seriously.

As Peter spoke, Maddie added her own silent petition that they would be protected from natural as well as human dangers. She reached up to feel the bump under the fabric of her bodice where she had hung Roland's ring on a chain. She would wear it around her neck for safe keeping until they camped at the spot where Roland was killed and she would say her final good-bye to him. The prayer ended, and Maddie reluctantly pulled her hand away from the almost unnoticeable lump where the ring lay.

"Thank you," Ellen murmured, and the other adults nodded in agreement.

"I'm glad to see I didn't miss you," came a voice from behind the wagon.

Edward. Maddie whipped around, startled at his sudden appearance. He came to her, hands outstretched. When she put on a smile and put out her own hands, Edward drew her close and pecked her cheek. Maddie flushed hard, hoping that no one was watching.

"Oh, young love!" cried Caroline, clapping her hands.

Edward glanced up and grinned. "If you'll excuse us for a moment," he said, taking Maddie's hand and drawing her several feet away. She was painfully aware of everyone's eyes boring into her back—and of the ring burning into her skin under the dress. He led her to a spot under a tree, then pulled her close again. She hoped the clump of branches blocked their faces from view. "I had to come say good-bye," he said, standing so close that he breathed into her hair. Maddie's stomach became a swarm of nervous butterflies.

"It was good of you to come," she said. An awkward pause followed, and Maddie broke it with, "I'm sorry this isn't our wedding trip. I know you had hoped it would be."

She looked up to see Edward's eyes smiling down at her. "Don't you fret about that for one moment," he said, squeezing her hands in his. "I understand why it can't be, and after thinking about it, I want it this way. When we get married—and then sealed—I want it to be a happy time for you, not something that will bring you distress."

"Thank you, Edward," Maddie said, standing up on her toes and kissing his cheek.

"I'll miss you," he said.

Maddie nodded in agreement, but didn't say the words. "When I return, we will begin our wedding plans, and I will be all yours." Her throat tightened after she said the words, as she realized Edward might recognize them as a confession—that until she returned from saying good-bye to Roland, she wouldn't be fully his.

But Edward said nothing and instead leaned forward and kissed her lips briefly. "Good-bye, Edward," she said, smiling up at him.

"Good-bye, Madeline. God speed your journey."

CHAPTER 17

For the first part of the day's trek, Abe kept his distance from Maddie. While she hadn't given any indication that she still harbored fears about his being Indian, he didn't want to take a chance. Besides, she was already engaged to be married to that Edward fellow who had come to say good-bye.

As Abe walked along the dusty road beside the wagon and the cow, he looked at her, walking ahead of him and carrying Mary on her back. He sighed. Ever since seeing her at the school festival, he had wished to talk with her about her own lost love. After such a recitation, she must have one. They'd be able to empathize with each other. But he feared any overture of friendship on his part would be inappropriate.

Around noon, they stopped to water the animals and get a bite to eat. Abe stood next to one of the horses by the river and watched Maddie. She crouched at the riverbank and helped her niece and nephew. She filled tin cans with fresh water and let them have their fill while she took a handkerchief and dunked it in the water.

"Look at your faces," she said, wiping down Lorenzo's dusty hands. "You're covered."

"And will be again within the hour," Peter said as he approached with the other horse.

"True," Maddie said, working on Lorenzo's face. "But that doesn't mean we can't make an attempt at looking civilized."

Mary sat to the side, pulling at her shoe. "A pebble's in my shoe. It hurts."

"I'll get it out in just a minute," Maddie said. Lorenzo squirmed under his aunt's rubbing, but Maddie held him firm until she finished. She turned back to the river, where she rinsed the cloth and rung it out.

She began working on Mary's dusty face, and just then the little girl's efforts at her shoe finally paid off. The offending shoe flew through the air and landed in the river—which proceeded to carry the shoe down its course, bobbing along the way.

"No!" Maddie cried, watching it float away.

Abe jumped into action. He leaped into the water and swam toward the shoe, reaching out and snagging it with the tips of his fingers. He stood up and walked back to shore, the water at chest level. His foot slipped on a rock, and his head disappeared under the water. With a gasp and ice-cold pain shooting through his head, he resurfaced and held up the dripping shoe. The small group on the bank cheered.

"Yea!" Mary called out, jumping up and down on one foot. "He got it! He got it!"

His clothes hanging from him with the extra weight of the water, Abe climbed out of the river—careful not to slip again—and brought the shoe to Maddie.

"Thank you," she said, taking it from him. "It's getting cold. Too cold for bare feet anymore. She couldn't have walked without this. I don't know what we would have done."

"You're welcome," Abe said. "I'm happy to help."

Their eyes locked, and Abe thought he saw the beginnings of a smile at the corners of her mouth. At the very least, her eyes didn't show fear. But he had no desire to press the issue—or his luck—so he simply nodded and went back to the horse. Even so, he couldn't help but notice that for the rest of the day, he saw more of Maddie. Often she would walk closer to him, sometimes even making small talk about the landscape and Abe's recent travels.

Who knew a wet shoe could make a friend.

* * *

Thursday morning Clara sat at the vanity table and tried to put up her hair. As a knock sounded at the bedroom door, her hands fumbled, and a pin fell to the table. "Come in," she said, picking up the pin and trying again.

Miriam opened the door a crack and peered inside. "Are you almost ready?" When she noticed Clara's trembling hands, she hurried to the bed, where she deposited an armload of clothing. "Let me help you with that." She took the pin from Clara's hand and two more from the vanity table, then she secured Clara's hair in a pretty knot at the nape of her neck.

"Thank you," Clara said with a wistful smile. "I've done my hair every day for as long as I can remember. Never needed help before."

"It's a fitting day to be pampered," Miriam said with two pins between her teeth. One by one, she pushed them into the bun, then smoothed Clara's hair and nodded. "You're beautiful," Miriam said in a reverent tone. "It's almost as if the Spirit has already come to be with you today, as if the Lord knows you're about to go to His house."

"He does," Clara said, looking in the mirror at her reflection. For the first time in more than a decade—perhaps longer—she thought she looked almost pretty. It was something in her eyes. They caught each other's gaze in the mirror and smiled.

Miriam sniffed and turned to the bed. "I brought my temple clothing for you to wear," she said, lifting a white dress and shaking it out.

"Then what will you wear?" Clara asked, fingering the different pieces lying on the bed. She didn't know what they would be used for, and she couldn't wait to find out.

"The matron says the temple has some spares. I'll wear one of theirs. You deserve to have something special for your first time."

"Thank you," Clara said with a touch of awe in her voice. She smoothed a wrinkle on some of the fabric, then pulled her hand away gently, as if the clothing were part of the temple and deserved as much reverence as the building did. "They're so beautiful."

Old hopes bubbled up in her—hopes that had stayed with her since Nauvoo. The feeling of pride as the temple was built, the overwhelming disappointment when she and Bart were turned away from it. And here she was, preparing to receive all those blessings she had only dreamed about. It was as if all her life had been pointing toward this day.

"Thank you, Miriam," she said, her heart ready to burst with joy. "I can't wait to wear them."

"I'm glad we're the same size," Miriam said. She leaned down and hugged her friend.

Less than an hour later, Clara was on her way to the temple for the first time. She wanted to walk, but in spite of her recovery, Charles refused to let her go on her own two feet.

"You'll need your strength for the temple itself," he had said. And when she began to protest, he merely put up his hand and shook his head. "Miracle or no miracle, you aren't walking." And that was that. He had hitched up his buggy and driven Clara and Miriam to the temple.

When the elegant building came into view, Clara gasped and clutched at her collar. Charles reined in the horse.

"What's wrong?" he asked, reaching to feel Clara's forehead and check her pulse.

Clara hardly noticed his touch. Her heart raced as she gazed at the white temple. Above the door stood a beautiful, tall dome and a spire reaching heavenward. She shook her head, emotion overcoming her. "It looks so much like Nauvoo," she said, her voice almost a whisper.

The two buildings weren't exactly twins, but the shape and feel of the St. George Temple felt like an echo of the one in Nauvoo. How she had pined to go inside those walls. The ones that stood before her looked so similar—and she was about to enter them.

"Thank You, Lord," she said under her breath. Then, "Please, Charles. Let's go."

CHAPTER 18

"The temple is so beautiful," Clara exclaimed as the buggy approached the tall, white structure. It looked like a fortress with its corner towers and battlements along the top—one significant way the building differed from Nauvoo. Arches around the windows looked perfectly round and smooth, as if they had been carved out of fresh cream.

"It *is* beautiful—now," Miriam agreed.

"Oh? Wasn't it always?" Clara asked, shifting her position to look at her friend. "Hasn't it always looked like this?"

"Not quite. Brother Brigham wanted it this way, but it didn't happen right at first. They say he got his way after he died, though."

Charles laughed and adjusted his hat. "Great story, that one."

"You tell it," Miriam said with a chuckle of her own.

"The original dome and tower were much shorter," Charles began. "Brother Brigham took one look at it and declared they were ugly and made the whole temple look short and squatty."

"I can't imagine that," Clara said, gazing at the temple as they approached. "The tower is perfect. So stately and elegant. Prettiest building in hundreds of miles, I'd wager."

"No question about that," Charles said with a firm nod. "When the temple was finished, Brother Brigham hadn't the heart to order the Saints to fix the dome or the tower, even though both were squat and stubby. The people had sacrificed a lot to finish the tabernacle while building the temple. Everyone was plumb wore out."

"What happened for them to change it? Did they finally agree with President Young?"

Miriam chuckled. "In a manner of speaking."

The wagon reached the east side of the temple, and Charles pulled the horses to a stop. He rested an arm on the back of the bench to finish his story. "Like I said, Brother Brigham didn't have the heart to make them change it after all their sacrifices, though he made no bones about hating the short, ugly thing. He died not long after the dedication. Then, almost exactly a year later, we had one of the worst storms ever. Lightning hit the temple smack on the tower."

Clara gasped involuntarily, her hand coming to her mouth even though she sat beside the temple, which was perfectly fine and obviously not seriously harmed. "What happened?"

"Well, word has it that the strike should have destroyed the whole building. Instead, it just burned the dome." Charles and Miriam began laughing, and Clara relaxed and joined in on the joviality.

"Let me guess the rest." She held her stomach to avoid laughing so hard that she'd start coughing. "They saw the lightning as a message from the grave and made haste rebuilding it in the manner President Young first wanted."

"Pretty much," Charles said, pushing his hat higher with a knuckle. "In fact, you're in luck that you came down when you did. They just finished the dome last May, so this look is new to all of us. Well, we're here. Time to go. Are you ready?"

"Am I ever," Clara said, already gathering her things and standing.

Charles got out and helped her down from the wagon, and Miriam followed behind with the clothing, which was carefully folded inside a linen bag to keep it clean. Charles shifted from foot to foot, obviously wary of letting Clara leave his sight even for the day.

She noticed his hesitation and stood at her fullest height, with her head erect—but she didn't come close to matching the stature of her younger years no matter how straight she tried to make her back.

"Look at me," she demanded. "I'm fit as a fiddle, as they say. And I'm standing on holy ground with every intention of going inside." She waved the back of her hand at him. "Now git."

The corners of Charles's mouth lifted, and a snicker escaped. "Very well," he said, lifting his hands in surrender. "I'll 'git.' But only because Miriam will be with you. And don't overexert yourself. Sit whenever you can. Promise at least that much to your physician."

Clara raised her eyebrows and planted a fist on her hip. "I believe I said git!"

"No more protests from me," Charles said, climbing back onto the wagon. He gathered the reins, brow furrowed as he eyed his patient. "Miriam, take care of her, please."

His wife nodded. "I will." Then she grinned. "Now git!" Both women waved as Charles clicked his tongue and snapped the reins, and the horses moved out.

"You have your recommend?" Miriam asked, shifting the clothing in her arms.

"In my pocket," Clara said with a nod.

She paused on the walkway, making Miriam stop and turn around. "What is it?" she asked with a concerned tone in her voice.

Clara stared at the eastern side of the temple with its elegant white dome and tower reaching heavenward. "Brigham was right, wasn't he?"

"He was." Both of their voices had turned reverent, away from the gaiety of a moment before. Miriam pointed to the southeast corner of the temple. "That's where we stood when the site was dedicated." With a shake of her head, she added, "I can scarcely believe it was nearly twelve years ago."

Without any words, they both instinctively left the walkway and headed left, toward that side of the temple. Clara gazed at the grounds, which were clean and cared for, if simple. Red rocks rose behind them, the deep rust color sharply contrasting with the brilliant white of the building's walls.

"What was it like?" Clara asked in a hushed whisper. "Being at the dedication of the site?"

They paused at the southeast corner, and Miriam gazed as if she could see right through the white-plastered walls to the bare ground that had been there more than a decade earlier.

"It was peaceful. Joyful. Glorious. I remember George A. Smith saying the prayer, kneeling right there." She pointed at the corner of the foundation. "Then a brass band played, and Brother Brigham took the first shovelful of dirt. Several other priesthood leaders followed with the shovel, and then some of the congregation." She smiled. "I got to move a little dirt too."

The hairs on Clara's arms raised at the thought that her friend had anything to do with the building of this temple. Once again she was brought back to her time in Nauvoo as they tried so desperately to finish the temple there. But although such images bombarded her memory, she didn't say a word as Miriam recounted the events of more than a decade ago.

"As the temple went up, I assumed it would be the color of the sandstone they were using," Miriam said, her eyes tracking the wall and rising to the tower. "But when they plastered it white, it almost seemed like the temple had been baptized. It looked beautiful, white and pure." Her hand went to her chest, and her eyes grew watery.

I hadn't seen this as my temple, Clara suddenly realized. Until this moment, she had yearned for the one in Nauvoo—a temple that no longer existed—knowing she would never enter its doors. Here in the middle of the dry, hot, redrock land of St. George, she was determined to receive her temple blessings. But she held no deep love for the structure itself—until this moment.

Miriam went on as Clara dabbed at her eyes.

"I remember Brother Brigham standing on a chair for the dedication. Rickety old thing it was," she said, a tender smile toying at her lips. "Then he raised a white handkerchief and led the crowd in the Hosanna Shout. I remember waving my handkerchief and shouting the words as loudly as I could. Felt like my heart was near to bursting. I believe the very power of God was in the midst of us. You could almost see it, touch it." She shook her head slightly. "I'm sorry. I didn't mean to go on like that. I had forgotten all about some of those things."

"No. Don't apologize," Clara assured Miriam, touching her arm. "That's what I needed to hear today. To be honest," she said, lowering her head, "I had feared that I wouldn't feel the Spirit. I had such a deep love of the Nauvoo Temple that I feared that not having any connection to this one would dampen the joy of my day."

She put her arms around Miriam and squeezed tightly, saying, "Thank you for sharing your memories. I feel as if I was there that day too."

Miriam clung to Clara for several seconds, and when the friends pulled away, the sentiment touched them both, and they sniffed. Clara squared her shoulders, pulled her recommend from her pocket, and said, "Well then. I'm ready. Let's go."

* * *

The Hampton party was a few days into their trip when they reached Sunset Crossing, where several roads converged into the main one. Peter left the road and went to the center of town to purchase some axle grease, sugar, and a new tinderbox. Ellen went with him on Caroline's suggestion. The children had trouble sleeping at night, and she said that sachets of lavender would help them rest. Ellen hoped to find some in one of the stores.

While they shopped, Caroline sat in the shade of the wagon box and played peek-a-boo with Lorenzo and pat-a-cake with Mary. Watching them, Maddie couldn't help but think that it was fitting— Caroline seemed so childlike herself. Maddie moseyed along the edge of the road, where they had stopped the wagon in a broad, grassy area. She decided to take in some air and enjoy the change of scenery now that there were people and houses instead of the road and its ruts. Plenty of pine trees grew along the road, and Maddie enjoyed the fresh breeze.

"Mind if I join you?"

She turned as Abe approached from behind. "Please do," she said, and he fell into step beside her. They walked in silence for several minutes, and Maddie began to feel awkward. Should she thank him again for rescuing Mary's shoe the other day? They had pretty much exhausted talking about the weather. What else was there to discuss with a perfect stranger?

"So," Maddie said, grasping for something to say, "do I understand correctly that your mother isn't from St. George?"

"That's right," Abe said. "It's a temporary arrangement."

"Oh, I see," Maddie said, wishing he would have volunteered more information. "Where is she from originally? What . . . um . . . tribe?"

Abe hesitated for half a second and glanced her direction. "We lived in Salt Lake. She's white," he said. "I was adopted as a boy."

Maddie flushed bright red. She had been wondering how he had grown up, what Indian traditions he practiced, whether he spoke another language, how he had come to look so civilized. "I—oh, I'm sorry," she said, touching a hand to her nose. "It's really none of my business. I just assumed—"

"It's a natural assumption." With a shrug, Abe said, "I was adopted by Mormons. But I'm not one."

"Oh, I see," Maddie said for the second time. She felt as tongue-tied as some of her students as they recited poetry in class.

"I've—I've been meaning to tell you that I enjoyed your performance at the festival," Abe said after an awkward pause. "It was remarkable."

"*You* were there?" Maddie pulled to a stop and furrowed her brow. "I didn't see you."

"I was in the back," Abe said. "Come to think of it, Edward was back there too, although I hadn't met him at the time. He seemed to really enjoy the final scene. Shakespeare, wasn't it?"

She nodded. "Yes, it was."

"But to me, your recitation was the best part of the evening. You see," Abe went on, "I lost someone I loved a few years ago." He looked up at the sky in thought. "She ended our relationship and married someone else. And that poem—or rather, your delivery of it—captured my feelings exactly. I wanted to tell you that."

"Thank you," Maddie said, her face turning pale. She turned back to the road and began walking briskly, unsure if she wanted to continue the conversation. She felt as if her privacy had been invaded, when in reality, dozens of people had heard her recite that evening. But that night held so many feelings that she wanted to keep it the way she remembered—as if she had been reciting the poem to Roland. She simply hadn't expected anyone in her audience to respond this way—to see into her soul that way—especially a perfect stranger.

"I'm sorry," Abe said, not following her. "I meant no harm," he called louder.

Maddie stopped, knowing she was being rude. She closed her eyes and took a breath before turning around. "No, I'm the one who should apologize." She walked back, closing the gap between them. She could see genuine concern on his face, and suddenly she wanted to explain the situation. "The truth is, I almost didn't recite that particular poem. It . . . it has a lot of meaning for me."

"I thought it must."

They both looked at the ground, Maddie avoiding his eyes.

"Did you . . ." Abe's voice had lowered to almost a whisper. "Did you lose someone too?"

Maddie didn't look up, but she nodded, unable to speak. She wiped her eyes and nodded again, this time managing to say, "Yes." She raised her head and looked into his eyes—so dark they were almost black. Different from Roland's green ones, but just as kind and good. "My fiancé. He died two and a half years ago."

She stepped along the path and wiped at her eyes again. Abe followed beside her as she regained her composure, then quietly asked, "What happened?"

How could she tell Abe about Roland's death? And yet she wanted to. She looked away and bit her lips together. "It was on the way to be married in St. George. We were about halfway there when he was killed." Searching for a way to explain the tragedy without offending Abe, she paused in her step and turned to him. "I'm sorry I reacted as I did the first time I met you. It was . . . because of *how* Roland died."

Instead of the surprise she expected to see, Abe nodded. "An Indian?"

"Yes," Maddie said, feeling as if her heart had begun beating again. He didn't seem unsettled at all. Somehow he made her feel comfortable talking about these things, as if they had known one another for ages. She began walking again, and Abe stayed at her side. "He was shot point-blank in the chest, and the Indian took his horse." A shudder went through her.

"I am so sorry." Abe shook his head sadly. "Coming on this trip must be so hard for you. And I thought *my* loss was tragic."

Maddie just shrugged. She turned around to head back toward the wagon. "Ellen needed me to come. Besides, it's been long enough that I should be able to move on with my life."

They walked silently for several minutes. Then Abe said, "When you stood on that stage, I knew you understood what it was like. But I didn't have any idea just how much you had suffered."

She smiled at him, feeling a sudden lifting of her burden, which surprised her. Granted, Abe was still about as close to a stranger as a person could be. Yet they had a unique connection, the two of them, and Maddie wanted to understand it better. In all the time since

Roland's death, plenty of people had expressed their condolences. Most had gone on about how she would love again, or how she would see Roland in the next life.

No one had truthfully—believably—said, "I understand." Abe was the first. And he was an Indian of all things. The irony wasn't lost on Maddie.

She hesitated for a moment, wanting to know more about Abe and his lost love. "Abe, would you—would you tell me about her . . . sometime?" She was scarcely able to believe that she had asked such a personal question of someone she had met only a few days ago.

He thought about it for a minute, then slowly nodded. "If you'll tell me about Roland."

The request was only fair. And after all the time that had passed since Roland died, the thought of sharing the details with someone who understood was a welcome relief.

"I'd like that," she said.

* * *

Clara's day in the temple proved to be one of the happiest of her life. Miraculously free from all ailments for several blessed hours, she went from room to room and learned more of God and made covenants. She felt more joy than she could ever remember experiencing in a single day. As she passed by a mirror on the way to the dressing room at the end of her session, she almost didn't recognize herself. Stopping, she stared at the image and examined her reflection. She looked younger, less careworn. Even her wrinkles looked smoother, and her eyes sparkled. It was as if she had dropped ten years from her age. Or more.

Amazing what the Spirit can do. She smiled as she entered the dressing room. Not much later, as she and Miriam headed for the doors, Clara leaned in and confided, "I'm sure glad I fasted today. It brought the Spirit so close."

"You *what?*" Miriam stopped short and stared at her friend.

They had paused before the doors, and with the smile of a child caught in mischief, Clara shrugged. "I know Charles said my body couldn't stand it, but I also wasn't about to sacrifice my day in the temple for any overprotective instructions, even if they did come from a doctor."

For a second, Miriam could do nothing but gape at her friend. "Then what—what happened to the breakfast I brought up this morning?"

"I slid the tray under the bed," Clara said, turning back toward the doors. She waved a hand toward Miriam. "Oh, stop looking at me like that. As you can see, I'm perfectly fine. A tad weak, but nothing a good supper can't fix."

With a furrowed brow, Miriam followed Clara, who had reached the doors and was opening them. "I suppose," she said reluctantly. "But you shouldn't have taken such a risk, and without telling me or Charles. You could have—Clara!"

Her friend had collapsed on the threshold. Miriam rushed forward, where she held the doors open with her back so they wouldn't press upon Clara's prostrate form.

"Help! Someone, please!" she cried.

A brother dressed in white hurried to them and held the door, freeing Miriam to kneel and help her friend. He leaned forward and asked, "What's wrong?"

Miriam ignored him and patted Clara's cheeks. "Clara, can you hear me?"

Her chest rose and fell shallowly, so at least she was breathing. But her face was pale, and she remained unresponsive. Another brother appeared and helped Miriam carry Clara back into the temple foyer and place her on a couch. "I'll find a blanket and water," he said, hurrying away.

Miriam stood, staring at her friend, feeling torn about what she should do. She needed to fetch Charles, but at the same time, how could she leave Clara's side? Her hand rubbed at her forehead, which had begun to throb. With sudden decision, she turned to the tall, thin man who had held the door. He stood behind her, somewhat out of the way but looking eager to help.

"Please," Miriam said, determined to stay with Clara, "fetch Dr. Willis. Do you know where he lives?"

The man said nothing, but gave a quick nod before rushing out the doors.

Miriam's attention turned back to her friend. She raised Clara's eyelids and looked in them as she had seen her husband do to patients. She had no idea what she should be looking for, and wouldn't have known what to do anyway.

Several decorative pillows from the couch had fallen haphazardly onto the floor. Each had been intricately embroidered especially for the temple. Feeling only a slight pinch of concern over soiling them, Miriam gathered three pillows and put them under Clara's feet. She remembered Charles propping up patients' feet and hoped it would help today.

When the other brother arrived with the blanket, Miriam shook it out and placed it over Clara's cold form. "Thank you," she told the temple worker as she took the glass of water from his outstretched hand. "Could you find some food?"

"I'm sure I can find something," he said, then hurried off.

Miriam tried hard to keep her voice even and her emotions from running wild in panic. She knelt beside the couch and held Clara's cold, limp hand between both of hers, trying to warm it up. Every so often she glanced at the doors.

Charles, where are you? Please hurry.

CHAPTER 19

The following day, Friday, Caroline insisted that she walk part of the way. "Those horses are getting plenty of work as it is," she told Peter as he tried to help her up onto the wagon bench before pulling out of camp. She put her fist on her hip, refusing his offer, and shook her head. "I might not be able to walk far, but I'm dag-blamed if I don't do my best as far as I can today."

"Suit yourself," Peter said, as if he had a choice in the matter. Maddie laughed, and Abe couldn't help but chuckle too. If Caroline didn't *want* to ride, no one in this life could make her.

Six hours and nearly twenty miles later, the entire company was pleasantly surprised to find Caroline still tromping along, walking better than any of them had ever seen her walk in all the years she had lived in Snowflake.

"Do you need a break?" Peter called over his shoulder from the bench.

"Not hardly," Caroline yelled back from the side of the wagon. "Must be the air closer to the temple that's making me feel younger with every step." They weren't yet halfway to St. George, but she inhaled deeply through her nose and let out a hearty breath through her mouth. She turned to Abe, who walked behind her, and demanded, "Isn't the air just full of the Spirit?"

"Um, well . . ." Abe stammered, unsure what to say. What he *wanted* to say was that the air felt dry and hot and miserable for both man and beast, but he wasn't about to make Caroline feel bad. "It sure is clean air," he managed. Maddie grinned back at him, her shoulders trembling with laughter, surely knowing what he was thinking.

As they walked along, Abe had an urge to put his arm around Maddie's shoulders or to take her hand in his. For several minutes their arms had occasionally brushed one another, making him feel more connected to her. He had some idea of what she had felt when she lost Roland, and he wanted to protect her from feeling so unhappy ever again.

Whoa, he told himself, and unconsciously took a half step to the side, away from Maddie. *I won't do* that *again.*

He took off his hat and fanned his face, which suddenly felt more flushed than before. She was engaged! Besides, feeling anything more than friendship toward a Mormon woman was absolutely, unequivocally, out of the question. He had done that once and ended up with a broken heart.

But thinking back to their walk the other day, he couldn't help but know that he understood her feelings, at least to some extent. While their stories differed, they had both lost a love and bore the scars to prove it. Some of his happened to be on his face—from pulling Lizzy out of a fire in Logan years ago—but more remained deeply etched on his heart.

That common ground was proving dangerous. The more he felt himself drawn to Maddie, the more he risked his heart. Years ago, his mother had warned him that a mixed-belief relationship could spell trouble. She was right. And he would *not* toy with such things again.

"Ellen!"

Maddie's sudden cry tore through Abe's thoughts, and he instantly became alert. About fifteen feet ahead, Ellen had stopped walking, her eyes closed, her hands clutching her belly. At her feet lay spatters of blood. Maddie rushed to her sister's side as Abe sprang into action.

"Peter!" he yelled, racing forward. "Stop the wagon!"

With a hearty yank at the reins and a yell of, "Whoa, there, boys," Peter stopped the horses and the wagon, then leaned over, eyebrows raised as Abe reached him. "What is it?"

"Something's wrong with Ellen," Abe said, but already Peter had seen her face and the growing puddle of red in the sand.

Without a word, he braced himself on the edge of the wagon and jumped off, then flew to his wife. Caroline and Maddie had both reached her, supporting her weight under their own. Ellen's face looked drawn and white, pinched with pain. She tried to take a step, but the effort made her face screw up even more tightly, and she stopped.

Peter swooped in, making Maddie and Caroline move aside. He gently picked up his wife and marched to the wagon, disregarding the blood soaking through her skirt.

"Move those oat sacks!" he yelled. Abe rushed in to help, heaving bags of oats and stacking them beside the wagon, then rearranging the rest of the items in the wagon to make a spot for Ellen.

"Mary, you and Lorry go play with your aunt," Peter called to his children. They sat in the wagon box, huddled to one side, eyes wide as their father commanded them to play. They climbed out of the box onto the bench, but didn't leave, instead watching as the adults moved around earnestly and spoke to one another in abrupt, sharp tones.

"The baby," Ellen whispered through the chaos, expressing what everyone else thought.

Abe suddenly noticed the horses snorting and sidestepping on the ground, their eyes wild. They could sense something wasn't quite right. He hurried to the wagon and took the reins. Speaking softly, he tried to calm the animals. He stroked their necks and waited until they were under control. With the tension in the air, the last thing they needed was runaway horses.

"Is she all right?" he called.

Peter glanced at Abe across the wagon box. Sweat beaded on his forehead, and a look of helplessness crossed his face. "I don't know what to do."

Caroline pushed Peter and Maddie away from the back of the wagon as if she were swatting flies. "Make room for me," she said. "*I* know what to do." She huffed and shook her head at them. "Heavens. Let a woman have some space."

She didn't look at all concerned as she leaned over Ellen. "When did the pains start?"

"An hour ago, maybe," Ellen said with a grimace. She blinked hard, then added, "But I didn't think they were serious. With my other babies I had some beforehand, but the real ones never started *this* early . . ."

Caroline gave a nod of certainty. "It's not uncommon for later children to come earlier."

"Two months early?" Peter demanded.

Caroline shrugged. "Exercise can begin the process. Perhaps she walked too much."

"The faster I walked, the worse they got," Ellen said, then stopped and grimaced.

Peter's jaw clenched; he was obviously getting antsy, and discussing the problem wasn't solving it. "So what can we do?"

Caroline merely patted him on the arm. "It's quite simple," she assured him. "I have just the thing—cramp bark. Paid for it to be brought to Utah all the way from the East. I carried it to Snowflake when we moved here. Cost a pretty penny, I might add. Used it all the time when I worked as a midwife."

She began looking around the wagon, brow furrowed, as she pushed various items aside and looked under others. "Maddie," Caroline said, turning to her, "where did you put my bag of herbs?"

Maddie's face drained. Her hand flew to her lips. "It's still in the kitchen cupboard! I forgot to pack it. I'm so sorry, Caroline . . ."

With a disappointed sigh, Caroline merely shook her head. "Told you it was important, didn't I? Somehow I knew we'd need some of my remedies. Next thing you know, someone's going to break a bone or come down with consumption, and there won't be a thing I can do about it." She huffed in disgust, then clamped her lips together, staring over Abe's head, likely at some fluffy white cloud in the otherwise clear sky.

She chewed on the inside of her cheek and squinted one eye hard, then demanded of Peter, "Any chance you men could find me some nettles or alfalfa in these parts? Or both? They're not as good as cramp bark, but they might help."

"If they're out here," Peter said, "we'll find 'em." He looked ready to bolt into the desert in search of the plants, but Abe called out to him before he could leave.

"First let's find a place to camp for the night. That way Ellen can rest while we search."

Fearing for his wife, Peter hesitated. But Caroline broke in. "Abe's right. Ellen needs to lie still. That'll help stop both the pains and the bleeding. A bumpy wagon won't help matters."

With a shaky nod, Peter scanned the area and pointed toward an open, relatively flat spot. "Let's camp over there. We can find a spring or dig for water later."

With a cluck to the horses, Abe snapped the reins, and soon the wagon moved slowly toward the spot Peter had indicated, an area away from the main road. Abe couldn't help but think that this predicament would have been better handled yesterday, before they left the banks of the Little Colorado and headed more north toward Tuba City. They had to be pretty close to the town, he figured, and therefore water couldn't be too far away, but they'd have to look for it. As the wagon jolted forward, Ellen lay in the back and moaned periodically with pain, hands over her belly. Abe looked at her and grimaced, feeling uneasy.

The moment they were somewhat settled, Peter and Abe left to find the plants Caroline had requested. As Maddie watched them leave, she felt a twinge of concern at the thought of the women and children being left without a man to protect them. She glanced around the countryside as if she could spot a group of Indians waiting in ambush. But just as quickly, she shoved the thoughts aside, knowing that she was being ridiculous. She needed to help Caroline with Ellen, tend the children, and see to a hundred other things. Fearful thoughts would serve as nothing but a distraction.

If only Abe would have stayed behind.

"Madeline," Caroline called from the wagon in a sweet voice. "Would you be a dear and milk the cow?"

With a glance at the lowing animal, which was tethered to the wagon on the far side, Maddie tilted her head in exasperation. With such scatterbrained behavior, could they trust Caroline with Ellen and the baby?

"It's not time to milk yet," Maddie said, crossing to the wagon. "She might dry out." She bit her lip to avoid adding, "I'd think someone who grew up on a farm would know that."

Caroline poked her head out of the wagon cover and groaned in frustration. "Sakes alive, you'd think I'm a child asking for a piece of cake. Ellen needs to drink milk *now.* You've got to trust me here. I've seen the same thing happen with mothers a hundred times if I have once. The water barrels are empty, and milk's better for these things anyway. So unless you've got a rod like Moses did to make a fountain from a rock, I suggest you get milking."

"Sorry," Maddie said, feeling penitent. Scatterbrained or not, Caroline did seem to be thinking clearly—and she knew what needed to be done. Maddie found a pail in the wagon box, then urged Mary and Lorenzo out so they wouldn't disturb their mother. "Let's see if you can find some really pretty rocks," she said, hoping the challenge would keep them occupied. She picked out two large cups from the dishes and handed them to the children. "Use these to collect the rocks. When they're full, bring them back and we'll look at them together."

"Can we use that?" Mary asked, pointing at the pail. "It'll hold more."

"True," Maddie said, "but if you filled it up with rocks, it would be much too heavy for you to lift."

"Then I suppose these will do," Mary said, a phrase she surely got from Ellen. The children each snatched a cup and hurried off.

"Don't go far," Maddie called. "Stay where I can see you. And keep your brother close."

"I will," Mary said, pulling Lorenzo along by the hand. He toddled after her as quickly as he could but tumbled once or twice on the uneven ground. Mary let go and bent down, examining a rock. She pointed it out to her brother. "Look at this one! Do you want it for your cup?"

Lorenzo gave a big nod and held it up for Mary, who plopped the bright red sandstone into his mug. And the two were off in search of more rocks. With the children no longer underfoot, Maddie went to the back of the wagon. "Ellen, how do you feel?"

Caroline gave one look at Maddie and threw her arms up in exasperation. "Why aren't you milking the cow?"

"I will. In just a moment," Maddie said, holding up the pail for evidence. "I just wanted to check on my sister."

Opening her eyes, Ellen smiled. "I'm a little better already. Lying down helps. The pains aren't as strong. Caroline's been rubbing my feet, and that eases them, too."

Maddie just stood there for a moment. She needed to get Ellen some milk, but she didn't want to leave her sister's side. When

Caroline looked up, eyebrows arched impatiently, Maddie nodded. "I'll be back with some milk in a minute."

The next few hours were spent taking care of Ellen and praying that her baby wouldn't come yet. Maddie had brought the milk— still worried about stripping the cow for fear of drying her out. Peter and Abe returned an hour or so later with nettles but no alfalfa. By that point, Mary and Lorenzo had tired of collecting rocks and sat on the ground, their stashes dumped in piles. They sorted and compared rocks, Lorenzo occasionally stealing from his sister's pile to add to his own.

On Caroline's orders, the men made a fire pit. While Peter gathered kindling and wood, Abe went in search of water and ended up having to dig to find anything drinkable and not filled with red sand. They built a fire and boiled the greens to make a drink for Ellen.

She rested in the wagon for the remainder of the day. They didn't dare move out again, and Caroline advised that they not travel the next day, either. "Let her body mend," she said. "And let the baby catch his breath."

But that meant no traveling for two full days. Tomorrow was Saturday, and of course they wouldn't journey on the Sabbath. Even Abe knew that. So they'd be here until Monday morning, assuming Ellen would be well enough to travel by then. While Maddie and Caroline cared for Ellen, Abe and Peter sat around the campfire. Mixed emotions gnawed at Abe as he stared at the flames. On one hand, he wanted the best for Ellen Hampton and her family—which, of course, included her unborn child. That meant staying as long as needed for Ellen to rest.

But then there was his mother. Abe had no way of knowing her condition. Had she recovered? Had she experienced a turn for the worse? Had she passed on without him saying good-bye? He gazed northward at the endless stretch of road before them, deep ruts from all those who had already traveled this way. He had hoped to arrive in St. George in two and a half weeks. With a baby threatening to come and an elderly woman along, the trip would take three weeks or more.

Please sustain Mother that long. Abe looked at Peter, who sat across the fire from him, forehead lined with worry. His eyes looked haunted as he stared blankly, and dark circles made his face look haggard and aged.

"I'm sorry," Abe offered, not knowing what else to say.

Peter gave the slightest hint of a nod. "Thanks. I'm trying to have faith. But in these situations, it's really in God's hands, isn't it?"

"I suppose it is," Abe said. A thought popped into his mind, one that surprised him, but it felt right nonetheless, so he verbalized it. "Have you given her a blessing?"

"No, I haven't," he said, raising one shoulder in a shrug. "I'm the only elder—" He cut off.

"Don't worry," Abe said, smiling to ward off any concerns. "I know I don't hold the priesthood."

Peter returned the smile. "It's supposed to be two," he said. "I'm the only one."

Abe could hardly believe he was saying this—or that he knew enough about Mormon beliefs to say what he was about to say. "True, but my understanding is that in a pinch, when only one elder is available, the Lord accepts the blessing anyway."

"You're right," Peter said, his head tilting with the realization. "I hadn't really thought of it that way. I've never been in a situation where I couldn't call on another brother."

"Then that settles it," Abe said with a nod. "You have consecrated oil, don't you?"

Who is this speaking? Abe thought. *This is so unlike me, encouraging a priesthood blessing. Since when do I believe any of that stuff?*

But it was the best he could do to comfort Maddie and her family, and if he had known of more he could do, he would have done it. He and Peter dug through a bag in the front of the wagon, then went to the rear where Maddie sat holding Ellen's hand. The children slept soundly, covered with quilts, under the wagon box. Caroline, apparently exhausted from her trek and tending to Ellen, had fallen asleep beside Ellen and snored deeply.

"Peter's going to give her a blessing," Abe said in a whisper. Maddie's eyes locked with his, and she smiled in gratitude as if she knew it had been his idea. He took off his hat and bowed his head as Peter placed a drop of oil on his wife's crown and pronounced both the anointing and the sealing.

The words weren't anything unusual, but as Peter removed his hands, a feeling a warmth and peace permeated the very air. For several moments, no one moved or said a word. Abe didn't know the reason everyone else stayed silent, but he knew why he did. His heart had been touched at the depth of peace and emotions hovering in the air, and he wanted to experience them longer. For one of the first times in his life, he grasped why so many were drawn to religion, and to the Mormons especially. It was this warmth and peace, this joy. Because even with Ellen's pain and the uncertainty of what would happen with her baby, that feeling—peace—existed.

"Thank you," Ellen finally said quietly. Peter leaned down and gave her a kiss. She put her arms around him, hugged him tight, and the two wept together.

The sight brought a knot to Abe's throat. This was the kind of life he wanted to have—someone to care about. Someone to care *for*. Someone to be with through the inevitable trials of life. He felt painfully aware of Maddie standing only a few feet away and the fact that the image in his mind of his future wife wore Maddie's face. He forced himself to replace her picture with someone else's—some faceless woman, a shadow he did not yet know.

Peter pulled back, his eyes glassy. He brushed some damp locks of hair from Ellen's forehead, and she closed her eyes at his touch. Leaning down, he brushed her cheek with his lips.

Abe's eyes began to burn, and he blinked several times to clear them. He turned his head to the side so no one would see, then walked back to the fire, hoping that no one had noticed his tears. If they did, he could always blame it on the smoke.

CHAPTER 20

Bright light pierced through the crack between the window and its shade, landing on Clara's face. She cringed and turned away, but the sudden movement sent shards of pain shooting through her head, and she gasped.

"She's awake!"

The voice seemed familiar, yet so far away, like someone was calling from across the ocean. The sound was followed by footfalls and the gentle pressure of someone sitting on the mattress beside her. "Clara?" A hand came to her forehead, and the voice spoke again. "Clara, how do you feel?"

She tried to open her eyes, but they felt like heavy lead weights. Giving up, she tried to speak, but through her parched throat managed only a scratchy, "Mmm."

"Praise the Lord; she can hear us."

Miriam, she suddenly realized. It was her voice she heard. At least Clara thought it was. Her mind was clouded in confusion, as if she were trying to see through a murky haze.

Where was she? Why did she feel so weak? And why did she feel so much pain?

Miriam placed a cup to Clara's mouth, and a mouthful of water seeped in, moistening her dry tongue. Eagerly, her lips opened for more, and this time Miriam tilted the cup again and allowed a drizzle to enter her mouth. Clara swallowed, grateful for the water. An awareness of ravenous hunger hit her, and she wondered how long she had been lying here.

Through the haze, a beam of light fought through her mind—a dim memory returning. As Clara focused on it, the images grew clearer in her mind. The temple. She had been in the temple. Somewhere near the doors. No, *at* the doors. Holding one open and crossing the threshold. Then a feeling of faintness had washed over her, and her legs had gone out. All went dark as she collapsed. Darkness—that was the last memory until this moment.

Had she been leaving the temple or coming to it? The question sent fear clutching at her heart, and she searched her memory for an answer until one surfaced. Standing in the temple, dressed in white, making covenants. At the memory, she almost shuddered with relief.

She *had* received her endowment. The sealing to Bart had yet to take place, but that couldn't happen until after Charles performed Bart's ordinance work anyway. All was well. A stuttered sigh escaped her lips, and she sank further into the pillow. She turned her head to the window, where the sharp light shone right into her eyes again, and she turned away in pain.

"Sun," she said, the single word tearing at her throat.

Miriam scuttled over to the far wall and drew the curtains, which blocked the bright rays and made the room dimmer. Clara attempted a smile as her thanks. She wanted to say the word, but her throat wouldn't let her. Swallowing, she tried to moisten it, and Miriam must have understood, because she brought the cup to her lips again. The process was repeated twice more, by which time Clara felt she could muster a word or two.

She forced her heavy eyelids open and asked, "How long?"

Miriam placed the cup in her lap. "Since Thursday evening." When Clara closed her eyes and tried to calculate the time, Miriam went on. "The sun is setting, and it's Saturday. You've been asleep for over forty-eight hours."

No wonder her stomach felt hollow. *Sleeping? Just sleeping?* She knew better. Her health was failing. It was easy to see that her days were numbered. But the pressing anxiety of living to do her temple work had passed, so the thought didn't upset her much.

That is, until another, more pressing thought gripped her mind.

"Abe?" she whispered.

"Not here yet," Miriam said. "Soon, I'm sure." She took Clara's hand and gently stroked the top of it. "The weather has been good, and it's the safest time of year to make the journey, judging from other travelers we've talked to."

Clara nodded, wishing she could know where her son was, what he was doing, feeling. Whom he traveled with. Whether he was safe. Her mind swirled with questions, and probably would until she saw him again, held him in her own arms, and knew he was well.

"Would you like some vegetable broth?" Miriam asked.

Nodding weakly, Clara let her eyes droop closed so she could rest. "Mmm-hmm." The interchange with Miriam, brief as it had been, felt as taxing as the walk to St. George.

Miriam scooted her chair back, and Clara heard footsteps, then the door opening as her friend left to fetch the broth. But Clara didn't know if she'd be able to eat; she felt weaker than ever, as if moving so much as her thumb were as much work as hauling hay. Her back ached, but the sheer thought of trying to adjust her position was more daunting than facing the discomfort. So she let her heavy eyelids stay closed and tried not to think about the aches all over her body. They were a sign, she knew, of her body slowly winding down, like a clock.

Abe. She set her thoughts on him, imagining his dark hair and warm eyes. Kind eyes. Her mind turned back the years like the pages of a book, and suddenly she held him on her lap as a boy of eight when she first adopted him, sadly thin and small for his age. Suddenly he was grown, and it was last summer, just a few months ago—or had it been a lifetime?—when they had sat on the same swing. She had been the smaller one then, resting her head on his grown shoulder every night before he left.

With the Lord's help, they would be reunited shortly.

Bless my son, she thought. *Please protect him and bring him to me.*

Once more the darkness washed over her, and she surrendered, falling into a deep sleep.

* * *

The Hamptons took the next few days slow and easy. Ellen had rested all weekend, and everyone felt good about traveling again. Peter made sure they didn't tax her unduly. By Wednesday, Ellen felt like herself again; the contractions and bleeding had stopped, and she expressed a desire to walk once more.

"Over my dead body," Caroline said brusquely. "And I know that might not be too far into the future, as old as I am. But until then, or until that baby's here safe and sound, you're riding." With a harrumph, Caroline nodded her head with resolution and stalked off.

So Ellen rode during the day but was given permission by Caroline to cook morning and night and to care for the children. Peter had indicated that on Thursday they would travel only half a day, to the base of Lee's Backbone.

The next morning, the children slept in as late as they wanted to. Ellen made hotcakes for breakfast, but Caroline insisted on oatmeal for herself—stuck to the ribs better than hotcakes, she said. Instead of Ellen doing more work, Maddie stepped in and made a pot of oatmeal, also planning to wash all the dishes so Ellen could get back to the wagon and rest. As they readied themselves, they were calm and relaxed, knowing they wouldn't have to go far.

They were gathered around the morning fire when Caroline shoved a spoonful of oatmeal into her mouth and asked, "Peter, why don't we cross Lee's Backbone today? Get the blasted thing over with."

"No, no," Peter said from across the fire as he cut his hotcakes with a fork. "We tried it in the evening last time."

The mention of "last time" almost made Maddie choke on her food. She hadn't realized until that moment just how close they were to the site of Roland's death. They had been on the road a week and a half already; she should have anticipated it by now.

"Took longer than we thought to get up and over," Peter went on. "The horses were ready to give out by the time we reached level ground. Besides, I've heard far too many stories about crossing that thing to attempt it late in the day when we're tired and it might grow dark on us. We're going over in the morning when we're fresh and have a full day ahead."

Caroline nodded, apparently accepting his reasoning. She swallowed, then asked, "In that case, I assume we'll be camping on the other side?"

"I'm not planning on it," Peter said.

Maddie's food got stuck in her throat. "We aren't?" The other side was the very spot where Roland had been attacked, and where Maddie had planned to say her final good-bye.

With the side of his fork, Peter cut into a hotcake. "Oh, I figure we'll cross the river first. That way we can head on in the morning right away. Why do you ask?"

Unable to find her voice, Maddie just shook her head. She didn't want to answer the question and expose her heart. The other side of the river would have to do for her farewell.

Caroline scooped the last bite of oatmeal from her bowl. "After the Backbone is Lee's Ferry, you know. I've heard plenty of stories about that, too. The horses may be spooked after getting over and down that steep ridge—don't know as I'd be up to making them cross a river on a ferry the same day." She punctuated her statement with her spoon, inadvertently lobbing the ball of oatmeal onto Peter's trousers. She went on as if she hadn't noticed. "Of course, I'm not the one driving the team. If you want to spook the animals, I suppose that's your prerogative."

"We'll see about Lee's Ferry when we get there," Peter said, flicking off the oatmeal with two fingers. "But it's not high water this late in the year, so I don't anticipate problems crossing the river, even with the horses. It's not like we have a hundred head of cattle to swim across. I've heard stories about *that.*"

The rest of the day passed uneventfully. They made camp at the base of Lee's Backbone, with several hours left before dark. After the initial busywork of settling into a new place, Maddie stood and looked at the daunting pass: steep and rugged, without a clear path visible, at least from where she stood. She wondered if you could see broken wagons or horse remains from the top, since so many people seemed to have toppled wagons or lost animals while trying to cross it. Turning away, she decided not to give Lee's Backbone another thought until the morning when she had to face it. Maddie went to bed that night after saying a sincere prayer to help Ellen get across easily, and for help with Mary, Lorenzo, and, of course, Caroline as well.

* * *

The following morning dawned gray and unusually cloudy.

"Perfect weather!" Peter proclaimed when he woke. "After all the heat and wind we've endured, it's a relief to have some cloud cover, don't you think?"

They ate breakfast, broke camp, and loaded their supplies back into the wagon. Before they knew it, Maddie had Mary, Lorenzo, and

Ellen settled in the wagon box, since the nearly four-mile climb up the rocky pass would be particularly difficult on them. Caroline sat beside Peter on the bench, and Maddie ended up walking with Abe—an arrangement that suited her fine. They moved along the first, sloping edges of Lee's Backbone. The other side was only a mile and a half down, so they'd make better time on the way down.

The higher they went, the slower the horses pulled. Some of the switchbacks were tight and unnerving, but the party climbed and walked for some time without any real trouble—breathing hard, stopping for water breaks, but nothing unusual. A significant distance up the mountain, the horses hit a steeper grade. They pulled and strained against their load. The wheels creaked as they moved inches at a time. Maddie slowed down to make plenty of room between her and the wagon. She glanced at the sky, which had grown a dark, forbidding gray.

"Everybody out," Peter called as he stopped the horses. They stumbled, sending a shower of pebbles down the rocky embankment. Maddie's stomach lurched. She looked down and saw just how far they had gone—they were well over halfway—and how steep the mountain looked below. She felt grateful that the children wouldn't be riding in the wagon after all. Peter went on. "The horses can't pull this much weight. Everyone will have to walk." He got off and reached for Mary.

"But Lorry and I are too little walk to the temple. You said so lots of times."

"It won't be for the rest of the way," Peter assured her. "It's just over this mountain."

"We all walk? Even you, Pa?" Mary's innocent face had a teasing gleam in it as he lifted her down from the wagon.

Peter ruffled her hair and kissed the top of her head. "You caught me. I suppose *I'll* get to ride for a spell. But only because the horses need a driver. Unless *you'd* like to drive the horses so I can walk."

"Pa!" Mary said, laughing. "That's silly."

"Come here, Mary," Maddie said, taking the girl's hand. "Walk with me."

Mary took no more than a step up the slope when she shook her head and reached out her arms. "Carry me. I'm too tired to walk."

Shaking her head, Maddie said, "No. Maybe closer to the top if you get really tired." When Mary stuck out her lower lip in a pout, Maddie said, "Mary, you're so big you get to walk most of the way, but I'll have to carry Lorenzo. He's so little he can't do it himself like you can."

"Oh, all right," Mary reluctantly agreed.

Maddie crossed to where Lorenzo tugged on his mother's skirt. Ellen bent to lift the child. "Ellen, you can't carry him," Maddie declared, gently pushing her sister aside.

"But someone has to," Ellen protested. "He certainly can't walk all the way up."

"I know that," Maddie said, scooping Lorry into her arms, "but you need to take care of your growing baby. Walking up a mountain is more than you should be doing. Carrying a two-year-old at the same time is a really bad idea."

"Maddie's right," Caroline said from her perch on the bench. Peter helped her down, and she landed on her feet with a thud and a big sigh. Then she tromped over to the sisters. "Ellen dear, don't you even *think* of carrying that little boy," she said, wagging a finger. "Lorenzo will be fine. And so you know, the moment Peter says it's safe for you to be in the wagon, you're getting back inside for the duration. Is that clear?"

"Yes," Ellen said demurely.

Maddie had a wicked urge to add, "Yes, Mother."

Caroline stared at Ellen for a moment, as if searching her eyes for intent to disobey. But finally satisfied that her orders would be followed, Caroline turned to little Mary. "How'd you like to walk with me?"

"Sure," Mary said, and reached her soft, pudgy hand into Caroline's thin, wrinkled one. "If Aunt Maddie doesn't mind."

"I don't mind at all," Maddie assured her niece. If anything, she was grateful for Caroline's assistance as they crossed the ridge.

"Stand back," Peter called from the wagon. They stopped and backed up, then waited for further orders. "Perfect," Peter said. "You ladies wait there while Abe and I get the wagon over the top. I just don't want anyone behind the wagon if it rolls backward."

Peter urged the horses forward as Abe helped steady the wagon and its contents. The lighter load seemed to help, but the horses still slipped and struggled on the dirt and loose rocks.

Thunder clapped loudly overhead, making everyone jump. Lorenzo buried his head in Maddie's shoulder. Mary ran to her mother and hid her face in the folds of her dress. Moments later, large raindrops began falling, turning the ground into mud and slick rock.

Had they just started going up the pass, they would surely have turned back. It would have been easier to attempt the climb tomorrow when the ground dried out from the storm.

Maddie looked back, then up the incline. It was steep going, and unsafe even if they could have turned the team around, which was impossible. They had no choice but to go on.

"Caroline, take Lorenzo for a minute," she said, handing over the little boy. The heavy drops turned into a torrent of rain so thick Maddie could hardly see. She ran up to the wagon in spite of Peter's admonitions to stay back. She reached inside, her feet slipping on mud. The wheels were buried several inches in mud and slipped and turned instead of moving forward. Maddie held onto the wagon box and pulled out some blankets. She released her hold and waited for the others to join her.

"Wrap Mary in this one," she called to Caroline, then put a blanket around Lorenzo and took him in her arms. Propped on her hip, his body shook with cold, and his wide eyes showed fear as Maddie picked her way across the ground, trying to step on rough stones and plants that would give her more of a foothold. She went slowly, keeping her balance by grasping onto tall rocks and shrubs, and sometimes even the edge of the ridge itself. Twice she slipped and almost lost her grip on the boy, but she held tight and kept going, not daring to set him down. If she could take a misstep, a toddler certainly could, too. She shuddered to think of him falling down the rock-strewn ridge.

Agonizing slow step by slow step, the wagon moved forward. Sometimes the wheels locked in the gluelike muck, then slipped backward several feet while the women and children waited, clinging to one another until the wagon moved forward a safe distance. Maddie found it increasingly difficult to make out any trail and to pick the best places to avoid slipping. She looked forward to see where the top was. No matter how many steps she took, it always looked the same. It seemed they would never reach it.

The wagon wheels stuck in the mud again, and as Abe heaved against the wood and metal to free them, Maddie felt grateful that he had come. They couldn't have made the trip without him. The wagon lurched forward again, and they continued trudging up the mountain. Maddie's feet felt like they had turned to ice, and she could hardly tell where she placed them. She adjusted Lorenzo's position in her arms and touched his feet. They were freezing, and so were his ears and hands. She adjusted the blanket around his head better and continued, hoping that Mary's feet weren't too cold—and that Ellen hadn't given in and decided to carry her daughter.

She glanced back to double-check and was astounded to see Caroline carrying Mary.

The old lady looked grumpy enough—but plenty strong as she grumbled, "To think you were about to carry her." By the look of exasperation on Ellen's face, Caroline had been giving her an earful for several minutes.

"Might as well toss yourself and the babe inside you off the edge, for as much good as it would do you," Caroline went on, adjusting Mary on her ample hip. "Heavens to Betsy. I have to carry her if that's the only way to keep you from doing it."

Maddie turned back, rain dripping off her face and hair. She smiled, thinking that Caroline had become another helper on the trip, not a burden. The Lord had watched over them. As she reached the summit and looked down the north side of Lee's Backbone, she gulped—then remembered what she had just told herself. The Lord had protected them thus far, and He would continue to do so. It wasn't as steep or as long as the south side, but going down was quite different from going up. She didn't even want to think about what it would be like traveling back home—going down the longer, steeper side they had just crested.

Please protect us, she thought. *We'll need help getting down.*

Everyone paused at the summit and looked at what awaited them. Seeing the drop, Abe whistled. "This will be an adventure," he said in a flat voice. Then he pointed toward the Colorado River in the distance below. "And then we get to face that."

"I hope the ferry will make it an uneventful crossing," Peter said. "Let's get moving again before the wagon and horses get mired too deep in the mud."

He eased the horses forward down the embankment, and Maddie watched every hoof's placement, holding her breath that neither of the horses would slip. The cow was still tied to the wagon, and she bellowed and groaned whenever the rope pulled her along.

They managed the first switchback without trouble, but at the second one, the weight of the wagon sent the whole thing racing forward. Abe grabbed the back of the box and dug his heels into the ground to slow the descent. The cow moaned even louder as it slipped, its hooves sinking into the mud while being dragged down the mountain. The horses' feet scrambled forward in the muck to escape the wagon as it pummeled upon them.

Without a conscious thought, Maddie thrust Lorenzo into Ellen's arms and raced to Abe's side. She too held onto the wagon with all her might, digging her heels in. Her weight had some effect, but not much, and the wagon dragged her along at a frightening pace while Peter struggled with the horses up front. She could only imagine the fear shooting through him, because stabs of terror were coursing through her own body.

After an eternity of jostling and bumping, the wagon reached a more level spot and slowed. Maddie and Abe let go and caught their breath. Her arms felt as limp as bread in milk, and her entire body trembled.

"Thanks," Abe said between breaths. As if in silent agreement, the two of them went back to help Ellen and the others. Abe took Mary from Caroline, who gratefully surrendered the four-year-old, and Maddie retrieved Lorenzo from his mother.

"Well, that was exciting," Caroline said as she continued on past Abe.

Excitement I could have done without, Maddie thought as she followed behind. They still had a good half mile ahead of them, but the remaining grade wasn't nearly as steep or dangerous. They all walked leisurely to catch their breath and calm their nerves.

"Reminded me of coming to Zion," Caroline said, nodding toward the wagon ahead. "We'd tie a big log to the back of a wagon to act as a sort of brake. Some Gentile folks even called it 'the Mormon brake.'" Caroline chuckled. "But I don't think we ever used *people*."

Maddie tried to laugh, but her body was still shaking from exertion, and she hadn't gotten her breath back yet. Even holding wiggly Lorenzo became difficult. She and Abe walked side by side, picking their way down the steep path, each with a child in their arms. As the rain let up, Maddie studied Abe. He held Mary like it was the most natural thing in the world, as if he carried children around every day.

Walking beside him with Lorenzo, Maddie could almost imagine they were the parents of these children. As she had a thousand times, she imagined holding a child of her own. For the first time, the baby didn't have brown or blond hair. The child's hair was black. The image made her stumble on the trail and shake her head. *That* wasn't something she could let herself think about.

CHAPTER 21

The group trudged through the mud to the edge of the Colorado River, then stopped. No one said a word, but by the looks on their faces, Abe could tell they all had the same thought—no one wanted to face crossing the behemoth of a river.

Abe stared at the band of water before them. It wasn't *that* wide, he reminded himself—just wider than any river he had seen before. And the water wasn't remarkably fast. Nothing about it looked particularly dangerous. A breeze passed through his rain-soaked shirt, and Abe shivered. He knew that even though the river was quiet, the water flowing in it had to be very cold. The thought didn't exactly make him anticipate the crossing that lay ahead, regardless of how safe it was.

The house on the other side seemed so far away that, without the ferry, it might as well have been on another continent. Abe had heard his mother tell about the times she crossed rivers coming to Zion— the dreaded Sweetwater in particular—and suddenly he had a much better understanding of what a feat that had been. Had the Hampton party been the first pioneers coming to Utah, how would they have gotten their wagon, horses, cow, five adults, and two small children across a river? *At least we have a ferry to call on,* Abe thought. The first Mormon pioneers didn't have that luxury.

"I suppose there's nothing but doing it." Peter raised his rifle and fired it into the air three times, the signal for the ferryman that someone needed to cross. The blast sent Mary cowering into her mother's skirts, and at her reaction, Lorenzo started to cry. Moments after the rifle shot, a man emerged from the house across the river.

"Ho there!" Peter called, cupping his mouth with his free hand.

The man on the other side waved both his arms in response as he went to the ferry dock.

"Is this really safe?" Maddie asked no one in particular. Abe turned around. Maddie stood beside a big, red rock, where she had been wiping mud from her boots. Wet hair hung in her face, and several inches of her hem were soaked with mud. She wiped a strand out of her eyes and looked over the river. "That's a pitifully small ferry. I'd rather stay on this side with firm ground under my feet, thank you very much."

"I think we all would," Abe said. "But Peter says hundreds of people and animals have crossed on it."

"Animals aren't that smart," Maddie responded dryly.

"I'm sure we'll be fine."

"And remember," Peter said, coming over to join them. "This is the season for low water. Spring is when the river is high and choppy. It's much less dangerous in the fall."

"*Less* dangerous?" Maddie turned to her brother-in-law. "The sentiment is so comforting." Abe bit his lips together and stifled a chuckle, but then all three burst into laughter, a welcome release of the mounting tension.

"Aw, this is nothin'," Caroline called from the wagon. She tried to hop down but instead dismounted slowly. Then she let out a huff, brushed off her skirts, and joined the group, pumping her arms as she walked. "This is a little stream compared to the Mississippi," she said, waving her hand as if shooing away a fly. "I could cross this with my arms tied behind my back." Amusement at the image tickled the edge of Abe's mouth. He was tempted to ask whether she could also cross it with one leg tied, too.

Instead, Peter said, "The river's too deep to walk across, so don't think of crossing it yourself, Caroline. We're loading up the ferry, taking it over, and that'll be the end of it."

Abe was glad Peter had been so direct; you never knew what idea Caroline would get herself set on. True to form, she folded her arms firmly and shook her head.

"Nope. Those horses shouldn't be on that excuse for a boat today. I told ye before that getting over that pass would be enough for them.

Don't put them through that, too. Horses hate water and rafts. Wait 'til tomorrow or let 'em swim across today."

Abe turned his head so no one would see him rolling his eyes. *As if swimming in frigid waters would be less trying on a horse than ferrying across.*

"You don't suggest we pull the wagon onto the ferry ourselves, do you?" Peter asked. He glanced at Abe, who knew from the sparkle in Peter's eye that he was enjoying the banter with the older lady. Maybe it kept his nerves at bay as well.

"I don't care how you get that wagon on," Caroline said. "But the horses won't like it, I'll tell you that. I'll say it again—it's better to let them swim across. Much kinder."

At that, Maddie turned to Caroline. "But it's so *cold*. You can't seriously think it's kind to the horses to make them swim through ice-cold water?"

"Oh, fiddlesticks." Caroline tilted her head stubbornly. "They wouldn't suffer from the cold. They'd thank you for the exercise."

No one knew how to respond to Caroline, so instead they watched the ferry draw closer to the shore. Abe wondered if a swarm of moths had erupted in everyone's stomach as they had in his. He wished he were already on the other side, sitting inside the ferryman's home and talking about how simple and quick the crossing had been—and how silly they had been to worry about it. The ferry docked, and the man on it secured the craft before approaching them. Peter went down the shore, and Abe followed close behind.

"Peter Hampton," he said, extending his hand.

"Warren Johnson," the ferryman answered. "Good to meet you." He looked over the group. "Is this everyone? Just one wagon, one team?"

"That's all," Peter said with a nod. "We've also got my wife, her sister, and a friend, so it's five adults, two children."

"Then we can go over in one trip easy enough," Warren said. "With bigger parties, we're going back and forth all day." He lifted a shoulder and smiled as he added, "On the other hand, I'm paid per trip, so extra work doesn't hurt. Now then." He nodded and gestured toward the ferry, then clapped his hands together. "Let's get the team and the wagon on first. After they're settled, everyone else can climb on. I want to hurry back; don't want to miss my Polly's birthday party. She's turning six, and her mother baked a special strawberry rhubarb pie—my favorite too." He headed toward the river, then paused and turned back. "My wives tend to cook more than we need. See, we get regular visitors, as you can imagine. So you're welcome to join us for pie, if you'd like; I'm sure there's enough."

"Thank you kindly," Peter said, tipping his hat. "We'd enjoy that."

"Enjoy" is an understatement, Abe thought. After days on the road with the same bland food, "relish, savor, and devour" were more like it.

The three men got to work, with Peter driving, Abe in the back calling directions, and Brother Johnson in front guiding the way and giving orders. They slowly eased the wagon onto the wooden boards with room to spare.

"Everyone ready?" Warren hollered.

Maddie called for Lorenzo to come to her. He protested, wanting to run the length of the raft. "No chance of that, my boy," she said, scooping him into her arms. "I'm not having you get wet." He kicked and squirmed, but only for a moment, knowing his aunt meant business.

Warren Johnson pushed a long pole into the water and used it to propel them away from the shore. The first movement sent a jolt through everyone and everything on the craft. The horses pawed the floor and pulled at the reins as Peter tried to calm them.

"Steady, boys, easy there," he said.

Maddie lost her balance, and Lorenzo slipped from her arms. She gasped, and Abe shot out his arm to grab the boy. Maddie had fallen to her knees and now clambered to her feet, hands shaking. She paused for a moment, catching her breath and getting her bearings as the ferry moved with surprising speed away from the shore.

"Thanks," she said breathlessly as she struggled to place one foot under the other. "I almost—"

Her words broke off as she stepped directly on a wet patch and her foot slid out from under her. Maddie's hand flew out, reaching toward Abe. He leaned forward, Lorenzo held securely in one arm, but just missed the edge of her skirt as she fell off the ferry, calling for help. She disappeared into the dark water with a splash.

"Maddie's overboard!" he yelled. Not knowing how deep the river ran, but knowing it wasn't shallow, he thrust Lorenzo at Caroline. "Stop! Overboard!" he cried again to Warren.

The ferryman had already heard the shout and was pressing his pole hard into the riverbed to slow the craft. A jolt like the first followed as they reduced speed, and as the horses shifted forward, they kicked and pawed, neighing with complaint and fear as the wagon pressed its weight against them.

Abe didn't waste a moment; he looked around for something he could put out for Maddie to hold onto, but found nothing long enough at first glance. "Maddie!" he called, racing to the back of the ferry, which was a good twenty feet away from where she had fallen in. "Maddie!"

Her head rose above the surface, and her hands flailed before she went back under, clearly unable to swim. With two swift movements, Abe yanked off his boots, then dove into the river after her. *Please, Lord, don't let her drown.*

Abe's brief prayer was followed by the most intense effort he could muster. He swam as fast and hard as he could, and found himself swallowing water. He had never been a good swimmer, but it was apparent she couldn't swim at all—and her heavy skirts were probably weighing her down.

A brief image flashed into his mind of the water-logged fabric pulling her down to the depths of the riverbed and holding her there. He shook his hair out of his eyes, then focused on the spot where he had seen her last, only a yard or two away. Swimming toward it, periodically he treaded water, searching for her and shouting, "Maddie! Maddie, where are you?"

Taking a gulp of air, Abe dove. Blackness surrounded him, and he could see nothing but a faint light from the surface. His lungs felt ready to burst as he floundered, reaching and twisting, trying to find Maddie. Unable to stay under any longer, he kicked to the surface and gasped for air. Then he quickly went back under, deeper this time.

Help me find her, he prayed. *I can't leave her here.*

His hands searched the water, back and forth in all directions. Once he felt something, then realized it was only a plant swaying in the current.

The current. She had probably gone downstream. After another breath at the surface, Abe kicked downstream, arms outstretched, eyes closed, and mind focused. His fingers brushed something that felt like another plant, and he was about to move on when he stopped and, not knowing why, reached out to it again.

Hair. It's Maddie's hair. Heart pounding, Abe took a handful and pulled. Maddie's limp form came to him. Wishing he could cry out, he instead put an arm under hers and kicked to the surface as hard as he could. His legs felt like hot coal, and his lungs were ready to burst by the time he broke through the surface.

Shivering, he yelled to the others. "Here! I found her!"

He held Maddie's blue-tinged face above the water and kept kicking to keep them both afloat. *I can't keep going much longer,* he thought as his left leg began cramping. *Hurry!*

The ferry arrived not a moment too soon. Warren, his face red with exertion, had the pole dug into the riverbed as hard as he could, trying to keep the ferry from going downstream. The horses were skittish and pawing the boards as Peter left them to lean over the side and reach for Maddie.

He hoisted her up and rolled her to the center of the raft, where Ellen and Caroline waited anxiously. The moment Abe grasped Peter's arm, his entire body gave out, and he felt like a bag of sand, unable to climb out himself. Once Peter dragged him onto the ferry, he lay beside Maddie, coughing and sputtering, his chest moving rapidly up and down.

Weakly, he turned his head toward Maddie, where Caroline was at work. She had shooed Ellen back to the wagon to contain the children. She rolled Maddie to her side and pounded on her back to release the water from her lungs. Abe couldn't see Maddie's face, but she still wasn't moving. With a shaky hand, he reached out and put a hand to her back, then closed his eyes and tried to feel a heartbeat.

Very faint, oh so faint, but there it was. His arm fell to his side with a sigh of relief.

* * *

By the time they crossed to the other side, Maddie was breathing well. Over the next couple of hours, her color returned. Caroline insisted that Maddie needed her rest and ordered Peter to leave the wagon far enough away from the Johnson home that she wouldn't be disturbed by noise.

"Please let me stay with her," Abe said, trying to move past Caroline to the wagon.

The old lady's arms were deceptively strong—or perhaps Abe was still weak and spent from his own exertions. She held him back and shook her head. "Not yet. Go inside and leave her be. She needs peace and quiet."

"But I'm not going to—"

"Hup—" Caroline cocked her head to the side and stopped him midsentence.

"I'll be—"

"Hup—" she said again, this time putting up a hand.

"Very well." Abe surrendered, looking at the wagon and wishing he could see more of Maddie than the tips of her quilt-covered toes. "You'll come get me as soon as it's all right to?"

Caroline gave a deep nod. "I promise."

Abe gazed at the wagon again, then sighed and turned toward the house, where the Johnsons were celebrating six-year-old Polly's birthday. Warren had just gone in after Peter gave him payment for the crossing. Ellen stood beside her husband at the door with a handkerchief to her face. She looked like she had been crying.

"Is everything all right?" Abe asked, looking from Ellen to Peter.

Ellen nodded. "We're just so grateful . . ." But her voice cut off before she could finish, and she pressed her lips together to ward off more tears.

"What Ellen means," Peter said, putting a hand on Abe's shoulder, "is *thank you* for saving Maddie's life today. For risking your life for hers."

The horror of that moment washed over Abe again—the frantic search for Maddie in the water, his desperate effort to reach her, his cry to the heavens for help. He let out a breath to steady himself and shake off the feeling. "You're welcome." What else could he say? Ellen came forward and threw her arms around him in a big hug.

"Thank you," she whispered into his ear. "Thank you so much for coming. We couldn't have made it this far without you. You've been a godsend." She pulled back and wiped her nose self-consciously. "I suppose we should go inside and be part of the festivities."

Abe turned the handle and held the door open for Peter and Ellen. After quickly smoothing her hair and catching her breath, Ellen stepped inside, Peter and Abe following behind.

The main room was full of noise and children. Two boys were chasing a younger sister around the room with a squealing mouse, and their mother, Samantha, had to call them back.

"Jeremiah! Frank! You boys know better than that! Put that filthy thing outside and sit down. It's Polly's day. Give your sister an hour of fun instead of terrorizing poor Lydia to death."

The boys sheepishly looked at their father, who raised one eyebrow and glared at them. That's all it took. The boys ran outside, released the rodent, and came back in penitently, heads down. They found a spot on a bench and sat quietly, but couldn't resist poking one another in the ribs.

Abe slid onto the bench beside them and scanned the room. "Looks like you're the only boys in the family."

Jeremiah, the older of the two, nodded grumpily. "Not fair, is it? How'd you like to live with *nine girls?*"

"Nine!" Frank echoed, emphasizing the depth of their tribulation. "Three from our Mama Samantha, and six from Mama Permelia."

He shook his head woefully as Jeremiah piped in, "We was hoping that Mama Permelia would have a boy, but last month we got *another* girl." He pointed at the cradle, where one of the daughters was rocking quietly by the wall, away from the bustle of the birthday celebration.

Frank leaned over and pointed at Samantha, who was serving the dishes of pie that her sister wife, Permelia, was cutting. Frank whispered, "My mama's having another baby come spring. Jeremiah and I are praying for a brother."

"I hope you get it," Abe said. "But you know, I think siblings are fun, no matter what kind. I was an only child. Didn't have any brothers or sisters."

The boys reached out for their plates of pie, and each took a huge bite. They chewed thoughtfully before Frank turned back to Abe. "Not *one?*"

"Not one," Abe said, accepting a plate from Permelia. "Thank you, ma'am."

The boys swallowed their bites, took another, and swallowed again before Jeremiah answered thoughtfully. "I suppose a sister's better than nothin'. It'd be pretty lonely all by yourself, wouldn't it?"

"It would," Abe agreed. *It was.*

He took a bite of pie, fully expecting to relish the home-cooked treat, but he couldn't keep his mind from wandering to Maddie. His knee bounced in anticipation of Caroline granting him permission to see her, and he decided that as soon as he finished his pie, he'd visit Maddie, with or without Caroline's consent. As he ate his last bite, the door opened, and Caroline came inside. Everyone turned to her and waited for her report. "Madeline is doing fine. She could stand a visitor or two, maybe. But not a long visit, mind you. She'll be fine, but she needs some rest."

Ellen smiled her thanks, and Peter murmured his appreciation.

"Now I need some pie," Caroline announced. She trotted to the table.

"Here, have my seat." Abe stood and gestured toward it, and Caroline sat herself down with a flourish. Before her dress hit the bench, Abe was through the door, racing to Maddie's side. He climbed onto the wagon bench and peered inside the box, not daring to say anything at first. There she lay, her hair dry and spread out under her head like a halo, her eyes closed. Blankets covered her from the neck down, with only the hint of a sock-covered toe sticking out the bottom.

She took a deep breath, then let it out. Abe pulled himself back, hoping not to disturb her, but her eyes fluttered open, and she took in her surroundings. She looked as if she were trying to get her bearings and remember where she was—and why. Her gaze fell on Abe, and she started. "I'm sorry," he said. "I didn't mean to frighten you."

He made a move to leave, but Maddie said, "It's all right. I just thought I was alone."

"Do you . . . want to be?" Abe asked, poised to leave.

"No." Maddie clamped her eyes closed for a moment and shook her head. "I don't remember what happened. Caroline said I fell into the water."

"That's right." Abe relaxed his grip on the edge of the wagon and settled into the bench, facing backward. "Gave us a bit of a fright. How do you feel?"

She thought about the question before answering it. "Weak. But all right."

"Good."

"I'm glad you're here." She smiled up at him and tried to adjust her position so she could see him better. Abe scooted closer so they faced one another.

"Abe . . ." Maddie cut off, licked her lips, then went on. "Did *you* save me?"

His throat grew tight as he thought back to the terror he felt at being unable to find her in the water. He nodded, but couldn't say anything.

She reached for his hand and touched it. "Thanks."

Her hand stayed there, and she closed her eyes. She was obviously tired, so Abe didn't try to keep her talking. Instead he sat there as the evening turned dark, letting her hand rest on his. Her fingers were still cold, so he turned his hand over and clasped hers.

She needed to be warmed up. At least, that's the excuse he gave himself.

CHAPTER 22

The day after Maddie's fall into the river, the travelers remained at Lee's Ferry. She had gotten most of her strength back over the course of the day, so they planned to leave Monday morning. Abe asked her to come with him on a stroll, but when he headed for the river, she backed off.

"I've had enough of the Colorado," she said, waving her hands. "If you don't mind."

"I need to get water for camp," Abe said. "Come with me?"

Maddie hesitated for a minute, but finally nodded. "Only if you promise I don't have to get anywhere near the edge."

"You have my word." Abe grabbed a couple of pails and headed toward the river, glancing over his shoulder to confirm that she was coming. He grinned and continued picking his way through dried grasses and sagebrush. He reached the bank and looked back. From where he stood, the Johnson home and their camp were out of sight, and it gave him a strange sense of isolation.

When Maddie joined him, he pointed at the river. "You know, a few days ago I would have thought it would be great fun to put my feet in there to cool off. But I think I've had enough of it, just as you have."

Maddie chewed her bottom lip for a moment, then said, "You know what? It's hot and dry, and there's no reason this river should dictate what we can and cannot do. I say we cool off in the water anyway."

Abe grinned, liking the way she thought—refusing to let fear decide for her.

"Splash your face," Abe said. "That's a good start."

"Only if you stay by me so I won't fall in."

He was more than happy to agree to that. Maddie stepped to the edge, knelt, and filled her cupped hand with water, then splashed her face. "That does feel nice," she said, standing up. Abe took off his boots and socks, then sat at the bank, and, with relish, plopped his feet into the rushing water with a hearty splash. "Oh, that's cold!" he said at the sudden shock.

Maddie laughed out loud. "You knew that before."

"Join me?"

She put a hand on her hip and raised her eyebrows. "I thought I was going to splash my face. There was no talk of disrobing."

"Disrobing?" A full-blown laugh erupted from Abe. "It's boots, for Pete's sake. I'm sure your feet are as hot and dusty—and sore— as mine." When Maddie gave him an unconvinced snort, Abe drew his foot across the water, nice and shallow, and flicked the water right at her.

A spray flew through the air and caught her in the face. "Whoa!" She backed away and wiped it off, laughing nonetheless. "What was that for?"

"You said yourself it felt nice and cool on your face. Imagine it on your feet. Unless, of course, you're yellow."

Maddie stared him down, lips pursed. "Yellow, is it?" She marched the remaining few feet and sat down. Then she untied her boots and, with a flourish, pulled them off and tossed them aside, then blushed as she stared at her bare feet. "I never thought anyone would be able to convince me to show my ankles to a strange man." She lifted her skirts as she scooted to the edge of the river, her pale skin sticking out under the hem. Beside his tan feet, hers looked like cream. She peered over her shoulder toward camp. "How you managed to coerce me to go away from everyone else *and* be so immodest, I'll never know."

"It's a gift," Abe said with a smirk. "Besides, we've been traveling for nearly two weeks. I'm no stranger."

Maddie sat down and slipped her slender feet into the rushing water, and after the initial moment of shock at the cold, her eyes glazed over with pleasure. "Oh, it's pure heaven."

Abe couldn't help but laugh. "That nice, huh?"

"You have no idea," Maddie said, then, looking at his feet beside hers, added, "Or maybe you do." She closed her eyes in enjoyment, moving her feet in a gentle kicking motion. Abe noticed for the first time just how dark her lashes were against her skin.

"I don't know about you," Abe said, moving his feet back and forth in the water. "But I'm half tempted to stay here for the rest of my life."

"I could second that," Maddie said, a smile hovering on her lips.

For a moment, Abe's mind flitted to that image—he and Maddie sitting here at the edge of the river together, just the two of them, for the rest of eternity.

She opened an eye a crack. "It's been a while . . . will you tell me about . . . her?"

They both knew who and what she referred to. Not since Sunset Crossing had they brought up their past loves. Travel wasn't particularly conducive to private conversation, and with the party moving out again on Monday, this might be their only chance for some time.

Abe nodded and began crossing and uncrossing his ankles in a figure eight, sloshing water to the sides. "Lizzy and I were so much alike," he began. The pain was several years old, not quite so fresh and raw, but just as deep in some ways, especially since he had been away from Logan only a year. "Sometimes I wonder whether, after all this time, we're still alike at all."

"In what ways?"

"Does she still devour books and poetry? Our interest in books is what drew us together in the first place." He stared into the water, which was constantly moving and changing. Lizzy might have changed over the years. Had he? In some ways, absolutely. In others, not so much.

"How . . ." Maddie cut off and hesitated, unsure how to ask the question hovering on her lips. "What drew you apart? You said before she married someone else."

Abe leaned back and stared at the sky, pale blue and cloudless. "She changed in a very significant way." He wondered whether he should explain the change to Maddie. Probably not; she was like Lizzy in that way. A believer. Instead of clarifying, he plunged on. "She changed to the point that we didn't have enough in common anymore. Actually, *she* thought we didn't. At the time, I was sure it wasn't anything serious. We had known each other for a long time. So I protested, thinking we could still be happy together."

"But?"

He shook his head. "But I couldn't convince her. And you know what?"

"What?" Maddie squinted against the sun as she looked at him.

"I've done a lot of thinking since then, and, rather reluctantly, I came to realize that she was right. Had we gotten married, *I* might have been happy, at least at first. Maybe we both would have been, for a time. But eventually she would have been miserable. And that would have made me miserable, too—because I really loved her."

He shrugged, lying back on the ground and blocking the sun with his arm. "But knowing that this is how it needed to turn out doesn't make the reality much easier to live with." He lay there, blocking Maddie's face from his vision. He had never talked much about Lizzy. Doing so brought up old feelings, and he wasn't sure how he felt about them or what emotions would register on his face.

"Did she love you too?" Maddie asked quietly.

"At one time, yes." Abe sighed again. "But then came those changes . . . She chose someone who believed as she did. They had more in common—it was a better match."

Maddie pulled her feet out of the water—they were bright red—and pulled them under her knees. She turned to face Abe. "Do you believe, then, that similarities—having things in common—is the most important thing?"

Abe sat up. "What do you mean?"

"Are similar beliefs or interests the most important thing? Does love mean so little?"

He considered. "I think love is important, too, but it can't be the only thing to base married life on."

Her right hand went to her engagement ring, and she twisted it back and forth. Abe caught the action and eyed it with interest. She avoided his face as she said, "But what if a couple has everything else that spells a good match—similar beliefs, goals, social position? Everything *except* love."

Maddie looked up and caught Abe's gaze. He seemed to see right through her, and she had to swallow hard suddenly. "Never mind. I—

I shouldn't have said anything." She stood and gathered her shoes and stockings in her arms, then headed toward camp. Abe had a sudden realization of what her words might mean.

"No, wait." Abe stood as he called out to her. Maddie stopped, head bowed as he went on. "You don't love Edward, do you?"

Maddie paused. Her shoulders dropped, and she gave a miserable shake of her head. "No. At least, not in the way I think a woman should feel about her betrothed." She turned back toward Abe, her face pinched with pain. "But I tried following my heart once, and look where it got me."

"Tell me about him?" Abe asked, echoing her earlier question. Maddie looked back toward camp, then at her hands, and finally at Abe. He offered his hand, as he would if helping her out of a wagon. She hesitantly put her hand in his, and he eased her back to a seated position on the ground. She pulled her hand away, placed her shoes and stockings beside her, and held both hands in her lap. Abe didn't say anything, waiting for her.

"I—I've thought more of Roland in the last few weeks than— than anytime since he died," Maddie began. "In a strange way, I've given myself permission to dwell on him during this trip." She let out a strained chuckle. "I had no idea how painful it would be."

"Why now?"

"Because we're here, on the road where he died." She looked up, taking in the landscape, the clumps of pine trees in the distance, the desertlike features between. Wind swept her hair, and she smoothed it back. "I'll allow myself to think of Roland for a little while yet." She sniffed and looked up as if willing the sun to dry her tears. Abe wanted to know what she meant by *yet*. Why now and not later?

"Last time we came this way, we camped on the other side of the river, over there," she said, fingering a piece of dry grass. "We planned to cross in the morning, but then Roland died, and we headed home." Maddie sighed. "I have a feeling that's the real reason Peter wanted to make the crossing right away—he didn't want to camp there again for my sake—but I wish we would have."

"Why?" Abe asked, amazed.

She adjusted her position, getting onto her knees as her voice took on energy. "I have held onto Roland for so long. It's not fair to Edward. It's also no way to enter a marriage. So the only way I can think of is saying good-bye to Roland properly—back at the place I last saw him."

She reached for the chain around her neck and withdrew it, showing Abe the ring. "I've worn this ever since the school festival." She turned it over in her hand and smiled sadly. "I hope Edward hasn't noticed." She slipped her finger into the band in remembrance and pressed her lips together. "I've decided to give this back to Roland, in a manner of speaking. You see, I reread one of his letters recently—and although he didn't mean it this way at the time, I took from it that he was giving me leave to find happiness with someone else. But I can't just walk away. I have to say good-bye to him first."

It somehow made sense to Abe. He knew that Maddie's plan might sound preposterous to someone else, but he felt honored that she shared with him something so sacred to her.

"I understand." Abe paused, digesting what she had said and realizing that he might have gotten over Lizzy quicker if he had said good-bye to her properly.

Maddie stared ahead at the river. "I wish I could do it on the other side, but this one will do. I'll say good-bye tomorrow."

They sat in silence for several minutes as Maddie stared across the river at the place where her fiancé had died. "It happened so suddenly."

"What . . . did happen exactly?" Somehow Abe knew it was all right to ask the question.

And she answered. When she spoke, it was as if she were reliving the events, as if she could see them play out again in the babbling water before her.

"Roland went to water his horse," she said. "I meant to join him, to fetch water for camp. But I got distracted. Ellen was expecting Lorenzo and was so tired that when we stopped for camp, she took a nap right away. Mary was not quite two then, and she ran off without her shoes. She stepped right into a bunch of prickly weeds. While Roland took his horse down to the river, I stayed behind to pull the thorns out of Mary's feet. He went by himself."

Her tone was one of regret, or possibly guilt. Abe's brow furrowed. "You don't blame yourself for what happened, do you?"

Maddie had continued to stare into the water, but Abe's voice made her blink and break the connection. "Some days I have. I've thought that perhaps the Indian wouldn't have attacked if a woman had been there. Or that I could have alerted the other men—strength in numbers, you know. But Roland was alone. So was the Indian. Only he was armed, and Roland wasn't."

Her voice trailed off, and she closed her eyes. A tear rolled down one cheek, and Abe didn't press her to continue. She took a moment before going on. "I finished with Mary and got the buckets, then headed for the river. And I—I saw the gun go off. Roland collapsed. The Indian saw me, and looked like he might shoot me too, but he just took Roland's horse and rode away."

Maddie flinched and turned her head at the memory.

"I'm so sorry," Abe said. "You don't have to tell me all this."

But she shook her head and reached for Abe's hand. She looked deeply into his eyes and said, "No, I want to tell you. I haven't spoken of it, ever. There hasn't been anyone I felt I could discuss it with. Peter and Ellen always avoid the topic as if it were a disease, and the entire community still gives me looks of sympathy—but not understanding." She squeezed his hand, and Abe gripped hers in return. "But *you* understand, don't you, Abe?"

He nodded, eyes burning and threatening tears of their own.

Maddie smiled through misty eyes. "I'm so glad I can tell you, especially now—here."

At the sorrow in her eyes, Abe's heart felt ready to burst. The ache was combined with a desire to share more; he could tell she wanted to talk about it. "What happened next?"

"I dropped the buckets and ran to him. He had already lost a lot of blood, so I tried to staunch the wounds, but it just kept coming." Tears coursed down her cheeks as she remembered the scene. "Every breath he took made a horrible gurgling sound, and bubbles came out of his chest. It was dreadful. I screamed for help at the top of my lungs."

She shuddered, brow furrowed. "I put my arms around him, trying to comfort him and keep him alive until Peter and his brother James came." Maddie put her hands up as if reaching for Roland. "I remember holding his face in my hands—his beautiful face. He had turned pale from losing so much blood."

Maddie cried so hard she could scarcely speak. She wiped at her tears with both hands.

"I'm so sorry," Abe said in a whisper. Losing Lizzy hadn't been nearly so traumatic, but somehow he could still relate to Maddie's feelings. He wanted to reach out and take Maddie into his arms to comfort her, but it wasn't his place to do so—not yet, anyway.

And even as Abe felt empathy for Maddie, another understanding came to him. For the first time in his life, as he looked at the agony in Maddie's eyes, he could see why Lizzy's mother—and so many other people over the course of his life—had hated him simply for being Indian. Lizzy's mother had lost loved ones in a manner similar to the way Maddie had lost Roland. It would have been more surprising had Lizzy's mother *welcomed* him at first sight. He had known about this before, but until now he'd never truly understood.

"You know," Maddie said after taking a breath and another sniff, "there are times I've wished the Indian would have killed me too. Then Roland wouldn't have been the only one to die. And we'd still be together." She looked up at Abe and shook her head. "Isn't that terrible?"

A lock of hair had fallen into her eyes, and Abe pushed it away. "It would only be terrible if you decided not to live the life you were granted to keep, to only live in your memories with Roland. But you already know that, which is why you're going to say good-bye to him." In response, Maddie nodded silently. Abe continued, "It will free you to truly live your life with someone you love."

And Maddie deserves love, he thought. Edward or no Edward, Abe had a crazy desire to make sure she got it.

"You really *do* understand, don't you? I didn't expect to find a friend like you." Maddie gave a slight shake of her head as if she couldn't quite believe her fortune. She looked up at the sky as if trying to remember. "'Oh, the comfort—the inexpressible comfort,'" she quoted, "'of feeling safe with a person—having neither to weigh thoughts nor measure words, but pouring them all right out, just as they are, chaff and grain together—'"

"'Certain that a faithful hand will take and sift them,'" Abe broke in, continuing the line, "'keep what is worth keeping, and then with the breath of kindness blow the rest away.'"

"That's right," Maddie said, managing a smile through the remainder of her tears. "How did you know?"

"Dinah Craik. One of my favorite passages." Abe pulled a piece of grass and began fiddling with it. Perhaps Maddie loved books as he did. Over the years he had met plenty of women who chose to teach out of convenience without enjoying the job. That number included his own teachers from childhood. He had met so few people like himself over the years that it had never occurred to him that Maddie might be a kindred reader.

"So, are all schoolteachers as well-versed as you?" he asked wryly.

"Only those of us who can't keep our noses out of books," Maddie said, managing a smile through her watery eyes. "We're more rare than you might believe in spite of making our students read and recite."

"Oh, I believe it," Abe said.

Maddie suddenly put a hand to his cheek, sending a charge through Abe as she said, "Thanks again for listening. I'm grateful you came with us."

"So am I."

She opened her mouth, about to say something more, but instead she bit her lips together and turned to picking up her stockings and boots. With her belongings in her arms, she faced Abe. Holding her shoes in one arm, she leaned forward and gave him a hug with the other.

Her touch made Abe catch his breath. His eyes closed as he put an arm around her, holding her in return and relishing the moment. All too soon, she pulled back. But instead of releasing him completely, Maddie still held onto his shoulder, and her face stopped inches from his. Her fingers curled around the edges of the boots. Her eyes locked with his for several seconds, sending Abe's heart thumping hard in anticipation.

Friendship is Love, without his wings. The line from Lord Byron jumped into Abe's mind. *What I feel is more than friendship. I am falling in love with this woman.*

The look in her eyes practically shouted an additional possibility into his mind. *And I think she cares for me.* Without looking beyond the moment, he tilted his head forward ever so slightly. Maddie didn't pull away. She took a quick glance at his lips, hesitated, then leaned forward.

A thrill went through Abe as he closed the gap between them and gently pressed his lips against hers. She kissed him back, and for a brief moment, all that existed in the world was the two of them and the rushing water, which Abe felt echoed the joy coursing through him.

Maddie pulled away, closing her eyes. Her eyelids fluttered open, and she looked up with flushed cheeks. She smiled, then without a word, scrambled to her feet and hurried away, one hand holding her skirts. Abe watched her go, his heart still beating furiously.

Come back, he wanted to say, but instead another thought surfaced.

Careful. You've made a mistake. He had just put his toe in water that he had promised he'd never enter again. Leaving Utah certainly hadn't solved *this* problem. Living anywhere with Latter-day Saints would bring him face-to-face with Mormon women. He rested his arms on his bent knees and looked at the river—the only witness to their kiss.

I have to be extra careful, or I'll repeat the past.

CHAPTER 23

The next night when it was dark and the children were asleep, Maddie quietly left the fire pit and headed toward the riverbank. The moon was full and bright, lighting her path. Her heart beat heavily as she thought of what she was about to do, something she had planned from the moment she agreed to come on this trip with Ellen's family.

She wasn't a hundred feet from camp when she heard footsteps brushing through the grasses behind her. Maddie turned to see Abe following her. A lump went to her throat, and her heart sped up. For a moment, she could think of nothing but the kiss they had shared earlier.

"Are you all right?" he asked.

Maddie tried to smile and reassure him. "I'm fine. I'm just—" Her voice caught.

"Are you . . ." Abe hesitated, eyebrows raised in question. He glanced at the river.

She nodded, eyes watery. "I'm going to go say good-bye to Roland."

"Do you want me to come?"

She shook her head. "Thanks, but no. This is something I have to do alone." Her fingers went up to the chain and fingered Roland's ring. Her knees already felt weak at the thought of what lay ahead, and she hoped that touching the ring would give her strength. She wrapped her hand around the tin band, making a fist.

"You're sure?" Abe asked. "You know I'd be glad to come with you."

She nodded, biting emotion back. "I know," she managed, lifting her chin bravely. "But I have to do this myself."

Abe took a step away as if telling her he understood. "I'll be over by that boulder downstream if you need me."

Maddie managed a smile of gratitude. It was kind of him to remain nearby, just in case. Her heart swelled with warmth. "Thanks."

He squeezed her shoulder as she faced the Colorado River. "Good luck."

She gave him a grim smile of determination, then walked toward the riverbank. With each step, her feet felt heavier, although the night around her was quiet and peaceful. Moonlight shimmered off the water as it moved. The river looked the same, yet Maddie knew it wasn't; in the last two years, water must have carved out new pieces of land and carried them away. The river always changed—ever moving, never constant. Yet for this moment, she felt transported back in time.

Twenty feet from the shore, she shivered. Word had it that there had been no Indian skirmishes since last summer, and Roland's death was the only one to ever happen this far north—but that certainly didn't mean it couldn't happen again.

Perhaps doing this at night wasn't the wisest decision, she thought. Every image she had tried to push away for two and a half years returned. Closing her eyes, she could almost hear the rifle shots blasting into the air. Before her, Roland collapsed onto the ground. Maddie saw herself running to his side, screaming for help, watching him die in her arms.

Opening her eyes, she walked the last few feet and looked across the river. She could see the exact spot where it happened, recognized it from three large rocks on the bank. She turned away, the pain of Roland's death so real, so fresh as she stood so near the site.

Despite the pain, she couldn't leave, not without fulfilling her purpose for coming. She reached for the chain and unclasped it, then slipped Roland's ring into her palm. Her fingers curled around the metal band, and for a moment, she didn't think she had the strength to do what she knew needed to be done. She took a deep breath to steel herself and climbed onto a pile of rocks similar to the ones he had fallen onto.

"Roland, I will love you always. You know that," she whispered, clutching the ring tightly in her fist. "But I feel that you have released me so that I can find happiness with another man. And now I must release you so I can find that happiness."

She looked down and opened her hand. One finger trembled as it traced the outline of the ring. She brought the ring to her lips and kissed it, then with all her strength, flung the tin and glass into the river. A moonbeam caught a glint of the glass as the arc peaked, sparkling like a diamond, and she thought she heard it plop before being carried away by the current.

Maddie stared into the water, arms wrapped around herself and tears rolling down her face. She'd let go of the one treasure linking her to Roland. She was supposed to feel free now—free to go on with her life.

So why did she feel as if her heart had broken all over again?

She wiped the tears away with both hands, but another wave of crying came over her. The pain was more than she could bear by herself. She ran, tripping on sand and weeds as she sobbed, clawing her way to the spot where Abe waited. Blindly, she raced into the shadows, where she saw him standing by the boulder. Hearing her approach, he turned, worried and anxious.

"Maddie?" At the sound of his voice, she felt relief—as if she had received a promise that her burden would be eased. Just as quickly, the pain returned, and with it a gaping emptiness where Roland's ring had hung beneath her dress. Her hand pressed against the spot where it had been, and despair washed over her. She covered her mouth again as another sob escaped, and she almost turned away, not wanting Abe to see her like this. When he had offered to help her with her good-bye, this surely wasn't what he meant.

But then he raised his arms and opened them. That was all she needed. She stumbled the remaining feet and fell into his embrace. He wrapped his arms around her, then leaned his head against hers and whispered, "Let it all out. Just let it out."

An intense cry ripped from her throat, and she wet his shirt with her tears as she sobbed against his chest. "It's not fair. We were supposed to be *happy* and *married*. I loved him."

"I know." Abe stroked her hair and back, drawing her closer. "I know."

She cried harder, in great, wracking heaves. Not since she wept over Roland's body at the river had she allowed herself to so openly express the searing pain. Not until now, when it all came out, as fresh and raw as it was so long ago.

Maddie's sobs lessened, increased, and lessened again. Abe held her the entire time, making it safe for her to feel and express the deepest sorrows of her heart. Eventually her cries quieted, leaving her breath catching as it came under control. Only then did Abe lead her to the boulder, where they sat while Maddie wiped her eyes and leaned her head on his shoulder. She stared into the river and remembered.

They stayed there for so long that she lost track of time. With her tears finally spent, Maddie sat upright and looked into Abe's eyes. Anyone else would have given her the same empty platitudes she had heard innumerable times. Those people never seemed to understand that even if heaven was "a better place," it wasn't better for her when Roland went there. That she hadn't wanted to marry just anyone. And that Roland's death cut a hole into her heart that would never entirely heal.

Somehow Abe knew it all.

"Thank you," she said, "for not trying to make it better or telling me it'll be all right, that Roland's in a better place, and that I'll still marry someday."

"You're welcome." He wiped some remaining moisture from her cheek, his brow furrowed. "I wish I knew what to say besides being sorry for you."

Maddie rested her hand on Abe's cheek and managed a smile. "That's the only thing I needed to hear. That someone is sorry and cares. Not that it'll be all better."

"Because it won't."

She nodded, touched by how deeply he understood. "Because it won't."

* * *

The following morning, Maddie emerged from the wagon after putting her hair back into a simple bun. She stepped onto the ground and was sliding in the last pin just as she caught Abe's gaze, an action that made her stumble on a rock. He smiled at her as he arranged wood in the fire pit, and she felt awash with gratitude and warmth as she remembered the day before. She had been so close to him, not just by being held, but with her soul.

"Morning," he said with a nod.

"Morning," she said, then opened her mouth to say something more, but nothing had been left unsaid last night. "Thanks again." She smiled back, then glanced around to make sure no one had heard. She didn't want to explain to anyone what had happened. Not yet, at least. She headed for the wagon to get the little ones ready for the day.

"Maddie," Abe said.

"Yes?" she said as she pivoted to face him.

His eyes were lined with concern. "How are you this morning?"

"How am I?" she repeated the question and looked at the ground. After all she had felt in reliving Roland's death, she was surprised to realize that she now felt peace. And happiness. Her memories were not just ones of sadness, but of comfort in Abe's arms. She raised her head and smiled. "This is the happiest I have felt in two and a half years."

Relief came over his face, and the warmth she had seen in his eyes the night before returned. "Good." He paused, nodded in thought, then repeated, "Good."

"Aunt Maddie, come get me dressed!" Mary called from under her quilt.

"I'm coming," Maddie said. She reached for Abe's hand and gave it a squeeze. "Thank you. For everything you did for me last night. I couldn't have gotten through it without you."

They smiled at one another, then silently parted ways to continue the morning's work. Maddie headed for the wagon, under which Lorry still slept peacefully. After Maddie gently pulled Mary out from underneath, the little girl willingly let her aunt help her, slipping her nightclothes over her head, arms raised. The nightgown was replaced with her dress. Maddie buttoned her up, then set her on the edge of the wagon box to do her hair.

After a moment of brushing, Mary said, "Aunt Maddie?"

"Yes?" Maddie continued brushing out snarls.

Mary winced at a stubborn tangle before saying, "You're as good a mother as Ma."

Maddie smiled to herself. She had hoped her efforts to care for Ellen's children had been well received, especially since the further Ellen progressed in her pregnancy, the more tired she became and the harder it was to perform daily chores. "Thank you."

She cocked her head and turned partway to her aunt. "So why aren't you a mother?"

Midtangle, Maddie's hands paused, and the brush drooped. How was she to answer that question? Her eyes darted to Abe at the campfire and back again. Fortunately, he was busy stacking kindling and didn't notice. "I . . ." Finally she managed, "I hope someday I will be."

She hurriedly braided Mary's hair, tied on her boots, and lifted her onto the ground. "There you go," she said, urging her away. As she watched her prance off, Maddie thought again of Mary's question and then to the events of the night before. Her stomach flipped over. Abe's back was to her, and he was talking to Peter. She put her hand to her middle and turned away.

What had she done last night?

She had taken a leap that wasn't hers to take. Edward was at home waiting faithfully for her. What right did she have to break that trust? And to heap on the coals, she had broken that trust with a virtual stranger.

No, not that, she thought. *Abe's not a stranger. He's a dear, dear friend, even if I've only known him a short time, and—*

But she stopped her thoughts there, waving her hands in decision. *No. I can't think of this now.* For the moment she needed to help get the party moving for the day. She would have plenty of time to think over what had happened both times at the riverbank yesterday—and what would happen next between her and Abe. They might have two weeks behind them on the trail, but they had at least a week ahead of them yet; neither of them could pretend nothing had happened.

And what in the world did she *want* to happen next?

Her confusion made her keep a distance from Abe during the morning meal and cleanup. He caught her eye more than once, and each time she couldn't help but smile in return and feel a fluttering sensation in her middle. But he didn't try to sit beside her and—and what? They had no understanding about what their relationship did or did not mean. Fortunately, the fact that Abe didn't act differently in front of the group made the morning much simpler.

They started on the road slightly earlier than usual, although the time felt longer to Maddie; she wanted some time walking alone to sort out her thoughts and feelings. Peter was determined to reach Jacob's Pools today. That meant starting early, everyone riding most of the way, and few breaks.

Abe drove the team while Maddie rode in the back of the wagon. She spent most of the time staring at the back of his head with that black hair, and at his strong arms controlling the animals. She forced herself to look away and examine her heart.

I must decide what I feel about Abe. And what I should do about him. And about Edward.

Why had she allowed herself to get into this situation? It wasn't the proper thing to do.

Abe wasn't like any other man she had ever met. Nothing at all like Edward. Somewhat like Roland, but different in many ways, too. If she allowed herself to think far enough, she could imagine herself loving Abe.

But he wasn't a Latter-day Saint. That counted for something.

And then there was Edward. He counted for something too.

Maddie rubbed her forehead, where a giant headache had begun throbbing. She took a deep breath, closed her eyes, and thought hard. *What do I want?* She made a mental list, picturing the items written on one of her students' slates. A good husband. Children. A stable life.

Not good enough. She mentally wiped the slate with the side of her hand and tried again. *I truly want a husband I love with my very soul. A husband I not only respect and admire, but yearn to spend my life with. A good man with good values. A kind man. A hard worker.*

The list went off on its own, no longer on her mental slate but spinning around and around like thread on a spindle.

I want a man who gives me chills when he kisses me.

I want a man like Abe Franklin.

She opened her eyes and smiled at the thought. *I'm ready if you are,* she thought. She wouldn't hop off the wagon and announce to him that she wanted to be his bride. But she would make sure he knew she was open to exploring the possibility.

The thought made her smile, and her headache dissolved into the air.

CHAPTER 24

Clara lay in the dim light of the spare room, coming in and out of consciousness—at least Miriam thought so; it was hard to tell. Clara rarely opened her eyes, and when she did, her lids hardly lifted, her gaze focused on nothing. Any sounds she made were few and did not consist of intelligible words.

Miriam sat beside Clara, wiping her hot brow with a moist cloth. The fever hadn't responded to her care, and nothing else she did seemed to have any effect. Each day Clara seemed to get slightly worse, and Charles was running out of ideas. With a sigh, Miriam let her hands drop to her lap. She wouldn't have admitted it—perhaps even to herself—but the action represented resignation. She looked over at Clara. By candlelight, her wrinkles and bony figure appeared even more pronounced. And her chest moved so slowly.

The door creaked on its hinges, and Miriam raised her head. Charles stood there, his hand on the edge of the door. "Any change?"

Miriam gave a shake of her head and bit her lips together. She should be grateful there had been no change—while it meant that Clara hadn't improved, it also meant that she hadn't taken a turn for the worse. But somehow the thought felt hollow.

"Will you give her a blessing?" Miriam asked, her voice breathy and tight.

"Of course," Charles said. "I'll go fetch another brother and some oil. Brother McKinney is probably home tonight."

Miriam spent the next several minutes gently rocking back and forth on her chair to ease the worry. The seat below her creaked with her movement, the only sound in the room.

"I always meant to come up north to visit," she said suddenly. "Ever since we left Salt Lake City. But a good time never came, with the trip so far." She paused, wondering if she were talking to herself or whether Clara could hear her words. "I've missed you, Clara. It has been so wonderful to see you again."

Miriam began wringing her hands. "Where did the years go? Weren't we just newlyweds walking to Zion?" A sad laugh escaped her lips. "Yet here we are, gray and wrinkled."

After rocking for a few more minutes, Miriam began speaking to Clara again. "I'm a great-grandmother. Did I tell you that?"

She told about her grandchildren and the two great-grandchildren, then stopped as her list ran headlong into Ruth, her third-born. The thought of her made her heart ache. "You know, I wish *you* could talk to Ruth. She married nearly sixteen years ago and can't seem to bear children. Her sister-wife has at least seven, if I remember correctly. It's been quite a trial . . . I'd bet you could have been a greater comfort to her than I have been. You know what it's like not to have children." Her voice trailed off, and she stared out the window, where the sky was dark and stars were peeking through, like pinholes in black paper.

"Abe."

Miriam's head whipped around and she leaned toward the bed. "Clara?"

The word wasn't repeated, and for a moment Miriam wondered if she had imagined that Clara had spoken. Miriam continued talking. "Abe will be here soon, I'm sure." She took Clara's hand in hers. It was cold, and she began rubbing it, hoping that her friend could hang on long enough for Abe to reach St. George. But then she noticed the creases in Clara's forehead. Something troubled her. And then Miriam realized what it was.

"I'm sorry. That was insensitive of me. You *do* have a child," Miriam said penitently. "I didn't mean it like that. Just that you would be able to relate to Ruth's inability to bear children."

"Abe . . . is enough."

"Yes, he is," Miriam said, her voice choking up. "And he'll be here soon."

The two sat in silence, the only sound Miriam's occasional sniffs as she held Clara's hand. A few minutes later, the door creaked again as Charles arrived with Brother McKinney.

Miriam crossed to her husband with hope in her heart. "She spoke," she told him. "Twice."

"She did?" He moved past her to the bed to do his own examination of the patient. As Miriam watched him gently check Clara's fever, her breathing, and her pulse, she couldn't help but marvel at what a combination her husband was—a man of science and a man of faith. He'd do everything he could medically to save Clara, but he also knew that nothing he could do was as powerful as what God could do, if He so desired.

Charles gestured toward Brother McKinney, who went to the far side of the bed and anointed Clara. Charles then continued with the blessing. Miriam folded her arms tightly and closed her eyes hard as she listened to the words.

You shall be healed. Say it. Miriam waited for the statement or something like it. Perhaps, *Your mission is not complete,* or *Your prayers are answered.*

But nothing like that came from her husband's mouth. After beginning the blessing, he paused for what seemed like ages. He then took a breath and went on, describing the valiant woman that was Clara Franklin. He enumerated elements of her righteous life and her efforts to live the gospel. He spoke in length about how beloved she was of her Father.

Beautiful, all. Miriam cried as each word was spoken and hoped Clara could hear them too; it was impossible to tell if she was still conscious.

The blessing did not say a word about health until the very end, when again Charles paused. His voice caught, and he hesitated before saying, "Clara, your time is at hand."

No! Miriam wanted to cry out at the top of her lungs. But a simultaneous calmness in her heart told her that Charles was only the mouthpiece. It was Clara's time.

If only she can hold on long enough to see her son.

* * *

Over the next several days, the Hamptons' wagon traveled across more rocky terrain, through House Rock Valley, with the Vermillion Cliffs on one side and the Kaibab Plateau on the other. All along the trail, the land was barren except for scrubby bushes and some grasses interspersed with rocks. Then out of the blue they'd see beautiful rock formations jutting from the horizon—tall cliffs with colors from red to purple.

They came across few people and settlements on their way, but moved quickly downhill toward one nestled at the base of more towering layers of rock. The weather became warmer, and their only real concern was the periodic return of Ellen's contractions, which slowed the progress of the party somewhat.

"You need to rest now," Caroline said as she pushed Ellen back down on the blankets. She had been sitting to read from the Bible, but Caroline insisted that any movement at all could hasten the baby's arrival. If she had her way, her patient wouldn't do more than blink and breathe for the next few days. With hawklike supervision, Caroline managed the contractions with the nettles concoction and an extra day of rest.

Two days later, when the Hampton party traveled again, Ellen hinted that she could walk, and Caroline nearly flew into a rage at the very idea. "Do you want that baby to come right now?" she demanded. "Well, *do* you?"

Peter raised a hand to quiet her as he turned to his wife. "Caroline is right. I'd like to make up for lost time, and having you walk is not the wisest way of doing that. Just ride."

"Can we ride all the way too?" Mary asked, pulling on her father's shirt as she held her little brother's hand.

Laughing, Peter scooped her up and placed her into the wagon. "I don't see why not, seeing as you've spent most of the trip in there. Just don't bother your mother."

"We won't," Mary promised solemnly. "We'll just tell her stories all day."

Maddie lifted Lorenzo into the wagon beside Mary. The two of them clapped and cheered as if they hadn't ridden much already. They plopped down on either side of their mother. Lorenzo leaned in and rested his head against her, and Mary began jabbering away, telling her mother all about the game she and her brother had invented that morning with rocks and weeds. The game had more rules than Maddie had students, and she turned away from the sight with a smile on her face. It would be good for the children to spend time with their mother.

For days the air had been dry, and Maddie had wished there would be a little wind. For their first several days on the road, the wind had gusted so hard it was a wonder no one had blown away. Now, as they traveled through the Buckskin Mountains, the weather was cooler and much more temperate, with pine trees and a pleasant breeze. Maddie enjoyed seeing the dark green of the trees after so much dry, brown landscape.

Maddie spent some of the afternoon walking beside Abe. Days had passed since the evening by the river, yet neither had said a word about it since. They had gone past House Rock Spring without having a decent conversation. First they had no opportunity; it seemed they were never alone, especially when Peter insisted they all ride to save time. Today they traveled side by side behind the wagon, but Maddie didn't know what to say. Tall pine trees provided shade, and every so often a bird or squirrel made noises high up in the branches.

Finally she ventured to start a conversation. "You know," she said, looking over at him, "you never did tell me about your childhood. How did you come to live with Mormon folk in Salt Lake? And how come you're not one of us?"

Abe hooked his thumbs behind his suspenders. "It's a long story. Sure you want to hear it?"

She absolutely wanted the entire story—every detail. Who was this man she had come to care for, who had kissed her, had held her on the riverbank when she was broken inside? Instead of saying all of that, she merely replied, "Tell me."

Abe launched into how his Shoshone mother had sold him to the Hutchings family as an indentured servant when she fled from her jealous husband with another man. How the Hutchings family didn't want him and eventually offered him to the Franklins, who had no children of their own. How Clara Franklin had been the parent of all children's dreams—and how her husband had been exactly the opposite.

"I suppose it's his fault I'm not a member," Abe said with a shrug. "As a boy, I decided that I wanted nothing to do with a God who approved of such a man."

"And whoever said God approved of him?" Maddie demanded.

Abe stopped on the trail as the thought struck home. "I suppose *he* did." He looked at Maddie and shook his head. "But Mother's beliefs were different. She believed in a more gentle God. She didn't outright condemn Brother Franklin, at least when I was young—I think she feared him in those days as much as I did. So I hated him for hurting us both, and I hated the Church for letting him be pious on Sundays and act the part of the faithful Saint and hold positions in leadership—all those things were so hypocritical to me."

"How horrible," Maddie said. "I don't blame you for hating him."

"You know, I don't hate him anymore," Abe said with a shrug. "He's dead, and even his memory has no more power over me. He was a bitter, pathetic old man. I pity him."

Maddie read between the lines and hoped she interpreted correctly. "So does that mean your view of the Church has changed, too?"

Abe let out a cynical laugh. "Not exactly. My adoptive father might have started the ball rolling, but plenty of others have kept it moving at a good pace. I've never been in danger of letting down my guard. Fact is, I've seen and experienced a few too many things in my days, a few too many people like Brother Franklin. It's some of those things that made me leave Logan, and then Salt Lake City." His eyes clouded, and Maddie wanted to ask him what he was thinking about to bring such a troubled expression into his eyes.

At that point, Peter stopped the horses and called out that it was time for a break. Everyone gathered around one of the water barrels for drinks, and it wasn't until after Abe and Maddie had their metal cups filled that they meandered some distance away from the wagon and kept talking. She sat at on a rock at the side of the road, and Abe made do with a patch of dirt.

"Technically, I was baptized," he said, then took a drink of water.

"You were *what?*" Stunned, Maddie leaned forward at his sudden declaration.

Abe laughed at the expression on her face. "Right before the Hutchings family passed me on to the Franklins. No one explained what had happened or what it meant. There was a large group of people getting baptized the same day in a river—and I didn't even remember it until about four years ago when my mother got hold of the certificate."

Maddie leaned back, resting her hand on the rock. "So, Abe Franklin is a Mormon."

He gave a quick shake of his head and held up a finger to correct her. "No, I'm not. For one thing, I don't think God would accept such a baptism, when the person didn't even know what it meant. I made no covenants that day. If anything, I racked up another sin by getting so angry at the man baptizing me that I think I left him with a black eye." He smiled sadly, then tilted his cup, which was empty except for a couple of drops that wet the ground. "Besides, the certificate was destroyed."

"How?"

But Abe didn't answer the question, and Maddie didn't feel she could pry as he went on. "I doubt any other record exists of it, and certainly not in my name. It listed me as, 'Abraham Michael *Hutchings*.' I don't think they had really adopted me, so that's just not right." Resting his arms on his knees, he grew more serious. "Fact is, at one time I thought the baptism was enough for me to be with Lizzy. Technically, I was a member, right?" He shook his head sadly. "But it wasn't close to enough. We didn't believe the same things, hold the same things dear in our hearts, have the same view of the world, the same hopes."

A quiet stillness descended over them, and for a minute, Maddie felt her heart sink. What had their kiss implied, if anything? What had their time that night meant? Did they have no future together? She thought for sure he did believe, and yet . . .

It took a moment to form the words, but she finally said, "And what if you had started to believe the way she did? What then?"

By now Abe wasn't looking at her. He gazed staring into the tree trunks around them and kicked some pine needles with his boot. "Then I would have gotten baptized—for real—and made promises to God." He lowered his head, still avoiding her eyes. "Then perhaps Lizzy and I would have married."

A call from Peter broke the moment. "Time to move out! Everybody back to the wagon!"

Maddie brushed some dirt from her skirt and made a move to stand. Before she could leave, Abe grasped her hand and stood to face her. "I never thought I'd find myself caring about another Mormon girl."

Her face flushed. She opened her mouth to speak, but nothing came out.

Instead, Abe lowered his voice and said, "Maddie, if there's anyone who could make me change, it would be you."

He released her hand and headed for the wagon. Maddie's heart raced as she watched him go. What did he mean? That she could change his mind about marrying a Mormon girl? Make him decide that his baptism was valid after all?

Or that she could change his mind about the Church?

A smile curved her lips. She didn't know which he meant. But she was bound and determined to find out.

* * *

Later, as they approached Kanab, Caroline began hobbling, and when Peter finally managed to convince her to ride with Ellen, she agreed. She climbed into the wagon, all the while cursing her rheumatism and a supposed storm brewing despite the clear sky.

"At least I can keep an eye on Ellen," she said reluctantly as Peter supported her into the wagon. "That's some comfort. I'm afraid she's been trying to move around too much."

Once Caroline was in the wagon, Maddie still didn't have another chance to talk with Abe. More often than not, he drove the team through the mountainous area while Peter watched over Mary and carried Lorenzo on his shoulders to ease the cramped quarters of the wagon.

That night at camp, both Abe and Maddie had more duties than before, since neither Ellen nor Caroline was in good shape. Of course, Caroline insisted that she stay with Ellen solely to supervise her, not because of any pain or other problems she herself might be undergoing.

Another day of travel brought them to Pipe Springs—only two or three days out of St. George. As they got ready to head out the next morning, Maddie stopped by as Abe harnessed the horses. "Good morning."

His head popped up, and a grin spread across his face. The scars on his cheek always moved when he smiled, and she had come to like seeing that. He nodded her direction and tipped his hat. "Morning to you too."

"You've got a much heavier load, don't you?" Maddie said. "Although I suppose we're moving faster now that Caroline's riding instead of walking."

"We are," Abe said, slipping a bridle over one horse's nose. It opened its mouth to let in the bit, then lowered its head and nickered. "But it's a shame *your* hip isn't acting up."

Maddie flushed and turned away, unable to hide a smile. She had thought the same thing more than once; if she had an excuse to ride, she'd be able to sit on the bench beside Abe. She had wondered if sitting behind him as Caroline did each day would be conducive to conversation, but Abe answered the thought before she said anything else.

"She's a sweet lady, but she's got a tongue on her that doesn't stop moving." He buckled a leather strap and moved to the other side of the horses.

"I tend to have a tongue of my own," Maddie said, stroking one of the horses' necks.

"But I doubt I'd ever get tired of hearing it."

Maddie lowered her head, biting her lips together to keep them from grinning too broadly. She was grateful that the other horse stood between them so Abe couldn't see her burning cheeks. The memory of their kiss returned, coupled with Abe's words that she could change his mind, sending an extra dose of heat climbing up her neck.

She set to petting the horse more vigorously, and it responded by nuzzling her arm. Still, neither Maddie nor Abe had said a word about their kiss—what it did or did not mean, what it might imply, or not imply, about the future. And this moment wouldn't last very long, so it wasn't the best time to bring up such a hefty topic.

But she wanted to talk about it, to know what lay in Abe's heart, to tell him what she felt in return. Instead everything was ambiguous. She was sure of nothing besides the fact that she kept wishing he'd kiss her again. And each time it crossed her mind, it was quickly followed by a feeling of betraying Edward.

"Looks like we're done here," Abe said and patted the back of one horse.

"I should go help Ellen." Maddie took a step to leave but hesitated. Abe did the same, and for a charged moment, they just stared at each other. The look in his eyes was deeper than anything Maddie had experienced with Edward, and a single word came to her mind—*love*.

I think I love him. The thought came suddenly, surprising her. Another followed. *And I don't love Edward.*

Her ears were bright pink, she knew, and she could hear nothing but the pounding of her heart as her right hand twisted Edward's ring. Abe broke the moment by leaning forward and brushing his lips against her cheek as he moved away to help Peter finish loading the wagon.

Maddie whipped around to watch him leave, her heart racing. She looked down at the ring, and on impulse, took it off and closed her hand around it. No matter what happened between her and Abe, she now knew one thing for sure—he had reawakened a part of her heart that she thought was dead. He had shown her what love could be again, had reminded her of what it felt like. She could never again consider marrying just for security.

She made a fist, squeezing her hand tightly around the ring. In spite of all his careful devotion, Edward wasn't really in love with her, either. She felt sure of that. The look she just saw in Abe's eyes was one she had never seen in Edward's. Breaking off the engagement would be better for both of them. Edward had pursued her because they seemed like a good match, because they were comfortable together. Now she wanted more, for herself, and hopefully for him as well. He deserved to have someone who adored him. She couldn't give him that. She'd tell Edward about her decision as soon as she returned to Snowflake.

* * *

Hurricane Cliffs and the Rock Canyon Dugway loomed in the distance, a barrier between travelers and St. George. The actual distance to the city wasn't that far, but with steep switchbacks—which were reportedly almost as bad as Lee's Backbone—this wasn't an area they could cross in a couple of hours. They made camp, though they were far from a river or spring, in an area where Abe and Peter had to dig down for water, as they had several times already on the trip. Night fell, and Peter kept the fire stoked while Ellen rested. It wasn't long before she began crying out in pain and calling to her sister. Maddie and Caroline rushed to her side, and the former midwife declared, "That baby's coming tonight whether we like it or not."

Peter jumped from his seat by the fire and rushed to the wagon, but Caroline tried to push him away. "Let me take care of her. A birth is no place for men."

He grasped Ellen's hand and said, "Are you all right?"

"No." She gripped back with force and shook her head.

Caroline put both hands on his chest and forced him back to the fire. "I'll let you know if there's anything you can do to help. In the meantime, let us womenfolk have our privacy."

Peter swallowed hard as he stared at the wagon, but finally bit his lower lip and nodded. "I'll be at the fire. Let me know." He walked back, taking looks over his shoulder and clenching his fists nervously.

Caroline and Maddie turned their attention to Ellen, who already had sweat forming at her hairline.

"We're so close," she groaned as another contraction came on. "We left plenty early enough. Why couldn't the baby wait?" As the pain intensified, she stopped talking and began squeezing her sister's hand tighter. Maddie braced Ellen and helped her through the pain, while Caroline calmly gathered supplies and prepared for the birth.

"It's no use balking about the timing," Caroline said as she folded a towel and put it on a pile of several others. She talked like Ellen was merely complaining over grass stains in the wash rather than being in the middle of childbirth. "We did our best to keep that babe where he belonged, but in the end, it's not our choice."

Ellen whimpered and cringed at the pain, her face contorted until the contraction passed and she collapsed on the quilt. "Neither of my other babies came this early," Ellen protested. "And this one was supposed to be born in the covenant."

Caroline snapped a towel before folding it and returned with, "You might as well save some of your crying energies. Chances are you'll be laboring all night. You'll need your strength." She turned around to the water pail and muttered, "If they hadn't forgotten my herbs, we would have made it at least another day or two." With that she walked away to fill the pail and boil some water. Maddie scowled at her back. Caroline might know a lot about birthing babies, but she had a lot to learn about making a patient feel comforted. Or maybe she had lost the ability in the years since she had last served as a midwife.

No, Maddie decided as she smoothed Ellen's hair away from her face. She couldn't imagine Caroline being anything but the slightly off-kilter person she was. Normally her eccentricities didn't bother Maddie, but this was different. Ellen was in real, intense pain, and there was no use in "saving" her cries for later; they were real *now.*

Another contraction came on, and when Ellen's grip tightened, Maddie clung back. A wave of guilt swept over Maddie for forgetting the bag of herbs. As the contraction peaked, Ellen's face pinched, and she covered her face with her hands, tears leaking from her eyes. "I can't do this, Maddie," she said through her teeth. "It's too much."

"Yes, you can," Maddie said. "You're strong." But she didn't know if her words were true—and even if they were, did they feel empty to her sister? If only they had Caroline's medicines. Maddie kept trying. "You've done this twice before. You can do it again."

After the contraction eased, Ellen lay back in temporary relief. "This time feels different. The pains got hard much faster. With the others, I labored hours before I hurt like this."

At her sister's words, Maddie's stomach twisted. She didn't know the first thing about birthing babies or what to do if something went wrong. For that matter, she probably wouldn't even know that something was wrong. She wished now she had been present for Ellen's previous births; at least then she'd know what to expect. As it was, she felt inept and underfoot.

As Caroline walked farther away, Maddie called out to her. "Caroline! Come back. Peter or Abe can get the water."

The elderly lady stopped where she was, turned, and put a hand to her hip. "I know what I'm doing," she said. "I've been fetching water for a good seventy years. Land sakes." She was about to turn away again, when Maddie called out a second time.

"But I need you here. And Ellen needs you. Anyone can boil water, but they can't help us with the baby. *You* can."

Caroline seemed pleased at the acknowledgment of her skill. "Well, that's true enough. Very well." She gave a dramatic sigh as she handed off the pail to Peter, thumping it into his chest. "Fill that up and boil the water for at least five minutes. Then call me, and I'll come get it from you." She raised a finger at him. "And don't you try bringing me the water. You aren't coming anywhere near the birthing wagon."

Peter grabbed the bucket. "Consider it done. But please let me know what's happening over there. If you do, I promise I won't interfere."

"Of course." Caroline wiped her hands against each other with satisfaction, then headed back. "I hope the children will be able to sleep through all the screaming," she said bluntly as she reached them. "The cries are only going to get louder."

Maddie had to resist the urge to send Caroline away; deciding between birthing knowledge and bedside manner became a difficult choice. If only Caroline would stop saying such heartless things. But she probably had no idea how her words sounded, and Maddie clung to the hope that Ellen would be so focused on her baby that she wouldn't hear or remember most of them.

Caroline scuttled Mary and Lorenzo toward the campfire, then awkwardly climbed onto the wagon and sat at Ellen's feet. "Now let me check how close you are," she said. "You're between contractions, right? Don't want to do this when you're in the middle of one. *That* would hurt." This she confided in Maddie, who merely nodded. At least Caroline would attempt to spare Ellen some physical pain.

"What should I do?" Maddie asked.

"Just hold her hand," Caroline said, getting into position. A moment later, she declared, "Mercy, woman! You've moved quickly. Yer nearly there. No wonder you've been in so much pain. The baby'll come in just a few minutes, I warrant."

Tension shot through Maddie. "But what about the water? Don't we need it first?" She was ready to jump out of the wagon and chase Peter down.

Caroline put a hand on Maddie's arm and shook her head. "We'll be fine, young lady. I think Ellen will need you at her side more than any bucket of water."

Maddie hesitated a moment, but Ellen's hand reaching up for hers convinced her to stay. She sank back down beside Ellen just as the worst contraction yet came on and her eyes shot open at the sudden increase in pain. She shut them tight again as she gasped. Caroline rubbed her hands together in anticipation.

"We're close. Really close. Next thing you know, the baby will be here. Third babies are always the easiest. First and second ones pave the way. Wonder why it didn't occur to me before. Let's push."

With a strangled moan, Ellen bore down. Maddie supported her body, encouraging her with what she hoped were comforting words: "You're doing well," "You're strong," "Keep going," and "Almost there."

Caroline led Ellen through the pushing process, then between each contraction, she physically pushed Ellen back to the pillow, saying, "Save your energy between the pains, now."

Not ten minutes later, a wet, red, screaming bundle slipped into Caroline's hands. She grabbed a towel and expertly wiped the baby's face free of fluid. High-pitched cries began, first quiet, then escalating into loud, demanding wails, a sign of a baby breathing well. Only at the sound of the insistent cry did Ellen flop back to the bed and take a breath of relief. It was over, and her baby was fine.

"You did it, Ellen!" Maddie cried, tears of both joy and relief falling down her cheeks. "You did it! You're a mother again!"

Ellen nodded, her hair wet and flattened against her head. "And listen—what a set of lungs! Is it a boy or a girl?"

Caroline had tied and cut the cord and was cleaning off the baby. "It's a boy. He's got good color and loud pipes, which is something."

"A boy," Ellen said. She closed her eyes, relieved that it was over. "William Peter."

Caroline put baby William in a small blanket. She kissed his head in an uncharacteristic show of affection and handed him over to his mother. "He's a precious one, he is," she said. "I can tell by the swirl of his hair."

The midwife went about her business cleaning up and tending to Ellen. Maddie stroked the little baby's shock of blond hair and said, "I'm sorry he wasn't born in the covenant."

Ellen looked up at her younger sister and shook her head. "I'm not." At Maddie's surprised look, Ellen shrugged. "We'll be sealed, and that's all that really matters. He came just in time to be part of the temple trip with the rest of his family. I think he wanted to enter the city with us, to be born almost in the shadow of the temple."

Maddie leaned forward and kissed the top of little William's head. "I like that thought."

CHAPTER 25

Maddie stayed at her sister's side long after baby William's arrival. His body was tiny, without the rolls of fat that Mary and Lorry had on their legs and arms as newborns.

"Small and skinny's to be expected with an early baby," Caroline told them with authority. "I've seen babies this young have trouble breathing and eating, and some simply don't make it. You're lucky this little one doesn't have any of those problems. He's a little cuss but a strong one, for sure."

Caroline helped Ellen change clothes and get more comfortable in the wagon. Maddie gave William a thorough bath in the water Peter had boiled and let cool. She used a soft cloth and a bit of lye soap. William's arms and legs flailed, and he cried in insistent wails. Maddie quickly dried him off, then wrapped him first in a thin cloth to bundle him tightly, followed by a warmer blanket. She picked him up and brought him close, resting her cheek on his perfect head and sandy blond hair, never wanting the moment to end.

Caroline scuttled over from the fire. "Peter needs to see the baby, and quick, because the little tyke needs to nurse right away."

At her voice, the sweet moment popped like a bubble, and Maddie nodded. She returned to the wagon, where Peter waited with his wife. Maddie gently handed over her brand-new nephew to his father.

"He's beautiful." Maddie's arms ached with longing for her own child.

"Isn't he?" Ellen looked happier and prettier than Maddie could ever remember her. Ellen and Peter's faces seemed to glow as they looked on their son. As Maddie witnessed the perfect scene, she yearned to experience the same thing, yet felt grateful for the honor of witnessing her nephew's birth. Someday her time would come. And it couldn't arrive soon enough.

"Now then," Caroline said, a hand on her hip. "Are you going to be all right in feeding the baby? That can be tricky."

Ellen smiled and nodded. "We'll manage. William *is* my third child."

"Now you call if you need help," Caroline said, then turned away and murmured, "I have to check on these new mothers myself. They think they're as indestructible as the three Nephites." She paused, then turned around and came back. She unfolded a quilt and tucked it around Ellen. "That's better. A chill is the last thing you need."

Caroline shifted from one foot to the other, hesitant to leave. Maddie finally wrapped an arm around the lady and shepherded her toward the campfire, leaving Ellen and her baby alone in the privacy and quiet of the wagon. "She'll be fine," she said to Caroline. "I think what she needs right now is some sleep."

"I suppose so." Caroline looked over her shoulder and shrugged. "Just as long as she does call when she needs me. I know a sight more than she may give me credit for—just 'cause I haven't been a mother doesn't mean I don't know how to care for one." She blew out a huff of air as they reached the fire pit and sat down. The circle of rocks was made by a previous traveling party, and probably used by dozens of others journeying along the same road over the years. Maddie wondered what stories those other travelers could tell about their trips.

Abe poked at the embers and added a piece of wood, sending sparks into the night air. A few minutes later, Peter returned. As he sat down, he gestured toward a pot in the hot ashes, wrinkling his nose. "I tried to make something for supper, but it's not quite up to the standards of what you womenfolk cook up."

"Sorry we weren't able to help," Maddie said with chagrin as she picked up a metal spoon. She stirred the beans but had to pull back at the burnt smell.

"Hey, we gave it our best attempt," Abe said, laughing at the look on Maddie's face.

Caroline grunted with disapproval. "That's gonna take some serious elbow grease—assuming the pot isn't a total loss." She stood and marched away, adding over her shoulder, "I'll make up some biscuits for everyone. And please, men, don't you try cooking again, for all our sakes."

As she walked into the shadows, Peter leaned toward Maddie and spoke sheepishly. "I gave the children dried apples and beef jerky before putting them to bed." He glanced over his shoulder where they slept under a blanket together. He looked up hopefully. "Is that all right, do you think? They had a cup of water each, so I doubt they'll get bellyaches, but it wasn't a hot meal, and—"

"It's fine," Maddie said. "Thank you for taking care of them while we were with Ellen."

Peter pressed his lips into a line. "Had to do something . . ." He nodded, biting his lower lip in thought. "Thanks—for helping her and our baby."

"You're welcome," Maddie said, catching his eye. They smiled at each other, then Caroline returned with her biscuit ingredients and a frying pan. She whipped together the batter, dropped it into the pan of grease, and in a short time they were chewing on hot, delicious biscuits.

"Know what we need?" Caroline asked as Peter finished off the last biscuit. Without waiting, she answered her own question. "Music."

She revealed a harmonica hidden in her pocket and waved it back and forth. "I knew this would come in handy. After a big day like today, we need to celebrate."

Maddie wondered why Caroline hadn't played it before now, but the lady explained on her own. "I don't use this much. I reserve it for special occasions. And by golly, a birth is the *most* special of occasions." She put the harmonica to her mouth and began to play. Her foot tapped the ground, and she rocked side to side with the quick rhythm. Maddie clapped along as the music filled the air.

Midphrase, Caroline pulled away from her instrument. "We're missing something. A celebration isn't complete without dancing. Peter, dance with Maddie."

"Very well," Peter said obediently. "Maddie?" His hand was outstretched.

"Sounds fun to me." She took his hand and together they danced a cotillion pattern as Abe clapped and encouraged them on. When Caroline finished her song, Peter wiped his forehead with his sleeve.

"You're a fine dancer," Caroline said, nodding with approval. "You two up for another?"

Peter's eyes wandered to the wagon, and he shook his head. "I want to check on Ellen and the baby. If you'll excuse me."

"Of course," Caroline said, then raised her voice as she added, "Don't wake them if they're sleeping."

Peter smiled at her order and walked toward the wagon.

"Well, I suppose that leaves you, Abe." Caroline's mouth pursed to one side in thought. "Maddie, I don't suppose you know how to play the harmonica? I'd enjoy a dance myself . . ."

Maddie had to press her lips together to avoid smiling. At the beginning of their journey, Caroline seemed to have eyes for Abe, but she hadn't given any hint of it on the trail until now. "I'm sorry, I don't know how to play."

With a sigh, Caroline nodded, although Maddie noticed her cheeks were pinker than they had been a moment before. "So Abe, I assume you can dance with Maddie, then? Because we certainly aren't done marking the occasion."

"I sure can. I'd be happy to oblige." Abe looked more serious than Maddie knew he felt. She could see a gleam of humor in his eyes as he reached for her hand. His hand closed tightly around hers as she stood, and her heart thumped so hard that for a moment Maddie was sure Caroline could hear it.

She didn't seem to notice and instead began another fast-paced melody. Abe gave Maddie a proper bow before leading her in a makeshift quadrille at first, and eventually improvising as they went. They danced—twirling, skipping, and laughing—as Caroline played song after song. Maddie had no idea how long they danced—the evening felt timeless, as if no one and nothing existed besides the two of them and the rhythmic music. Her cheeks flushed from the exercise, and she breathed heavier, but she had no desire to stop.

They went around the rocks, weaving in and out, Maddie twirling under his arm. As Abe led her around, Maddie's foot caught on a protruding rock. She let out a yelp and began falling, but Abe reached out and caught her. The feel of his arm around her waist sent a rush though Maddie, and she sucked in her breath.

"Are you all right?" he asked, leaning in close. "You're trembling." His forehead sparkled with perspiration, and his breathing was heavier than normal. Perhaps that's why he seemed to be trembling too.

"I'm . . . I'm fine, thank you," Maddie said, knowing that she shook because of his touch rather than the near fall. He lifted her to a standing position, but instead of moving away, they stood close and gazed into each other's eyes. Maddie could hardly breathe as Abe's hand tightened around her waist. Her eyes flitted to his mouth, sending her insides burning. She tore her gaze away from his and swallowed.

Abe leaned close and whispered in her ear, "I think I love you, Madeline Stratton."

A warm wave rushed through Maddie, and she opened her mouth to answer, when a different voice spoke instead.

"Shall I play another one? You're not hurt, are you?"

The moment evaporated. Maddie was brought back to the present—Caroline watching them, the cold evening air, the wagon a ways off. Abe standing inches away from her. "I'm—I'm fine." Feeling embarrassed and exposed, she coughed, her face burning to the tips of her ears. "I think I'll check on the baby too." She gently pulled away from Abe and walked out of the circle of firelight into the darkness. His fingers lingered on hers just a moment as she stepped away.

She passed Peter, who was coming back. Had he seen what happened between her and Abe? It was the first time outside of their rare private moments that they had shown what they felt for each other. If Caroline recognized what had happened, she didn't show it. Peter's gait paused almost imperceptibly as they passed, and he opened his mouth as if to say something. Maddie's stomach tightened in anticipation, but he didn't speak. Instead his mouth curved into a knowing smile, and he kept walking.

Eyes lowered, Maddie increased her pace, feeling lightheaded as she neared the wagon. She clutched the edge of the box and turned around, biting her lip as she looked back to where Peter, Abe, and Caroline sat around the glowing fire. Abe seemed to be looking over his shoulder straight at her, but the light of the fire put his face in the shadows, and she couldn't read his expression.

"What's happening between you and Abe?"

Maddie whipped around and faced her sister, who had raised up on her elbow. Baby William lay in front of her, sleeping.

"I . . . we . . ." Maddie hesitated, staring at her sister for a moment. She let out a sigh and covered her face with her hands. "I don't know."

With a quieter voice, Ellen asked, "What about Edward?"

Maddie clasped her fingers together and lifted her shoulders in a shrug. "I can't marry him, that's what. I know that now."

"Because of Abe?" Ellen pressed.

"Yes. No." Maddie shook her head to clear her mind. "I mean, because of Abe, I've realized I can't marry Edward."

Ellen craned her head to peer at the group around the fire. "So you and Abe . . . have plans?"

"Not at all," Maddie said, somewhat helplessly. How could she explain what she didn't even know herself? "I care for him. He understands me better than any female friend I've ever had. I want to be with him, and yet . . ."

"Yet he's not a Latter-day Saint," Ellen finished.

Mentally grasping for something to put her sister at ease, Maddie nodded. "On the other hand, he *was* baptized as a child."

"He was?" Ellen's forehead crinkled. "I thought—"

"He says he doesn't believe," Maddie acknowledged. "But I'm sure it's only a matter of time."

Ellen reached forward and took Maddie's hand. She squeezed it and looked deeply into her sister's eyes. "You can't be sure of anything. You know that, don't you?"

Maddie looked away, unwilling to answer. She turned back toward Abe, silhouetted against the yellow firelight. Seeing him brought back the feel of his arm around her, the sound of his voice in her ear. "Maybe I can't *plan* on it," she said quietly. "But I can certainly *hope* for it, can't I?"

"Just be careful where you place your heart," Ellen said.

"I know." Maddie nodded in agreement, but secretly she struggled. Her mind might know that hope was all she had, but her heart insisted on planning for a future with Abe Franklin, Latter-day Saint.

* * *

They had only one more hard day of travel before reaching St. George: climbing Hurricane Cliffs, which were almost as steep and unnerving as Lee's Backbone. Abe and Maddie worked together to help everyone up and over, especially the children and Caroline, whose hip seemed to be getting worse. The wagon pulled into St. George on a Wednesday as afternoon brushed against evening. When the city came into view and they began passing houses, Abe's stomach tightened.

Hurry. Faster, he thought, aiming the sentiment at the wagon. He had been over three weeks on the road, managing to not think too often about what his mother's condition might or might not be, since he could do absolutely nothing about it. But now he was so close to her that every inch of his body tensed in worry and anticipation of finding her.

Let her be well, Abe thought. *She has to be well.* Any number of things could have happened since Dr. Willis sent his letter. Abe considered leaving the wagon altogether and racing off to find his mother.

"Are you feeling all right?" Maddie asked suddenly.

Abe looked over, surprised. He hadn't realized that his emotions showed so clearly on his face. "I need to see my mother. Do you think anyone would mind if I leave to find her?"

"Of course not. Are we close?"

He pulled out the letter from Dr. Willis, unfolded it, and passed it to her. He had the directions memorized. "I think it's close to the temple," he said, nodding toward the tower still a distance ahead.

"We're headed for a hotel on Main Street," Maddie said. "You can come get your things later. Go."

She nudged him forward, and Abe nodded, grateful she understood. He trotted to Peter at the front of the wagon and said, "Maddie and I are going to find my mother."

Maddie was taken aback. "You want me to come with you?"

"Of course," Abe said, then turned back to Peter for his response.

"Absolutely. Go," Peter said, glancing over from the team. "We'll be at the hotel."

Together, Abe and Maddie rushed ahead and through the city streets. They didn't speak at all, just studied street signs and eagerly hurried around corners and along streets. Abe felt grateful that Maddie sensed his need to hurry. He took her hand and pulled her along as he ran.

"I think that's it!" she called suddenly, pointing across the street. She reread the directions. Abe already knew the two-story house matched the description, and as they ran closer, he could read the sign hanging above the door: "Dr. Willis, Physician."

He reached up and knocked as both of them tried to catch their breath. After perhaps half a minute—but what felt like much longer—Abe knocked again. They heard footfalls, and the door opened, revealing an elderly woman. She looked tired and worn, her eyes weary. Wisps of gray hair framed her face as if it had been a long time since she had done her hair.

"May I help you?"

"Good evening," Abe said, taking off his hat. Instead of polite formalities, he wanted to burst through the door and race inside, but he forced himself to speak slowly and say, "I'm Abe Franklin. I'm looking for my mother, Clara Franklin."

The woman's hand went to her mouth. "Abe! I'm so glad you're here. She's been asking for you. Come in, come in."

He had found the right house, and his mother was inside—asking for him. Abe felt as if his knees would give out at any moment as relief washed over him. "How is she? May I see her?"

"Follow me." The lady ushered them into a room that looked as if it served as the doctor's office and closed the door. A bench stood on one side for waiting patients. On the other side was a desk for reception work and a hall down which Abe assumed were examination rooms. Miriam led the way up the stairs to the living quarters. Normally Abe would have held back and let Maddie go first, but feeling his urgency, she stepped to the side and let him pass. He gave her a grateful look as he climbed the stairs.

"She's hanging on," Miriam said over her shoulder. Then, when they all reached the top, she turned. Abe nearly ran into her and wanted to push her aside to find his mother. But she held up a hand to ease his rush and said, "When her party arrived, Charles didn't think she'd make it through the night. It's thanks to a blessing, I think, that she's still here. She had quite a turnaround those first few days. It was a miracle the way she regained her strength for a time—even went to the temple."

Abe grasped Miriam's arm. She turned around, and he clarified, "She made it to the temple? She's had her endowment?" Abe knew that was his mother's greatest desire, and it would have broken his heart if she were unable to go after all her efforts to get there.

Miriam smiled. "She did. And it was a glorious day." But Miriam's eyes clouded. "Right after that, though, she took a turn for the worse. Ever since, she's been hovering between . . ." She sniffed, motioned for them to follow, and said, "Come with me. She's in the spare room. When I left her a moment ago, she was sleeping."

Miriam led them through the sitting room to a closed door. She softly knocked on it, then opened it a crack and peered inside. "Clara?" she whispered. Abe could hear no response. Miriam opened the door a few more inches and stepped inside. "Clara, Abe is here."

He heard a sharp intake of breath from the room and could no longer restrain himself. He shoved the door open and all but ran to her, leaving Maddie at the door. At the sight of his mother's weak body, he had to stifle a cry of surprise. He pulled up a chair, took her cold hand in his, and said, "Mother, I'm here. It's me, Abe."

Clara's fingers pressed ever so slightly against his hand, and she managed to slowly turn her head in his direction until her eyes found him. "Abe." Her voice cracked and was so quiet that had Abe not been listening for it, he might not have heard it. He leaned forward and put his arms around her tiny, frail form in an embrace. He wanted to squeeze her hard, but had to satisfy himself with holding her gently in his arms.

"Oh, Mother," Abe said, his throat tightening. "I'm sorry I wasn't here sooner."

Her face looked ashen, almost gray, her skin as thin as an onion's.

"The temple," she said, the slightest glimmer in her weak eyes. "I went."

"I heard. I'm so glad." Abe had to cough to clear his throat, and he felt tears burning against his eyelids. "I'm so glad."

She managed a barely perceptible nod. "Beautiful."

"I bet it was."

"Not sealed, though." Her fingers pressed on Abe's again, and she gazed into his eyes. "Get me sealed. Will you?"

"You'll do that yourself," Abe said, holding her cold hands between his strong, warm ones. "You'll see."

"No, I won't." Her head shook back and forth, but it moved less than an inch either direction. "I won't be here." She blinked sadly, then urged again, "Get me sealed."

Abe swallowed the huge lump that had formed in his throat. This time he didn't argue, although inside he didn't want to believe her. "I'll make sure it gets done."

She closed her eyes and let out a sigh of relief. "My son."

"My mother." Abe's voice was high and strained.

"I want you sealed to me, too." Her mouth tightened into a fine line, and Abe felt the yearning that his mother did for such a sealing. If families were indeed forever, he would give anything to be Clara Franklin's son throughout eternity.

"That—would be nice," he said, knowing it would be cruel to give her false hope.

Clara's gaze shifted, and she noticed Maddie standing at the door. "Who's that?"

Abe turned to Maddie and smiled. He held out a hand, and she walked to his side. "This is Madeline Stratton," he said. "Madeline, meet my mother, Clara."

Maddie stood beside Abe, who held her hand. She bobbed her head in respect and said, "It's an honor. I've heard so much about you."

"You have the advantage," Clara said. A cough took over her body, and her eyes squeezed shut at the stabbing pains. Abe stood and looked around helplessly for what he could do. The attack subsided, and his mother breathed in deep and relaxed. After several seconds, she opened her eyes and spoke to Abe.

"Like Lizzy?"

He felt as if a hand had just clutched at his heart. He knew what she meant and was unsure how to answer. Yes, Maddie was a believing Latter-day Saint. All those years ago, his mother had been right when she predicted that he and Lizzy wouldn't be happy together if they weren't of the same faith.

How was this time with Maddie any different?

It was different because he loved Maddie more, in a deeper, more mature way than he had cared for Lizzy. He knew that now. His and Lizzy's relationship was based on secret meetings and excitement. Even though it lasted much longer than he had known Maddie, his feelings this time were different.

Yet the fact remained that they were of different faiths. His hand relaxed, and Maddie slipped hers away from his grasp. The action sent a stab into Abe's heart and yet—had he learned nothing? Yes. And for a time, he had fought against this very thing. He should have fought harder. His mother was right.

"Like Lizzy?" she pressed again.

"Yes," Abe said reluctantly. Maddie took a step backward, away from the bed, as if knowing she didn't belong here.

Clara frowned. "Don't hurt yourself again." She pleaded with him more with her eyes than with her words, and it tore at his heart.

He knelt beside her and took her hand in his. "I won't, Mother. I promise."

She took a stuttered breath and smiled with satisfaction. "My son," she said again as she closed her eyes. She said nothing more, the exchange exhausting what little energy she had.

Without a word, Maddie retreated from the room, for which Abe was grateful. He wasn't sure how to react after making the promise to his mother. Under any other circumstances, he would have gone after Maddie, but he couldn't leave his mother.

* * *

Maddie quietly stepped out of Clara Franklin's bedroom and closed the door with a click. She stared at the knob as her fingers slipped off it, her mind filled with questions, her heart battling conflicting emotions.

"Is everything all right?"

At the sound of Miriam's voice, Maddie started. "It's fine," she said. "Everything is fine." As she faced Miriam, she hoped to wipe any look of worry from her face. "I thought they should have some privacy."

"That's considerate of you." Miriam gestured toward the kitchen. "Would you like something to eat? I think I have some cookies in the pantry."

"No, but thank you." Maddie didn't remember when she last ate. She supposed the pit in her stomach might be partially caused by hunger, but she didn't want food. She noticed that the light outside the window was quickly fading, and used it as an excuse.

"I should probably go," Maddie said, nodding to the window. "My sister just had a baby, and she has two other little ones, and I don't think I'm needed here—"

Her voice cut off, and her head turned to the bedroom door again. She felt torn between staying here for Abe and leaving—also for Abe. He promised his mother that he wouldn't repeat the past. That likely meant he wouldn't pursue a future with Maddie. Her fingers gripped the sides of her skirt. As much as she hated to admit it, Clara Franklin had a point. It was something that had been whispering in her mind every time she and Abe talked.

"I—I'd better go to the hotel," she said, backing toward the stairs. "Thank you so much for everything. Will you please tell Abe good-bye for me?"

The moment the words left her mouth, Maddie's throat went dry. Her step paused, and for a moment, she wondered if it would be good-bye for the night or for much longer. Would Abe return to Snowflake? Would he follow his mother's instructions to the point that he would never see her again?

Maddie moved to the stairs and raised her skirts, hurrying down and leaving the house as quickly as she could—hopefully without drawing attention to the upheaval of her emotions. When she stepped outside, the cool night air hit her face, and she shivered. Holding her elbows with her hands, she stepped into the street and headed toward the center of town. But a few seconds later, she felt compelled to stop and turn around. There was the Willis home, where at that moment Abe sat vigil by his mother's bedside. An upstairs window had a soft golden glow, and the lacy curtain made her quite certain that it was the room they were in.

"Lord, bless them both," she said under her breath as she headed down the street. Abe was suffering, and would suffer even more as he watched his mother pass into the next life. Maddie felt selfish even worrying about what the future would hold for her and Abe at a time like that.

Yet she could think of nothing else.

She chastised herself, and not just for the inappropriate timing. She needed to be realistic. She shouldn't keep thinking about being with Abe, no matter how much she cared for him. Not when their beliefs were so different.

But they aren't so different.

The thought struck her with such intensity that she stopped walking and whipped around to look at the house again. She gazed at the halo around the window. It looked almost heavenly.

Appropriate for the moment at hand, she thought. But it was more than that. Abe believed more than he would admit; Maddie was sure of it. When she pictured Abe, he was a baptized, faithful Saint. She couldn't quite get herself to recognize—even though she knew it was the truth—that he wasn't those things.

With a sigh, she turned away. No amount of assurance that he really did believe or would eventually be baptized could change the fact that for now, he wasn't a member of the Church. And she was. She realized that entertaining thoughts of spending her life with Abe were pure folly—unless circumstances changed. Which they might. But they hadn't.

With her seesaw of thoughts, she threw up her hands in frustration and trudged down the street. She felt as if what was meant to happen couldn't be after all, simply because of a timing error. If only he had recognized his faith before coming to Snowflake. Or if they hadn't met until he had acknowledged his budding testimony. Of course, in that case, she probably would have gone ahead and married Edward, and it would have been too late to meet Abe. She shook her head, wanting to stop thinking in circles—and going through such wrenching emotions.

Several blocks later, Maddie found the temple and knew the hotel had to be nearby. She was about to head around the corner, using Peter's directions, when she paused and turned around. There stood the temple in its majesty and beauty.

Warmth washed over Maddie, and she breathed easier. *Abe will go inside with me one day.* All would work itself out. She felt she needn't worry. Abe *did* believe. Someday he'd recognize that, and then they could move on with their life together.

What if he doesn't?

She shoved the thought into a dark corner and headed for the hotel. She found it without any trouble and went inside to rest for the night. Tomorrow she would need to find Abe and support him. She wouldn't mention his promise to his mother or what the implications might be.

Surely he would see the reality of his own faith. He wouldn't give her up.

CHAPTER 26

Hours passed, and Abe kept vigil beside his mother's bed. As the sunset waned, Miriam came in unobtrusively to light a few candles, then left mother and son alone once more. Evening wore into night, and Abe sang her favorite hymns—songs distinct with Mormon doctrine. He had heard her sing them countless times as a boy, but he had never sung them himself.

As he sang, "The Spirit of God," he remembered how much that hymn meant to his mother. She told him it was sung at the Kirtland Temple dedication, and that ever since, the song brought back memories of that day and her desires for temple blessings. She had finally received them. Abe brushed some hair from his mother's face as he sang, taking in every curve of her features, the smile lines around her eyes, the white hairline. He was grateful that her face no longer looked pinched with pain. The music seemed to soothe her, and her breaths grew easier but farther apart.

By the time he began to sing, "If You Could Hie to Kolob," tears coursed down his face, and he didn't attempt to stop them. His voice caught here and there on the tune. At the last verse, Abe felt a sphere of love around the two of them, a warmth they shared together. "There is no end to glory; There is no end to love; There is no end to being; There is no . . ."

He stopped, unable to sing the words for a moment. His lips pressed together, and he finally managed, "'There is no . . . no death above.'"

With the back of his hand, Abe wiped his eyes, feeling for the first time that death really wasn't the end. To his own surprise, he knew that when his mother passed, she would be looking down on him instead of being gone forever. Just as she had always taught him.

"I found a home for us in Snowflake, Mother," Abe said between sniffs. "It's beautiful, with a porch perfect for watching the sunset."

He didn't know why he was telling her these things; seeing her so weak, he knew they wouldn't be returning to Snowflake together. "We'll sit there and read together," he went on, remembering the hundreds of times they had done that in the creaky swing at their old house.

"And we'll talk about *Rasselas* and read new books and—"

"Abe." She spoke for the first time in hours.

"Mother?"

"It's true." She swallowed slowly and weakly, speaking with her eyes closed. "I know it."

He had heard many people "bearing testimony" in his life. But this was different. A fresh batch of tears brimmed in Abe's eyes and fell down his face. His mother's five simple words pierced deeper than any other testimony he had heard. In her last moments, she was bearing one last witness to her son, after bearing witness all throughout his life.

That was all she said. Abe didn't know how to respond, so he just held her hand and hoped she'd keep talking. But she didn't say anything else, and Abe didn't leave her side. He was oblivious to the fact that Maddie was gone, oblivious to everything around him except for his dying mother. This was the end. Her face had no color in it. Her breathing grew more shallow by the minute, stopping altogether at times, only to start again with a deep rattle.

If it weren't for the subtle rise and fall of her chest and the occasional movement under her closed eyelids, she would have appeared gone already. Many, many times in the past he had held one of her hands between his and warmed it up; her fingers had always been cold. But tonight they felt colder than usual.

At least there's the next life. At least she'll have a perfected body someday.

The thoughts washed over Abe so suddenly that he hardly realized what they were until they had passed. He was about to mentally debate the thought, as was his lifelong reaction—almost a reflex, by now—when he stopped. He looked at his mother again and remembered her brief yet powerful witness—*It's true. I know it.*

If ever there was a time to allow faith into his life, this was it. The idea wasn't as strange as it should have been. He realized that over the past several weeks, a chink in his anti-religion armor had developed, and the hole had grown.

How many times had he said quiet prayers in his heart and mind? Rarely in a set format, never formal, but always speaking to God nonetheless. It had happened more times than he could count. And many of those prayers had been answered—most importantly, the one he gave when he begged to find Maddie in the river. From outside the bedroom door, a hushed voice broke into his thoughts.

"It's a miracle she's lasted this long."

"Or sheer stubbornness," came the reply. "She refused to go until she saw her son again."

Miracle or stubbornness? Abe didn't particularly care which it was. The thought of his mother passing before he arrived sent a chill through him. At least he was here with her. But she was still dying, and there wasn't a thing he could do about it.

The actual moment of her passing escaped Abe. He was warming her hand one moment, trying to ignore the voices in the hall, and the next he realized her hand was limp. Looking up, he waited to see the ribbon bow on her nightgown move with her breath, but it didn't. It was as if she had slipped quietly away, not wanting to make any fanfare or draw attention to herself.

Abe's throat tightened, and he placed his hand over her heart, hoping to feel a beat. Nothing. The moment had arrived as expected, but the disappointment was bitter all the same. He leaned over her as if there were something he could do to make her come back, his heart breaking but his mind refusing to believe what he saw.

It took several moments for him to acknowledge that it was over. She was gone. He leaned down and kissed her cheek. "I love you, Mother," he said with a choked voice. He sat in the chair and continued to cradle her tiny hand in his as if he could still warm it. For some time he sat alone with his grief, until Charles came in.

His step came up short when he registered the scene. "How long ago?"

Abe shrugged. He lowered his head, and a heavy tear dripped off the tip of his nose. "I'm not sure."

Charles reverently drew the sheet over Clara's body. The finality of the action sent Abe's shoulders shaking. He covered his eyes with one hand.

* * *

The following morning Maddie was tried to the core in her attempt to be pleasant and happy for her sister. Ellen and Peter should enter the temple of their God with joy—without even a tiny cloud to dampen their day. Knowing that Clara Franklin had been on her deathbed the night before would do that very thing. So would any knowledge of what Abe had promised his mother and what it might mean for Maddie. She helped them prepare for the day by getting the children ready. It would be a challenge keeping baby William happy without his mother being able to nurse him for several hours.

An impatient knock sounded on the hotel room door, followed by an equally impatient voice. "Are you in there? It's Caroline. We don't want to be late."

After smoothing Mary's bow, Maddie crossed to the door and opened it. "Good morning, Caroline," she said. "Come in. We're just about ready."

Caroline swooped in. Instead of sporting a regular bun at her nape, she had spent considerable time on a hairstyle that she must have worn as a young woman. Maddie hadn't ever worn her hair that way before, and neither had anyone her age. Caroline's hair was parted down the middle and smoothed down over her temples. Coils of graying braids covered her ears, into which some wild flowers had been inserted for decoration. Maddie smiled in spite of herself. Caroline looked ready to go to a ball or to meet her beau. To top off the grand entrance, a floral scent wafted as she entered.

"Let's go, let's go!" Caroline announced, clapping her hands for attention, but her gloves muffled the sound. She gave the room an indignant look as if they had let her down, then demanded once more, "Come on, let's go!"

"We've got plenty of time, Caroline," Ellen said, putting on a gold chain necklace that had a pendant in the shape of a rose. It was her fanciest jewelry, which she had brought for the occasion. "The carriage isn't even here yet."

Caroline went to the window and stared out at the street, arms folded, to watch for the carriage. Maddie was suddenly grateful. She didn't want to look outside—it brought back thoughts of walking through the streets last night.

"Ready," Ellen said.

"Finally," Caroline said, turning. "And the carriage has just arrived."

"Perfect timing," Peter said.

Ellen raised her eyes to her husband's. As they gazed at one another, they had nothing but pure happiness on their faces. The sight made Maddie's throat tighten and her eyes sting.

That is what she wanted—that kind of happiness with a husband, and an eternal marriage. Was she being naive to think that Abe could be such a man? Her mind told her *yes.* Even so, the image in her mind of him being a member of the Church was so strong she couldn't shake it.

And yet—

Emotions running amok, Maddie's hand went to her stomach. "Children, hug your parents good-bye. You'll see them this afternoon when you go to the temple to be sealed to them."

Mary raced to her mother and threw her arms around her legs. "Will you tell me all about the temple tonight?"

Ellen lowered herself to Mary's height and laughed, a sparkling, tinkling laugh of happiness. "You're coming there too, you know."

The girl shook her head. "But I want to know what you're doing *before* I come."

Her mother stroked Mary's sweet, round cheek and answered, "I'll tell you what I can. Even what it looks like—all the paintings and decorations. But some things in the temple are so special they can't be talked about unless you're inside."

"Like what?" Mary asked, her brow furrowed and her lips pouting.

"I haven't been there yet, so I don't know," Ellen said honestly.

"Oh." Mary nodded. "But you can tell me about it when Lorry and I come to be sealed this afternoon. We'll all be inside the temple then."

"Not exactly," Peter interjected, ruffling Mary's hair. Maddie raised an eyebrow at the gesture—she'd have to fix Mary's hair. It was all mussed up, not fit for a temple sealing. Peter went on. "You'll understand someday when you grow up and come to the temple too."

"Very well." Mary said the words with the pathos of a four-year-old, followed by a deep sigh. But then she trotted—apparently not completely crushed—to Maddie's side and held her hand. "We'll have fun today, won't we, Aunt Maddie?"

"Yes, we will," Maddie said. "But you must promise not to muss up your dress."

"Oh, I promise," Mary said solemnly.

"The carriage is waiting," Caroline said from the door, where she stood holding it open.

Maddie hugged Ellen. "Have a wonderful day. I wish I could be there with you."

"So do I," Ellen said. "Thanks again for coming with us."

They left none too soon for Caroline—and right around the time Maddie's emotions were about to get the better of her. She closed the door behind them, then brought the children to the window to watch their parents drive away. The carriage was something Peter had wanted for Ellen—to ride in style even though the temple was well within walking distance. It was more like celebrating the ride to their second—eternal—wedding, he had said. At least, that was one reason. The other was so that neither Ellen nor Caroline would have to walk any farther.

Maddie would be walking to the temple later that day with the three children. She would take them to the sisters working inside. Then she'd wait alone in the front area for the new, eternal Hampton family to emerge.

Over the next several hours, Maddie entertained her niece and nephews and tried to get baby William to eat from a bottle, nap, and stay happy. A few hours past midday, Maddie decided it was time to leave. They would arrive early, but she simply couldn't abide sitting in the hotel room any longer.

Maddie washed the children's faces and hands, changed William's diaper, and soon headed down the stairs and out the hotel doors. She walked along, holding Lorenzo's hand and carrying William. She didn't have a hand free for Mary. "You stay close by," she urged. "No wandering off."

They walked toward the temple and managed quite well for a few blocks. That's when Mary glanced around a corner, pointed to a bakery sign hanging over the street, and ran off in that direction. "I want a sticky bun!" she shouted over her shoulder. "I'll get there first!"

"Mary, come back here at once!" Maddie tried to scurry along, but Lorenzo couldn't quite keep up, and she couldn't run fast while carrying the baby. Plus, her dratted skirts kept getting in the way, bringing her perilously close to falling headlong onto the dirt road. "Mary. Come back!"

The little girl came to a stop before the bakery window. She pressed her face against the glass and gazed longingly at the treats behind it, their smells wafting out the door. Maddie marched over and grabbed her hand. "Mary, you are never to do such a thing again," she began, then stopped as a sight down the road caught her eye. There in the distance was the Willis home—and Maddie could see the upper story windows. Black drapes hung in them.

A hand flew to her mouth. She had known that Clara Franklin was dying, but seeing proof of her passing . . .

"What's wrong?" Mary asked, turning in the direction Maddie stared. "Oh, look! It's Abe! Hi, Abe!" Mary pulled her hand free from Maddie's suddenly limp one and raced down the road. Abe had just stepped out of the house. He was too far away for Maddie to read his expression, but the very sight of him sent her heart beating heavily. With dread? Expectation? She couldn't name the emotion.

She walked down the road to fetch Mary, who had just jumped into Abe's arms. As Maddie approached, she could tell he was trying to smile for Mary's sake. His eyes were ringed with red, with dark circles under them; he looked like he hadn't slept at all. Maddie suddenly felt guilty for sleeping soundly in a bed—the first comfortable rest she had experienced since leaving home.

Abe set Mary on the ground. The little girl kept chattering about everything that had happened to her since she last saw him—the hotel room, how the baby had spit up all over her, how Lorenzo kicked her in the bed all night. How she missed him.

"I've missed you too," Abe said quietly, but he was staring at Maddie.

She lowered her eyes. Looking up at the black drape, she said, "I'm—I'm sorry."

He lowered his face and nodded, then cleared his throat as if unable to speak.

"I'm glad you were here," Maddie went on.

"Me too," Abe managed.

Neither spoke again for a minute. Maddie didn't know what to say, though her heart was full to bursting. They both seemed to sense that things weren't quite the same as they had been yesterday when they walked the streets of St. George, looking for the Willis home.

"The funeral is tomorrow morning," Abe suddenly said. "Ten o'clock at the chapel."

"We'll be there," Maddie said firmly. His eyes looked like wells of pain, and Maddie wished she could reach out and hold him, comfort him as he had comforted her at the bank of the Colorado. But something held her back, a barrier between them that she didn't know how to cross.

"I promised to fetch some bread for Sister Willis," Abe said suddenly, gesturing toward the bakery.

"I want a sticky bun!" Mary proclaimed. She put her hand in Abe's and pulled him to the bakery. "Abe, will you get me a sticky bun?"

Maddie slowly followed the two of them to the bakery, where Abe bought three sticky buns—one for Mary, one for Lorenzo, and one for Maddie. Their fingers brushed as he placed the third bun in her hand, and Maddie had a wild desire to take his hand, to hold onto it and stay with him all day as he mourned for his mother.

But it wasn't her place, so instead she merely said, "Thank you."

He opened his mouth as if he were about to say something, but then clamped it closed. "I'll see you tomorrow."

"Yes, tomorrow," Maddie repeated—as if she couldn't form an intelligible thought on her own. She watched him buy two loaves of hot bread and leave the bakery with them in a paper bag, then head to the Willis home without a look back.

Maddie let out a breath she hadn't realized she had been holding. She looked around to regain her bearings as if the last few minutes had been a mirage, then cleared her throat and tried to get back to business.

"Let's go," she said to Mary and Lorenzo. "Follow me. And don't get any sugar on your best clothes. You need to be all clean for the sealing, you know."

* * *

After taking the children to the temple, Maddie wanted to wander the grounds and sort out her emotions about what to do next. But that wasn't an option. Within moments of the temple sisters taking the children inside, Caroline came out, radiant and grinning with joy. She put her arm through Maddie's and walked her bodily out the doors.

"It was so wonderful!" she gushed. "It was heavenly. Glorious. So amazing. Florence was right in wishing she had come earlier. I'm so glad I didn't put it off. The trip was absolutely worth every miserable step, sleeping with rocks in my back, and sunburned cheeks to boot."

"I'm so glad you had such a wonderful day," Maddie said.

They reached the road, and Caroline stopped. She turned back, looked at the temple, and sighed. "I wish I could stay here forever. I don't want to leave."

Maddie patted her hand, and they turned onto the street, the shadow of the temple covering them as the sun lowered on the western horizon. "Living near a temple would sure be something, wouldn't it?"

Gritting her teeth, Caroline's eyes narrowed, and her step became deliberate. "I don't want to leave," she said again, only this time more firmly. She stopped and caught Maddie's eye in earnest. "I want to stay."

"But what about your new home in—" Maddie began, then cut off when she saw the intensity in Caroline's eyes.

"Home," she said, as if the word were foreign. She pointed over her shoulder toward the temple. "*That* is my home. I've never felt such belonging in my life." Searching Maddie's eyes for understanding, she went on. "What's left for me in Snowflake? Or worse, Woodruff? I have no family there. Florence is gone. There's Pearl, of course; I'll miss her. But she'd be fine without me." She paused, looked at her knotted hands, and sniffed. "I want to stay."

CHAPTER 27

The chapel was nearly empty. Abe sat at the front, waiting to give his mother's eulogy. The sight of so few people tore at his heart. He remembered how the funeral of Lizzy's cousin Jimmy had been and wished the same for his mother.

It wasn't that the world held few people who loved her; he knew that. It was that he had taken her away from her home, to die apart from her dearest friends. None of her lifelong neighbors knew of her passing, none of her friends. Not even Joanna.

Abe was the only person in the room who had known Clara Franklin for any significant amount of time. The Wilson family was here; they had met her a few weeks before. Dr. and Miriam Willis had known her years ago but hadn't been in contact for decades. And then there were the Hamptons and Caroline Palmer. They hadn't even met his mother, but came as his friends.

And Maddie. She sat alone on a pew on one side of the chapel. She had met his mother briefly, and he couldn't say the meeting had gone well.

After the bishop announced Abe, he stood and went to the podium. He tried not to look at Maddie and the pain in her eyes, which would only magnify the grief he was already suffering.

"Clara Wallace Franklin was born in Rochester, New York, on April 22, 1805," Abe began. He read the words, not looking up, because he knew that if he did, he'd lose all composure. His mother deserved a dignified service. "She was the third of nine children born to Clive and Beverly Wallace, and the first to reach adulthood. At the age of twenty-seven, she was baptized a member of The Church of

Jesus Christ of Latter-day Saints and moved to Kirtland, Ohio, to gather with the Saints. There she met Bartholomew Franklin. They married three months later, and over the years endured persecution as they followed the Saints, eventually settling in Salt Lake City. They were unable to have any children of their own."

At this, Abe's voice caught. He closed his eyes and had to breathe hard to ward off tears. There was a reason he'd been brought into their life. For his sake and for hers. Only now did he realize what it must have meant for her to have a child after years of being barren. "In 1865, she and her husband indentured an eight-year-old Shoshone boy, but Clara raised him as her own." By now Abe couldn't go on. His eyes were too blurred by tears to see the words, but even if he could have made them out, he didn't want to. Dry facts weren't enough to reflect the life of Clara Franklin.

He quietly folded the papers and spoke from his heart. "My mother was a wonderful woman. She taught me compassion, hard work, and loyalty. She taught me faith in myself and in God. Not all of her lessons were perfectly received, but she never stopped giving them. She rarely taught with words, and never with lectures. Almost always, it was her quiet deeds that spoke volumes. That could *fill* volumes. I wish—I wish that all of the hundreds of people she touched in her life could know that she has passed. That they could be here with us, honoring her life the way she honored them by her love and her service."

Abe finished, then ventured a glance up and saw that everyone in the small congregation had tears in their eyes. He pushed away from the podium and sat down. He rested his head in his hands to hide the tears that fell down his cheeks.

* * *

Sister Willis served a light supper to everyone who came to the service. The party was small but somber. Maddie tried more than once to speak with Abe. Each time something got in the way—either another person reached him first or her gumption gave out and she backed away.

What can I say that would help? Maddie sat on a window seat and thought long and hard, wanting so badly to ease his pain. *I can't,* she realized. Grief is part of the process of living and dying. She had learned that first when her parents died days apart from each other, and again after Roland's death. What would she have wanted from friends when she was going through the same kind of pain Abe was?

Certainly not what she received—assurances about seeing them in the next life, of how they were in a better place, or how God needed them more. None of that had calmed her pain or eased her mind. What she would have given for a friend to give her a hug and simply say, "I'm sorry," the way Abe had at the riverbank.

She lifted her head and scanned the room for him. Of all the people who learned about Roland, Abe understood. And he had shared his story about Lizzy because *Maddie* understood. He needed that same understanding now. He wasn't in the kitchen, on the back porch, or in the sitting room. She looked down the passageway toward the front of the house and saw him standing at the base of the staircase. He held a glass of juice in his hand but seemed oblivious to it as he stared up to the top floor.

He stood on the spot where they had first entered the Willis home, gone up the stairs, and seen his mother lying on the bed. Maddie wondered if he were remembering that moment too— wishing it had ended differently, with his mother walking down the stairs healed and well again.

"Abe," she said, coming into view.

He started, almost spilling his drink, then focused on her. "Maddie."

Their eyes locked as she crossed the space between them and did what she had decided he needed most. She put her arms around him, hugged him tight, and whispered, "I'm sorry."

Abe set the glass on an end table and returned the embrace. His head lowered near hers, and she could hear him crying into her shoulder. "It's my fault," he said. "I took her away from her home."

"No, Abe," Maddie said, remembering Caroline's pure joy at receiving her blessings. "You gave her a great gift. She left this world with what she wanted most. You could have done nothing to make her happier." She pulled back and held his face between her hands. The sight of his tears sent a new wave of emotion through her, and she struggled to go on. "You did that."

He closed his eyes and turned away, sniffing. Maddie had to force herself not to throw her arms around him again. With a sleeve, he wiped at his eyes. "I miss her already. Strange, isn't it? For months I was away from her. In the past, I've been apart from her for years at a stretch, seeing her only on rare occasions. And yet . . ."

"It's different now, because you know you *can't* see her," Maddie finished.

Abe came back around and nodded. "You've already been through this, haven't you?"

She nodded sadly. "I know how it feels. I'm so sorry."

"I needed to hear someone say that." He took her hand and brushed his thumb across the top. "That was one of the most intense nights of my life."

"I can imagine . . ."

"I mean *besides* the sadness over Mother's passing. That room must have held more emotion and love than anyplace I've ever been." He touched his fingertips to his heart. "Deep inside I felt—" But he cut off, and lowered his eyes to the floor.

Something made Maddie's stomach flip in anticipation. That night at his mother's bedside, he had felt something strong—something of heaven, she was sure of it. "What?"

Abe didn't look at her for several moments. When he finally raised his eyes, he said, "Thanks again, Maddie. For understanding."

She swallowed down her disappointment that he wouldn't admit he had felt the Spirit. "You're welcome."

* * *

It was evening, and Abe knew he needed to talk to Maddie, to explain things to her. Doing so would just about kill him, but what else could he do?

He walked to the hotel well after dark, when Charles and Miriam had retired for the night and when he was sure that the Hampton children would be asleep. Caroline too, he guessed. No one would miss either him or Maddie, so it was a good time to talk.

He found her room easily enough and knocked. Shuffling sounds made it through the door, and soon it opened. The look on Maddie's face made it clear that she had expected Ellen, not him. Her hair was down, cascading in waves around her shoulders. She wore a dressing gown, which she held to her chest with one hand while holding the door in the other.

"Abe?" she said, her voice catching. "What are you doing here?"

Besides obvious surprise at seeing him, he couldn't read her face. What was she thinking?

"I know it's late," he said. "And I'm sorry to disturb you. Would you come for a walk with me?" Dim candlelight in the room made a halo around her—she looked like an angel.

Yet he was about to cause her pain.

I must be an idiot, he thought, then reminded himself, *but it'll be best for both of us.*

Maddie nodded stiffly. "Just give me a moment to change."

She closed the door with a quiet click, and Abe waited in the hall. A few minutes later she emerged wearing her dark blue dress with her hair in a bun. Without a word, she walked toward the steps, wrapping her shawl around her shoulders as Abe followed her down to the front door.

Once outside, they walked side by side for a couple of blocks, neither saying a word. Maddie clutched the shawl tightly as if she was cold. They might as well have been miles apart because of the awkward tension between them. He didn't know what to say, exactly, or how to say it. Yet he must speak. *What* was she thinking?

He eyed her from the side, aware of her jaw working, her hands clenching and unclenching. "I know why you've come," she said suddenly. Her eyes flashed as she looked over, then quickly away.

"Oh?" Abe hadn't expected this.

"I heard what you promised your mother."

He had hoped to work his way into the subject, to talk about their time together and how much his decision had already pained him. To tell her how much he cared for her and how the choice he made today would save her pain in later years. Instead he had to be content with saying, "Then—you see her wisdom."

"Perhaps I would if you were someone else." Maddie tightened the shawl around her shoulders. "But you're just as stubborn as a mule. You've lived among Saints your entire life, yet you refuse to do the simplest thing of asking God if there's a shred of possibility that the Church might have the truth. And I know—" Her voice cut off, and she stopped walking abruptly. Abe's step came up short, and a knot formed in his throat as he faced Maddie with her wild eyes. She had a finger pointing at him, and her eyes watered. "I know that if you would take half a minute to ask God for the truth, you'd admit you already know it, and this wouldn't be an issue. We could be together, and that would be the end of it!"

She ran ahead of him, leaving Abe speechless in the street.

He went after her without the slightest idea of what he was going to say when he reached her. "Maddie!" She slowed, and he caught up, then had to catch his breath. "Maddie, you have to hear me out." He reached for her arm, but at his touch, she slipped a step away and turned her head.

"What?" Her voice was low and shaky, as if she had been crying.

"Maddie, it's not that simple. If only it were. But the fact is, you can't know what's in my heart. Wishing for something to be there is not going to change reality."

"You already know, Abe." Tears streamed down her cheeks. "But you've spent your entire life avoiding the Church and everything about it. Your pride won't let you admit that it's gotten into your heart in spite of your efforts." She turned away, and Abe wished it were light so he could see her reflection in the shop windows. As it was, all he could tell was that her hand covered her face, and she was crying.

Abe had to force himself to remember his promise, to think of how much he and Lizzy were both hurt back in Logan. He couldn't repeat the past. "Maybe I am like a mule in holding my ground on this one. But sometimes stubbornness can keep a body from making a foolish mistake you'll regret for the rest of your life."

Maddie spun around and pointed her finger at him, face on fire. "Are you calling *me* a foolish mistake? Something to *regret?*" She pushed past him in a rage, letting out a cry of frustration and walked on, heading back for the hotel and pounding the dirt road with each step.

"No. That's not what I meant," Abe said, trotting to catch up to her. As he approached, her pace slowed, and she finally stopped, wrapping her arms around her body. She did care for him, of that he was certain. Angry as she was, she couldn't ignore him.

Boots covered in dust, she lowered her head and asked in a small voice, "Then what *did* you mean?"

"I meant—" Abe cut off, struggling to put his emotions into words. "The future. That mixing our lives would be a mistake, a painful, horrible mistake. For you more than for me. I want to spare you that."

She raised her face, and Abe's heart ached at the pain in her eyes, redness visible even in the moonlight. "Shouldn't I be the one to decide that?"

"No." Abe shrugged helplessly. "I've lived through this once before, Maddie, remember?" His eyes smarted and burned, and he swallowed hard. "All it got me was pain. I'm not going to do the same thing again, because it's not just me I'd hurt this time. It'd be you, too. I care too much about you to do that."

She didn't answer right away, and Abe paused, struggling to go on. "I know it's crazy to say such a thing only weeks after meeting you, but I love you, Madeline. I love you. And I refuse to do something that I know will hurt you. Not today, perhaps, but down the road. And then you'd hate me for it. I can't live with that."

"I could never hate you," Maddie said quietly. "I love you too."

With everything in his soul, Abe wanted to reach out and gather her into his arms—to hold her as he had that night by the river—a time he still let himself believe they could have a future together. His hand raised to touch her, but he paused and pulled it back. Instead of comforting her, he knew he had to make their parting final. Doing this earlier would be less painful than waiting months or years, when their attachment had grown even deeper. As wrenching as it was to say the words, he added a new argument but tried to do it softly. "Maddie, you've already promised yourself to another man. What about Edward?"

Her hair bobbed as she nodded miserably and sniffed. "He also deserves someone who loves him completely. Even if I never saw you again, I could never marry him."

She turned back and looked at Abe. She was heavenly to him even with her red eyes. They had gotten to know each other better in a matter of weeks than most couples ever managed with months of formal courting. Struggling together in the wilderness revealed character much quicker than visits in the parlor or evening buggy rides ever could.

Swiping at her cheeks, Maddie said, "I can't go on thinking I'll never see you again. And yet how can I live in the same town, seeing you on the street and pretending we're mere acquaintances?"

Her words mirrored his feelings from Logan exactly. That's why he had to leave Cache Valley, why he went to live in Salt Lake City with his mother. To think that he had already caused the same pain in someone else—someone he cared deeply for. *Poor Lizzy.* He had never contemplated what she must have gone through when she told him good-bye.

Maddie spoke, her voice pleading. "If you'd just see that you can be a part of the Church. That you really do believe . . . That what you felt in the room with your mother was—"

"You can't know what I believe," Abe said, his voice suddenly growing tight.

Yet standing firm in the face of Maddie's pleading face was proving harder by the moment.

He had no desire to start an argument about his beliefs and his desire to keep every inch of himself out of the Church. So Abe did nothing but nod, not trusting himself to speak. If he weren't careful, he'd open his mouth and profess his love again—or worse, admit that he had actually prayed a few times—and they'd be back where they started.

He drew his mind to the evening when he brought Lizzy up the scaffolding of the Logan Temple to one of the towers. He remembered her words as the sun set over the valley and she told him a final good-bye. Surely that memory would give him the strength to hold Maddie at bay.

When she gazed into his eyes, his heart all but melted at their deep brown sorrow as she spoke. "You say you want to keep from hurting me?"

"More than you know."

She stepped closer and gripped his shirt between her hands and spoke every word slowly and with intensity. "Then don't push me away."

Before Abe could respond, Maddie rose onto her toes and pulled his face to hers. She pressed her lips against his, kissing with more fervency than she had at the riverbank. It sent Abe reeling. His heart sped up, and he found himself kissing her in return with equal intensity.

She pulled a few inches away and stayed there for a moment, hands cradling his head as she tried to read his eyes. A symphony of emotions crashed through Abe, and he could do nothing but stand there and force himself into silence.

I love you, Maddie. I want to be with you. Thoughts could not be stopped, but he clamped his teeth together to prevent them from escaping. *I just can't be a Mormon.*

When he said nothing, Maddie spun on her heels and ran back into the hotel, hands covering her face.

Abe stood rooted in place and watched her go, wishing with his whole heart that he could go after her, take her in his arms, and kiss her again.

CHAPTER 28

"Thanks for helping Miriam with the office work," Charles called to Caroline as she headed into the office with his wife. "We've been a bit shorthanded of late, so we truly appreciate the help."

Caroline waved the idea away. "Oh, it's nothing. I'm glad to help."

He waved good-bye, and he left for a walk with Abe, who closed the door behind them. "I don't know how you talked me into this," Abe said as they reached the street.

"Doctor's orders," Charles said for the umpteenth time. "You agreed because I'm your doctor, and I say you need the exercise, the fresh air, and the distraction." He nodded to someone as they passed in the street.

The distraction? As miserable as Abe felt, he didn't *want* to stop thinking about his mother. She may not have given him physical life, but in so many ways she had breathed life into what otherwise would have been nothing more than existence. Clara Franklin had been more of a mother to him than anyone else could have. And if mourning her meant feeling so desperately sad that he wanted to do nothing but sit on the Willises' family porch all day, so be it. But Charles wouldn't leave Abe alone—at least not until he went out for a bit, so here they were.

They walked in silence for several blocks, then Abe lifted his head and looked around for the first time. Until then he had been following Charles but paying no attention to their surroundings. They rounded a corner, and the temple tower became visible.

"What are you doing?" Abe stopped walking.

Charles grabbed his arm and tried to keep the two of them moving. "Oh, come on."

But Abe ripped his arm away. "My mother just died, and you have the gall to try proselyting?" He turned and headed down the road, taking broad strides as anger and heat climbed up his throat.

"Abe, no," Charles called after him. "Please stop. That's not what I intended. Not at all."

Abe was about to turn the corner they had just gone around but hesitated at the sincerity of Charles's voice. He put a hand on the brick of the building he stood beside and looked back. "Then what *did* you intend?"

Charles took a few steps toward Abe, hands raised in surrender. "To keep a promise I made to your mother."

Abe's eyebrows drew together. He wasn't sure whether he should be curious or irate at another trick. "What kind of promise?"

"She asked me to show you around the temple grounds and tell you about the temple. She wanted you to know what it meant—to her and to the Saints."

"Don't you think I *know* what it meant to her?" Abe snapped. "It's the one thing she was willing to sacrifice everything for."

Charles pressed on. "'Tell him the tower story,' your mother said. She thought you'd get a good laugh out of that one. 'Tell him about your working on the foundation.' And I promised I would." Charles looked over his shoulder at the temple rising into the sky.

The evening breeze picked up, sending a shiver down Abe's back. He tried to decide if the plea from Charles was genuine. If it was, he needed to honor his mother's request.

He finally let out a deep sigh and nodded. "Very well. Tell me."

As he returned to Charles's side, his pace wasn't nearly as fast as it had been a moment before. Abe felt oddly reluctant to follow Charles to the temple block, as if doing so would mark the end of one thing and the beginning of another. Neither said another word until they reached the temple. They walked onto the grounds, and Abe followed Charles to the front, where he craned his neck to look up at the tower.

"So what about the tower?"

"Do you believe in the spirit world?" Charles asked.

Abe remembered the warm feeling at his mother's bedside when he sang and felt for sure that death wasn't the end. But why had Charles asked the question? Abe braced himself to cut off any attempts at conversion. "I suppose I believe in an afterlife," he answered vaguely.

"Well, a lot of folks in these parts think Brigham Young had a hand in making that there tower—from beyond the grave." Charles pointed at the dome and the tower rising above it. "This new one was finished last spring. If you look careful, you can tell it's new."

Abe squinted and nodded, noting a slight color difference between the dome and the rest of the building and the fact that it didn't look weathered or dirty in the least. "What did it used to look like?"

"Short and squatty. That's what it used to be," Charles said. "Trust me, it's much nicer this way." He went on, describing how Brigham Young had hated the dome and tower, how he wanted it changed but didn't have the heart to insist on it after the members' sacrifices.

"And here's the part your mother thought you'd get a laugh over," Charles said. "Brother Brigham died, see, and almost exactly a year later, lightning hit the temple smack dab on the tower. Didn't damage hardly anything else. When folks saw that, they figured they'd better rebuild it the way Brother Brigham first wanted it."

At the image, a chuckle escaped Abe. His mother was right; he was glad she had made sure he'd hear the story. It was the first time he had laughed in days. He looked at the tower again. "I can't imagine it smaller."

"It was. Ugly thing, too. But it's not the tower that I worked on."

When Abe lowered his eyes to meet Charles's, the latter pointed to the base of the temple. "That's it. What you can't see. The foundation. And what's under it—what we had to do to get *ready* to make a foundation. Hoo-eee, was that one big, nasty job."

Abe felt in no mood to take the bait, but he decided to humor the man. This story might end up interesting like the one about the tower. "Why is that?"

"Come sit over here and I'll tell you." Charles motioned for Abe to follow, and he led the way to a bench beside some hedges that bordered the temple fence. Abe reluctantly went along, hoping the discussion wouldn't be lengthy and overly serious.

"The north end of the lot was easy to dig out," Charles began. He leaned back, crossed his feet at the ankles, and went on. "But the other three sides were somethin' else—nothing but water, mud, and muck." He shook his head at the memory. "Not unlike what I hear Nauvoo was before they drained it."

"So why didn't they just move the site a little bit north, to drier land?" Abe folded his arms as if Charles had begun debating him. It felt to Abe as if his beliefs—or lack thereof—were about to be under attack, although rationally he knew otherwise.

"We couldn't move it," Charles said with a shrug. "President Young wouldn't hear of it. Said that's where the temple was to stand and that we'd have to find some way to make it work."

Ridiculous Latter-day Saints, Abe thought. He rolled his eyes and bit again. "All right, the temple is standing, so I know you solved the problem."

"Problems," Charles corrected, emphasizing with his hand. "We managed to get a drainage system going. I imagine it'll be there as long as the temple stands—can't have that water coming back, you know."

"What else?"

"Turns out that besides dealing with soggy soil, we also had to find a stone for a base to put the foundation on, something that wouldn't rot away from all the water and minerals. We couldn't use sandstone or limestone, which was a shame—they're so easy to find, even here. No, those stones wouldn't last. No sirree."

This time Charles paused, and Abe didn't break the silence. If his companion wanted to keeping talking to himself, fine. Abe would sit and politely listen for his mother's sake. He was having a tough go at not blaming the towering white structure for his mother's death. Or himself for sending her to it. Hearing about its construction didn't exactly fill the cockles of his heart with warm embers.

Charles reached up and adjusted his hat, then leaned forward and rested his arms on his legs. "President Young found the stone we were to use for preparing the ground. It was left from a volcano." Here Charles seemed to pause for effect before adding, "Had to build a road to it over a ridge, then haul in the rock. Sometimes it was in small pieces no bigger than my hand. Other times it took an entire team to pull a single boulder. We had to pound that rock into the ground. *Then* we built the foundation on top of that."

Abe's voice burst out in spite of himself. "So much work just to keep this site? That's crazy."

"The entire idea of building this temple in the middle of the desert might have been called a bit . . . impractical . . . by some," Charles said.

That's an understatement if I ever heard one, Abe thought.

"At least we got to use sandstone on the exterior." He pointed at it. "The walls are just stuccoed white, you see. They're sandstone underneath."

"Well, at least there's that," Abe said. Using some local, softer stone was *some* consolation for all the back-breaking work on the foundation, he supposed.

Abe shook his head in wonder. What was it about Brigham Young that made his followers so passionate about temples? Why were his demands about temple sites so precise and rigid? Why did the people always find a solution whenever he insisted they solve a problem? Abe noticed that Brigham Young didn't always offer the answer, but certainly expected to get one.

"You know, Brother Brigham was quite the prophet and leader," Charles said as if hearing Abe's thoughts. "He was right about the volcanic rock. It worked well, and the temple is as strong and stable as if it were built on granite. But building the temple was tough, no question. Lots of supplies were scarce—lumber among them, as you might imagine. Had to haul that in, too. The temple took people from all over Utah donating men, food, money, supplies. Everyone made sacrifices. It was quite a feat."

He picked a piece of grass, slid it between his teeth, and sat back to admire the temple. He seemed to feel some ownership in its success, and Abe realized that was part of the reason so many of the people had sacrificed for it; the temple became theirs.

Abe shifted on the bench, looking straight at Charles. "So how exactly did you get the volcanic rock into the ground?" He had done a little work on the Salt Lake Temple and a considerable amount on the Logan one. With all that work behind him, his curiosity got the better of him. In Logan the temple sat on a bed of gravel, of all things, and Brigham Young had declared they could dig for dozens of feet and still find no bedrock, so they might as well not try. Here stood another temple with an unusual story about its foundation.

"We used a rather unusual pile driver." Charles grinned.

Abe hated to admit that he really wanted to know, and he nodded.

"We filled the driver with lead, then the horses raised it up on ropes. It'd be released, and down it'd go, plunging that black rock deeper every time." Charles leaned conspiratorially toward Abe. "But I bet you can't guess what we used as the pile driver. I'll give you a hint—it was made of brass."

Abe finally laughed as he hazarded a guess. "Something you can fill up, made of brass, in the middle of the desert? How about I make a ridiculous guess and say it was part of a ship? Even better—a *battle*ship?"

"Good guess," Charles said, slapping Abe on the knee. "You got the battle part right. The pile driver was a heavy, old cannon used by Napoleon's own troops. Once we filled the thing with lead, it weighed nearly a thousand pounds." Charles folded his arms and sat back, giving Abe a look as if daring him to top that.

"Wait. Napoleon?" Abe repeated. "As in—"

"As in Bonaparte. The French emperor who lost at Waterloo." He nodded with satisfaction. "The very same."

"But how—" Abe looked at the temple, then back at Charles, confusion written all over his face. "How in the world did one of Napoleon's cannons get here?"

"He abandoned it after his defeat in Moscow. It was taken into Russia and eventually over to Alaska and down to California. Don't know all the details, but it was brought to Utah as payment for some of the Mormon Battalion folks from Sutter's Mill. When we needed a pile driver, someone had the idea of using the old cannon. It wasn't fancy, but it sure did the trick."

Charles laughed aloud, and so did Abe. The bizarre connection of the St. George Temple to a battlefield in Moscow seemed so out of place and unreal to Abe as he sat in the middle of the American desert. They settled into a jovial silence, both taking in the view of the temple. Abe folded his arms, and every so often he'd glance at Charles and then back at the whiteness that contrasted so sharply with the red rock rising in the distance.

"Let's go back," Charles said, rising. Abe followed suit, and as they headed back, he kept thinking. This hadn't been the kind of discussion he expected. Abe had assumed they'd be talking about priesthood ordinances, and the only true and living Church. Yet here they were laughing over lightning strikes from the grave and a lead-filled cannon.

But those were exactly the kinds of stories that Abe appreciated hearing. They still showed him what his mother probably hoped he'd get out of them—that this was a people who would build their temple no matter what. And in the manner their leader told them to.

And that they'd have plenty of divine help along the way.

"Thanks for telling me those stories," he told Dr. Willis when they reached his home.

"My pleasure," he said, tipping his hat as he went inside.

Abe leaned against the house, still contemplating the stories of the tower and the cannon. "Even *I* can't call both of those coincidence," he murmured. "One or the other, perhaps. But both?" He felt a tingling sensation in his heart and brought his hand up to it. But before he could allow the feeling to last, he cleared his throat and brushed it aside. Pushing away from the house, he walked toward the street.

Caroline Palmer peered around the doorway and watched him leave. She smiled to herself and patted her heart. "He felt the Spirit," she whispered. "I know it. Won't Maddie be pleased?"

* * *

The Hampton party had been in St. George for nearly two weeks, much longer than they had originally planned. Clara's funeral was part of the reason—it was on a Friday, the last day of the week for endowments. To complete temple work for Florence and Bart, they had to wait for the following Thursday. But no one begrudged the extra time, given the reasons.

Caroline insisted on doing temple work for Florence, and Charles kept another promise to Clara by getting Bart's work done as well. It was Maddie's idea to get her parents' temple work completed, which Ellen and Peter performed the same day as the others did the additional work.

Thursday evening, Peter and Abe loaded the wagon to get ready to leave the following morning. Abe had his mother's farm money, so he helped restock the wagon for the return trip, since most of their rations had been used on their extra-long journey up and their prolonged stay. In addition to the money from the farm, Abe added one other item to the wagon, a large basket with some of his mother's belongings. He planned to come back and retrieve her other things—dishes, some furniture, and other heavier items—from the Willises' stable someday. In the meantime, Abe needed to have a few mementos of his mother with him.

Friday morning dawned crisp and clear. Maddie kept herself busy to avoid thinking about spending significant amounts of time with Abe over the next three weeks. They hadn't spoken more than a few stiff pleasantries since their argument on the street. While Maddie hated that, she didn't know what either of them could possibly say that wouldn't make the other feel worse. The trip home would do that well enough on its own.

For once, Caroline wasn't buzzing about, trying to direct everyone. Instead, she stood at the door of the hotel, wringing her hands and staring forlornly down the street.

"What's wrong?" Maddie asked. She looked around and realized that Caroline hadn't put a single thing into the wagon.

"I don't want to leave." Her voice had risen a notch and sounded panicky.

Maddie put an arm around her and tried to calm the old lady as if she were a small child. "I'm sorry it didn't work out for you to stay, but—"

At that moment, a buggy sounded, and Caroline clapped her hands, her face brightening. "They've come!"

Confused, Maddie turned around to see Charles driving and stopping in front of the hotel. "Are you ready?"

"Oh, yes!" Caroline practically skipped her way over to the buggy and got in as Charles retrieved her things.

Peter, Ellen, and Abe had stopped working as well, all of them staring. Peter got the use of his tongue first. "May I ask what this is all about?"

"I didn't want to say anything until it was for sure," Caroline said from her perch in the buggy. "Because I just knew that if I said a word about it, something would happen and it would all fall to pieces."

Her answer didn't clarify the situation, so Charles filled in the details. "Yesterday, as Caroline and Miriam were leaving the temple, they got to talking. Turns out Caroline wants to be a temple worker and stay here, and we could really use some help in the office. She's been a great boon to us the last while, and with the town growing, I won't be able to keep up all by myself. We've got an extra room, so we offered it to her."

"Isn't it perfect?" Caroline clasped her hands together, beaming pure joy. "I get to stay."

Maddie smiled at Caroline's excitement. "You get to stay home."

"Yes! That's it exactly!" Caroline's face clouded for just a moment when she added, "I'll miss you all, naturally. Pearl too. But she doesn't need me. I think it'll be a relief for her to not have to worry about me anymore. She does, you know . . . worry about me, I mean. Oh, and I hope you don't think I'm not grateful for all you've done for me. I truly am. If it weren't for you, I wouldn't be here at all." She stopped when she ran out of breath, and Peter ventured to answer.

"We wish you only the best," he said. "It's been a pleasure to travel with you."

She shook his hand in return, but then leaned down from her seat and hugged him tight. In surprise, Peter nearly lost his balance as she squeezed his neck hard. She pulled back and gave his cheek a big, wet kiss, then patted it. "You be good to that wife of yours, you hear?"

"I will," Peter said with a nod as he retreated.

A moment later, Charles sat beside Caroline in the buggy. He flicked the reins, and they soon disappeared down the street. Everyone seemed to sigh collectively. Maddie felt a tad melancholy. Caroline had a way of livening any situation and making even difficult moments seem lighter. Maddie would miss that.

"All right," Peter said. "I think we're ready. Let's go."

They all loaded onto the wagon, Maddie in the back with the children, Ellen in the middle with the baby, and Abe beside Peter. As the wagon lurched forward, Maddie looked out the rear and watched the temple disappear from view. The purpose of their journey was accomplished. So much had happened since they left home that Maddie felt like a different person. It wasn't all that long ago that she hadn't known Abe. Now she wanted nothing more than to be with him for the rest of her life—if only he'd accept what he already knew in his heart. Sometimes she toyed with the idea of marrying him even knowing he wasn't a believer—yet. But she knew as well as Abe did that it was a bad idea, even if she could convince him to do it.

For the first time in weeks, Maddie thought of Sister Brown and wondered how she had fared with the students in Maddie's absence. How would she handle losing another housemate? Would she go on to Woodruff alone? The thought was sad and disheartening at best.

Such thoughts occupied Maggie's mind as St. George grew smaller and eventually faded into the horizon. When she could no longer see any sign of the city, Maddie sighed, adjusted her position, and looked toward home.

CHAPTER 29

On that first day of travel, they faced going back up and over the steep switchbacks of Rock Canyon Dugway. They climbed higher until they passed through Canaan Gap. As the horses strained against the load, everyone got out of the wagon to walk. A couple of times Maddie ended up near Abe, but neither of them spoke. She had Lorenzo to worry about. Besides, breathing heavily and choosing solid places to step provided good excuses to not speak.

But they didn't stop Maddie from thinking plenty. And this time it wasn't about the beauty of the Hurricane Cliffs or the towering red and purple walls they passed through at Canaan Gap. It was about Abe.

Both of them spent much of their time avoiding one another, because neither could see the point in rekindling a friendship. Sunday the party rested just outside of Kanab. That day was harder for Maddie than the previous ones, as she had no excuse to avoid mingling and talking with everyone. She wasn't keeping Lorry in line or urging Mary to keep moving. And she couldn't just walk on the far side of the wagon to avoid Abe.

She spent much of the day apart from the camp, several hundred feet away, looking toward the spectacular cliffs rising out of the ground behind Kanab. She clutched her Bible and Book of Mormon to her chest until she found a good spot, free of prickles and with a rock for a seat. With her back to camp, she spent time reading her scriptures and thinking about her life since she had said good-bye to Edward under the tree the morning they left Snowflake.

She mourned for the friend Abe had been a few weeks ago, the person she could tell anything to. He had understood her heart in a way no one else ever had. It was as if a good friend had died, and the reminder of that death was constantly thrust into her face every time she laid eyes on him.

They reached Lee's Ferry midweek. The sight sent Maddie's heart racing. She clamped her eyes shut and turned away so her gaze wouldn't meander toward the riverbank where she and Abe had first kissed, across from where Roland had died, and where she had nearly drowned. With all the emotions tied to this place, Maddie wished she could live the rest of her life without ever seeing Lee's Ferry again.

Warren Johnson came out to meet them, smiling broadly. "Welcome back!" he called as he came out of the house. "How was your time at the temple?"

Peter hopped down from the wagon, and they shook hands heartily. "It was wonderful," Peter said. "Wouldn't trade it for anything in the world."

With a nod, Warren glanced over his shoulder at the house and a couple of the children who were peeking out the door. "Family's everything, isn't it? I'll tell you, seeing folks' faces like yours after being sealed, well, that's what makes my mission here worth doing. There's a reason the Lord called us here, and it's not just to help those going down to Arizona. It's to get those who are already there back to the temple."

It didn't take long for Warren, Abe, and Peter to get the wagon onto the ferry—which was blessedly dry and without any slippery spots. Even so, Maddie sat *inside* the wagon with the children as they crossed. She tried singing songs and playing silly finger games with Mary to keep them—and herself—calm as they crossed the water. When the ferry bumped into the far shore, her stomach turned over, and it was all she could do not to cry until she had hard ground under her feet again. On the other side, they said good-bye to Warren and made camp.

The sun set quickly behind Lee's Backbone, and as the light gave way to dusk, Maddie sat beside the fire, unwilling to sleep. She had half a mind to ask Peter why he decided to camp at Roland's place of death on their return trip. More than once her eyes drifted toward the riverbank and pulled back. Then she looked up at the ridge to the south, remembering all too well what it had been like to come up and over Lee's Backbone last time.

She dreaded what tomorrow would bring as they faced going down the other side. On their way north, she and Abe had worked together to keep the wagon from racing down the mountainside. She thought of how her feelings for Abe had begun to bud. How they kissed the day after he rescued her from the water.

Home. She just wanted to get home and put the past behind her. And yet, reaching home meant facing Edward. She stared at the flickering flames before her, dread in her stomach. Going home also meant seeing Abe in town, at least until he settled affairs with the house and Sister Brown. Would he leave then? She hoped so. And yet she wanted him to stay. But for what?

In frustration, she stood and stalked away from the fire to be alone. She had taken only a few steps when she saw Abe's shape in the darkness as he stood by the wagon. It made her pull to a stop.

"Hello, Maddie," he said, as if they had just met walking along a city street.

"Hello." She turned and began walking the other way.

"Maddie?"

Again, her feet stilled, and her hand went out to steady herself on the wagon. "Yes?" She stared at the ground, waiting.

Abe came around the wagon, and the sound of his footsteps made her knees shake. He stopped inches away from her. "I'm sorry. I really am."

Her throat tightened, and she couldn't speak. For an answer, she nodded, then managed, "I should have known when you told me about Lizzy and the certificate."

She pushed away from the wagon and ran off.

* * *

The next morning, Lee's Backbone rose into the sky, a forbidding structure. Looking at it from the north, it was clear how it had gotten its name. The ridge looked like a crooked spine going up toward the sky, as if some huge creature had died there eons ago.

"Are you sure you'll be able to walk?" Maddie asked Ellen as they sat among the bedrolls. "Maybe we'll be able to carry you over in the wagon after all."

"That's ridiculous and you know it," Ellen said. Baby William lay cradled in his mother's arms as he nursed.

"But you walked almost the entire way up Rock Canyon Dugway," Maddie protested. "You overdid it then and need to rest now."

"That was days ago," Ellen said. "I've been riding most of the way ever since we passed through Canaan Gap, so I can surely walk a couple of hours. And there's no chance anyone can force me into that wagon up there anyway," she added, pointing at the steep slope.

Maddie nodded, granting Ellen that point. Coming over it the first time had been hard enough, and they had been lucky, all things considered. No overturned wagon, no injured horses, just a few rattled nerves and chilled feet. They had fared much better than so many others who had crossed Lee's Backbone and survived with frightening stories and scars.

Ellen finished feeding William and set to burping him, while Maddie put Lorenzo's boots on the toddler. Abe approached them, and Maddie turned slightly away, avoiding his gaze. "The horses are ready," Abe said to Ellen. "What about the wagon? It's pretty empty now. Are you sure you want us to carry everything else?"

"Sure do," Peter said, coming up from behind. He put a hand on Abe's shoulder and pointed at the piles of supplies he had made. "Considering how tough it was on the horses getting up the other side last time—and then having the same weight bearing on them coming down the other—I think it'll be best for them to have as light a wagon as we can manage this time around."

"Lighter probably is better," Abe agreed.

Peter turned to his wife. "Ellen, how are you feeling?"

She gave the baby a kiss on his towhead and smiled. "We're doing just fine."

Peter leaned down and stroked his tiny son's head. He leaned in to Ellen and kissed her forehead. "You take care." Then, to Abe, "Let's go. Thanks for getting the horses ready." They walked to the wagon and finished arranging supplies in the order they should be brought over. "I'll follow in the wagon."

Abe grabbed two sacks of feed to carry over the mountain. "Glad to help." He headed on up the trail, carrying the sacks and taking long strides.

Peter planned to take the horses and wagon across as Abe and Maddie carried supplies. When the wagon and horses were over, Peter would help with the remaining load, and then they'd all return to help Ellen and the children. The process would take the entire day, but they weren't in any rush. Especially, Maddie thought with a pang of sadness, since Clara Franklin was no longer waiting for them at the end of their journey.

As Maddie surveyed the supplies, she was secretly glad Abe wouldn't be walking beside her. Truth be told, he was probably avoiding her as much as she was him. Peter urged the horses forward, and Maddie waited, a stack of pots and pans in her hands. She would follow behind, using the wagon as a barrier between her and Abe. He had managed to get quite far ahead already—deliberately, Maddie realized. He wanted her to be more comfortable. She sighed and adjusted a frying pan, then started up the base of Lee's Backbone.

If only he'd say a blasted prayer and get the answer that was already in his heart. If only he'd let go of pride he had developed as a boy, and just admit that he knew. The mule!

Tears threatened to well in her eyes, and Maddie gritted her teeth angrily to ward them off. Abe had said what he did because he thought it would give them both a chance at happiness in the future, that it would save them both pain. In reality, her heart felt shredded. But she couldn't be angry at Abe for that, not when it was his goodness and his love for her that made him do it.

As the grade increased, the horses slowed and dug their hooves in. Maddie paused, waiting for them to keep going. Perhaps they remembered Lee's Backbone from before.

"Come on, boys," Peter said, urging them forward. One horse slipped on the rocks and reared in panic, and Maddie took a couple of nervous steps backwards. Peter calmed the horses with his voice and the reins, and eventually they obeyed, moving slowly and scattering pebbles and dirt over the edge with each step.

For some reason, the way up the mountain felt longer this time. Maddie wondered if it was because this time she walked the path alone—and carried a burden. No, two burdens. Besides the pots, she also had an ache in her heart for Abe that made each step difficult.

Stop thinking such things, she chided herself. *Focus on the trail.* She glanced over her shoulder at Ellen and the children, a sight that grew smaller with each step. Ellen would get some much needed rest while she waited, Maddie thought. But climbing the mountain would be a challenge. Of course, Abe would help . . .

Abe again. She shook her head again and walked faster.

By the time Peter and the wagon neared the summit, Maddie's arms ached. She paused and set the pots down to rest her arms. She was grateful that Abe had already gone down the other side and she couldn't see him—at least for the moment. A couple of minutes later, the wagon crested the top and dropped out of sight.

Maddie sighed and leaned down to reach for the pots again, when a sudden yell from Peter shattered the air. Her head snapped up as her heart leapt into her throat. Sounds of rocks falling, thumps, and more yells followed, and she gripped her skirts.

What now? Abandoning the pots at the side of the path, she clambered up the mountain, scattering rocks in her haste. When she reached the summit, a cry ripped from her throat.

Several yards ahead, Abe lay perfectly still. His legs were bent at odd angles, and blood stained the ground. The wagon had finally come to a stop at the end of the switchback, unharmed from all appearances. Peter alighted, shaky and pale, and ran back up the path to Abe's side.

"No!" Maddie cried in terror and raced down the rocky terrain toward Abe. "Help him!" she screamed at Peter. She threw herself down beside Abe, who groaned softly. She closed her eyes in relief. He was alive. "Abe," she said, bringing his face around with trembling hands. "Abe, can you hear me?"

"Maddie?"

Tears sprang to her eyes, and her heart increased its pace. "Yes, it's me. Hold on, all right? You've got to hold on."

Abe's eyes were hard to read, disoriented; he couldn't focus on her face. Panic filled her as she looked at him, unsure of his injuries besides his broken legs. He grasped at his belly and moaned. Lifting his shirt, she saw bright red patches where the horses had trampled him. The angles of his legs made Maddie shudder; the wagon wheels had all but cut them to pieces. His entire body would be a collection of huge bruises in another day or so—if he lived that long. Maddie covered her mouth, knowing he surely had severe injuries to his insides as well.

She hadn't the slightest inkling what to do, but she knew Abe needed a doctor—now. And she would do everything in her power to prevent losing a second man that she loved. Resolutely, she stood and marched to Peter. He stood a pace off, still trembling, just staring in shock. With Roland's death, Maddie had been the one unable to think or move when faced with the situation. Peter had been the man of action.

"Is he—all right?" Peter's voice sounded tight.

"Not if he doesn't get help," Maddie said. "We've got to carry him to the wagon."

"The horses are still skittish," Peter protested. "They can't be driven until—"

"Then Abe will die," Maddie said, spitting the words out without softening them or her tone. "Help me!"

Peter numbly secured the reins around a large boulder, then followed Maddie to Abe's side. "You've got to carry him," Maddie informed her brother-in-law. "I'm not strong enough."

Silently, Peter obeyed, sliding his hands under Abe's limp body. The latter cringed and gritted his teeth at the increased pain. At Abe's obvious agony, Peter stopped.

"Now!" Maddie yelled at him.

With a nervous nod, Peter secured his grip and took painful step by painful step to the wagon. As he placed Abe inside, Maddie untied the reins and went to the horses. Rubbing their noses, she closed her eyes and whispered, "Father, please calm these animals. I need them. Abe needs them."

She opened her eyes and took a deep breath to calm herself. It didn't work. Impatiently, she waited for Peter to return. She eyed the sun—as if that meant anything at the moment—and found her hands gripping the leather straps so hard they bit into her skin. "Peter, hurry!"

A moment later, Peter came around to the front, tucking something into his pocket. Maddie was about to ask him why he moved slower than a tortoise when he said, "Sorry I took so long. Thought giving him a blessing would be worth it."

Maddie's protest stopped on her lips, and she was suddenly contrite. "Oh. Thank you for thinking of that." She bit her lip nervously, then added, "What did the blessing say? Is he going to be all right?"

One shoulder rose and then fell. "I don't know. All I was prompted to say was that he wouldn't be in too much pain and that God's will should be done."

A tight knot formed in her throat. In her experience, "God's will" tended to mean the person was about to die. At least, that's what it meant with her parents. She hadn't been reconciled with God's will back then, and certainly wasn't today, either, if it meant Abe losing his life. She didn't dare pray for God's will to be done. *I lack the faith this time, Lord. Just don't take him.*

Peter tilted his head toward the wagon. "Not much I could do to make him comfortable, but I tried. All the blankets are back with Ellen but one."

"I know," Maddie said, her middle feeling heavy and queasy at the same time. She fingered the reins, eager to get moving, to do something for Abe. "Thanks for trying."

"He doesn't look good," Peter pressed.

"I *know*," Maddie shot back.

Peter noticed the reins in her hands. "What do you think you're doing?" he asked, snatching them from her.

She grabbed them back. "I'm saving Abe. And *you* are going to stay with your wife and children."

"Maddie, you don't—" Peter began to protest. "He's not—"

But Maddie ignored him and climbed into the wagon. She might not be familiar with these horses—or remember much about driving a wagon. But that didn't matter. One look in Peter's eyes showed her that he thought Abe had no hope. The fact was, no one else would do everything in their power to save Abe. If no one else had hope, fine. As long as she could do something at all for him, she had hope. Doing this was her job, because no one else loved him as much as she did. Even if he *was* a stubborn old mule.

"I'll send the wagon back as soon as I can," she said, sitting on the bench and making sure her skirts were clear of the wheels—remembering that much. She gave a quick glance at Abe. His belly had started to swell—and the pain in his eyes ripped at her heart. With determination, she forced herself to look away and drive the team. She flicked the reins, and the horses took off down the next switchback and the road that would eventually lead toward the rutted trail and Bitter Springs.

Fitting name for today, Maddie thought. As the wagon gained speed, fear crept up her back and set the hairs on her neck on end. What if the horses took their head and she lost control? What if they wouldn't obey her? What if she gave the wrong command? What if they could sense she wasn't their master and didn't really know what she was doing?

As they went around another turn, she pulled on the reins to slow the horses. But a moan from Abe made her look at him. His face was turning pale, and another knot formed in her stomach. The sight cemented her determination. She turned back to the horses and flicked the reins to speed up the wagon.

If I let my nerves get the better of me, Abe will die. She held onto her courage, trying not to count how many years it had been since she had driven her father's team. To break the tension in the air, she began talking.

"Don't you dare die on me, Abe Franklin," she yelled over her shoulder. "You can't do that to me. You hear?" A few miles down the road, they left the mountain and headed fast down the wagon road. The horses picked up speed. The wind whipped Maddie's hair as she headed into the wilderness without water. Without food. With nothing but Abe and a shred of hope.

She gulped at the thought. If anything were to happen to her or the wagon, they'd be stranded in the middle of nowhere. And it wouldn't be just Abe's life that hung in the balance.

"Let's both do some praying," she said to Abe. "Harder than we've ever done before."

* * *

Bitter Springs.
Maddie thought that was the first settlement after Lee's Backbone. How many more hours of travel did she have ahead? Every so often

she took a peek at Abe, hoping he was still all right. The jostling and bumping must be absolutely horrific for him, but she didn't dare stop. Instead, she gritted her teeth and kept going, constantly reminding herself that making Abe hurt now might save his life if it meant reaching a doctor sooner.

The horses pulled the wagon along at a brisk trot, slower than the near gallop she had pressed them to before. When perspiration had begun foaming on their fur, she knew they needed a break and let them slow their pace, but she didn't dare let them stop altogether. Her eyes searched the landscape, hoping to see a blur in the distance that would mark a settlement, but saw nothing.

What had their trip north consisted of? She tried to remember details, but every day seemed so similar to the last that they all blended together. They hadn't traveled a full day from Bitter Springs to Lee's Backbone. She remembered that much, because Peter had made a point of keeping them at the base overnight so they could start up the ridge in the morning, rested.

Rested. What a foreign word that seemed. She couldn't contemplate resting for one moment. Instead, her entire body tensed as she sat ramrod straight at the bench and held the reins between her cramped fingers. No matter how fast the horses had gone before, it wasn't nearly fast enough for her. And she waited impatiently for the horses to be ready to speed up again. But as she sat there telling the horses what to do, she realized just how simple the task had become, as if she had always known how to drive a team.

Thank you, Lord, for helping me, she whispered, suddenly grateful. She had been so upset when she first jumped onto the wagon and took off that she hadn't recognized the hand of the Lord in getting her this far.

Thank you, Lord. But please—keep Abe alive.

The road crept by at a tortoise's pace, and Maddie wished for wings. Once more she looked behind at Abe, just long enough to make sure he was all right. Most times she just glanced back, saw the pinched look on his face, and returned her attention to the horses. But this time he lay motionless, his entire body sagging. Heart racing with fear, Maddie stopped the horses completely. She whipped around in her seat to check on him.

His face registered nothing, and even his jaw was slack. A hideous fear gripped her entire body, and she stared at his chest, nothing else in the world existing. At long last, his rib cage rose slightly, fell, and a few agonizing seconds later, finally rose again. Maddie let out a shaky breath. She turned to the horses, realizing she had been gripping the bench.

"Abe," she said in what she hoped was a comforting voice. "Can you hear me?"

No response. But his chest still rose and fell, and Maddie had to satisfy herself with that much. Perhaps he had fainted from the pain. A mixed blessing. The thought allowed her to return to the horses and get them going again, closer to Bitter Springs with every step. She couldn't help checking his breathing every so often. Once, a look at Abe registered a new concern. His belly looked more distended every time she checked on him. What did *that* mean?

With a shake of her head, she blinked hard several times and forced herself to focus on the rutted road before her. Worrying about Abe would slow them down, and if time could save him, she didn't want to be the cause of losing a moment.

But how much longer until they reached Bitter Springs? No dark line appeared on the horizon yet. She was on the right road; there were plenty of ruts to prove it. As each minute passed and the road crawled by, always looking the same as the last mile, she kept checking everything time and again.

The horses—Abe—the road—the horizon.

There must be a way to determine the distance, she decided. So she steered her thoughts back to their journey toward St. George. They had traveled from Bitter Springs to the base of Lee's Backbone in a little more than half a day. They also started out the day later than normal, she reminded herself, so the actual distance was probably twenty miles or less.

Maddie looked behind them. Lee's Backbone was nowhere in sight, and although it reassured her that they had traveled a considerable distance, it also made her feel more alone than ever. She had to reach Bitter Springs. She had no supplies, not even water in the barrels. Peter had emptied them to lighten the load before crossing Lee's Backbone.

Stop worrying, she told herself. *I need to figure the distance. I'm a teacher, for Pete's sake. I can solve an arithmetic problem.* She figured they must have averaged between three and four miles an hour on the way up from Snowflake. Since leaving Peter behind, she must have driven the horses at least twice that fast.

Maddie forced herself to clear her mind. How long had she been driving the team? It felt like hours and hours, but she knew that was due to her anxiety. If she was right in figuring the distance to Bitter Springs and how fast she was going, they might already be more than halfway, with another hour and a half to go.

Another glance behind her showed that Abe was getting worse fast. Would he make it that long? His face was pale, as if he had lost a lot of blood. Another prayer escaped her lips. *Lord, don't take another from me. I cannot bear it again.*

The horses seemed able to keep up the pace, although she knew they must be thirsty. "Sorry, boys," she called, urging them on. "In spite of the name, there's plenty of water at Bitter Springs, even if it's not the tastiest." She flicked the reins. "Let's go. You've had it easy long enough."

The talk of water made her realize that her entire body felt hot and parched. It was more of an observation than anything, since such things simply didn't matter. She might be thirsty, but Abe was in agony.

She looked over her shoulder. "You can wait too, you know," she told him, trying to hold back fear. Her nerves held her emotions so close to the surface, she found herself being terse and saying with almost a twinge of anger in her voice, "You're just going to have to hang on, you know. Be a mule."

Maddie turned back to the road, but then glanced at Abe again, realizing that his face had more expression than before. He had pulled his arms up around his chest, and his lips moved ever so slightly. His eyes were closed, but he was definitely conscious. She snapped the reins again to get the horses moving a little faster, the tiniest hint of a smile on her lips.

I think he's praying. Just like I told him to.

CHAPTER 30

There it was—Bitter Springs. At first Maddie could make out only a dark blur on the horizon. She pressed the horses to full speed, knowing that they hadn't far to go. They could make a final push, giving Abe a few extra minutes, which he might need to survive.

Heart beating heavily in her chest, Maddie snapped the reins again. "Faster! Let's go. Hiyah!" She practically stood up, leaning forward as if that might bring her a little closer to the settlement.

The blur had grown larger and darker. As Maddie stared at it, willing it to draw ever closer, she could make out shapes of buildings—a fence over here, a steeple of a church beyond. *Almost there,* she thought. *Hang on, Abe.* She hazarded a look over her shoulder and gasped. His face was white, and his eyelids were barely open, showing that his eyes had rolled into the back of his head. His lips no longer moved, his hands no longer clenched and unclenched like they had as he fought the pain. She could make out no sound of pain or moaning. Panic surging through her, Maddie kept whipping her head from the road to Abe and back again, checking on him, hoping to see his chest rising. She didn't.

"Abe!" The cry ripped from her throat, and it was all she could do not to throw the reins away and jump to his side over the bench.

She was nearing the first homestead of Bitter Springs, set apart of the town proper. She wanted desperately to stop and check on Abe, but instead she gritted her teeth and flicked the reins to get the horses moving even faster. "We're almost there," she called to both the animals and to Abe. "Just a little farther."

The animals whinnied in protest, hooves kicking up more dust as they tried to speed up. So quickly she could hardly register what happened, the gray on the right stepped in a hole and tripped. As the horse stumbled and tried to regain its footing, the wagon lurched violently to one side. The force caused its companion and the wagon to leave the road, then veer back. Maddie grasped onto the box just in time to save herself from being thrown off. The wagon headed straight toward a pile of rocks, and she grimaced, bracing herself and trying to steer away.

"Left!" she screamed at the horses, untangling the leather straps and turning them that direction. They obeyed, turning toward the east. With relief, Maddie saw the front wheel clear the stack of rocks. But a moment later the back wheel smashed into the pile. Spokes snapped, a wheel broke, and the back corner of the wagon crashed to the ground.

"Stop, you stupid horses! Stop!" Maddie yelled at the top of her lungs, pulling the reins and crossing her arms against her chest to help her lean against their force and keep from letting go. The wagon scraped against the ground as it gradually came to a stop. Every second felt like an hour to Maddie; every heartbeat was filled with terror. With another look over her shoulder, Maddie saw Abe huddled in the broken corner of the wagon. Finally they came to a blessed stop, although the horses kept pawing the ground and pulling against their bridles.

Maddie jumped off the wagon and wanted to race to the cabin some hundred feet away, but she didn't trust the skittish horses to stay put with Abe crippled behind them. She quickly freed the horses, not caring that she had no place to tie them. She'd need some other way to travel besides the wagon anyway. And all that mattered was Abe's safety.

She ran to the back of the smashed box, where she found Abe still crammed into the back corner that had dragged on the ground. He was still breathing. With both hands, she tried to help him straighten out. It took all her strength to lift his almost lifeless torso even a few inches.

"Abe," she said, "can you hear me?" He flopped to the side, still white, but his eyes had a slight pinch around them, as if they were contorted with suffering.

His broken legs! Maddie thought. They had to be in excruciating pain, tucked under him like that. Her hands trembled with mixed emotions as she gingerly tried to free his legs without hurting him further.

At least I know he's alive, she thought.

"I'll be back with help," Maddie said, leaning down and brushing some hair from his eyes. She hoped he could hear and understand. She hesitated, not wanting to leave.

What if I go, and while I'm gone he . . . no. I'll find help. And he'll be here when I return.

She leaned over the wagon edge and kissed his forehead, swallowing back emotion because she knew she had to be strong. Breaking down in tears would help no one. "I'll be back soon, Abe, I promise," she said. "Don't you dare go anywhere."

Once again lifting her skirts, Maddie bolted down the dirt road toward the cabin. When she reached it, she rapped hard on the door. "I need help!" she cried, out of breath. "Please!"

A middle-aged man opened the door, brow raised. "What's the matter?" He looked beyond Maddie at the mess of a wagon on the road and the free-roaming horses.

"My friend got run over." She turned and hurried toward Abe, beckoning for the man to follow. "He needs help, but the wagon's broken, so I have no way to move him."

The man nodded. "I can bring you into the city. Met a lady who moved in not a fortnight ago. She's practically a physician. Name's Julia Stoddard. Wait here." He hurried behind the house to a small stable in the rear, then came back several minutes later with a single horse and a small cart.

"It's not much," he apologized.

"It's enough," Maddie said gratefully, following him toward her damaged wagon.

"I'm Murray York," he told her as he hopped off the cart and crossed toward Abe.

"Madeline Stratton," she replied.

Murray and Maddie lifted Abe, who, to her relief and horror, moaned. Murray placed him in the cart, and she climbed in beside him. She held his hand and stroked the top of it, hating the sound of his painful cries. One time he stopped moaning, and her heart lurched. She held her breath as she waited for a sign that Abe wasn't going the way of all the earth. She noticed his forehead crumple with discomfort, and she let out her breath. Abe was breathing and feeling and thinking. And maybe he could feel her hand holding his, and she got some comfort from that.

The cart jostled more than the wagon had, and as they bumped along the rutted road, Maddie watched with angst as Abe's contorted legs slammed into the floor of the cart again and again. Finally in the city proper, they reached a whitewashed house, where the cart stopped. Murray tied up his horse and scooped Abe in his big arms. He kicked the house door open unceremoniously and walked right in. Maddie followed close behind.

"Julia? Julia!" he called out. "Hurry! Got a patient who needs you something terrible."

An instant later, a woman appeared. "What's going on?" she asked, tying an apron around her waist. She looked up and saw Abe's nearly dead form in Murray's arms.

"On my heavens!" she cried with a hint of a British accent. "Over there now."

"Are you—are you a doctor?" Maddie asked tentatively.

"Midwife and nurse," the lady answered in a curt tone, turning her back on Maddie and going to the table where Murray placed Abe. "But I've done a whole lot more than that at times." She began probing and inspecting Abe, oblivious to Maddie and Murray, who had backed away to give her room.

"Julia's worked beside some of the greatest surgeons in London," he said under his breath. "She was part of the war between North and South. Had to do some surgeries herself then—things like amputating soldiers' legs 'n' such."

Maddie shivered and looked at what she could see of Abe's form lying on the table behind the nurse. If his legs were too damaged, would they have to be cut off? More importantly, would he even live?

Julia inspected Abe's legs, belly, scrapes and wounds, then raced to the door, barking orders to the kitchen and up the stairs for family members to fetch supplies. She whirled around and headed back inside, her boots clomping on the wooden floor. The sound stopped abruptly, and Maddie looked up. Julia had turned at the doorway, face flushed.

"Wait out there," Julia said, pointing at the entry. "Surgery isn't for the faint of heart."

Surgery? The word gripped Maddie's insides, and she looked at Abe in a panic. "Will he be all right?"

Julia didn't answer right away. She swallowed and considered her answer. "It's his only hope, I'm afraid. I've got chloroform."

Maddie nodded, biting her lips together. She supposed the news of chloroform was supposed to make her feel better.

"I won't lie to you," Julia said. "I'm afraid for him."

"Will he keep his legs?"

"I—I hope so. I'll do my best, I promise." Julia touched Maddie's arm in a gesture of comfort.

"Thank you," Maddie said, her throat so tight her voice came out in a whisper.

Two people raced into the room with supplies Julia had called for, and she turned to get ready for the task at hand. But she paused before leaving and said, "Pray for him. And for me."

"I will," Maddie said.

Julia nodded silently, opened her mouth as if about to say something else, then shook her head and hurried to a sink in one corner, where she washed her hands and arms. Maddie turned her head, unable to look at Abe. She and Murray stepped into the entryway, and she closed the door behind them.

"Thank you, Mr. York," she said. "We couldn't have gotten here without your help."

"My pleasure," he said. "Or rather, it would have been a pleasure under other circumstances." He peered at the door and asked, "Were you coming from the Mormon temple?"

"Yes," Maddie replied. She almost added an explanation about how it was Peter and Ellen who got sealed, when Murray went on.

"You know, I see lots of people going past my house on the way up to St. George. I'm not a Mormon, but I can't help but admire you folk for making sacrifices for what you believe in." He shook his head sadly. "I sure hope he pulls through. It'd be such a pity to lose him after going all the way to the temple together."

"Oh, no," Maddie said, shaking her head. "Our party went to St. George, and some of us went to the temple. The two of us aren't . . ."

She lowered her face and bit her lips as emotion flooded her. The two of them *weren't* married, but they might be . . . someday . . . She didn't want to consider ever parting from Abe again.

For hours she had been strong for Abe, but after reaching Bitter Springs and getting him in the most capable hands in the area, there was nothing more she could do for him. His future was out of her hands, so being strong or weak made no difference. Her wall of resolution crumbled.

"We aren't married," she said, her voice cracking. Then she added, "Yet."

Murray patted her shoulder. It felt like her father's hand, and Maddie suddenly had a deep ache to see her parents again. A sob caught in her throat.

Murray's hand felt warm and secure as he said, "I hope you're married soon."

"So do I," she said quietly.

"Is there anything else I can help you with? Anything you need?"

"I don't know." Maddie couldn't think clearly, and nothing existed besides the moment.

"Where's the rest of your group?" he asked. "Do they need anything?"

"Ellen and Peter!" A hand flew to Maddie's mouth. "Yes, they'll need help. They're on the north side of Lee's Backbone waiting for me to return with the wagon."

A line cracked Murray's leathery, wrinkled skin. "That contraption of yours doesn't have any more miles in it," he said, patting her shoulder. "Don't you worry. I'll get them."

"Thank you," Maddie said with a wan smile. "You're so generous to help a total stranger who came banging on your door."

Murray shrugged at the compliment. "You call on me if you need anything. Anything at all. But first I'll go fetch your family." Before Maddie could utter a word, Murray stepped out, and the door clanged shut behind him.

Her emotions running hard, Maddie found a bench against the stairs and collapsed onto it. She dropped her head into her hands and closed her eyes. The tears refused to stay back, so she finally just let them come.

There was only one thing she could do for Abe. Lips moving silently and tears dripping onto her lap, she prayed harder than she ever had in her life.

* * *

Maddie didn't move from the bench for hours. At first she listened for any sounds coming from the other room. Every so often Julia barked an order, and someone would come out, thunder up the stairs or rush past Maddie into the kitchen, and moments later hurry back—carrying water, a container with a spray attachment containing some liquid, towels, a sharp knife. Sometimes the runner would be a young woman who looked to be somewhere between fifteen and twenty. Each time she came out, she'd pause awkwardly before Maddie, then bob her head with a mumbled, "Excuse me," before she shuffled away.

Other times it was an older gentleman, his heavy feet shaking the wooden floors as he barreled past, brow heavily creased and Maddie apparently invisible. He wore an apron with fresh blood spots on it. The sight sent a shiver of dread through her.

Each time she heard the door, Maddie sat up in anticipation—heart reeling and fingers grasping the edge of the bench—as she hoped to see Julia emerge and give her news about Abe's condition. But after several hours, Maddie grew so fatigued that her grip on the edge of the bench lessened, and her posture began to sag. The errand runners appeared less frequently, and Maddie could hear nothing from the room. She began staring at the opposite wall in a foggy mental haze.

She was unaware of the light fading outside the windows until she could hardly make out any shapes in the home's entryway, and everything began looking like dark shadows of varying blackness. A door opened, and Maddie's head instinctively went up again. Her head throbbed, and she put her hand to her forehead as she looked up, fully expecting to see yet another person racing out of the side room, but instead, it was the front door that had opened. Maddie squinted to see who stood in the doorway.

"Madeline, I've brought your sister," came a deep, gravelly voice.

"Murray?" The haze around Maddie's mind began clearing ever so slightly.

"Maddie!" Ellen pushed her way around Murray and ran into the entryway. Maddie stood and rushed into her arms, and the sisters grasped each other hard, crying together.

"I'm sorry I left you behind," Maddie sobbed into her sister's shoulder. "I'm sorry I broke the wagon, and—"

"It's all right," Ellen interrupted, rubbing her sister's back as she might have done to baby William. "It's all right. We're all fine. Don't worry." She pulled away and held her sister by the shoulders. "Really."

By then, Maddie had completely broken down and sobbed uncontrollably. She gestured toward the closed side door and shook her head. Ellen followed Maddie's finger. "Abe?"

Maddie nodded miserably.

"Is he . . ." Ellen's voice trailed off, not able to finish the thought they were both having.

Maddie wrapped her arms around herself and sniffed. "I don't know."

"I hate to interrupt," Murray said, stepping closer. "But Ellen, how 'bout I take your family back to my place for the night? I'm no great cook, but I can find some bread and cheese and warm up some potato soup. You must all be hungry and spent."

"Thank you," Ellen said, confirming with a nod to Peter, who stood in the doorway with the children. "We'd love a place to stay."

"Then let's pile in the cart and get back," Murray said. He took a step closer to Maddie and leaned toward her. "Haven't heard any word, then?"

She shook her head and lifted her chin in an attempt at bravery. "Nothing."

"Nothing means there's hope." He put an arm around her and added, "I suppose you want to stay here."

Not trusting herself to say much, Maddie managed only a nod, grateful that Murray understood. "Thanks," she whispered hoarsely.

He gave her a weak smile. "You remind me of my daughter," he said. "And I'd do anything for Betty." He turned to Ellen and Peter, then called, "All right, then. I'll take you folks back, and I'll come for Madeline later."

Ellen took her sister's hands and studied her eyes. "Will you be all right alone? Peter can go ahead with the children, and I can stay here."

Maddie lowered her head; the pain reflecting in Ellen's eyes was too much to handle. "Thank you for wanting to stay, but I can manage."

Ellen nodded, but Maddie didn't know if that meant she understood. Ellen turned to Murray and said, "I brought a bag of jerky and a couple of biscuits with us in your cart. I'll bring them in. She'll need something to keep up her strength."

Maddie felt no hunger when Ellen brought in the two little sacks and put them on the bench. Food held no interest for her at all; the bags might as well have held sawdust for all she cared. How could she worry about something as trivial as her own comfort when Abe's very life was so uncertain?

"Promise me you'll eat something." Ellen scooted the sacks closer to Maddie, who lifted one shoulder in a halfhearted shrug. "Maddie," Ellen said fiercely, "when Abe comes out of there, he'll need you. And you need to be strong when that happens. Eat for him."

Something about her words cut through the void in Maddie's mind, and she nodded. "I will," she promised.

Satisfied, Ellen sighed and stepped back. "I'll be back in the morning."

Maddie nodded, wishing they would all just leave without any formal good-byes and pleasantries. Every moment she had to hold herself together was agony; she felt ready to fall into a million pieces, and it was all she could do not to cry out, demanding that they leave her alone.

Peter finally turned to the street, Murray followed, and Ellen went last. She paused at the door and said, "I love you, Maddie."

Maddie's voice choked up. "I love you too."

The door closed behind Ellen. Maddie's strength spent, she dropped to the bench and ignored the food beside her. With the tips of her fingers, she rubbed her forehead and tried to breath evenly. *I must be strong for Abe,* she thought, and repeated the words over and over.

The side-room door finally creaked open, this time slowly instead of with the abrupt clang it had made before. Julia stepped into the entry, and Maddie practically jumped to her feet. All fatigue vanished as anxiety shot through her body. She couldn't tell anything from Julia's demeanor; the nurse looked pale and bone-weary. She gripped the door frame as if she needed the support or she'd fall over. In her other hand was a candle, which spilled golden light across her apron, stained red.

"Is—is he all right?" Maddie asked. She held her breath, feeling as if the rest of her life hinged on the answer.

"I hope so. I *think* so," Julia said. She ran a hand over her face and blinked heavily. "I've never seen anything like that before."

She walked into the hall, where she sat on the bench that had kept Maddie company all evening, then set the candle down beside her. The room took on eerie shadows and shapes, giving Maddie the urge to blow out the candle and return the entryway to peaceful darkness.

Julia spoke again, this time more quietly. "You prayed for me, didn't you?"

"I have been praying for you and Abe ever since he went in there," Maddie said, nodding toward the room.

"Thank you." Julia gave a slight shake of her head and added, "I did things I didn't know how to do. I knew what was wrong with him—I could see it in my mind—and I knew what to do." Exhausted and emotionally spent, she dropped her hands to her lap.

"What *was* wrong with him?" Maddie asked in a reverent whisper. "What did you do?" She crossed and sat beside Julia, whose head still shook back and forth in disbelief.

"For starters, he was bleeding inside, with nowhere for it to go. That's why his belly was so large. It would have killed him had you not gotten here when you did. Frankly, I'm surprised he hadn't already bled to death when you got here."

Maddie didn't pause to consider the role she had played in saving his life, instead wanting to know what had happened while she waited on the other side of the closed door. "How did you stop the bleeding?"

Julia's brow furrowed. "It's all rather complicated, but let's just say that I knew what part was causing the problem and that I had to take out his spleen."

Maddie didn't know what a spleen was or why a body could do without it, but she trusted the nurse. "So the bleeding is stopped?"

For the first time, Julia's lips curved. "I think so." She turned to Maddie and took her hands. "I've assisted surgeons attempting the same operation I just performed—and failing. To be honest, we won't know for a few days if the operation was a success. Patients often have problems after, and with his legs . . . " Julia's voice trailed off, and she took a deep breath before going on. "You see, they're severely broken. One fracture almost punctured an artery." When Maddie's face registered no understanding, Julia explained, "In that case, he would have bled to death. Often with fractures this serious, amputation is the only option."

Eyes wide, Maddie's hands gripped Julia's. "But you fixed them? He still has his legs?"

"He stayed under the chloroform longer than anyone I've ever seen. I was able to set every bone properly and get them secured with plaster." She sighed hard. "He'll have a long recovery ahead, from the surgery and his mending bones. And someone will have to regularly swab all his wounds with antiseptic." Julia looked hesitant to claim victory, but she gave a smile and put a hand on Maddie's shoulder, giving her some hope to cling to. "As long as he doesn't get an infection, I think he has a good chance of recovery."

Maddie put a hand over her chest, where emotion bubbled up. "Thank you so much."

"Thank you for your prayers." Julia patted Maddie's leg. "I think they did it, not me." Julia stood, removed her apron, and took a step toward the kitchen. "I need to get something to eat, then I'll watch over him through the night. My husband is with him now." She took another step toward the kitchen, then paused. "Do you want to have a bite with me? And of course you can spend the night in our spare room."

"Thank you," Maddie said. "I'd like that." She remembered the two sacks Ellen had left before and felt slightly guilty for not keeping her promise; it hadn't been intentional. "Can I see him first?"

Julia nodded. "I think so. Just be prepared for him not to be his normal self."

The prospect of seeing Abe again—alive—sent Maddie's heart beating hard. "Thank you," she said. "I'll join you in the kitchen before long."

"If I finish before you come, I'll leave something out for you," Julia promised before ducking out of the room.

Maddie reached for the doorknob and noticed her hand trembling. She clasped her hands together and tried to stop it. Her emotions had been stripped raw during the day, and going to see Abe brought up as much fear as joy in her. Was she prepared to see him?

Forcing such thoughts out of her mind, she reached out and took hold of the doorknob, turning it soundly and pulling the door open. At the far side was a long table, beside which an elderly gentleman sat, reading the Bible by lamplight.

And on the table, most of his body draped with a sheet, lay Abe. As Maddie stepped inside, she could see that his legs were encased in plaster casts, and they were rigged up on some sort of device. She couldn't see evidence of his abdominal surgery through the sheet, although both the floor and sheet had blood stains that testified of it. His eyes were closed, as if he slept peacefully. His chest rose and fell easily. After all the times in the wagon that Maggie checked his breathing—hoping to see his chest going in and out—the sight of his smooth breathing brought a knot to her throat. She covered her mouth with a hand to stifle a cry.

Julia's husband raised his eyes from his reading, face lined with concern for her. "I'm so sorry," he said, standing beside her. "This must be such a trial for you."

She merely nodded and blinked, sending two plump tears down her cheeks. Leaning over Abe, she combed her fingers through his thick, black hair, then kissed his forehead. "You're going to be well again, just you wait and see," she whispered. "You can't leave me. I won't let you."

And she kissed his forehead again.

CHAPTER 31

Abe stayed in Julia's makeshift parlor-hospital room for several days, until she felt certain he was well enough to be transported to someplace more comfortable. Not only would more peaceful surroundings be good for Abe, but Julia needed her examination room back. Fortunately, Brother and Sister Hatch, who lived across the street, offered their home to both Abe and Maddie. Their children were grown, and they had the space.

Carrying Abe up the stairs to the Hatches' spare room was a challenge that took four men. But once Abe was settled, the soft bed and cozy atmosphere lifted his spirits in spite of his constant pain.

Maddie stayed with him virtually around the clock, following all of Julia's instructions and doing anything she could think of to ease Abe's discomfort. Julia came twice a day to swab his incision and other wounds with antiseptic solution and change his bandages, but Maddie did most of the other things. The only time she left his side for any length of time was when Peter and Ellen left town. With their wagon beyond repair, they had borrowed another family's wagon with promises to return it soon or send money to pay for a new one.

"Are you sure you don't want to come home with us?" Ellen asked on the doorstep to the Hatch home. "What about the school?"

"They're in good hands with Sister Brown," Maddie said. "I think she'll be fine—provided Avery isn't causing too much trouble. She wanted the work."

Ellen nodded, still unsure, and Maddie wondered if her sister's concern was for another reason. "Do you need me to come home with you?" Maddie asked. "I know it'll be a little tough going home with three children instead of two, and fewer adults to help."

Ellen turned her head away so Maddie couldn't see her expression well. "It's not that," she said. "We're past the toughest part of the road. I just worry about you. We've never been apart."

Maddie hadn't realized that. "Goodness, you're right. I'll miss you too, but I won't be gone long. Just until Abe can come home." *Home.* Snowflake was his home now. She wondered what he would think of that, especially coming back without his mother. Again she wondered if he'd stay.

Lowering her head, Ellen nodded, studying her hands. "There's something else I'm worried about. What will happen with you and Abe?"

"I don't know," Maddie said.

"What about Edward?" Ellen pressed. "What should I tell him?"

Maddie considered, then finally sighed. "It's not your duty to tell him anything. It's on my shoulders. No matter what happens with Abe, I'm the one who needs to talk to Edward."

Neither sister said anything for a moment. There was nothing left but to leave, and neither was ready for that. "I'll see you soon," Maddie said, unwilling to actually say, "Good-bye." She leaned forward and gave her sister a hug. "Thank you for everything. God speed your journey."

"We'll pray for you—and Abe," Ellen said, pulling back and holding Maddie at arm's length. They squeezed hands, smiled at each other, and let go. Ellen went to the borrowed wagon, where Peter and the children waited. He handed baby William to Ellen, and she snuggled him into her arms. Peter snapped the reins, and they were off.

Maddie stayed on the porch, waving at her niece and nephew, who were in the back of the wagon frantically waving back and jumping around. When they were out of sight, she sighed and went back into the house. She would miss her sister and the children. Not just while she stayed here with Abe, but in the future, because even if she went back to live with them, it probably wouldn't be for long, but only as a temporary guest.

She still clung to the hope that she would leave their home as Mrs. Franklin, but if that didn't happen, she would still leave Ellen and Peter's house. If Abe stayed in Snowflake, would she be able to bear living in the same town? The thought cut into her heart, and she tried not to dwell on it as she climbed the stairs to the spare room, where Abe had been taking a nap.

Pausing in the doorway, she gazed at him lying in the bed, eyes closed. In the quiet of the moment, she thought through their argument on the street, when Abe put an end to their relationship. Not her hope of one, however. Most days she went on, optimistic that someday Abe would come around. But at moments like this, when all was quiet and she wasn't busy nursing him back to health, a different future presented itself to her, and she had to face that it could come to pass.

Although in the private spaces of Maddie's heart she wanted nothing more than to be his wife, she knew the most important thing now was to focus on getting Abe better. Even if her dreams would later be dashed, she'd always be able to look back, knowing that she had done everything in her power to make them happen. She went in, sat again at the chair by his bedside, and took his hand in hers. It was cold, so she began rubbing his fingers to warm them.

I'm not going to do the same thing again because it's not just me I'd hurt this time. It'd be you, too. Abe's words returned to her.

She pushed a lock of hair behind her ear and kept rubbing his hand. *I'm already hurting, and it won't stop anytime soon.*

Maddie looked at Abe's sleeping face, and her fingers paused in their work as she remembered something else he had said: *I care too much about you to do that.*

The thought made her lips press together with determination. It was the knowledge that Abe cared about her that kept her hope alive. If he had said he didn't have feelings for her, she would have mourned in private and moved on. She sighed. If only she knew what the future held.

Abe suddenly squeezed her hand, and she looked over to see him awake and smiling.

"Good morning," she said, putting on a smile. She hoped that her turbulent emotions wouldn't be apparent on her face.

Abe eyed the window. "Is it? Still morning, I mean."

"For another hour," Maddie said, moving toward the side table. Her thoughts of what tomorrow would hold were brushed away as she went into action and became Abe's nurse once more. "Sister

Hatch brought up some soup with bread and butter. Would you like some?"

"Yes, thanks." Abe gave Maddie a grateful smile. She could see pain in his eyes that he was trying to hide. That made her ache, but she refused to let him see her worry, so she turned to the food and began feeding him, since he couldn't do that himself yet. One arm was in a splint because of torn shoulder muscles, and he couldn't sit up at all because of his abdomen. He lay propped up by several pillows, and Maddie had to help him eat and drink as best she could.

Halfway through his meal, an elderly neighbor peeked her head around the bedroom door. Maddie looked up when the woman spoke.

"Hello there. I'm Sister Clark, a friend of Sister Hatch."

"Oh, hello," Maddie said, scooping more soup into the spoon.

"I just came by for tea," Sister Clark went on. "Sister Hatch tells me you've been by his side night and day."

"I sure have," Maddie said with a smile and a look at Abe. "I've even learned how to shave him." She patted Abe's smooth cheek, which she had shaved just that morning. He grunted, but she could tell he wanted to laugh.

"Only nicked me twice this time," he said.

Sister Clark clutched at the lace at the neck of her dress and sighed, leaning against the door frame. "That's so wonderful," she said, apparently not noticing the banter between Abe and Maddie. "It's certainly heartwarming to see young married people treating each other so well."

"Thank you so much," Maddie said, ignoring the look from Abe when she didn't correct the woman. The comment stung her heart, but she decided to make light of it instead of showing the reality. "Of course, I've only done what any wife would do."

"Oh, I wouldn't say that," the gray-haired woman replied with a firm shake of her head. "You're one special girl." Then she addressed Abe and wagged a finger at him. "You get well soon, so you can take care of her. With a heart of gold like she has, she deserves it."

"Yes, ma'am," Abe said with an obedient nod. When she left down the hall, Abe licked some broth off his lip and said wryly, "You lied to that woman."

"No I didn't," Maddie said, putting the soup bowl on the side table and reaching for the water glass. "I simply didn't correct her assumption."

"May I ask why?" Abe's mouth twitched with amusement.

"Because one shouldn't argue with one's elders, especially about matters that are really only a matter of time. Water?" She held out the glass for him. Even though she kept her tone light, she ached for the words to be true and for Abe to say something to make them so.

Abe ignored the offer. "We're not married."

"Well, no, not yet," Maddie said in response, putting the glass back on the table. "But we will be, or that makes *you* a liar. You promised her you'd take care of me." She stopped and held her breath, but wore a slightly smug look on her face as she waited for his response. She arranged his blankets, smoothing them out, then met his eyes.

"I didn't say that," he countered.

"Yes, you did. You said, 'Yes, ma'am.'" Maddie gave him a napkin, still businesslike.

"What makes you think I'll change my mind?" Abe asked, taking the napkin and balling it in his one free hand. His tone had gotten serious, although she could tell that it was easier for them both to talk about such a serious issue in playful terms. "You have done so much for me since the accident. I know I'll never be able to repay any of it. And you know I love you. But as far as our faiths go, we're still in the same situation as before. I don't want to hurt you like I did Lizzy."

She took the napkin and paused for just a moment, his blunt statement taking her aback slightly. Had *nothing* changed? She couldn't believe that. Her entire life had turned upside down since the accident. And she simply couldn't imagine life without Abe. Would more change? Would he insist they stay apart?

She sat beside him where she'd sat for so many hours over so many days. She tried to lighten her tone to hide her fears. "First of all, Abe, I saved your life and have nursed you back to health. And like it or not, I'm staying by your side as long as you need the attention."

"Yes, you did and you have, and as I said, I'll never be able to thank you enough, but marrying you—"

Maddie held up a hand to stop him. "Words and platitudes aren't enough. You *owe* me something for all that." She eyed the ceiling. "Hmm. I think a lifetime at your side should do. But there's more."

Abe folded his free arm across his chest—which lacked the power such an action would have had with two arms. "I can't wait to hear it." Amusement danced in his eyes.

Happiness went through Maddie as she remembered the feeling that Abe was praying because he believed in a God who would answer him. "The truth is, Mr. Franklin, you aren't the unbeliever you purport to be."

"What?" Abe looked sincerely perplexed and almost offended.

"And you called *me* a liar."

"Maddie," he warned her. "We've had this conversation before." He tried to sit up, but the pain forced him back down to the pillows with a wince. "How can you possibly know what I do or do not believe?"

Maddie smoothed his hair back and cupped his cheek in her hand. She took a deep breath—heart pounding as she took the plunge. "You've shown me your faith along the trail. Remember Ellen's blessing? Then there were those feelings you had with your mother before she passed. And before we left, Caroline told me something else—that she overheard you after your walk with Dr. Willis. You felt something when you walked around the temple with him."

"That gossip," Abe muttered.

She studied his face, saving her best arrow for last. "And after the accident, you prayed in the wagon—didn't you?"

Their eyes locked for a moment. Maddie didn't need him to admit to anything. She had no desire to trap him, just to point out something he hadn't realized on his own. And he didn't deny it. His eyes confirmed the truth of her words.

"You *do* believe in God," she said. "And that should be enough."

He reached up and took her hand from his face. "What about a temple sealing? Don't you still want that?"

"Of course I do. But I also want—you. And if you'd stop being so stubborn, you'd admit that I could have both." She stopped, her heart ready to burst if Abe didn't agree.

"But—"

"But nothing," Maddie said, putting her fingers over his lips. They had discussed the situation numerous times, and always came to the same place. "You need to rest and heal up. We'll talk about it later." He had a crumb of bread on one of his lips. Maddie gingerly reached over and wiped her thumb over his mouth. "Stubborn old mule."

Abe turned his head and kissed her hand. "Read to me?"

"Of course." She retrieved a book from the floor that held a bookmark in it. They were halfway through Dinah Craik's *Life for a Life*, which they had borrowed from the Hatches' personal library. They had reached the moment when the heroine discusses scripture with Dr. Urquhart, and how he believed that the one main doctrine throughout the Bible was repentance.

"'Thus ended our little talk: yet it left a pleasant impression. True, the subject was strange enough; my sisters might have been shocked at it; and at my freedom in asking and giving opinions.'" Maddie could relate to this sentiment; she and Abe had shared many conversations on a variety of "strange" subjects.

As she continued to read, Abe reached out and took her left hand with his free hand. She looked over in surprise, but his eyes were closed. A smile broke across her face, and she continued, not realizing until she reached it what passage came next.

"'Oh, the comfort—the inexpressible comfort of feeling safe with a person—having neither to weigh thoughts nor measure words, but pouring them all right out, just as they are, chaff and grain together; certain that a faithful hand will take and sift them, keep what is worth keeping . . .'"

He opened his eyes, and they smiled at each other. Together they finished the line. "'And then with the breath of kindness blow the rest away.'"

* * *

Mornings came and passed into evenings over and over again, while Maddie cared for Abe. Julia continued to come daily to dress Abe's wounds and give Maddie instructions on his care. Sister Hatch kept Maddie under watchful eyes, making sure everyone knew that the two young people were chaperoned. Sister Hatch also spelled Maddie when she was tired. Abe and Maddie talked little about spiritual things, mostly because they ended up arguing more often than not.

After several weeks, Abe was feeling better, and Maddie spent more time in the evenings alone by the fireplace with a quilt wrapped around her. She gazed into the flames and thought hard about all the things they were leaving unspoken—all the things about their future. Her future.

Somehow, in a way she couldn't explain and wouldn't even try, she felt her options didn't amount to two: Abe *or* a temple marriage with Edward. She had learned enough over the course of this trip to know that whatever else happened, she had to give Edward his ring back. A third option presented itself to Maddie, one she tried to avoid thinking about: temple marriage to someone other than Abe or Edward. The thought was almost unimaginable, and she brushed it aside, unwilling to give it space in her mind. She still clung to the hope that Abe would soon be able to give her all she wanted.

After all, he had more faith than he wanted to admit. He had prayed, and by all accounts had received what he had asked for. Surely Abe would take her to the temple someday. Deep inside, he already had a testimony. He just had to fight against a lifetime of pushing the Church away to see it.

But what if he never did see beyond the pains of his past? Maddie shook her head and looked away from the fire. She began picking at the stitches in the quilt, reluctantly admitting to an idea she didn't want to acknowledge—that perhaps a future lay before her without Abe in it.

Then why have I felt that sticking with Abe has been the right thing to do? She pulled the blanket tighter, as if it might offer her the comfort she sought. For weeks now she had followed a path that she felt peace about—complete assurance about. Deep in her heart, she knew she could never marry someone who didn't embrace the gospel, that God wouldn't condone her doing such a thing. Abe joining the Church was the only way she could reconcile her peaceful feelings about their relationship while keeping true to her convictions. Surely if the Lord brought them together, it was only a matter of time before Abe joined the Church. And yet . . .

I feel like a child, she thought. *I don't know what to do, and I'm afraid of what's coming next.* She thought back to her mother and wished she could climb into her lap and be held, that her mother could sing a lullaby and make everything better. Maddie remembered how safe she felt with her mother, even doing everyday tasks. Life was uncomplicated then, consisting of schoolwork, chores, and those quiet moments of stitching with her mother at her side. Sitting beside her mother, Maddie would watch her make tiny, even stitches and wonder if her large, lumpy ones would ever look so neat.

In such quiet moments, her mother would talk of the future, of the past, or of the troubles in young Maddie's life. It was on one of those days when Maddie had come from school upset because her best friend had abandoned her for another girl, spreading rumors about her that were wholly untrue. Maddie could hardly see her needlework for her tears. "It makes me so angry, Mama," she said with a sniff. "I just want to go to school and invent mean gossip about *her* and—"

"It's sometimes hard to do what you know is right," her mother said quietly. "Especially when you've been wronged and you hurt so much. Isn't it?"

Maddie nodded and wiped her tears with the back of her hand. She knew her thoughts weren't good ones, and she was ashamed of them, but they were how she felt.

Her mother put her work on her lap and reached for Maddie's hand. "You're eight years old now. You've been baptized. So I know that no matter how much you're hurting, no matter how much you'd like to get back at her, you'll do what's right. And the Lord knows it too."

Now as Maddie sat before the Hatches' fireplace, with Abe sleeping upstairs, she felt like that eight-year-old girl again. She could almost hear her mother's words.

I'll know you'll do what's right. And the Lord knows it too.

So what *was* the right thing to do? She hadn't been doing the wrong thing so far; she knew that in her heart. But how long was too long to sit and wait for Abe to come around? Maddie closed her eyes, and a tear tumbled down each cheek as a heartrending but perfectly clear feeling washed over her.

Any longer is too long. Now was the time. Time for her to go home and move on to the next stage of her life, even if that meant going without Abe. Her time with him had served a purpose, of that she was sure. Maddie hoped to someday know what that purpose was. But for now she would have to trust in faith that she could do what she needed to do—walk away.

She sighed heavily. *Walk away.* It sounded so simple. Maddie's hands covered her face.

Oh, I miss you, Mama. I wish you were here to hold me.

* * *

Julia came into the bedroom carrying a brand-new cane. "This is for you, Abe," she declared, coming across the room and standing at the foot of his bed. "Today I'll take your casts off, and you'll be walking with this for a while."

"That's wonderful!" Maddie said, clapping her hands together. The news sent a thrill through her. By the looks of him, Abe wanted to jump off the bed right away and walk all over town. Since he had seen nothing but the four blue walls of the room he'd lain in for two months, Maddie didn't blame him.

"Now, now," Julia said, coming to the side of the bed and pushing Abe back to his pillows. "Don't get too excited. Your muscles will be weak, and it'll take some time for your legs to regain their strength. Walking will be painful at first, I imagine. So don't get discouraged or try to do more than your legs are ready for, or you may end up right back in bed. And you'd better use the cane with every step."

She handed Abe the cane, and he tapped it on the floor. "I promise," he said, grinning widely.

Maddie excused herself so Julia could cut off the casts in private with the help of Brother Hatch. She waited just outside the door, biting her lower lip with eager anticipation. At Maddie's side, Sister Hatch seemed as excited as anyone. "He's become almost a part of the family," she said, clutching her chest and getting teary eyed. "It's such a relief to see him doing so well. He doesn't need us so much now, does he?"

She fell into Maddie's arms and hugged her, but her words struck Maddie and pierced her heart. Sister Hatch was right; Abe didn't need Maddie at his side as much anymore. He wasn't in ongoing pain. He could sit up and feed himself. Julia came over less often.

Sister Hatch pulled away, dabbed at her eyes, and scurried down the stairs to spread the news to her neighbors. As she left, Maddie turned to the closed door, suddenly heartsick. It was time to go.

A moment later, Julia opened the door to reveal Abe sitting up in bed, wearing trousers. He looked different, somehow, sitting all the way up rather than reclined. Stronger. More handsome. Maddie felt a love for him that overwhelmed her. She almost cried out at what she knew she had to do. But she wouldn't spoil Abe's moment for the world.

Abe, thrilled over his recovery, knew nothing of her turmoil. He couldn't stop smiling. "Can I try now?" he asked Julia.

"Almost," she said, gesturing for Brother Hatch to join her. They each supported one side of Abe's weight. Taking a deep breath, Abe steadied himself on the cane and slowly stood to his full height.

Tears sprang to Maddie's eyes as all the emotion from the harried wagon ride, Murray's help, and the surgery came back in a wave. Fear that he would never speak again, let alone stand. A hand went to her mouth. "Praise the Lord," she whispered.

CHAPTER 32

Maddie didn't sleep that night. Brother Hatch and Murray York were the only others who knew what the morrow would bring. She didn't mean to stay awake, but her thoughts and emotions kept swirling, preventing her from sleeping. She spent an hour writing a lengthy letter to Sister Hatch, explaining the situation and expressing her deepest gratitude for all the sister had done for both Maddie and Abe in opening her home. Maddie knew she'd never be able to repay the kindness, and she felt guilty knowing she would probably not see Sister Hatch in person to thank her properly.

When the parlor finally went from black to gray with the early light of dawn, Maddie got up, folded her blankets, and got dressed. She moved in a mechanical fashion, unwilling to think or to feel because doing so would make her cry all over again—something she had spent most of the night doing. She packed her meager belongings, then did her hair with the looking glass on the wall. She took in her reflection with sadness. Her eyes were puffy and red, with blue circles under them. She turned away and put her hair up without it.

After putting the last of her things in her bag, she stood, straightened her dress, and walked out of the parlor. She deposited the bag by the front door, placed the letter for Sister Hatch on the kitchen table, then went to the base of the stairs and caught her breath.

Lord, give me strength to do this.

She opened her eyes and took the steps slowly, wondering if anyone else was awake in the house. When she reached Abe's room, she knocked.

Some movement came from the other side of the door, followed by a weary-sounding, "Come in."

Maddie's stomach knotted. How many more times would she hear Abe's voice? She turned the knob and pushed the door open. His hair was disheveled, and he wore a look of surprise on his face. "Maddie, what's wrong?" He gingerly brought his legs off the bed and moved into a sitting position as if making room for her at the end of his bed.

Her feet felt rooted to the planks of the floor, and she stayed in the doorway. "Abe," she said, her voice catching. She cleared her throat. "I'm going home, unless anything has changed."

They both knew what she meant by that statement. Had anything changed in his faith? His brow furrowed, and he looked like he wanted to cross the room to argue, but couldn't. He looked around for his cane, but she stepped forward and interrupted just as he located the cane and grabbed it. "You don't need me here anymore. It's time I get back to my life in Snowflake."

Abe stared at her for a moment, trying to read her face. She looked away, and he spoke, his voice filled with hurt and confusion. "Back to your life? Do you mean back to Edward?"

For a moment, all she could do was shake her head. She wiped at tears forming in her eyes, wishing she could stamp out her heart so she wouldn't hurt this much. "No, Abe. You know me better than that. I'm returning his ring."

"But you can do that no matter when you go back," Abe said, moving to steady himself on the cane.

"And that's now."

"Why?" His single word hung in the air. Maddie gazed into his eyes, wondering if he really didn't know or understand.

"I can't go on like this, Abe. I've given you everything I have. The only thing I've asked in return is for you to seek for the truth, and you've refused to do that. You said yourself that we wouldn't make a good match with differing beliefs. I don't think our beliefs are all that different, but you do. So there's no point in either of us going on like this."

Abe sat back as if she had just delivered a blow. Clearly he had avoided thinking about what the future would bring between them.

For two months they had been living in the present, not thinking beyond the moment.

"I had hoped you would look past your father and the other pains in your life and see what your mother believed in." She hesitated, wanting so much to run to him and clasp him in a final embrace, but she didn't trust herself. If she felt his arms around her again, she might lose her resolve. Instead, she swallowed hard. "I'm so sorry, Abe, because I love you. More than anyone."

She backed out of the room, grasping the doorknob and pulling the door closed. When it clicked shut, her entire body began trembling. She raced down the stairs, grabbed her bag, and went onto the porch, slamming the outside door behind her. It was finished.

She waited, shaking and crying, until Murray arrived. For once she was grateful that Abe couldn't run after her. Even if he were well, though, would he? Not after declaring for so long that they didn't belong together.

"Morning," Murray said with a tilt of his hat.

"Good morning, Mr. York," she said, climbing up beside him.

"Should we wait to say good-bye to the Hatches?"

Maddie looked up at Abe's window and shook her head. "I left a letter explaining, and Brother Hatch already knows. I need to go now."

"As you wish." Murray flicked the reins.

Maddie moved out toward home, eyes closed and trying her hardest not to look back.

* * *

Abe spent the day in a stupor. Not even Julia could get him out of bed to take a turn around the room to strengthen his legs. All he could think about was Maddie telling him good-bye. None of his emotions made sense. Hadn't he been the one trying to convince Maddie that they shouldn't be together? Then why did her departure hurt so much?

Sister Hatch brought him food, but he didn't touch it. His breakfast tray was removed looking as it had when she placed it on the side table. The same with his other meals. He couldn't eat. He couldn't sleep. And in many ways, the ache in his heart was worse than the pain he had undergone from the accident.

As night approached, Sister Hatch came into the room with a glass of water. "Drink this." He gave a slight shake of his head and answered without looking at her. "I'm not thirsty."

"Drink it!" She held the glass to his lips and began to pour. He had to gulp the water to avoid drenching himself. With the glass empty, she nodded with satisfaction and once again left him alone.

The drink felt good on his dry throat, he admitted reluctantly. But what right did he have to feel any comfort when Maddie was somewhere on the road between Bitter Springs and Snowflake, her eyes red and puffy, just as when she'd stood at the door that morning.

"I'm so sorry," she had said. Hadn't Lizzy said exactly the same thing?

But this time was different. He still had Maddie's heart. With Lizzy, he had already lost it. In an odd way, knowing that Maddie loved him made it worse. He hadn't prevented anyone's suffering this time. Instead, he had landed both of them in terrible pain. How could he forgive himself for making Maddie hurt so much?

He thought through the weeks of his recovery. Many times he had woken in the night to see her hair trailing down her back and her feet tucked under her body as she slept on the stuffed chair across the room. Often her quilt had fallen to the floor, and Abe yearned to get out of bed and put it back over her sleeping figure, especially when the nights grew chillier.

When his pain grew intense in the middle of the night, as it often had, he tried to stifle any sign so he wouldn't disturb Maddie. Most times it didn't matter what he did; somehow she always opened her eyes right when he needed her soothing touch. She would get to her feet immediately and shuffle to his side. She'd sit beside him and say, "Where does it hurt?"

His heart swelled inside him at the thought of how much time and energy she had sacrificed for him.

Such thoughts were enough to drive one mad.

As night came on, Abe lay awake. He listened to the creaks of the wooden house and the wind in the trees outside, noises that belonged to another place and time, where people were happy. Moonlight spilled through the window above him, through the sheer curtains and onto his feet, and he couldn't help but realize yet again that it was truly a miracle he was alive at all. Despite his weak muscles, the bones had knitted, and someday, he hoped, his legs would be as strong as before.

In the quiet of the night, Abe sat and pondered Maddie's words. *I had hoped you would look past your father and the other pains in your life and see what it is your mother believed in.*

Maddie was right, in a way. Until recently, he hadn't even opened the Book of Mormon. When he'd had Ben's copy, he had read it regularly. He had even found some high points in it—like the prophet Samuel the Lamanite.

Abe noticed Maddie's Book of Mormon sitting on the end table; she must have forgotten it in her haste. He picked it up and thumbed through the pages.

The copy was much older than Ben's. Instead of black, the cover was tan leather, worn and cracked in places, and the entire volume was taller and wider. The text inside looked the same, but it wasn't broken into numbered paragraphs. The pages didn't have the cross-referenced scriptures along the bottom, either. Abe was surprised that he recognized so many differences; he didn't think he had paid that much attention to Ben's book. He flipped through it, remembering the times he had sat reading it, mostly to quell the nagging voice in his head.

Abe flipped all the way to the back of the book and stopped when he noticed—at the top of the second-to-last page—a section marked with a pencil. He held the book up to the moonlight, trying to read the text. He had to lean close and squint to make out the words:

> *And when ye shall receive these things, I would exhort you that ye would ask God, the Eternal Father, in the name of Christ, if these things are not true; and if ye shall ask with a sincere heart, with real intent, having faith in Christ, he will manifest the truth of it unto you, by the power of the Holy Ghost.*
>
> *And by the power of the Holy Ghost ye may know the truth of all things.*

Abe let the book fall to his lap. He stared into the shadowy darkness of the room, contemplating the words. Had he asked? No. He had prayed at times, as Maddie accused him of doing. More times than he would like to count, if he was being honest with himself.

His mind turned back to the inexplicable desire to read the Book of Mormon that had come over him on the train ride from San Bernardino. That had been the first inkling of desire he had ever felt to read it, despite growing up with a devout mother in a community of Saints. He remembered the nagging thoughts to read the words, and how he was finally able to sleep each time he gave in.

Feeling uneasy about where his thoughts were taking him, Abe closed the book and set it back on the table. Another volume lay beside it, and he picked it up, curious. The first part of the book had a series called *Lectures on Faith,* and Abe flipped through it, stopping here and there, then moving on. He hadn't had much faith. He felt a prick of guilt for his mother's sake. She had tried to instill faith in him in her own quiet way. But her husband's method of beating spoke louder.

The other section was called The Doctrine and Covenants, something Abe vaguely remembered hearing about. He turned pages randomly from the back to the front, stopping at passages that Maddie had marked.

> *Verily, verily, I say unto you, if you desire a further witness, cast your mind upon the night that you cried unto me in your heart, that you might know concerning the truth of these things.*
>
> *Did I not speak peace to your mind concerning the matter? What greater witness can you have than from God?*
>
> *And now, behold, you have received a witness; for if I have told you things which no man knoweth have you not received a witness?*

As he read the words, his entire body flushed warm, and he reread them. Again and again. Images flooded his mind from the past several months.

Finding Ben—and not only a place to stay in California, but a place to call home in Arizona.

His mother being able to receive her long-sought-for temple ordinances before her death.

The blessing Peter gave to Ellen for their baby and the intense joy and peace Abe felt afterward.

Begging God to help him find Maddie in the river—then pulling her from certain death.

The assurance at his mother's deathbed that told him she would live on.

The warmth burning in his chest when Charles took him on a walk around the temple.

Those moments and so many more crowded his mind. *What greater witness can you have than from God?*

The words gently but persistently repeated themselves in his mind. How many times had he been given a witness but brushed it aside, refusing to see it for what it was?

Can I deny what I've felt? No.

He thought of the quiet, patient teachings of his mother throughout his life. Of her burning testimony on her deathbed. All of the memories combined, sending waves of warmth through him. Despite the cold night, he felt a burning through his entire body as tears coursed down his cheeks.

I know what this feeling is, Abe realized suddenly. *I've heard it described all my life.* He sat up gingerly, stunned. The moment had approached subtly and unnoticed, yet inevitably, until like a magician pulls off a drape, the hidden secret was revealed. Abe knew. And had known for some time, if he had only let himself peek beneath the curtain. The warmth and happiness filling his body was almost overwhelming. The back of his hand came up and wiped at his tears as he held the book in his lap.

Maddie was right, he thought. *All this time she was right.* He looked at the chair, but of course, she wasn't sitting in it.

If he ever had feelings for Madeline Stratton—and he had, for months—they had only intensified since the accident. She had believed in him all this time. Why? Because she knew about his testimony before he did. She held onto the thought that it was just around the corner. Or lying under a layer of skeptical dust, waiting to be discovered.

But what about all the hurt, the bitterness he had experienced all his life? Could he really take a step and align himself with the very people who had caused him so much pain? Who had lynched Sam Harvey?

We're not all like your father.

Abe remembered his mother's words. So many people throughout his life—including Maddie—had first judged him because of what he was.

And each time he yearned to cry out, "We're not all like that. *I'm* not like that."

He had been the object of prejudice for so long that he hadn't realized he had been just as prejudiced in return—the exact thing he hated so much. How could he have been so blind and unfeeling to not see that he had done the same thing?

The realization didn't wipe away his adoptive father's actions, the wicked behavior of the mob, or the actions of uncounted people like them. But it did allow Abe to think in different terms.

If he got baptized, he wouldn't be joining *them.* He would be joining good people like Samuel the Lamanite.

Like his mother.

Like Maddie.

And that's something he could live with.

But Mother, can I live with the fact that I didn't open my heart while you lived?

CHAPTER 33

"I need to leave right away," Abe announced to Sister Hatch the following morning as she brought in his breakfast.

The elderly woman stopped midstep and cocked her head. "Oh, really? And what does Julia say about that?" She placed the tray on the side table and wiped her hands, eyebrows raised.

"I haven't spoken with her. But I need to go. Now." Abe made a move to get up, and Sister Hatch easily pushed him back. "You haven't gotten your strength back yet. You're in no condition to face a road trip. I'm not a doctor or a nurse, but even I can see that." She reached for a plate of toast and handed it to him. "Although I must say I'm glad to see you talking again. You're much better off than you were yesterday."

"Yes, I am." Abe didn't elaborate. The events of the previous night weren't something he could share with just anyone. He felt happy and peaceful about his newfound faith, yet at the same time anxiety riddled his mind. What if Maddie decided to accept Edward's hand after all? What if she didn't believe that Abe had discovered the truth on his own and still wouldn't have him? What if, in her sadness, she found someone else before he could reach her?

He bit into the toast, but it felt dry, like wood. It scratched all the way down, and he laid the toast back onto its plate. "Would you please fetch Julia as soon as you can? I must speak with her."

"Very well," Sister Hatch said, eyeing the toast with only a single bite gone. "But I don't know that it'll do you any good. You aren't leaving yet, and that's that."

Abe spent the next hour getting more antsy by the minute. Right when he felt ready to crawl down the stairs to Julia's office, the door opened, and she appeared. He didn't wait for her to speak. "I need to get back to Snowflake right away. It's urgent."

Julia smiled slowly and nodded. "And how do you expect to get there?"

"I don't know," Abe said, then lit up. "I can pay someone to take me. There's plenty of money in my—"

"You're going after her, aren't you?" Julia interrupted.

"Yes." Abe tried to read her face but couldn't. "Do you think that's foolish?"

"Not at all." She put a hand on her hip and laughed. "I don't suppose my opinion matters anyway, does it?"

"Not exactly," Abe said honestly, then rushed on. "It's not that I don't respect your opinion. You've done so much for me. You saved my life, and I will never be able to thank you enough for that. But I *have* to go to her."

Julia sat on a chair beside the bed. "Truth be told, Abe, you're a lot stronger now than I expected you to be. You've still got a long way to go, but you know that. If you go now, I'll worry; I won't pretend I won't. But I'll pray for you. And if you're careful and have someone who can watch out for you, I think you'll be all right, provided you don't leave for two more days. And that's final."

* * *

The day after Maddie reached home, she stood at one of the front windows, arms folded. With a pit in her stomach, she watched for Edward's arrival. She wished Abe could have been there for her, standing beside her as she explained the situation to Edward. It would have been so much simpler that way.

As things were, she would send Edward out of her life, not knowing if she would ever find another man who wanted to marry her. She took a deep breath, then went out, closing the door behind her. She shifted from foot to foot awkwardly. Exactly how was she to do this?

She sat on the stoop and waited. Edward appeared around the corner not two minutes later. As he approached, their eyes met, and he smiled, picking up his pace.

"Here we go," Maddie whispered under her breath. She wiped her damp palms on her skirt and waited.

Edward strode up the walk, and when he reached Maddie, he sat beside her and took her hands in his. He held them out and looked her over. "You're as beautiful as ever," he said. "And a little tanned from the trip, if I dare say it."

"Yes, I suppose I am. It's good to see you." Maddie hated how formal she sounded.

"It's *wonderful* to see you after so long." Edward's tone was more light and cheerful than she ever remembered, and he didn't stop smiling. He leaned in and kissed her cheek. Maddie closed her eyes and braced herself. How could she reject him?

"So how was your trip?" Edward asked, breaking the silence.

"Good, for the most part," Maddie said. "I suppose you've heard that Ellen's baby came early."

"I did. What a blessing Sister Palmer was there to help," Edward said.

"It was a blessing," Maddie agreed.

"I was disappointed when you didn't return with Ellen and Peter. They didn't explain much, just that a friend had been injured on the road and that you stayed back to help out."

"That's right," Maddie said, grateful that Ellen had kept the details about Abe to herself. "I didn't feel like I could leave him." She held her breath, wondering if Edward would notice the male pronoun.

Edward nodded, but by the look in his eye, he didn't seem to notice. He also didn't look satisfied with her response. She struggled to go on. "Edward, I—" She shook her head, still grasping at the best way to explain. She tried a different approach. "Will you answer me one question? And answer it with complete honesty?"

"Of course," he said, brow furrowing. "What is it?"

She licked her lips, hesitating for a second. "Pretend for a moment that I left for St. George and for some reason never returned."

Edward cocked his head as if completely confused. "Why wouldn't you come back?"

"It doesn't matter why. Just pretend for a moment," Maddie said, her hands clapped together. Her heart thudded hard against her chest, and she found it hard to take a deep breath. She was not in love with Edward, but she still cared for him as a friend. Hurting him was difficult, even if it was the right thing. "Pretend I'm on a trip and can't ever come back."

An eyebrow arched as he tried to guess where the question was going. "Am I supposed to pretend you've passed on?"

"No, not necessarily." She knew that an actual death and funeral would bring out a different kind of grief, and that wasn't what she meant to discuss. "Just pretend I'll never return." The look of disbelief in Edward's eyes showed that he didn't grasp the idea of a hypothetical situation. "Just pretend," Maddie insisted.

He leaned away slightly, wary. "All right . . ."

"If you knew I would never return, how would you feel?"

"I would miss you dreadfully, of course," Edward said, pulling back as if at something distasteful. "That's something I'd rather not think about, actually. Why do you ask?"

Feeling as if her stomach had a fistful of stones in it, Maddie struggled to go on. "I've done a lot of thinking, and I know what my answer would be if the situation were reversed."

Edward's eyebrows pulled together sharply. "What are you saying?"

"I'm wondering why we are engaged. Do you really love me, or is our engagement more a matter of convenience because we know one another well and seem to be a good match?" She searched his eyes for an answer, and he seemed to be searching for her intent in return.

"What is your answer to that same question?" His voice was painfully even.

Maddie's eyes dropped to her lap, and her heart thumped harder. "The trip made me do a lot of thinking," she began. "And I came to realize that it wouldn't be fair of me to marry you." Edward visibly started at her words, and she felt as if she had plunged a knife into his heart. Before she lost her gumption completely, she forged ahead. "It wouldn't be fair to marry when my feelings for you aren't as strong as I think they should be between a husband and wife."

He stared at her for a moment, and their eyes locked. Maddie's stomach twisted, and she wished he would speak. He finally bowed his head and nodded. "I've often wondered about that. I knew you would always love Roland more than you would me. But I hoped love would follow for us, in time. I wanted to make you happy. I think I still could." He raised his face, and Maddie's throat tightened at the sadness in his eyes.

"You're a good, good man." She struggled with every word but knew she had to see this to the end. "You deserve a wife who adores the very ground you walk on, someone who won't compare you to a phantom of her past. A woman who loves you just because you're Edward." She lowered her eyes sadly. "I see now that I can't do that. I don't think I ever could have. And I'm sorry."

Cheeks turning red with emotion, Edward cleared his throat but didn't immediately answer. He nodded heavily and cleared his throat again. "You deserve happiness too, Maddie. Don't do this just to be fair to me. I know how much you want to be a wife and mother. I don't need to have your whole heart to be happy."

"You are too kind, Edward," Maddie said. "I'm afraid you'll think less of me when I tell you the rest."

"The rest?" His head came up suddenly, eyes questioning. "What do you mean?" He shifted on the step, looking as uncomfortable as Maddie felt.

"The friend who was hurt . . . is a man. A man I have fallen in love with. I don't think we have a future together, and yet how can I marry you when I care for another?"

"Oh. I see."

There. It was all out. Even with the look of betrayal on Edward's face, Maddie couldn't help but feel as if a weight had been removed from her shoulders. She breathed out with relief. With the anxiety of telling the full truth gone, she could have collapsed on the porch. Without another word, she took the ring from her skirt pocket and placed it in the palm of Edward's hand. He looked at it, then closed his hand and looked away, his jaw working.

Maddie leaned forward, feeling his pain. "This is for the best. For both of us. I know you'll find someone else who will be happy sharing her life with you. Someone who thinks you are nothing less than the sun and the moon."

He avoided her gaze. "I hope you will be happy, Madeline."

"And I you." Maddie put a hand to his cheek and looked deeply into his eyes. "You really are a wonderful man."

Edward nodded and stood up. He brushed off his trousers and walked down the path, then paused with his back to her. Maddie wasn't sure how to say good-bye in such a situation. Instead of speaking, Edward turned enough to give his hat a tilt, then walked away.

As he disappeared around the corner, Maddie closed her eyes and breathed out heavily.

* * *

As promised, Julia let Abe leave two days after he made his demand to go home. She arranged the ride herself, much to Sister Hatch's horror. The party consisted of Martin and Ezra Tuttle, businessmen delivering goods to Taylor, just outside Snowflake. Abe paid them extra to take him all the way to Snowflake and the Hampton front porch. He wanted to go there first, not to the house he had bought. In fact, he had no idea how he'd get to the house after seeing Maddie. He certainly couldn't walk that far.

But he had to see her first.

The trip lasted over a week, Abe lying in the wagon next to an organ destined for some wealthy family. While the trip was long and dusty, Abe knew it was well worth the wait. When they pulled up in front of the Hamptons' house, Abe wished he could jump out and bang on the door. Instead he had to wait for Martin to help him down and walk beside him as he hobbled to the front door.

"Thanks for everything," Abe said. "I sure appreciate the ride."

"Our pleasure," Ezra said from his perch on the bench. "We'll be coming through Snowflake again this summer, probably. I'd like to know what happens with you and your girl."

"Let's hope it's a happy ending," Abe said with a forced smile. He knew that if Maddie didn't take him, by summer he wouldn't be in Snowflake anymore.

Martin and Ezra didn't move on until Abe knocked on the door and it opened. A gasp came from the other side.

"My goodness! Abe, is that really you?" Ellen cried. "Come in, come in!"

He turned and waved to his traveling partners, then carefully stepped inside, painfully aware of Ellen watching his every weak step. She hurriedly pulled out a chair by the kitchen table.

"This is such a surprise!" Ellen said, staring at Abe like he was an apparition. She kept shaking her head like she couldn't believe her eyes. "I'll . . . I'll go fetch Maddie. I think she's out back with the wash."

"Thank you," Abe called after her. As he waited, he thought through what he had planned to say to Maddie. He'd had plenty of time on the road to think about it.

But when she walked into the house, she took his breath away, and with it all his thoughts. Her hair was down, tumbling over her shoulders, and even though her dress was wet and her sleeves rolled up, he thought she had never looked more beautiful.

"Hello," she said, her voice shaky, as if she didn't trust herself. For a second, it all felt too much like the moment she stood in the doorway and said good-bye—when he couldn't rush to her and fold her into his arms to prevent her from leaving.

Instead of saying a word, Abe planted his cane firmly on the floor and stood. With slow, careful steps, he walked to her, his heart pounding. With each step he feared she would run away again, but instead, as he drew closer, he could see tears in her eyes.

"You're walking." Her voice cracked as she spoke.

"Maddie." The word felt like honey on his tongue. His legs began to feel weak, but he wasn't sure how much came from exertion and how much came from the emotion welling up in him. He plunged in. "Maddie, after you left, I felt I couldn't go on. But you were right. I had never seen past my pain to the truth."

They stood only a foot or two apart now. Abe could have reached out and touched her, but he didn't dare, not yet. She looked up at him with fear in her eyes. He hoped his words would wipe it away.

"I spent a long night with only my thoughts, your scriptures, and the Lord."

A flicker of something—hope?—crossed her eyes. "And?" Her voice was scarcely audible.

"You were right about a lot of things. If I had put aside my pride earlier, I would have seen that I already had a witness. Many witnesses. And now I know."

Maddie's face crumpled with emotion, and both hands covered her eyes, as if she had been hanging on to what little strength she had until the thread snapped. She lowered her hands and gazed into his eyes. "Really, Abe? *Really?*"

"I want to be baptized. It's not for your sake, and I understand if you think that. But no matter what happens between us, I *will* be baptized. I just wanted you to know. This time it will be with my own name, making real covenants."

She sucked in her breath and shook her head. "I—I don't know what to say. I—"

He reached for her hand and held it tight. "Maddie, say you'll marry me." He glanced at the floor. "I can't kneel. But if any man ever loved a woman and wanted to be with her, it's me."

"Oh, Abe," Maddie said, putting her arms around him. He nearly lost his balance, and she pulled back and steadied him. "I'll marry you with all my heart."

Abe felt like his heart could continue beating now. Balancing himself with his cane, he drew her in and kissed her. It was gentle but firm, and he felt like he had come home at last. When they pulled apart, their foreheads rested against one another's, and Abe said, "Promise me you won't tell anyone about my plans to get baptized."

She leaned back, curious. "Why?"

Feeling weak, Abe looked around for a chair. Maddie brought two over from the table, and they both sat. Holding his hand, she repeated, "Why can't anyone know?"

"It's for my mother's sake," Abe said slowly. Thinking of her brought the grief of her passing to the surface, and it took him a moment to go on. "She spent her life hoping I would turn to the gospel that she held dear—but she died without that happening. I want to make sure no one will doubt my sincerity. If I get baptized right before we get married, some will think I did it just so you would marry me. But I believe in the Church now, down to my core. And I want everyone to know that." Abe leaned in and kissed her. She willingly kissed him back, her fingers curling around his.

They heard rustling outside the door and whirled around. Ellen stood there, wiping her eyes and laughing. "It's wonderful! You two will be so happy, and—" She stopped, then added, "I'm sorry. I had to listen."

"You won't tell anyone about our secret, right?" Abe asked firmly.

Ellen made a gesture as if buttoning her mouth shut. "I'll keep it to myself. You can count on that."

CHAPTER 34

"Sister Brown is ready for you," Peter said, pulling the wagon up to the house that was legally Abe's. After giving Sister Brown advance notice that they would be coming, Peter had hitched up his wagon and driven Abe to his new home. Maddie rode beside Abe, unwilling to let him leave her quite yet.

"It's strange to think that it's going to be mine," Abe whispered to Maddie as the house came into view. "I haven't spent more than a few minutes inside."

"I'm grateful you arranged to buy the place before we left," Maddie said. "And that Sister Brown has agreed to be your house-keeper. We'll need to thank Ellen for arranging that."

Abe took Maddie's hand and corrected her. "She'll be *our* house-keeper, soon enough."

"Yes, *ours.*"

No sooner had Peter alighted from the wagon than the front door opened and Sister Brown appeared. "I'm so glad you made it safely," she said, coming down the stairs. "I've got some food ready for you. I hope you like ham and potatoes."

With Peter and Maddie's help, Abe managed to get out of the wagon and up the steps. Peter then took over and helped Abe to the second floor, where Sister Brown said there was a bedroom all made up and waiting for him.

Maddie wondered which room Sister Brown had put him in—had it belonged to Florence or Caroline? Or had she given up her own room and moved to a smaller one as their housekeeper?

When Abe was out of view, Maddie turned to Sister Brown. "Thank you so much. I don't know what Abe would do without someone to care for him. He can't get along by himself quite yet."

Sister Brown nodded and patted Maddie's hand. "It's my pleasure. I'm perfect for the job. An old lady like me won't raise any eyebrows if I'm living under the same roof as a strong young man, you know. Come in and help me get a tray of food ready for him."

Maddie followed her into the kitchen, which smelled heavenly. In the near future, she and Sister Brown would live under the same roof, cooking these kinds of meals together. The thought made Maddie feel as if she were truly at home.

At Sister Brown's request, Maddie scooped mashed potatoes onto a plate for Abe. "I'm glad you were able to continue at the school. I know that must have been difficult."

Sister Brown shrugged. "It wasn't so bad. Walking to the schoolhouse is what's so hard on me, and after Peter returned, he drove me each morning and picked me up each afternoon. Sweet man. So it was just fine. Don't worry your head about that. I was happy to do it."

Another concern bothered Maddie. She stole a glance at Sister Brown. "But the school days themselves must have been trying. I meant to warn about Avery Hancock and his antics. I hope he wasn't too hard on you."

Sister Brown burst out laughing, startling Maddie. This wasn't at all the reaction she had expected. "Oh, no," she said as she wiped a tear of laughter from her eye. "Avery wasn't hard on me. Not at all."

"But—but—" Maddie was speechless. Avery Hancock was the terror of the schoolhouse. He would surely see a helpless old lady as an even better target for his antics than he did Maddie.

"You see," Sister Brown said, a glimmer in her eye, "I have the upper hand with Avery."

Maddie didn't know how to respond. She just gaped as Sister Brown went on.

"What was it—five years ago—on Avery's very first day of school, he was so nervous that he wet his pants."

A hand flew to Maddie's face, and a giggle escaped. "Really?"

"Really," Sister Brown said with a satisfied nod. "It happened right outside the school door. I was the only one to see it, besides his mother. You should have seen his face. Absolute horror. He raced home and changed, and when he returned, he begged me, 'Don't tell anyone, Miss Brown, *please* don't tell.' It was quite pathetic, to tell you the truth." Sister Brown raised an eyebrow, and her mouth curled. "And do you know what I told him? That I'd never tell—as long as he behaved. And I've kept that promise until this moment. You're the first person I've ever breathed a word of it to."

"But what about when he did misbehave?" Maddie asked. Surely Avery couldn't have been an angel for all those years before she took over the school.

Sister Brown laughed. "Oh, all it took was one look from me, and he'd straighten up, pale as a sheet and terrified I'd spill his secret. Once in a while I'd have to say, 'Avery, should I tell the class a story?' He'd panic and obey in an instant."

"Sister Brown!" Maddie said. "That's blackmail!" She wasn't sure if she was more impressed or surprised to find such a sneaky bone in the old lady's body.

"Call it what you will, it worked, and without resorting to the switch," Sister Brown said. She poured a glass of milk and put it on the tray. "And it did the trick this fall, too. Avery hasn't forgotten, and neither have I."

* * *

"You must give me at least two weeks to put together a proper wedding," Ellen insisted. She couldn't stop grinning at the prospect of her sister's happiness. Even so, she wouldn't budge on the time line.

Fourteen days felt like an eternity for Abe and Maddie, but Ellen filled each one with preparations. She altered her own wedding gown for Maddie, adding some lace and a bustle in back. She also cooked like a madwoman, making cakes and puddings and breads and all kinds of foods for a wedding feast.

"You needn't make such a fuss," Maddie protested when she walked in on Ellen mixing up batter for another cake.

"Mother isn't here to do it," Ellen explained as she poured the mixture into cake pans. "It's my job, and I want to give you every-thing I had on my wedding day."

Eventually the time passed, and when the day arrived, Maddie rode to Bishop Hunt's home in Peter's wagon to avoid soiling her dress or shoes. She held a small bouquet of dried flowers, since no fresh ones were available in January. Eager to reach the bishop's home—and to see her groom—Maddie scanned the streets as they drove.

The horse's feet clip-clopped along as they passed a side street, which Maddie looked down. There was Edward—with Mary Jane on his arm. Maddie felt shocked at first, then recalled seeing them together after the school festival. They were heading the other direction, so Maddie couldn't see their faces, but they seemed comfortable together. Edward pointed up, where the moon was still visible in the sky. Maddie sat back and smiled to herself. *Maybe Mary Jane can fill his heart and see him as the sun and the moon.* She was young, but smart, sweet, and had a good heart. In time, it could blossom into a beautiful relationship.

Maddie arrived at the bishop's home a moment later. Peter helped her down from the wagon, and she walked inside, her stomach bubbly with nervous excitement. There, on the far side of the parlor, stood Abe. His hair was slicked back, and he wore a suit with a gray cravat. The image was a far cry from the disheveled, dusty man she had fallen in love with, and it made her take a breath. This was the man she was going to marry. In a few moments, she would be Madeline Franklin.

Abe smiled at her and held out a hand. She eagerly crossed to him and took it, never wanting to let go. They didn't have many guests, just Ellen's family, Sister Brown, Marie and Seth Ellsworth, and the bishop's wife.

"I'll bet your mother is here," Maddie whispered to Abe.

"I'll bet both of your parents are." They smiled at each other, knowing that their loved ones were looking down on them.

Bishop Hunt entered the room with his Bible and some papers, and he began the ceremony. Maddie was able to say, "I do," without any hesitation, and it thrilled her to hear Abe say the same words.

"As bishop of Snowflake, I pronounce you husband and wife," Bishop Hunt said.

Abe pulled something from his pocket. "This was my mother's," he said, opening his hand to reveal a ring. It was silver, with a small silver rose in the center, and a pearl nestled in the rose. He slipped it on Maddie's finger, then, leaning in, gave her a tender kiss. They grinned at each other with pure happiness—and a little mischievousness—knowing what Abe was about to do next. He turned to the entire company. "I have an announcement to make."

Bishop Hunt nodded, a knowing smile on his face. He was the only person Maddie and Abe had told. "Please tell everyone what we've discussed," the bishop urged.

Abe needed no coaxing. "I'm getting baptized tomorrow."

The entire room stood in stunned silence as the words sank in. A voice of choruses followed.

"Really?"

"How did that happen?"

"Where?"

Without elaborating on details, Abe simply said, "Peter, I'd like you to perform the ordinance."

"But . . . but . . ." Peter couldn't seem to decide whether to smile or look perplexed.

"It's not because of me, if that's what you're wondering," Maddie interjected.

"No, not at all," Abe agreed. "In fact, Maddie knew my intent all along. I decided on it weeks ago. I'm not getting baptized to get the girl." He looked at her, squeezed her hand, and kissed her cheek. "It just happens that I did get her. And I couldn't be happier."

EPILOGUE

Almost five years later—September 1888

Abe stood on the porch with his thumbs in his waistband. The sun's angle lowered in the sky, sending soft orange rays across the road. To the side of the house stood a wagon, fully stocked and ready to pull out come morning. Before him were two dark-haired boys playing in the road, chasing each other and laughing, tumbling over each other on the ground and getting themselves covered in dirt. Their mother wouldn't be pleased about having to bathe them tonight.

Yet the sight made Abe smile. The Johnson boys had been right—siblings made life much more fun, less lonely.

"Boys, it's almost time for bed," Abe called out to them. "You need to come in."

Timothy, the older boy, popped his head out of the cloud of dust and grinned, his teeth looking stark white against his dirty face. "Sure, Daddy. Just tell Matthew to stop tickling me! Aaack!"

Timothy let out a gale of laughter as his younger brother sat squarely on top of him and tickled with all his might. Abe didn't have the heart to stop their gaiety quite yet and instead watched them play a little longer.

He felt Maddie's arms slip around his waist, and he took her hands as she put her chin on his shoulder. "They're going to need a barrel of water dumped over their heads to get them clean," she said, but he could detect a note of laughter in her voice. She stepped to the side, and Abe put his arm around her shoulders. Without a word, they went to the porch swing.

"Are you ready for tomorrow?" Maddie asked quietly.

Abe didn't answer right away. He looked at the sun and instinctively began rocking the swing back and forth. The fact that his mother wasn't there with him still brought an ache to his heart—as Maddie said it probably always would.

There were his two beautiful, wonderful boys. They looked so much like their father, and yet they were so much like their mother in other ways—their smiles, their energy, their love of learning. Abe felt another ache, one that had become more common of late: he wanted to be able to claim Maddie as his wife forever, and he wanted their boys to belong to them forever.

"Yes," he said. "I'm ready."

Maddie took his hand in hers and rubbed her thumb over the top. "Have you decided about your parents?"

"I'm going to do it," Abe said with a firm nod, having to remind himself that the reason he would be getting them sealed wasn't because he thought Bart Franklin deserved the blessing. It was because Abe wanted to be his mother's son for eternity, and the only way to do that was to be sealed to them both. And, as he had later learned, his children's eternal blessings would come through a full line, not a broken one. If God deemed his adopted father unworthy of those blessings, He'd make sure Clara Franklin and her posterity still had theirs one way or another.

"I had a feeling you would," Maddie said, putting her head on his shoulder.

Abe leaned his head against hers. "You seem to have had a lot of feelings over the years."

"It's a gift," she said with a shrug. "I must have known you in the premortal life."

"Is there anything else you have a 'feeling' about that I should be aware of?" Abe asked with a laugh. "Do you happen to know what I'll be doing in, say, ten years?"

Maddie lifted her head and looked into his eyes. The sun had set farther, and it sent golden rays splashing across everything. "I have a feeling you'll be very happy with your wife and children," she said. "And I have a feeling that in ten years, one of those children will be oh, about nine years old."

Their eyes held for a moment, hers with a playful glimmer, his momentarily confused, until he grasped what she meant. "You're . . . you're . . ."

She nodded, her face splitting into a smile. "In May, I think."

"In that case, maybe we shouldn't travel. I don't want you to be under a lot of strain like Ellen was when—"

Maddie shook her head, took Abe's hand, and placed it over her middle. Their gaze followed to their hands, then again held each other's eyes. "It'll be fine. We're early enough that there shouldn't be any trouble like Ellen's. And I feel wonderful, better than I ever did with either Timothy or Matthew. I think it's a blessing to help us go now—so this one will be sealed to us the moment she's born."

Abe felt his eyes prick with tears at the thought. He had come to understand why Ellen and Peter had undertaken their trip to St. George when they did. And as he thought of being an eternal family, Abe could remember no time in his life that he had ever felt so happy. He had his wife at his side, his sons bursting with joy in front of him, and another child on the way.

Suddenly Maddie's phrasing repeated in his mind. "Wait. As soon as *she's* born?"

Maddie grinned. "Let's just say it's something I have a feeling about."

NOTE TO THE READER

I have always loved reading about the nineteenth century, and my favorite authors are from that period as well. So it shouldn't have been a surprise that I felt drawn to write about that era and the Logan Temple in *House on the Hill*, although prior to that, I had spent years writing contemporary novels.

The level of excitement from readers following the publication of *House on the Hill* was wholly unexpected—a gratifying experience on so many levels. In addition to all the wonderful feedback I received in letters, e-mails, and conversations, I got one overwhelming question over and over again: *What happens to Abe?*

To be honest, I didn't know. A lot of people were surprised to learn that I hadn't written *House on the Hill* with the intent to add a sequel. But my audience had a point. What *did* happen to Abe? I had come to love him as a character, and I wanted to find out what happened to him as much as they did. The most common question I was asked was whether Abe joined the Church. I replied, "I don't know. I'll find out."

When I began contemplating a follow-up book, I thought back on how rewarding an experience it was researching and writing about the Logan Temple. I knew that while the temple in Logan would always hold a special place in my heart, other temples must have rich stories behind them as well. I wanted to learn more about them, and that's why the St. George Temple served as a backdrop to the story, although it doesn't play nearly as big a role as the Logan Temple did in *House on the Hill*.

I hope readers enjoy following the next chapter of Abe's journey as much as I enjoyed writing it.

HISTORICAL NOTES

Much of the information I based this story on came from *Arizona's Honeymoon Trail and Mormon Wagon Roads* by Norma B. Ricketts. Until 1931, the trail, which started where many roads converged at Sunset Crossing, was generally referred to as the "Mormon Wagon Road." Will C. Barnes renamed it the "Honeymoon Trail" in an article he wrote for *Arizona Highways*, and the name has stuck ever since.

According to Ricketts, Barnes's article talked about his cattle ranch from where he could watch Latter-day Saints traveling to the St. George Temple, camping together and enjoying themselves despite the difficult trek. While he was not a Latter-day Saint, he had great respect for the Saints who braved the journey to the temple because of their beliefs. Barnes served as a model for Murray York.

While most of my characters are not based on real people, to create character names I often combined some of my favorite first and last names from individuals whose stories appear in *Arizona's Honeymoon Trail and Mormon Wagon Roads*. As such, similarities may exist between real settlers' names and those in the book, although they are coincidental and not intended to reflect people from history. The only actual residents of Snowflake that appear in the novel are Bishop Hunt and his wife, and any words or actions given them are invented. He served as bishop in the area for over three decades and regularly performed marriages in his parlor.

Unfortunately, Sam Harvey really was lynched in Salt Lake City on August 25, 1883. The men who responded to the incident arrived thinking it would be a relatively simple arrest of a drunk for public disturbance. The most thorough account I found was written by Harold Schindler of the *Salt Lake Tribune;* this account is found in his collection of Utah history articles, *In Another Time.* I used this for my main source about the lynching.

While some of the specific details of the event were invented for the novel, the basic facts are correct: the murder of Bishop/Marshal Burt at the pharmacy, Wilcken and Elijah Able restraining Harvey (Abe was not there, of course), Wilcken being shot in the arm, the crowd following the wagon to the city hall, Sam being beaten inside when word of the murder reached the officers, and Sam being dragged out into the jailhouse yard and, finally, lynched in the nearby stable shed.

Not mentioned in the scene is the further role of Officer Salmon. During the mob's chaos, W. H. Sells, a prominent Utahn, drove past in his buggy. Unaware that Harvey had already died, he got out of his buggy and insisted the crowd leave Harvey's fate up to the courts. The mob responded with anger, rushing forward to string Sells up beside Harvey. Officer Salmon quickly grabbed Sells and locked him in a jail cell for his own protection. According to Schindler, the *Herald* (presumably *The Daily Herald*) reported that Salmon's quick thinking saved Mr. Sell's life. The mob didn't disperse until the mayor confronted them as they dragged Harvey's body onto State Street.

While some people claim that Harvey's gruesome death was due solely to anger over his killing a beloved bishop, other accounts seem to point to his race as playing a role, and that's obviously my position. There's a good chance that had he not been black, he would have lived long enough to face a judge and jury for his crime. In addition, he most likely would have been buried in the cemetery instead of beside it.

It is important to note that Church leaders were vocal in condemning anyone involved with the lynching.

In early versions, I used the full name of Elijah Able and referred to him as Brother Able. But when early readers became confused between *Able* and *Abe,* I decided to refer to the former as simply "Elijah" or "Brother Elijah."

Geronimo was active in Arizona immediately prior to this period, and other Native Americans and their tribes also lived in the area. History records many skirmishes between settlers and Indians which began for a variety of reasons, including intense emotions and confusion when government land was given to settlers and later returned to the tribes. Several accounts exist of settlers—sometimes traveling the Honeymoon Trail—being attacked and sometimes killed by Indians.

The most tragic event I found related to Nathan Robinson, who died of a brutal shooting at the hands of some Apaches, then had his body dumped in a river and partially covered with rocks. Robinson wasn't traveling the trail at the time of his death, although the attack on Roland is based somewhat on these types of events. However, they generally happened farther south. To my knowledge, few, if any, skirmishes occurred at Lee's Ferry, and none are recorded after July 1883.

Warren Johnson was the ferryman at Lee's Ferry most of the time that it was in operation. Eventually the family had twenty-one children between his two wives, Permelia and Samantha. The family members' names and ages at the time of this story are accurate, but their personalities and actions portrayed are purely out of my imagination.

The baby that Samantha carried at the time the Hamptons arrived turned out to be yet another girl. Samantha ended up with four more children, two boys and two girls. Permelia later had three more boys.

The story of the Johnson family's later tragedy has been mentioned numerous times in General Conference, so it may be familiar to some readers: in May 1891, a family came through Lee's Ferry after losing a child to diphtheria. They interacted with the Johnson children and infected them.

In spite of the Johnsons' intense fasting and prayers, several children succumbed. Before the end of May, a five-year-old son, Jonathan, died. In mid-June, young Permelia (then nine) and Laura Alice (seven; the newborn in this book) died within four days of each other. Melinda (then fifteen, nearly eight at the time of the novel) also became ill. She held on until July, when she passed away.

Permelia, Warren's first wife, was the mother of all four children who died. She had previously lost a son at birth, making five of her ten children who did not reach adulthood. Miraculously, baby Joseph Smith Johnson (also Permelia's) who was about two months old when the family was exposed, survived, living to 1975 and the age of 84.

Some accounts indicate that there wasn't a good camping location on the north side of Lee's Backbone. However, the Hampton party was small, and with the events of the story, it made sense to have them camp on the north side of the ridge. So I took the liberty of putting them there both on the night Roland died and again on the second trip as they journeyed back to Snowflake.

Snowflake was known for its interest in the theater and performances. Since school festival-type events were common in the period in other locations, I assumed that they would have been particularly popular there. The first school in Snowflake was actually the upstairs of the old Stinson home, but I took the liberty of making a separate schoolhouse for Maddie.

The railroad through the upper half of Arizona was newly completed at the time Abe rode it from California. As a side note, the California city of Waterman is now known as Barstow.

A common misconception is that Native Americans don't grow facial hair. While some grow none, others do. It is common, however, for Native Americans to grow less than their European counterparts. Abe had much less of a beard than many men, but it's likely that after his travels he would have arrived in Snowflake with some growth.

According to *Church History in the Fulness of Times,* Joseph Smith used crutches for three years following his leg surgery and "sometimes limped slightly thereafter" (page 23). When he was tarred and feathered, the same volume reports that "[the mob] tried to force a vial of acid into his mouth, which chipped one of his teeth, causing him thereafter to speak with a slight whistle" (page 115).

The editions of the Book of Mormon described in the book are accurate, including the size, color, shape, and so on. Ben gives Abe the 1879 edition, which was edited by Orson Pratt. Royal Skousen, Professor of Linguistics at Brigham Young University, has done extensive research into all of the editions of the Book of Mormon. He states that the 1879 edition showed "major changes in the format of the text, including division of the long chapters in the original text, a true versification system (which has been followed in all subsequent LDS editions), and footnotes (mostly scriptural references)."

The story behind the St. George Temple dome and tower is accurate, including the lightning strike and the rebuilding of the dome and tower, much taller, like Brigham Young originally wanted them. The renovation was completed in May 1883, just a few months before Clara would have entered the city and seen the temple for the first time.

For details about the St. George Temple, I relied heavily on *History of the St. George Temple,* a thesis written by Kirk M. Curtis at Brigham Young University. Many people were called to settle St. George, often based on their professions. In his thesis, Curtis lists those professions and how many of each were called. I found no medical personnel included. However, a doctor made sense to me, so I took the liberty of giving Charles and Miriam Willis a call to settle the area and help with the temple construction because of his background.

Information about the temple lot's boggy soil and the cannon used as a pile driver on volcanic rock is found in many sources, including the thesis. According to Curtis, the water drainage system is still in place. Napoleon's abandoned cannon is on display at the St. George Temple Visitors Center.

Honeymoon Trail records the story of George Vernon Leavitt, an infant who grew gravely ill with pneumonia and was expected to die. His parents, who lived in Lehi, Utah, had the desire for him to be sealed to them. After a priesthood blessing, his health improved considerably, and the family was able to make the trip to the St. George Temple. Little George wasn't sick a single day of the arduous and long journey. The family was sealed, and they went home. Within weeks of their return, baby George's illness returned. This time he passed away. His story inspired my portrayal of Clara's experience of illness, recuperation long enough to receive temple blessings, and her eventual relapse.

Current Church policies for doing temple work on behalf of the dead require a one-year waiting period from the time of death. All of the sources I consulted agreed that this policy did not exist in 1883, but none could say precisely when it was instituted. Therefore, Caroline would most likely have been able to do temple work for Florence right away.

Marriages of convenience and necessity were common in this era. Living as a single woman was extremely difficult, especially if widowed and left with children. While Maddie's early view of marrying Edward must seem unromantic to twenty-first-century readers, to her contemporaries, it was her notion of wanting to marry only for love that might have seemed silly and impractical.

About ten years prior to the story, diamonds became widely popular—and much more available—for wedding and engagement bands, so Edward may well have been able to get one for Maddie.

The timing of Abe's baptism was inspired by Abel Alexander DeWitt, who came through Utah on his way to California. He met the Mormons and fell in love with Margaret Miller Watson, whom he married. He was baptized two weeks after the wedding and declared he did it that way because, "I didn't want anyone to think I joined the Church to get the girl." In 1879 he helped settle Arizona.

In my research for the first part of Abe's story in *House on the Hill,* Church historian Susan Easton Black explained some history to me in a personal e-mail. She indicated that during the era of Abe's childhood, it was common for children to be baptized without official interviews or other procedures that are in place today, and that Abe probably would have been baptized as a child regardless of his beliefs. That element played a part in the previous book, and of course had to play out in this one.

Rebaptism was practiced periodically as well, such as when the Saints first arrived in Utah and at other occasions when they wanted to renew their covenants. As a result, Abe's baptism as an adult would not have violated procedure, and as it stands, his baptism became a moment for him to actually make the covenants he had come to desire.

ABOUT THE AUTHOR

Annette Luthy Lyon was bitten by the writing bug when she was about eight and has never been the same. While she's been successful in magazine, newspaper, and business writing, her true passion is fiction. She graduated cum laude from BYU with a BA in English and served on the League of Utah Writer's Utah Valley chapter board for three years, including one as president. She received several awards from the League, including a Quill award and two Diamond awards. Annette and her husband, Rob, live in American Fork, Utah, with their four children.

She figures she must have read *Anne of Green Gables* one too many times as a teen, because all three of her daughters are redheads. Her son didn't get the red hair, but since brains seem to come with all colors, he doesn't mind.

Annette loves corresponding with her readers. She can be reached through her website at www.annettelyon.com or through Covenant email at info@covenant-lds.com or snail-mail at Covenant Communications, Inc., Box 416, American Fork, UT 84003-0416.